TO CAST A STONE

Recent Titles by Elizabeth Lord from Severn House

BUTTERFLY SUMMERS
AUTUMN SKIES
WINTER WINE

SHADOW OF THE PROTECTOR
FORTUNE'S DAUGHTER

COMPANY OF REBELS

TO CAST A STONE

Elizabeth Lord

This first world edition published in Great Britain 2007 by
SEVERN HOUSE PUBLISHERS LTD of
9–15 High Street, Sutton, Surrey SM1 1DF.
This first world edition published in the USA 2007 by
SEVERN HOUSE PUBLISHERS INC of
595 Madison Avenue, New York, N.Y. 10022.

British Library Cataloguing in Publication Data

Lord, Elizabeth, 1928-
     To cast a stone
     1.   Sisters - Fiction
     2.   East End (London, England) - Social conditions - Fiction
     I.   Title
     823.9'14 [F]

     ISBN-13: 978-0-7278-6513-7   (cased)

All Severn House titles are printed on acid-free paper.

Typeset by Palimpsest Book Production Ltd.,
Grangemouth, Stirlingshire, Scotland.
Printed and bound in Great Britain by
MPG Books Ltd., Bodmin, Cornwall.

One

The narrow width of Gales Gardens captured and held the reek of cooking, stale cabbage and urine. Men leaving the Salmon & Ball pub close by often used this ill-lit street as a convenient alley in which to relieve themselves of the pints they'd drunk. Some women, too, standing astride the grated drain out of the light of Bethnal Green Road to drag aside a bloomer leg, their errand hidden by a long skirt, trying to appear as if they'd merely paused for thought.

Ellie Jay, christened Alice Elizabeth but called Ellie, stood at her front door that opened directly from the single living room on to the cracked pavement and peered through the darkness towards the more brightly lit main thoroughfare. Her neighbour next door, Mrs Sharp, had gone for the doctor it seemed ages ago, but he was taking his time. No rush over a dead body.

There was singing coming from the Salmon & Ball, quickly drowned out by the rumble of a train passing over the railway bridge spanning the main road, its smoke drifting lazily through the curve of Gales Gardens to add another layer of sooty smuts to already blackened brickwork and the peeling paint of window sills.

A figure entering the street made her straighten up in anticipation, but it was just someone slipping into the shadows on a call of nature, his frame positioning itself for a second to face a wall. But seeing the light from her doorway he hastily adjusted his dress and hurried off.

Ellie pulled her short jacket closer about her against the cold, early-March evening. If the doctor didn't come soon she would have to go back indoors and start on the job herself, washing and laying out the body before the limbs set rigid. She'd seen it done, but this would be the first time she had ever done it herself. So far she had put the pennies on the eyelids to keep them closed and fastened a piece of cloth about the chin and forehead to prevent the mouth falling open; but the thought of stripping and washing the body made her cringe. Her mother had been a decent woman all her life, would never have dreamed of allowing anyone to see her naked, not even her husband, and would have been appalled at her own daughter looking upon her private parts in death. Mrs Sharp next door might have done it, being around Mum's age – forty; but she had no intention of letting a neighbour stare at her mother's nakedness, even with the best of intentions. If only the doctor would arrive.

She glanced down as the hand in hers tightened fractionally. She'd forgotten her thirteen-year-old sister standing beside her. Dora was three and a bit years younger than her, equally slender, dark-haired and green-eyed. Tears were glistening in those eyes and her voice was small.

'Do yer think Mum's orright on 'er own in there?'

Ellie wanted to retort that Mum had no cause any more to care if she was on her own. Instead she gripped the girl's hand a little tighter. 'Ain't a lot we can do till the doctor arrives.'

As if in reply to her remark, another figure turned into the street, this time his silhouette against the gaslight of the main road showing him to be carrying a sturdy doctor's bag. Ellie let go her sister's hand and hurried the few yards to meet him.

'I'm so glad yer've come,' she burst out. 'I've been waiting.'

'Yes, well, I've been busy with patients.' By his tone he might as well have said he'd been busy with the living. 'Where is your mother?' he asked brusquely.

'In the bedroom upstairs,' Ellie returned. Where else would she be?

He'd been told how ill she was and must have known that someone with pneumonia would be at death's door. But, with no money to pay for a doctor's visit, she'd been palmed off with a bottle of cough mixture for the few pence she had and advised to keep her mother as warm as possible while the illness ran its course. That was the lot of most people living in areas like this if they had no money. At least she hoped there'd be no charge to officially declare Mrs Jay deceased and write out the death certificate.

With Dora standing forlorn by the street door they went on

inside the empty house. 'Are you alone?' he asked. 'Where is your family, your father?'

'Gone,' Ellie replied tersely. 'He ain't coming back, neither. Nor is me brother. I don't know where they are so as to tell 'em me mum died.'

Saying no more she led the way upstairs to the larger of the two tiny bedrooms, leaving Dora downstairs on her own. At the doctor's enquiry a surge of bitter hate had raced through her against her father, walking out of the house two days earlier, leaving just her and Dora to cope with a sick woman. Her brother she could understand, after the fight, but her dad . . .

'I ain't sticking around ter catch 'er cold,' he'd declared. 'She's been moaning on about 'er ill 'ealth ever since I married 'er. I'm off to enjoy me own life, nor will I be coming back. I've 'ad enough of 'er always being ill.'

It wasn't true. Her mother hadn't always been ill – only these last two or three years, worn down by childbearing, only three now living, having had three miscarriages, one stillborn, three dying in infancy; that and working herself to a standstill to keep her family in food while he did nothing other than a few underhanded dealings – money he'd spend on himself, mostly.

Mum did outdoor work for a local hatbox manufacturer, bringing home the thin cardboard to make the fine boxes in which silk top hats were sold. On a good week she'd do three gross if work was there, half a crown a gross, though it took Ellie's help to achieve that. Repetitive, long hours sewing the bases to the sides and the same with the lids, Ellie pasting the white glazed paper to the finished article, stopping only for a midday meal and supper, Mum often working on into the night if she was behind with the work; and sometimes her fingers would be red raw from constant stitching. From what she earned she had to buy the paste, needles and thread herself, but she'd always try to put a little aside from what she earned, hidden away in case Dad found it. He'd never shown any appreciation of her hard work, and now his only thanks had been to up and leave her.

The real truth was that he liked not only his drink but his women too. Even at fifteen Ellie knew it. In his mid-forties, darkly handsome and always making sure of being well dressed while his family could go in rags for all he cared, on one occasion he'd brought home a fancy woman, taunting Mum and calling her an ugly, tiresome old bitch. Mum had cried.

True she was rake-thin, life's ravages plain on her face, but a framed, sepia photo of her showed her to have been extremely pretty when young, as Ellie was now, and Dora too. It was probably why Dad, with an eye for a pretty woman, had married her, but he'd never made her married life happy.

She should have left him, but where would she have gone? Despite it being the turn of the century, with people talking about it being a new world, there was nowhere for a married woman except at her husband's side, whether he was a good one or a thoroughly bad one; and James Jay, to Ellie's mind, was a thoroughly bad one with no scruples whatsoever where drink and women were concerned.

A couple of months ago he'd even turned his attention on her, his own daughter, reaching out to touch her young breast and remarking that she was growing into a beautiful girl. 'Like yer muvver was but she ain't no more. Always ill, no comfort to a man's needs.'

At first she hadn't understood, but as his hands began to grow bolder over the weeks, she soon had, dreading him coming near her and wondering how long before Dora took his eye.

Not long ago, her older brother Charlie had come home unexpectedly, catching his father with his hand up his older daughter's skirt as he sat next to her on the sofa, thinking himself safe, with her mother out shopping, Dora at school and she too scared to stop him lest he hit her. He was good at hitting people. He had belted Mum before now. Dora had felt the weight of his hand many a time. So had Ellie. Only Charlie was never attacked, being nineteen, taller and quite beefy.

Had he not walked in then, with Dad fondling her, before taking her upstairs, which he'd done on two former occasions – that first time slapping her face for trying to resist when she'd cried with shock and pain – she'd have been taken upstairs yet again.

Charlie had let out an enormous yell of horrified fury and sprung at him, dragging him up by his shirt front. There had been bouts of fighting in this house before, with furniture knocked around, even broken, but this time his fist had caught his father full in the face, sending him flat on his back, blood pouring from his nose. Charlie had stood back saying he'd had enough of this bloody family. He was leaving. He'd not been seen since.

Now her father had deserted them. Ellie couldn't blame her brother. Mum hadn't been ill then; but her father had left a desperately sick woman. For that she hated him with all her heart and soul, and as she sat in the room downstairs with Dora waiting for the doctor to finish his examination upstairs, she vowed that one day she would seek out her father and find a way of avenging his desertion of her mum.

The doctor was making his way down the steep, narrow stairs, the bare treads creaking under his rotund weight.

'Ah, there you are, my dears,' he announced as he came into the room. 'Your mother needs to be washed and decently laid out. I'll arrange for a woman to attend to it straight away. She lives nearby, so you'll not be too long on your own.'

Dora said nothing but merely sat staring bleakly into the low fire.

He turned to Ellie. 'Would you boil a kettle of water while you are waiting, young lady?'

As she nodded dismally, he came to lay a hand on her thin shoulder. Cringing slightly, she looked sharply up at him, but the eyes half-hidden by podgy cheeks held sympathy, not lust.

As he surveyed this slip of a girl in her faded dress and pinny, Doctor Lowe felt only pity as he surveyed the wan but pretty face framed by its mass of uncombed, dark-auburn hair. In the sickly light of the room's single gas lamp the eyes glistened clear and green with unshed tears. No doubt tears would eventually come as the enormity of her and her sister's plight finally took hold.

'Good girl,' he said quietly, moving his hand away, suddenly and inexplicably embarrassed by the way she had shrunk ever so slightly from his touch. 'If I can be of any help . . .'

He broke off as she shot him a strange look and gave a small, self-conscious cough. 'Perhaps you will kindly show me out, child.'

The door was closed on him immediately he stepped into the street. He turned and stared for a moment at the now closed door, then up and down the street, narrow as an alley.

Gales Gardens – what a name to give a place like this.

Gales Alley would have been more appropriate, so why such a grand name for such a miserable street? A leftover from brighter times, maybe, when Bethnal Green had been country, before London had expanded to swallow it up. He had a vision of a curving little road lined by cottages with gardens; hence the name that had stuck.

Hardly wide enough to drive a brewer's dray through, the pavements sunken and broken, little more than a foot wide, the street was curved so that from the far end the main road wasn't visible at all and, at this time of night, dim with a single gas lamp to pierce its entire length. The two girls he had just left had probably known no other home. And now they were alone. Two girls, one still a child, the other barely a woman, to be flung out into the world, virtually orphaned, their mother dead, their father gone God knew where, probably with little or no concern for their fate. How would they manage? He recalled the feeling that had gone through him as he'd said, 'If I can be of any help . . .'

Quickly he put the feeling behind him and, turning, hurried away.

The woman was there inside five minutes, just as Doctor Lowe had promised. Ellie had been sitting beside her sister on the old sofa, clutching her hand. Both sat in silence, Ellie staring into the low flame flickering in the grate beneath the kettle she had placed on a trivet over the coals.

She started violently at the dull rat-tat on the front door. Letting go of Dora's hand, she hurried to answer it. The woman in a black, shabby coat over a black blouse and skirt held a stained carpetbag. She was quite elderly and had the look of someone who had laid out an army of dead in her time.

''Ello, love. I'm the person what the doctor sent to come 'ere. Orright if I come in?'

Without a word, Ellie opened the door wider and the woman stepped inside.

'Me name's Daniels. If you'll just show me where yer mother's lying . . .'

Ellie found her voice. 'Upstairs in the front bedroom.'

'Fine,' the woman said and gave her a cheery, gap-toothed smile. 'No need for you ter come up. I can deal with things.

Just give me a basin with some 'ot water. I'll let yer know when I'm done.'

Leaving the woman to her task, Ellie rejoined her sister, who hadn't moved an inch. Taking Dora's hand again, she listened to the movements and faint creaking of the floor-boards above her.

After what seemed ages the woman came down and Ellie heard her go into the scullery to empty the basin.

'I've done up there,' she said cheerily as she peeped into the room, bringing Ellie to her feet. 'I'll be on me way now. I expect you'll sort out yer funeral arrangements tomorrer. Doctor Lowe said you two was all on yer own, so if yer want any 'elp, he said ter just let 'im know. Orright then, love?'

She was hovering, looking a little hesitant, and Ellie real-ized she was waiting for some payment for her trouble. Ellie's mind flew to the few precious shillings left in the house, all the more precious with Mum never again to bring any in. She pushed aside the catch of grief in her throat for her mother in order to think practically. Was there enough money to pay this woman?

'How much do I give yer?' she asked.

Mrs Daniels glanced around at the threadbare rug in front of the low fire, worn furniture, stained and faded wallpaper. 'A shilling'll do, love. From some I do ask more, but in your case, you two being on yer own, a shilling if yer can spare it. I wouldn't ask, but I do 'ave ter live. Yer do understand?'

Ellie lifted her chin in a gesture of dignity. 'Yes, of course.'

Going to the old sideboard she bent down and withdrew a flat tin from underneath it. It held part of next week's rent, but fishing out the coin she handed it over.

She saw the fingers close about it and knew the feeling. Every penny mattered in this neighbourhood and now she was shorter of the rent by a shilling. She should have swallowed her stupid sensitivity and let Mrs Sharp next door see to her mother instead. A couple of pennies for a glass of beer for her help would have done. Now, instead of indulging herself in her grief for her mother, she'd have to face reality and set to bringing in the rent making the hatboxes on her own.

Dora would have to help. She'd teach her, as Mum had taught *her*. But even between them they'd never do the number Mum had. Of course there'd be no men to look after. Charlie hadn't paid his way either, like his dad, lurching from one casual job to another, in his case betting away what he earned. All this, of course, was if Mum's employer thought fit to keep her on now her mum was gone. It could even be that he would dispense with her services with hardly a stab of guilt in his heart for her plight.

It was a thought, pushing away the grief in her. With no money for the rent she could be evicted. In fact she *would* be evicted. Landlords had no hearts either. Then where would she go?

Another month before she was sixteen, Dora not fourteen until the summer. They'd be classed as orphaned or abandoned children, homeless, to be taken by the authorities into one of the dozens of orphanages around East London or into that place in Bethnal Green Road that called itself the Home of Industry. Cheap labour more like. Boys taught a trade, it was said – blacksmithing and such; but more to become labourers, meantime working their little guts out for their keep. Girls went into the laundry, surrounded by steam, watched over by some soulless charge woman. They'd end up as kitchen skivvies in some better-class homes or in some sweatshop, sewing gowns for the wealthy for a few pence.

In her bitter frame of mind this was how she saw it. Other than that it meant sleeping where they could, going hungry, or worse. Two pretty girls could be picked up by the unscrupulous and sold into slavery. It happened.

Ellie tightened her lips and, with Dora having crept into their bed, she went to her mother's room to allow Dora a moment alone to give way to her loss. She stood for a while in the doorway, gazing at the covers under which her mother's body lay, still and silent, the sheet pulled up over the head.

Somehow it all seemed unreal. The whole room felt cold, dead. She too felt cold and dead. No tears, the only thought that came to her a practical one. First thing in the morning, she must go round to the undertaker's.

Closing the door gently, as if reluctant any sound might disturb the silence of death, she went to her own room. Quietly she undressed, this time not to disturb the living – Dora asleep, worn out by her loss.

Going over to the washstand she wiped a wet flannel over her face and armpits, dried herself on their shared towel, noting in the washstand's oval, pock-marked mirror her thin nakedness, which was steadily growing shapely with coming womanhood, that womanhood like all around here seeming to be delayed by poverty and lack of fresh air.

Ellie rinsed her mouth, donned her nightdress, which was old and becoming too tight around the breast, briefly combed her long, dark hair and finally slipped into bed beside Dora.

'Goodnight,' she whispered. Dora didn't answer. But she wasn't asleep, for Ellie could feel the bed shaking very slightly to Dora's silent weeping.

After a while it subsided, but rather than falling asleep herself more than half the night was spent awake, thinking of how she was going to pay for any decent funeral. In all this time she hadn't cried. It felt as if she couldn't – perhaps never would. Her insides felt empty – as though it was her body that lay dead.

Next morning she was up at the crack of dawn, dressed in her one Sunday dress, her hair combed until it shone, a damp rag to clean up her boots a bit.

'Mrs Sharp said you can go into her,' she told Dora as she left. 'I'm off to the undertaker's and don't want you staying in the house all on your own.'

'Can't I come with you?' Dora asked plaintively, her eyes still a little puffy from crying herself to sleep.

'I shan't be long.' It was a promise she knew would be kept. Her business with the undertaker wouldn't amount to much. No fine coffin to be selected, just a plain box wheeled on a handcart to a far corner in the church cemetery where paupers were laid to rest, several together in one grave.

Thankfully she wouldn't have to descend to that. Like a lot of people, Mum had for some years denied herself by putting away a penny a week into a burial fund which would give her and her husband a piece of ground of their own, if only a cheap plot far from those on the main pathway with its fine tombstones and imposing monuments.

No tombstone for Mum, though. The cheapest stone was around thirty shillings, well beyond the burial fund. Perhaps in time a wooden cross – who knows? – but at least there'd be a personal grave number to identify her, which was more than a pauper's grave got.

For some reason that last thought caught her suddenly, just as she opened the door to leave for the undertaker's, as if something in the depths of her heart had burst. Abruptly closing the door again against the outside world, she sank down in the corner in tears, silently weeping as she had seldom wept before, crouched there alone and in privacy, relieved that Dora was still upstairs in bed, most likely nursing her own silent misery.

Finally, her nose blocked and her throat aching, her eyes no doubt reddened, she stood up, wiping her damp cheeks with a not-too-clean handkerchief fished from her jacket pocket, and slipped out into the chill early-morning air, head now held high.

The arrangements didn't take long, as she knew they wouldn't, the lugubrious undertaker being interested only in clients with money to spend on a fine funeral with black plumed horses, ornate carriages and caskets, and even a couple of young, professional mute mourners.

On her return home Dora handed her a letter. 'Came fer you while you was out,' she said. 'Seems ter be something wrapped up inside.'

There certainly did seem to be: a single sheet of notepaper folded around something hard. As she opened it, the contents fell heavily on to the floor. On the verge of bending to retrieve it she saw it was a guinea – a golden guinea winking up at her. Ellie heard her sister gasp 'Oh, Lord!' but she had frozen, able only to stare down at it in disbelief almost bordering on alarm, not daring even to touch it.

'Did you see who sent this?'

'No. Whoever it was, they was gone by the time I found it lying 'ere.'

Reaching out, Ellie forced herself to tentatively touch it, withdrawing her fingers quickly as if it might burn her, while Dora stood by wide-eyed. Still wrapped in disbelief, she finally forced herself to pick the coin up. It lay heavy in her palm. Never in her life had she held a gold guinea. It felt cold, solid, almost evil.

'What's the letter say?' She vaguely heard her sister's voice. Coming to, she looked at the note again, sure that there must be some mistake – sent to the wrong address, not for her at all. But if this was a mistake, then it was providence. Why go to all that bother trying to trace the right recipient? Why shouldn't she keep it?

Painfully she scanned the writing. Her reading skills were not vast. Having left school at twelve, teachers having viewed the cane as the greater part of learning, it was good that she was for the most part intelligent or she might not have learned to read at all. She frowned at the difficult small writing and saw that her name was in fact there. Laboriously, she deciphered the words: '*I am sending this towards your mother's burial. You are alone now and need help. Please oblige me by accepting this, as it is my regret for not attending her in her illness. Doctor Lowe.*'

Opening her fingers, Ellie gazed again at the coin now warming in her hand. She could do such a lot with this money: twenty-one shillings – more than she'd ever held in her life, and all hers.

Dora too was gaping. 'Cor! It's a blooming fortune! We could really do with that.'

The words brought Ellie's thoughts back into line. She closed her hand abruptly over the guinea and glared at her sister.

'No, it's for Mum. A stone for 'er grave, just a small one. She worked 'ard all 'er life. She wanted respect 'spite all the odds and she never ever got none, not from Dad or Charlie. An' we all took 'er fer granted. And now she's gone, taken by pneumonia, which she didn't deserve, out in all weathers to take 'er work back and collect more, and working all hours God sent just to keep us. It just ain't fair. Now at least we can show 'er a little bit of respect by her 'aving a gravestone of some sort.'

She bit back a catch in her throat as she spoke, and turned viciously on her sister as Dora pouted, 'But what about us?'

'What about us?' she cried. 'We're still here. We'll fend for ourselves.'

'What on?' Dora retaliated, glaring up at her.

'We'll manage. But we should at least give Mum something to be proud of. She deserves that much. And if there *is* a bit left over . . .'

She suddenly stopped. What was she saying? This money didn't belong to them. She'd been about to take the doctor's money – money he'd sent so that he could ease his conscience. Well, she wasn't going to make it that easy for him.

'I'm returning this to the doctor – telling him we don't need his charity.'

'What?'

'No, I've made up me mind, Dora. Mum never took a penny off anyone she didn't earn honestly. She certainly wouldn't want ter start now. So I've decided. I'm sending it back.'

Dora was looking at her, horrified. 'What about us? We could do with the money. And what about Mum's gravestone?'

'She'd understand. I know we could do with the money, but I don't intend ter let 'er standards down now.'

Resolutely she folded the coin back into the note, ignoring Dora's protests. She would go there this afternoon, be polite but firm and hand it back to him, telling him thank you for the kind thought but she didn't need it. It would make her feel much better than if she kept it, even if it had promised to be a small bit of salvation to their plight.

Two

Doctor Bertram Lowe glanced up briefly to the tinkle of the front-door bell. Lowering his midday newspaper, he watched the chubby figure of Florrie, his housemaid, hurry past the open door of the morning room to answer it. Her high, youthful, slightly nasal voice rang out.

'I'm sorry, miss. The doctor's surgery is closed till two o'clock unless it's an emergency, and you must go round the back like everyone else.'

'This is a personal call,' returned a young voice, pleasantly low, but the accent strongly East End.

'I'm sorry, miss. Unless you're a personal friend of the doctor you've still got to go round the back.'

'I need to speak to 'im now.' The tone was becoming argumentative. 'It's a private matter. It ain't nothing to do with illnesses.'

'Well, I'm really sorry, love.' Florrie's tone had begun to match that of the caller. 'You must come back at two. The doctor's not available at any old time. He's just had his lunch and unless someone's urgently sick . . .'

'No, I need to see him now. Tell him . . .'

'Look, miss, if it's not nothing medical, I'm afraid the doctor can't help you.'

Bertram glimpsed his wife Mary hurrying past the room. 'What is it, Florrie?'

'A young lady, madam. She won't go away.'

Mary reached the street door. 'I'm Doctor Lowe's wife; can I help?'

There was a moment's hesitation. 'Would yer give 'im this?'

'What is it?'

'He'll know what it is. I've come to give it back.'

Bertram Lowe suddenly recognized the voice. Letting his

Manchester Guardian fall to the floor, he got up and lumbered out to the hallway.

'I'll deal with this, Mary. I know the young lady.'

The two women withdrew, Florrie gratefully, his wife reluctantly, as he turned his attention to the wan face looking up at him and smiled gently.

Again came that poignant sensation experienced on first seeing the girl. It had struck him how much like his daughter she was. Millicent had been taken from him and his wife eighteen months ago, despite all his efforts. He had tended hundreds of patients in his time yet had been unable to cure his own daughter.

This girl was about the age his daughter would have been now. Though Millicent, enjoying the advantages of good upbringing, had been healthy and robust, her blue-green eyes bright and sparkling until TB had claimed her, wasting away her health while cruelly bestowing on her cheeks that high colour that belied the ravages of the disease.

TB was rife among the poor. Called consumption, or the wasting disease, it could spread like wildfire in any cramped, unsavoury locality. Yet it was no respecter of persons: despite wealth or privilege, with upper- and middle-class people going to great pains to avoid contact with those among whom it played havoc, it could still sneak its way into fine homes.

As a professional man he could hardly avoid contact with those who had it but had done his best to keep his small family from the diseased. Then, five years ago, it had struck, taking from him his only child.

He'd sent her to a sanatorium as soon as he'd realized what it was, but it had been of no use. She'd become thin, listless, the flush of her cheeks not the rosy glow of health but the trademark of the disease; she'd died, pale and wasted, like this young girl standing on his doorstep, though this girl's pallor came from the smoke-filled atmosphere of London's East End, lack of fresh air and good healthy food. But underneath that, he knew this skinny waif was strong with a natural instinct for self-preservation. At this moment she was holding out a folded sheet of paper to him with a firm, determined hand.

'Thanks very much for yer kind thought,' she began, her green eyes a steady, almost aggressive stare. 'But we don't 'ave no need of yer 'elp.'

He experienced a moment of confusion. 'It was given with the best of intentions. You seemed as though you needed help in some way.'

'It would of been better 'elp if you'd of come when I called at yer surgery while me mum was alive. She might be better now if yer'd come when I asked. I know I didn't 'ave no money for a doctor's visit, but she's dead now. If I'd 'ad money then, she might still be alive, so I don't feel it's right you giving me money now it's too late, and I don't think I ought ter take it. So I'm giving it back. But thanks for the thought.'

It was a long speech and Bertram Lowe stood silent and stunned throughout, finally finding his voice.

'I want you to have it, child. With no one to bring in a wage – you said your father had left and your brother run off – you could end up destitute.'

'I can't remember saying me dad's left and me brother's gone.'

'Few remember what is said in the shock of bereavement.'

She shrugged off the comment. 'Anyway, I ain't that destitute as ter be obliged ter take charity.'

'It was not charity, child, merely given out of kindness of heart.'

'As I see it,' she broke in calmly, 'it was out of need to ease yer conscience at not coming when yer was most wanted.'

He stared down at her. She thought she had hit the nail on the head. How wrong she was. How could he tell her she bore such a likeness to his dead daughter that she had reawakened a grief he'd thought he'd begun at last to overcome? This gesture of helping her because God hadn't blessed him enough to help another had been his natural reaction.

He had spent his morning's surgery half-regretting having sent her that money. How else could she have taken it but in the way she had? She was nothing to him – just another child of the East End. Yet somehow he hadn't wanted to lose touch with her. Unknowingly she'd prompted in him a need to cling to the memory of his sweet, darling Millicent.

'I'd rather yer take it back,' she was saying.

He watched her bend down to lay the note he'd sent her with its contents on the lower of the two stone steps leading up to his door. But as she turned away he came to life, waddling down the steps, holding on to the wrought-iron railings for support, in time to catch her thin wrist.

'Please, my dear. Let me explain.'

She pulled against his grip. 'I ain't taking it back! I don't want yer blood-money!'

He hung on, thankful no one was passing, though perhaps curtains might be twitching. 'My dear, you look cold. Come inside for a moment. My wife will give you a warm drink. I didn't intend to insult you. I understand.'

He did understand this strange pride of the poor – at least, of those who had pride. Those who didn't had hands ever outstretched for easy handouts. This girl, he felt with an odd prick of satisfaction, wasn't one of them.

'Please accept my hospitality,' he urged.

He saw her glance over her shoulder at the cold-enwrapped street and her thin body gave a small shiver. She had ceased pulling against him, her pride dissipating, and he was able to draw her up the two steps and into the house, closing the door. Momentary panic flashed in the wide, green eyes as he did so, but faded as his wife returned along the hallway.

'You poor child,' she began. She held out a hand while he released his from Ellie's thin arm. 'I overheard what my husband said. I shall have a warming drink made straight away to take the chill out of you, my dear.'

She was a small woman. Her roundness made her look even smaller as she conducted Ellie gently across the wide, brightly lit hallway, the gas lamps lit despite it being daylight outside. It seemed to Ellie as astonishing that some people were able to burn gas with no thought at all to the cost.

The room she was shown into was bright, without need of lamps. There were two upholstered easy chairs and sofa in green brocade, flowery wallpaper with pictures and framed photos suspended all around the room from picture rails. Side tables held large potted plants. The sideboard held a clutter of family photos, vases and ornaments under glass domes, and there was a large oval mirror behind it – all typically Victorian; tasselled runners everywhere.

The mantelshelf above the fireplace, in which a huge fire blazed, held more ornaments, a gilt clock, also under a glass dome, and another mirror. A patterned rug almost covering the floor completed the sense of the room's being warm and cosy, if just a little overstuffed. Ellie had never seen such a room.

The doctor's wife guided her to the sofa, told her gently to sit down as she hesitated. 'I'll have our maid bring you a mug of warm milk. Or would you prefer cocoa?'

Cocoa. When had she last had cocoa? If Mum had a good day's work and she could afford some little luxury, perhaps.

Annoyed at herself for feeling a little overwhelmed, Ellie nodded. 'I'd like cocoa, please,' she said, trying to sound positive.

Going to the door to summon her maid, the woman paused, glancing back at Ellie. The fingers moved slowly to her lips and her eyes began to fill with tears; she turned her gaze towards her husband. Her voice shook. 'My dearest, she looks so much like our . . .'

'Mary, the cocoa,' he interrupted sternly.

She recovered herself with a start. 'Yes, dear, of course.'

As she departed, Doctor Lowe positioned himself with his back to the window's thick lace curtains and heavy drapes, surveying Ellie.

'My wife is an emotional woman. Some eighteen months ago we lost our daughter Millicent. Had she lived, she would have been about your age. My wife has never fully recovered from our loss and I am afraid she sees a resemblance to our daughter in every young girl she meets.'

He began to pace. With her own more recent grief to surmount, Ellie felt no particular interest in his. She let her gaze follow his portly figure and found herself wondering how two such plump people fitted into one bed with any comfort. Families she knew often crammed six or seven children into one bed, arranged top to tail or even sideways. But her parents had both been thin; plenty of room for them, though, in past times made room for a couple of little ones. But with Mum dead and Dad gone, the bed lay empty.

Skinny old cow, her father had called her. He himself was well built and muscular. Hard work had taken the flesh off Mum's bones while he strode around showing off to whatever woman caught his eye. The money to tog himself up, to treat them handsomely – them and his mates, who thought him a swell sort of bloke – came from his wheeling and dealing. Mum, on the other hand, saw very little of that money.

If she had a bad week, sheets and tablecloths and often her treasured jet brooch would be taken down to the pawnshop, her self-respect blown away, to be redeemed the moment more work came in.

He didn't care, so long as his self-respect remained intact, even walking out on her as she was dying. Though he hadn't known that at the time, the thought had flashed into Ellie's mind that if she did lay eyes on him again, she would swing for him for the way he'd treated Mum. If he knew she was dead, he'd no doubt put his hands together, being free to enjoy himself.

Her wish for revenge was swept away as Doctor Lowe's voice broke through. 'So you must forgive my wife's little outburst, my dear. I pray that some day she will find something or someone to take the pain from her.'

He turned abruptly to face her, a thoughtful light dawning in the piggy eyes. She noticed they were extremely light-coloured, like pale ale.

'I have been thinking ever since you turned up on my doorstep that you might be the solution to her grief.'

He smiled at Ellie's lifted eyebrows. 'With no money now, you could very well lose your home. There is the orphanage, or living rough under some archway until picked up by some unsavoury character for his exploitation. It happens, child. Many a young, homeless waif has been sold for slave labour of sorts for a few shillings. I'll refrain from mentioning the depths to which such practice can descend. But I may be a means of salvation.'

He paused while Ellie remained watching him, now suspiciously.

'What crosses my mind is that this house has a position for another staff member. Florrie, our housemaid, has been complaining about being asked to do work in the kitchen as well as her housemaid duties, and I do understand this. But cook can hardly be expected to do washing-up as well as making meals.'

Ellie sat silent as he regarded her contemplatively.

'I wonder,' he went on, '– what if I were to offer you employment as scullery maid? You would live in, no longer having to find rent; you would share Florrie's bedroom. She is from Norfolk – too far to get home. She's an extremely nice girl and could be a good friend to you.'

At last Ellie found her voice. 'What about me sister? I can't leave 'er.'

Doctor Lowe's face fell. Obviously he hadn't considered Dora.

But Ellie was ahead of him. All he wanted was someone who'd remind him of his dead daughter, trying to replace what he'd lost. It was such a ridiculous suggestion she almost laughed. She wasn't falling for that one.

'I ain't leaving me sister,' she said adamantly, keeping her face straight. 'I intend ter carry on the work me mother was doing.'

'And what is that?'

'She made hatboxes for shops what sold silk top hats. I 'elped her.' Quickly she explained her own part in the work. 'I know the job and me mum's employer might keep me on. So I don't need any—'

She was sharply interrupted. 'I think you'll find that will not work out as you hoped, child.'

'I beg yer pardon?'

'You and your poor mother did the work between you.'

'I 'elped,' Ellie interrupted rudely.

'Yes, helped. Which provided a larger output than had she worked alone. Working alone you'd complete less than half the number turned out by a skilled worker such as your mother was. Her employer needs full quotas from his outworkers. It is his business, my dear, to make a profit. There is no charity in business. You will find that out.'

She'd already found that out. Before coming here, she'd gone to the man. He'd looked down his nose at her, his smile oily.

'Sorry about your mum, love. I've lost a good worker. But I don't think you'll be taking her place. It's quotas I need. I can't afford people who turn in just a few here, a few there. I've a business to run. I'm sorry, love, you'll have to look for something else.'

'You're sacking me? Me and me mum turned in good work,' she had argued desperately.

'No, love,' had come the hardening tone. 'Your *mum* worked for me. You only helped her. You wasn't officially employed by me, so it's not a case of *sacking*. I'm sorry but that's how it stands. Goodbye.'

He had turned his back on her to stare down from his dusty office window at men in the warehouse moving stacks of hatboxes into waiting carts. She'd left, her visit over in four minutes flat.

Now she stood silent before this portly doctor, her dignity in being self-sufficient fading as the truth of his words sank in. Slowly came an idea that began to lift her heart. Work here. Live in. It had to be a godsend, but only if she could come to some arrangement for Dora.

She'd be cunning. Doctor Lowe wanted her for a reason. For that reason he would agree to anything.

'I couldn't possibly work for you if I 'ad to leave my sister on her own, Doctor Lowe,' she said quietly. 'She's only thirteen and we're alone now. I wouldn't want 'er to be even more alone. So I'll 'ave to refuse yer offer.'

His expression was almost one of dismay and fear and she knew she had scored. Unbelievable for a man to be so consumed by the need to keep alive a memory that should by now have been healing. She saw him pull himself up to his full, rotund height of five foot five.

'I could find something for her to do, I suppose, but I couldn't pay a wage. She would work for her keep – I can't say more than that.'

Ellie gave him the briefest smile of gratitude, that he'd not helped her mother earlier still in her mind. His strange glance in response to her smile made her wonder if that too didn't remind him of his daughter. She rather hoped so, perhaps a little heartlessly, but in her situation something like that could prove an advantage and allow her to play on it. She would find out just how as things developed. He owed her, came the thought – cut short as Florrie came with a steaming mug of cocoa for her.

There wasn't much to clear out of the house: a few bits of Mum's. Cheap trinkets, a few precious things she had hoarded, her beloved jet brooch which, as the years went on, had seen more visits to the pawnbroker's than time at her neck – these went into a cardboard box Ellie would keep by her to the end of her days. Merely holding them made the tears flow. Yet at the funeral she'd remained dry-eyed, walking behind the coffin on its handcart to the churchyard at St John's – a more prominent spot, paid for with the guinea Doctor Lowe had insisted she take back, as she would be working in his house from now on. This inability to shed tears as her mother's coffin was lowered into its grave she could only attribute to the hatred that was in her heart for her father and this wish she had for revenge. Dora, on the other hand, had sobbed enough for the two of them.

Ellie had protested about taking back the guinea until he had finally said that, if she insisted on being proud, he could take it from her wages if that was what she wanted. This she'd agreed to, feeling her conscience clearer, promising herself that she'd take nothing more from him but her wage and, from what she did earn, put a little by towards a stone for Mum – by herself, no one else, just her.

Most of Mum's clothes – which wasn't much – she took to a second-hand dealer, who gave her a few pence for them. A few bits she kept back for herself. Mum's jet brooch she fastened to the high collar of her dress and in her youthful way she promised herself she would wear it for ever in memory of her mother and as a constant reminder of the man she intended to make pay for walking off and leaving her as she lay on her sickbed.

The man who came to clear the house handed her a few shillings: daylight robbery maybe, but she had no option but to accept.

There was still no sign of her father. He didn't know Mum had died. There was no word from Charlie either, gone a good month now. In the past he had gone away, usually after an argument, though never for this long. He'd be terribly upset when he found out what had happened. She didn't care about her father, but Charlie was a different matter. She'd always felt close to Charlie.

She decided to leave word with Mrs Sharp next door, giving the new address where she'd be working. The Sharps' home was a muddle but jolly, even though Mr Sharp was seldom in work. There were several younger children. Dolly, nearly the same age as herself, she got on well with. And there was Ronnie Sharp, recently turned eighteen; she got on well with him too. She liked him a lot. But her quest today was his mother.

'Me dad – if he do come back, don't say where I am,' she

instructed her. 'See if you can worm out of 'im where he's living and drop a note in to Doctor Lowe so I know where to find 'im.' She didn't say why. That was her business. Nor did she believe for one minute that he'd turn up unless he got himself into trouble.

What belongings he'd left behind she refused to even soil her hands with by trying to sell them, but instead threw them all out into the gutter to lie there in the mud from a morning's rain. They'd been there hardly more than a minute before being pounced on by a cluster of women who appeared like magpies to paw over them. In five minutes flat the gutter was clear, not even a matchbox left. She'd much rather they'd been left to rot away, but they'd probably do someone some good. And she had washed her hands of him, though not of her determination to see him suffer for his treatment of Mum.

One day she'd find him wherever he was. She could be patient. Very soon she'd be sixteen – her birthday just over three weeks away – grown up; and she intended to find him and make him sorry for what he'd done to Mum, as well as to her, no matter how long it took.

What felt worse was the shame. Had she been partly to blame? Was it her? A phrase came dimly to mind, something said at some wedding or other: 'He who is without sin, let him cast the first stone.'

The words came out of the blue, pulling up sharp. Was she really without sin? Had she enticed him in some way? Should she have fought harder? But, still a child, she'd been too frightened to. He'd forced her. It wasn't her fault. But what if it had been? Those who are without sin . . .

Viciously she pushed the thought away from her. His sin, not hers!

Three

Watched by Doctor Lowe's housemaid though totally ignored by his ample-bodied cook, Ellie and her sister stood awkward and ill at ease in the large kitchen, which felt vast compared to the poky one they were used to.

Those days were behind them now. Their old home lay empty, awaiting new occupants. If their father went there in the next few days another family would be there. Mrs Sharp would tell him what had happened, of course.

Ellie wondered how affected he'd be, hearing of Mum's death. It would be a shock, obviously – he was human after all; but how long would it take for him to get over it? Not long she suspected. Would he feel any guilt about having deserted her when she'd been so ill? Ellie didn't think so. He might even feel relieved, able to get on with his own life without interference. Again came that curling tendril of hatred inside her.

What of the future? As she waited to be looked over by Doctor Lowe's wife, she wondered if she had been too quick in asking Mrs Sharp not to tell Dad where she'd now be living. Would he demand her and Dora back? Would he want a couple of kids around him mucking up his life? For her part she didn't need him spoiling her chance of a new life, if only as a scullery maid.

Something told her that this lowly position might not last too long. She could be on to something better. She kept thinking of Mrs Lowe's words, gasped out behind a trembling hand: 'She looks so like . . .' and the brittle way her husband had cut off what appeared to have been a reference to his daughter's likeness to herself. It might benefit her to play on that. Not too soon of course. Unable to cope with this apparent resemblance to his dead daughter, her new employer might dismiss her. She'd have to tread carefully.

She felt Dora's hand slip into hers. 'I feel really out of place 'ere,' Dora whispered. 'I wish we 'adn't come. I feel in the way.'

Ellie glanced down at her. 'We'll be all right. I'll make sure of it.'

Dora had been so excited when she had told her of their good fortune. 'So I won't have to go and live with Mrs Sharp after all,' she cried, having been told about their neighbour's kind offer to take her in.

'Only for a while,' Mrs Sharp had said. 'Until things settle. I couldn't have her for too long because there ain't much room for me own kids. But I couldn't see a child like her with nowhere to go or be stuck in an orphanage somewhere, poor little lamb, when I can be of some 'elp, at least until you find some work and somewhere cheaper to live.'

Dora had hated the idea, crying, 'I don't want ter live with strangers!'

'They're not strangers,' Ellie had said. 'They're neighbours and you're friends with Cathie and Bertie Sharp. You get on well together and Bertie's your special friend. You know he likes you a lot.'

'But not to live in the same 'ouse,' had come the protest. 'Their 'ome's crowded and I might be asked to share the same room with 'im.'

'No you won't,' Ellie told her. 'The girls sleep upstairs. Their brothers share the back room downstairs.'

Her sister's response had been an enormous shrug, but now of course there was no need to worry about that any more. Ellie stopped thinking of it as she saw the doctor's wife come into the kitchen.

Mary Lowe's gentle brown eyes took in the two young people standing in the centre of the room. They looked lost, while the kitchen resounded to the clash of saucepans that Mrs Jenkins was setting on the large black-leaded range in readiness for the family's midday meal. Mary gave each girl a smile that was as tremulous and awkward as their own response – that of the younger one shy, the older with a fraction more confidence.

None could have mistaken them for other than sisters, both of them auburn-haired and dimple-chinned, with narrow cheeks that would fill out and blossom with colour with some good food inside them. Both had the same firm set of the lips, the same pert nose, the same wide eyes with the darker rim of the iris quite sharply and startlingly defined.

But it was the older girl who drew her attention as if by a magnet and again she felt a lump inside her breast, the stinging threat of tears. There was no doubt her husband had engaged her because of this uncanny resemblance to their dead daughter. It was more than that. It was the posture, the smile, a movement. She'd argued against his engaging her but had finally given in, as she usually did before his stronger will; but deep inside she felt she would begin to regret it. What if this likeness started to affect her to such an extent that she'd be unable even to look at the girl.

She swallowed her doubts and said, 'I shall leave it to Cook to tell you what your duties will be, child.'

She turned to the younger girl. 'You, my dear . . . I'm sorry, I have forgotten your name for the moment.'

'Her name's Dora,' the sister said firmly.

'Yes, Dora,' Mary echoed without looking at the older girl. Already she felt dislike for her – not because she reminded her so of Millicent but because Millicent had been sweet and gentle. This girl was far from being that: hard, forthright rather than compliant and submissive as a domestic should be, especially one being taken on for such a lowly position as scullery maid.

'Come with me, dear,' she said quietly to Dora, who meekly followed her from the kitchen. She approved. Young people should know their place. She felt quite taken with her. And there lay the difference between the two.

'I hope you can sew and do simple mending,' she said at the door. 'I have a good outside seamstress for my finer things whom I would rather not burden with small everyday repairs.'

'I can sew,' came the ready response as Dora followed her into the hallway and up the broad stairs.

Mary Lowe smiled. The child was uncouth, ill-spoken, but she would set about teaching her as much as she could on how to be ladylike and speak nicely. Such a pretty little girl and not at all like her sister after all.

Left alone, Ellie felt suddenly jealous. Dora given sewing duties while she was left to scrub pots! It wasn't a nice feeling, jealousy, and she hurriedly turned her mind to the housemaid and the girl's ample physique.

It seemed everyone in this residence was well padded, from

her new employer and his wife down to the housemaid and their cook. She and Dora, being so thin, would stand out like sore thumbs in this house. Everyone here ate so well, judging by the food on the kitchen table at this very moment, it was no wonder they put on flesh. She wondered if, after a while, she and Dora would become as plump.

Came a momentary vision of her mother – thin, wiry, always going without. The memory brought a catch in her throat, which she forced back. She had to make her own way in the world now, she and Dora looking after each other. Giving in to tears would do no one any good. But tears there were, hovering unshed in her heart.

She almost jumped out of her skin as the cook, who'd been busy at the kitchen range, now turned on her.

'Right now, young lady, my name's Mrs Jenkins,' she said in a harsh, piercing voice. 'But you will call me Cook. Your employer you'll address as sir, and his wife as madam. Do you understand all that?'

'Yes,' Ellie replied, trying not to sound too meek yet not too forthright. 'And what do I call the housemaid?'

Mrs Jenkins's face relaxed, making her look almost pleasant but for the strident voice. 'You call her Florrie like the rest of us. And everyone will call you Ellie. Understand, girl?'

This was a relief. To have to call someone 'miss' when she was hardly older than herself would have gone against the grain, thought Ellie as she smiled back at Cook. She was aware that she had a naturally wide smile that revealed good strong teeth, not often seen in the sort of place she'd been brought up in. They were white and even, and the smile seemed to appease Mrs Jenkins, who said in a quieter tone, 'Very well, Ellie, get out of your things. Hang your hat and coat on a hook behind that cupboard door. Put the apron on you'll find there. Then you can take these used saucepans over to the sink. Fill it with water from that big kettle and put in a handful of the washing soda you can see on the draining board. Do you understand?'

'Yes,' Ellie said again, glancing at the several black iron saucepans. They looked huge and heavy.

'Make sure you scrub 'em absolutely clean. There's a dish-cloth and some wire wool to help you do that. I don't want nothing found stuck to the insides, you understand? Then let 'em drain a bit before drying 'em. I don't like wiping-up cloths to end up wringing wet. You understand all that?'

Ellie nodded. It seemed to be Mrs Jenkins's stock remark – asking if she understood, like she was some foreigner who couldn't speak English. She had almost taken offence at it, but then realized this was going to be asked of her for the rest of her stay.

Happening to glance at Florrie, she saw the girl give a comical grimace, a brief and significant downturn of her chubby lips with her bottom lip thrust ludicrously outward and downward, the lips instantly returning to normal before Cook could notice. Ellie knew immediately that here was a friend and ally and no longer felt isolated as she quickly divested herself of her outdoor things and donned the apron.

Without a word she hoisted two of the three weighty cooking utensils and with an effort of her thin arms bore them to the sink, depositing the third one on top of them. Having sprinkled a handful of washing soda over them, she poured the boiling water from an equally heavy kettle, needing two hands to do it, and set to work.

Despite hot water and soda a scum soon formed on the surface as the baked grease and food reacted with them, requiring the addition of more soda. At this rate, she thought, as she scrubbed and scraped, her hands would be chafed red. It was as well they were already hard from her old environment or they'd have been well sore by the end of the day.

Even so, it was better than being out on the street or bundled into an orphanage. There she'd have had to do as she was told and no argument. Here she was still doing as she was told, but she was free to walk out any time she fancied. She didn't wish to, of course, but in this lay the difference. And who could say what the future had in store for her here.

'How did you get on?' Ellie whispered as she and Dora lay side by side in the narrow bed with its hard mattress. A similar bed by the other wall of this tiny attic room, leaving just enough space for a body to pass between, held only Florrie. But then the housemaid's plump girth took up as much room as two slim ones.

She'd fallen asleep the second her brown tousled hair had hit the unforgiving pillow and was already snoring, a soft, snorting, nasal inhalation followed by a sort of whiffled exhalation.

Ellie tried to ignore it as Dora whispered back, 'I like Mrs Lowe. She's very kind.'

Again Ellie experienced that earlier prick of jealousy. All she'd seen today was Cook's broad back or Florrie's full bosom and broad hips when she bustled into the kitchen to fetch something or other to do with her chores around the house. Not once had Ellie left that kitchen and it looked as though this would be all she'd ever see of the house, except to climb the back stairs to sleep, while Florrie enjoyed the freedom of the whole house and Dora was allowed to trail after her mistress like some little spoiled house cat.

'She gave me a boiled sweet from a dish in her bedroom,' Dora added to her sister's silent envy. 'And I was given my lunch and dinner in the ante-room next to hers where I'd been mending some sheets. How did you get on?'

'All right,' Ellie snorted tersely and turned over with her back to her sister. She had no intention of discussing her day, having to eat in the same place in which she worked. Even though it was a plate of delicious soup with new bread, Cook saying, 'One thing, dear, down here we do eat well, all the leftovers from cooking for the master and mistress and I make sure they eat well, don't you worry,' this said with a fat, crafty finger laid significantly alongside her stubby nose, Ellie had felt trapped.

'Don't you want to tell me what you got up to?' came Dora's voice.

'I need to go to sleep,' Ellie answered shortly, dragging the sheet and thin coverlet up over her ears. 'Goodnight!'

'Goodnight, Ellie,' came the quiet response and she couldn't help hearing a ring of bewilderment in it. Poor Dora, it wasn't her fault, but too late to explain now.

The next day proved exactly the same as the previous one. Day followed day, each spent endlessly washing up, scrubbing the wooden table free of flour and other bits of preparation, wiping down the side tables, blackleading the kitchen range and eternally scrubbing the flagstone floor. She found herself bitterly resenting tradesmen and carters who came in leaving muddy footprints. The nearest she came to breathing the open air was the small blast that followed behind someone entering through the kitchen back door.

A week passed. She hadn't seen hair or hide of her employer or his wife, nor had she been outside the house except to empty slops or pay a visit. She'd stand at the sink and stretch her neck to see over the opaque windowpanes to the clear panes above. That gave her a narrow view of sky and anyone passing along the back alley. She would stand there mesmerized until Cook called to her to get on with her work. She hadn't seen the sun for a week, the kitchen facing north so that the sun never came round at all. She felt trapped.

Added to this was a growing resentment when Dora told her one night that she and Mrs Lowe had visited her dressmaker, since Florrie, who usually accompanied her, was having her half-day off. Servants, it seemed, were allowed one half-day per fortnight and one whole day per month. At that rate she'd have to wait ages for her half-day. Even Dora had seen the great outdoors. It wasn't fair.

'Ellie, there's someone here to see you.' Mrs Jenkins's stern voice made her look up quickly from washing the kitchen floor. 'I made him stand outside. He says he's your brother but I don't—'

Ellie's squeal of delight cut her short as she sprang up, almost tipping over the pail of dirty suds in running past her to yank the door open. There stood Charlie. His ready smile faded as he surveyed her in mob cap and apron.

'What're you doing?' The question was harsh and sharp.

It was then she realized she still held a dripping scrubbing brush and that her apron was soaking wet.

'Washing the kitchen floor,' she said inanely, formal words already smothering what should have been excited reunion.

'Who for?' came another harsh question.

'I work here. For Doctor Lowe.'

'Scrubbing floors?'

'Not only that,' she replied, deflated. 'I work in the kitchen, washing up – that sort of thing.'

'A skivvy!'

'Well . . . yes. Dora works here too. She does sewing.'

She broke off, bewildered and angry at this turn of events that should have been full of joy. Instead here she was, being questioned by a brother who'd appeared completely out of the blue.

She fought the feeling of degradation with a show of outrage.

'What right've you got coming 'ere looking at me as if I was dirt?'

The question was ignored. 'What're you doing working for a bloody doctor when you should be at 'ome with Mum? And where are you all living? There's other people in our 'ouse.'

Ellie's face went bleak. He didn't know. He'd gone off in a temper after that fight with Dad. Now he'd come back to find his family not there.

'How did you know I was 'ere?' she asked stupidly. It helped give her time to recover from the shock of his having no idea what had happened.

'I went next door to ask. No one was in, but that silly old dear livin' the other side said you was working at the doctor's 'ouse in Old Ford Road and I could ask you what's gone on. She wouldn't say no more. So 'ere I am.'

Ellie was shivering. The late-March air was cold on her bare arms, still wet from scrubbing the kitchen floor, and she wasn't prepared to stand out here to tell him the news that their mother was dead, their father gone, and she and Dora homeless.

'Look, come inside,' she said.

As he followed her into the kitchen she said to a flabbergasted Mrs Jenkins that she needed to speak to her brother whom she'd not seen for ages, inside in the warm, and that what she had to tell him was an important and private matter.

Stunned by the look on Ellie's face, the woman gave a curt nod and retired to the hall, leaving them in the kitchen.

Once alone, Ellie turned to him. 'Mum died,' she said bluntly. There was no gentle way to say it. 'She caught pneumonia and died, three weeks ago. You wasn't here.'

She wanted to go on but couldn't for the moment. She let her voice die away as he stood looking at her in stunned silence. At his shocked stare she had to tell him everything, if only to combat the rage simmering away in her heart against her father, who had walked out on his family.

She began to relate that while their mother lay ill their father had calmly forsaken her for one of the floozies he'd often knocked about with.

'I don't know where he is now so I can't get in touch to tell 'im about Mum. As far as I know, he still don't know she's dead and, to tell you the truth, Charlie, I've got nothing but contempt for the likes of 'im.'

As she spoke she felt her blood boil. 'How could he be so vile knowing how ill she was? He even told her she'd been a drag on 'im for ages – Mum, who'd worked her fingers to the bone for him. He said he was glad to be rid of her and he wanted a life of his own, or something like that. Though I know one thing: if I ever see him again I will kill him!' She spat out those last words. 'I really will.'

Charlie had said nothing during all this. Finally he said in a low voice, 'Where's Mum buried?' It was as if he hadn't taken in a thing she had said, and there came a desire to hurt, to wound, her fondness for her brother flying out of the window.

'It could've been in a pauper's grave for all you care!' she burst out. But that wasn't fair. Ellie tried to curb her anger. 'I didn't have any money to bury her, but Doctor Lowe who I'm working for now gave me enough to have her buried properly.'

'Why should 'e do that?' came the suspicious query. 'What's 'e got ter do with you?'

'He wrote out the death certificate. I expect he was sorry for us girls.'

It sounded a lame excuse. She understood her brother's concern. Why would a man she didn't know, even a doctor, give her money for the burial of her mother? It would look odd to Charlie.

'I'm working for him to pay it back,' she lied hurriedly. She too had thought at first that he'd taken pity on her, but now of course she knew there had been more to it. But she couldn't tell that to Charlie. Already he'd begun to look belligerent.

'What've you been up to, to let some man give you money?'

'Nothing!' she shot back. 'I suppose he felt sorry for us all on our own with no money. You and Dad was nowhere to be found. We could have ended up in an orphanage. I didn't know where either of you was, did I?'

It was a bald accusation and he blinked, but she didn't care. She was fuming now. 'So you see, there was nothing in it, like what you think!'

She knew what he was thinking all right. 'And that's why I'm here, working to pay off the debt of Mum's burial in a half-decent grave.'

'Well it ain't right.' Again he hadn't really been listening to what she was saying. 'And I ain't 'aving you and your sister working in the 'ouse of some bloke what gives you money right out of the blue, debt or no debt.'

'So you'd be 'appier seeing us in an orphanage or out on the street?' she challenged.

'I'll look after yer. I've got money – won it boxing. I'll pay your debts and take you and Dora away from 'ere.'

Suddenly she realized she didn't want to be taken away from here. She might be a skivvy but she saw further into the future than Charlie could. What did he have to offer her? He made his living gambling, boxing, earning a bit here, a bit there; they could be on the poverty line for ever, moving from place to place. And when he finally met a girl and wanted to get married, what of her and Dora? At least here she could play on Doctor Lowe's obsession with her likeness to his dead daughter. It might take time but who knew what it might lead to?

'Look,' Charlie cut through her thoughts. 'I ain't standing 'ere in this bloody kitchen talking about it. I want ter see this employer of yours.'

'I don't think you're allowed,' she said in sudden panic.

'Sod what I'm allowed!'

Shoving her bodily to the door he opened it and pushed her ahead of him into the dim hallway with its wide stairs. Mrs Jenkins was standing there, a sturdy, rounded body, already prepared to bar his way. 'Oi, young man,' came her strident voice. 'Where d'you think you're going?'

But Charlie, six foot tall and burly with it, wasn't going to let some rotund if infuriated woman stand in his way. With one hand he thrust her aside, the other holding his sister by her upper arm. 'Where's this bloody so-called employer of me sisters? I need ter see 'im.'

'He's in surgery. He's busy,' cried Mrs Jenkins, hurrying after him, thoroughly infuriated at being so manhandled. 'You can't go in there when he's in consultation.'

'Can't I?' Charlie bellowed. His eyes had followed her brief glance in the direction of a door across the hall. Still hanging on to Ellie, he made for it, bursting through to startle the man's patient almost out of his skin. But Bertram Lowe had already become aware of raised voices in the hall and was ready for him. From behind his desk he turned to calmly face the intruder.

Four

Bertram Lowe looked towards his patient. 'I am so sorry, would you please excuse us for a moment, Mr Partridge?' he said in a quiet, polite voice.

As the surgery door closed, he turned back to take in his slim scullery maid and the burly, well-muscled man still holding her by the arm.

'Now, sir, who might you be?' he enquired in an unruffled tone.

'I'm 'er brother – that's what I am.'

'I see.' No two siblings could have looked more unalike. 'And what is it you want?'

Mrs Jenkins appearing at the door, all flustered, stopped whatever his visitor was about to say. 'I tried to stop him, Doctor Lowe . . .'

He cut her short with a wave of his podgy hand. 'That's quite all right, Mrs Jenkins. Thank you. You may carry on with your duties.'

'Do you want me to call for assistance, sir?' she asked, eyeing the big man.

'No, it's quite all right, thank you.'

As the woman left, he cast his pale gaze back to the pair. 'Now then, can I help you?'

Charlie took a deep breath in through his nose, his initial belligerence fading a little. 'I want to know what this one's doing 'ere.'

'As you can see, she is employed as a kitchen maid.'

'Scullery maid! Skivvy! I bet you ain't even paying 'er any wages.'

'Of course I pay her.'

'And what about what she says she owes you?'

'She owes me nothing.'

'Then what the bloody 'ell are you up to with 'er? I'm her

brother and I've got a right to know what you're up to. If you think you can—'

'My good man,' Doctor Lowe interrupted. 'If you are suggesting there is something underhanded in my employing this girl and her sister in my establishment, I assure you, you are entirely mistaken.'

'Then what you want with 'em?' Charlie bellowed. At that moment he looked and behaved so much like her father that Ellie leaned back from the hold he still had on her arm. But she stayed quiet in case a word from her would make matters worse.

Doctor Lowe remained completely unruffled. 'I happened to be in need of staff replacement and the two girls were looking for work, so I engaged them. There is nothing strange about it, as you appear to imagine.'

Some of Charlie's bombast again deflated a little, though he continued stubbornly, 'Then we'd better see what me other sister says. Where is she?'

'She is with my wife, upstairs in our living quarters.'

'Right! We'll see what she says,' Charlie said, letting go of Ellie at last to make for the door, yelling out, 'Dora, come down 'ere! I want yer!'

But Mrs Lowe had already come out of her room, having heard raised voices and Dora's name being yelled. Dora's hand in hers, she descended the stairs slowly. Seeing the small, plump, motherly figure and the trusting way Dora held her hand, Charlie's belligerence faded.

'I'm sorry, missus; I didn't mean to disturb you.'

The woman didn't reply, but Dora let go the hand and ran down the rest of the stairs to him, suddenly filled with emotion, tears in her eyes.

'Charlie! Oh, Charlie, we wondered where you was. Something awful happened while you've been away.'

'I know.' His voice had grown softer. He put both arms around the thin frame. 'Ellie told me. I'd 'ave given anything to be 'ere, but I didn't 'ave no idea.'

'We was in such a state,' Dora said, going into an instant torrent of words. 'There was only me and Ellie with Mum when she died and we didn't know what to do. Dad and you was gone and we 'ad no money and no one to care for us. We didn't even 'ave enough for a grave and we was already

way behind with the rent and had an eviction order weeks
ago 'cos Mum was ill and we didn't know where you or Dad
was. We was at our wits' end and no one could take us in
because they 'ad kids of their own. If Doctor Lowe hadn't
helped us out I don't know what we'd 'ave done.'

Hardly coming up for breath she told the rest of the story
in as fast a flood as before, ending with, 'He's been kind to
us and so 'as Mrs Lowe too.'

Ellie found her voice. 'We don't want to leave 'ere, Charlie.
We're both all right 'ere. If you take us away, where are we
going to live? In digs? I know you ain't got no proper job.
But I'm working now. I can hold up me head and earn me
own living.'

'As a blooming skivvy,' Charlie repeated, confused but on
the defensive still. 'A scullery maid.'

'If she does well while in my service,' Bertram Lowe put
in, 'she will inevitably rise in status, with higher pay. But if
they want to go with you, Mr Jay, I shall not stop them.'

Charlie seemed taken off guard. 'Well, I don't know,' he
muttered awkwardly. 'I suppose it'll be orright. But I intend
to hang around a bit, just to see 'em orright and be 'ere in
case they ain't.' His blue eyes flared for a moment, a warning
if things didn't go all right; but Ellie was ready for him.

'I don't want you interfering in our lives,' she said sharply.
'There was no sign of you when we needed you most, you
and Dad—'

'That wasn't my fault, Ellie,' he cut in. 'I wasn't to know
he'd walked off. You can't blame me.'

'I don't blame you,' she said. 'But I'd rather sort me own
life out, that's all.'

There was more to it than that. Her brother at nineteen was
so like his dad, and today she had seen that resemblance in
its full force. One day, as far as she could see, he would be
like Dad in every respect: selfish, overbearing, violent. There
was already hate in her heart towards her father, and a need
to avenge herself as well as Mum. She didn't want to feel the
same way about Charlie. The further he was away from her,
the better.

'I'm glad you come,' she said, drawing up her thin frame
with dignity. 'But me and Dora are all right.'

He was fidgeting awkwardly. 'I'll be off then. I'll keep in

touch, let yer know where I am time to time. I can't tell yer
'ow upset I feel about Mum. I can 'ardly believe she's gone,
it's such an 'orrible shock. She was such an 'ard worker and
an 'elp to all of us. I'm goin' ter miss her terribly – straight
I am.'

'Yes,' she said, flat-voiced. He could be as upset as he liked.

'Orright,' he said, and bending his six-foot frame took hold
of Dora, who'd let go of him, and kissed her on the top of
her head. He made to do the same with Ellie, but she moved
quickly away.

He straightened up, looking slightly offended, not understanding why she was being so cold towards him.

'Cheerio then,' he said gruffly and, receiving her stiff
response, allowed himself to be let out of the main door, a
sobered, dejected man.

Where he went Ellie had no idea. He had asked where Mum's
grave was and she'd told him, but when asked where he was
staying, all he had said was, 'Around.'

It gave the impression that it could be ages before she'd
set eyes on him again. So what? Dad was her real quarry. One
day she would catch up with him and make his life an eternal
misery. She didn't know how, but she would think of something when finally she found him.

One thing she did know: by the time she did find their
father, she'd be a lady. She had already decided upon that as
she went back to her kitchen duties, Dora going back upstairs
with Mrs Lowe, and Doctor Lowe returning to his surgery.

Whether it was to do with Charlie's belligerent attitude to her
being a mere scullery maid or not, the following afternoon
young Florrie came into the kitchen while she was up to her
eyes in rapidly cooling washing-up water and spoke in whispers to Mrs Jenkins.

Next thing Ellie heard was Cook's strident voice. 'Ellie,
leave that, love. You're wanted upstairs. The master wishes to
have a quick word with you. He's in his study. You know
where that is?'

'No,' Ellie admitted. The only part of the house she knew
was up the back stairs to the attic where she slept. Dora had
seen more of the place than her. 'Where is his study?'

'Up the main stairs, turn right along the landing and it's

the far door. Make sure to knock and wait to be called in. Understand that, girl? Don't go in until you're told to.'

'What's he want?' Ellie enquired.

'Never mind what he wants,' Cook said sharply. 'Get your apron off, wipe your hands thoroughly, take off your cap and tidy your hair, and then get straight up there. Hurry up now.'

Doing as she was told, her long hair, now released from its mob cap, tied neatly back with a bit of ribbon she kept in her skirt pocket, Ellie mounted the stairs, each step slower than the last, each with growing trepidation.

What did her employer want? Was it to tell her that her services were no longer needed? It could only be that after the way Charlie had behaved. And what about Dora? Did he intend to sack her too? After so short a time here would he even give them a reference? And where would they find work, two young girls with no skills? Even washing-up jobs like she'd been doing weren't easy to come by.

One question after another ran through her mind with each reluctant step. By the time she was outside the study door, at the dim end of the passage, her heart was thumping enough to make her feel sick. How was she going to break the news to Dora?

Well, this was it. If she was going to be given her marching orders, then she'd refuse to demean herself by hesitantly tapping, creeping in to hang her head and bob a curtsey. If she was to be told to go, then Doctor Lowe would see her as life had conditioned her, holding her head up and giving as good as she got.

She rapped on the door with her knuckles, louder perhaps than she had intended. For a moment there was silence, then Doctor Lowe's voice sounded, requesting she come in. Responding, she closed the door behind her and walked up to his desk. She was surprised to see that he was smiling up at her. Oh well, she thought, it's going to be done in good grace at least.

For all that, an apology was called for. 'I'm sorry me brother was so rude,' she began, hardly having reached the desk. 'He was just worried—'

'No need to apologize,' Doctor Lowe cut in with a brief lift of his hand. He was still smiling. Why was he smiling if he was about to dismiss her?

'I have asked to see you,' he hurried on as though her face had given away her thoughts, 'because I need to have a little talk with you. Do you like working here, my dear?'

'Do it matter?' she shot back at him. What did she have to lose? If he was about to get rid of her, it was best to come out with it and have done without this messing about trying to let her down lightly. It would add up to the same thing. As one who believed in straight talking, she was becoming impatient.

'Just tell me to go and let's get it over with!' she said.

'Go?' He looked suddenly bewildered, the small eyes in the podgy features going a little blank. 'No one is asking you to go.'

'Then why did you want to see me if it wasn't for that?'

'Simply to ask how you feel about working here. I wondered, perhaps, if your brother might have put ideas into your head and given you second thoughts about working here?'

It was she who was now bewildered. There was a momentary notion that he was inviting her to leave of her own accord, saving him the painful duty. 'I thought . . .' she began.

'That I intended to sack you?' he finished for her. 'Because of the incident with your brother?'

Ellie nodded. 'He can be a bit . . . outspoken,' she said, choosing a different word from the one that had first come to mind.

'As you are, my dear.' He waved away her instant protest. 'Yes, you are. It is what I admire about you, child. My daughter, whom my wife and I miss so much and grieve for, was always too ready to give in to everything. An exceptionally placid child but with no real spirit, I regret to say, though I loved her dearly.'

His gaze dropped away from Ellie's face, slanting sideways along some invisible, horizontal line, as if he were entering a world of his own.

'There were times when I wanted to shake some vigour or courage into her – times when I would have rejoiced to see my darling girl fight back when hurt or wronged. Perhaps that was why she so easily succumbed to her failing health. If only she had fought, had refused to let herself be taken from us, she might still . . .'

The rest of his words fell away into a shuddering sigh, his

obvious grief seeming to be getting the better of him. But, recovering with what to Ellie appeared to be a great effort, he turned his gaze back to her.

'I take it you have gathered how very like you are to my daughter in looks, age, height, colouring?' He said it almost belligerently, as if the apparent resemblance was her fault; but moments later his tone grew sad. 'I must admit that I was taken aback that first time I saw you, but I realize now, you are very different in character and spirit. You are as I would have given thanks to find her.'

Again his gaze wandered. 'It's very strange. You so resemble my sweet Millicent in looks; yet your sister, who does not physically remind me of her despite being like you in looks, is like her in manner – meek, quiet, easily controlled. You will never allow yourself to be controlled by anyone, my dear.'

He was right there. Ellie lifted her chin. 'But I'm not your daughter, am I, Doctor Lowe?' she reminded him, momentarily forgetting herself.

The remark drew his eyes back to her. For a moment she thought he was going to bellow at her to get out, he looked so deeply stunned. But the expression faded and he nodded, letting out his breath in a small, silent sigh of defeat.

'You were partially correct when you feared for your job here. My wife has been pleading with me to dismiss you. She says she finds it painful to look on you – that you remind her so of our daughter.'

'If I'm ter leave, what about me sister? If I've got to go, she's leaving with me. She won't 'ave her stay 'ere without me.'

He smiled at her forthrightness, his brief weakness over his daughter put aside. 'I have no intention whatsoever of dispensing with your services. I requested to see you to inform you that if you *are* happy here, I will seek a replacement scullery maid so that you may take up the duty of second housemaid. This house is quite large. Young Florrie is grossly overworked and she would welcome extra help.'

'But what if your wife insists on me going?'

Doctor Lowe drew himself up in his chair. 'I am the master in this house and have made up my mind. All I need to know is if you are happy working here. Now you may go, my dear, and tell Florrie the good news.'

Without waiting to be thanked, he leaned over and took up

a pen to dip it into the inkwell nestling on its stand to his right, proceeding to write something down on the papers that lay before him, thus dismissing her.

Ellie had no intention of thanking him. She was aware of what he was about, and what he was about needed no humble demonstration of gratitude from her. Indeed, though she saw opportunities of making the most of this odd resemblance Doctor Lowe saw in her to his darling Millicent, she was also made vaguely uncomfortable by it. It seemed to verge on the obsessive if not the morbid; moreover it held an element of something unnatural – that was the only word she could find for it.

She thought suddenly of her father as she made her way downstairs, hoping not to meet anyone coming up. The way her father had carried on with her – that too had been un-natural. She loathed him for his vileness, his utter disregard of her feelings. Every time she thought of it, it was like a slimy worm inside her stomach, slowly writhing its way upwards to eat at her heart – a sick feeling whenever she thought of him and what he used to do.

What if Doctor Lowe had unnatural thoughts of her too, in a different way, seeing his daughter in her, wanting to turn her into the little girl he had loved so much? Yet he was essentially a nice man, was probably not even aware of the strangeness in what he'd said to her. It made her cringe as much as did the memory of her father, but Doctor Lowe was a likeable man whereas her father certainly wasn't – a man she wanted with all her heart to see brought down.

In her mind's eye as she hurried back down the stairs she visualized her father grovelling before her in the most degrading situation – crawling in the filthy gutter covered in mud and horse piddle and the slime of other men's spittle, begging her for mercy as she stood over him in her revenge for all he'd done to her and Mum.

She had no idea how this would come about, but imagining it took away the strange feeling Doctor Lowe's words had given her.

Five

Ellie's eyes glowed with excitement as she told Florrie and Mrs Jenkins her news about being promoted to second housemaid under Florrie.

'Well good for you, dearie,' came Mrs Jenkins's strident voice. 'I just hope you appreciate it.'

'Yes, of course I do.'

'But don't you start putting on airs, miss, or you'll be back here in the kitchen working for me.'

The way she said that might have sounded ungracious and harsh, but she was genuinely pleased for the girl. All the while Ellie had been here – working like a little Trojan, she had to admit – not once had she ever seen that child smile, and it was about time she did. She'd had a raw deal, losing her mother like that, the brother disappearing and then the father walking out leaving the two young and vulnerable children entirely alone.

Now the brother had come here throwing his weight about. A lout he'd looked for all his flashy clothes, bought, she expected, with winnings from some gambling, but nothing permanent enough to see the girls in decent lodgings. Doctor Lowe had seen him off the premises, thank God, and perhaps, she hoped, the brother would never come back. Whether they'd ever see their father again was a different matter entirely, but the girls had a good home here, so long as they both behaved and worked hard.

She didn't know the rights of it, but something similar had happened to her when she'd been around young Ellie's age. She'd had two brothers as well, both younger than her, but they hadn't been as fortunate as Ellie and Dora in being taken in by a kind gentleman like Doctor Lowe.

Why he'd done it she'd no idea except that his heart must have been in the right place, seriously moved by the youngsters' plight. True, you can't save the whole world, Nora Jenkins smiled to herself, but it was good to have one kind soul to help you out when you most needed it.

There'd been no one to show her kindness or take her in when her father had died and her mother had become totally unhinged, admitted to a lunatic asylum. She and her two brothers had been separated, the boys sent to an orphanage and she taken into what was termed a 'haven' for girls where she had worked her little heart out. She'd never seen her brothers again.

Even today, at fifty-six, she often wondered where they'd ended up, what they looked like now and if they were still alive even, whether they'd married, raised families, perhaps now had grandchildren whom she would never see. At these times her heart would ache with questions and longing.

She'd never married. She had gone into service – not an exceptionally pretty child, yet she had come to the attention of one of her employer's sons. Falling pregnant, she'd been dismissed as if it was she who'd enticed him. She hadn't. She had been as scared as a rabbit each time he came near her, frightening her into secrecy and not admitting it was he who'd put her in the family way.

Of course they took his word against hers. Dismissed, she had looked for shelter. It had been winter. She had slipped on ice, fallen heavily and lost the baby. She was never sure whether she had pined or not, half of her in grief, the other half relieved and the guilt of feeling that relief plaguing her for years.

She'd found other employment, doing exactly what young Ellie had been doing, but, coming under the tuition of an excellent head cook, had learned her trade well. But she had kept away from men all her life, that single experience having been enough to make her never ever want to marry.

'You should be deeply grateful to Doctor Lowe,' she told Ellie sternly. 'You've been here only a few weeks and on no recommendation whatsoever. So don't you dare let him down or you'll have me to reckon with.'

'I won't,' Ellie said.

'If you do, and find yourself back here, I won't be as lenient with you as I've been so far. Of course, this leaves me with no help in the kitchen, so at times you might still be needed here until I'm found a replacement for you. Beats me why he's come to such an odd decision. I just hope you're grateful, that's all.'

'I am grateful,' Ellie assured her. Mrs Jenkins had no idea why he should offer this unexpected promotion, but *she* did and she couldn't help smiling to herself. This was the first step on her ladder and she saw no wrong in using her employer to achieve her aim of improving herself so much that when she finally met her father again, she would be in control. The very thought brought a glow to her cheeks.

Mary Lowe strode about her drawing room, turning every now and again to confront her husband sitting quietly in one of the comfortable armchairs.

He wanted to appear relaxed, but Mary's pacing was disturbing his mind. She seemed almost frantic.

'Why?' She paused and turned again to face him, her plump body held rigid. Well-fleshed as she was, her loose, biscuit-coloured afternoon gown of lace and chiffon gave her a regal appearance, adding to her display of indignation and betrayal.

'Why, Bertram? How could you promote that girl when you know full well how I feel about her? This interest in her is becoming an obsession with you. We both grieve for our darling girl. Millicent was our life. But you can't bring her back. This girl has gained a hold over you and she knows it. She is playing it to the full. What does she expect to achieve?'

'I don't think she expects to achieve anything. And why are you so much against her when you are so drawn to keeping her sister on?'

'Because I find Dora a sweet, even-tempered and willing girl. She has no idea what that sister of hers is up to.'

'I am not aware she is up to anything, Mary.'

'I am! I do not like her. I can never like her. I believe with all my heart that she is playing on this weakness of yours.'

'That is an unkind thing to say, Mary. She wouldn't stoop to—'

'Of course she would! She's clever. She is using your grief in order to better herself. She is using you, Bertram. She is playing you for a fool.'

Bertram stood up suddenly. 'Thank you so much, my dear, for those kind sentiments!' he said with acid sarcasm.

Since Millicent's death, there'd been many marital brushes

like this. If he was obsessed, as she said, with their loss, so was she – nothing of Millicent was to be moved. Even this claustrophobic drawing room, with its draperies and potted plants, had photographs everywhere of their child: studio portraits of her as a toddler sitting on his knee, her smiling mother standing behind them; older ones posed beside pedestals of various kinds; those of her in the garden playing with Tinker, her Yorkshire terrier. He could hardly bear to look at them, constant reminders of a child for ever lost to them.

'I'm not a fool!' he said harshly. 'You're the one growing obsessed. You miss her as much as I, but you can't let grief rule you. You've let your imagination run away with you and it must stop. I wish to hear no more!'

He could be firm when he wanted. A medical man had need to be firm against the malingerer, the manipulative or the merely bone-lazy patient. But he did have a tender heart and understood and felt for his wife's aversion to young Ellie. But Mary was becoming preoccupied by it and he needed to put a stop to it before it grew any worse. With Ellie kept on in this house, in time Mary would overcome her peculiar phobia and begin to accept her.

Telling himself this had the effect of dulling a little voice in his head that said his decision presented a unique opportunity to keep alive his daughter's memory. It had happened by sheer accident and a chance like this would never come again. He could even convince himself that Ellie reminding him so of Millicent might even, in time, take the sting out of his loss. She might, eventually, even take her place, said that insidious little voice in his head, though he tried to ignore it.

'A whole day to ourselves!' Dora cried as she and Ellie hurried arm in arm towards Victoria Park. 'We won't get another one for weeks and I want to make the most of it. Thank heaven it's a lovely sunny day. And warm too. You don't get many sunny days in April. We're so lucky.'

Dora was beginning to make sure to sound all her aitches, just as her mistress insisted.

'I want you to be a little lady, Dora, my child,' she'd told her almost with affection. 'A lady's maid – and that's what you may be some day – should speak nicely.'

Though Dora was still sewing in a humble role, repairing any rents in sheets and pillow cases, hemming towels that had become a little frayed at the edges, on the odd occasion she had been asked by Mrs Lowe to lay out the clothes she had chosen for the day, showing her how to do it nicely and neatly and with graceful movements, beaming at her as she achieved good results.

'In time you might act as my very own maid,' she'd said. 'Florrie is far too ungainly.' And of course there were the weekly jaunts to the market with her mistress, something she always really looked forward to. Last week Mrs Lowe had even bought her a little bag of toffees. She'd never treated her before and it had made her feel so very important.

When Dora told her, Ellie had smiled secretively but said nothing. The envy she'd once had was gone. Of course, now being under-housemaid, she too had been elevated. A few nights ago, as they lay in bed, she'd confided to Dora her hope of one day taking over from Florrie.

'She won't be here for ever,' she whispered. 'She'd want to move on or get married. Then I'd have someone working under me, wouldn't I?'

Mrs Jenkins had a new kitchen maid, a pale-faced girl of fourteen called Rose Holt, relieving Ellie of the extra chore of washing up. The only disappointment was that, contrary to what she'd expected, she still hardly saw Doctor Lowe except if he happened to pass while she was on hands and knees brushing the stair carpet or scrubbing the hall linoleum or cleaning out the fire grate, Florrie having taken it upon herself to do the cleaner jobs: polishing, dusting, cleaning brass, laying the table.

On the rare occasions when he did pass, she'd get to her feet to give a respectful bob. He'd respond with just a nod, passing on without speaking.

'It's so odd,' she said to Dora as they entered the park. 'He was so friendly to me when he took us on. Now he don't even seem to notice me.'

Not so much odd as worrying. She had read all sorts of things into this unexpected promotion. It had taken her a while to figure things out. Then she had rumbled it. Of course he wouldn't be so foolish as to commit himself by openly acknowledging her.

There was always someone about when he passed, on his way to either morning or evening surgery, or when surgery was over. Other times he'd be closeted in his study, though never when she cleared the ashes from the fire grate there or any other of the rooms; she up before six, the family not rising till two hours later. Even so, it seemed he was purposely avoiding her.

Only once had he come into his study when she'd been bent over the grate. She had looked up as a voice said, 'Excuse me,' in time to see his portly shape backing out, the door closing sharply on him.

It had left her with all sorts of questions. Had she misjudged his motives? Had he merely been kind to her and nothing more? She'd been so sure of her speculations. Or had his wife warned him to steer clear of her?

It was very obvious Mrs Lowe didn't like her. She had made that plain enough by totally ignoring her, walking by her as if she was invisible except for the set lips, the small double chin held high. Had she in fact advised that he had best avoid the one who reminded them so of their daughter?

If he heeded her, then all her plans would come unstuck. Worrying about it had made her miserable and her work here had become drudgery again. Even today with the April sun warm and promising, it wasn't easy to put all these questions to the back of her mind and unwind for an hour or two.

But it was good to be out of the place, if only for a few hours, to be back by four. Today, with no restriction, she could please herself what she did. She hadn't realized just how much freedom would come to mean. She'd known it all her life. Even in the shadow of poverty and hard work and in the constant wariness of a lascivious and violent father, she'd known freedom to a certain extent; but no longer.

At the beck and call of those over her, she'd become a prisoner; but maybe not for too long if the plans she had in mind could eventually be put into practice.

'Don't the park look lovely?' Dora's voice broke through her thoughts. 'What shall we do today?'

Ellie turned her face to her with a smile. 'Anything you like,' she said.

Six

It had been a lovely day exploring Victoria Park. In the very centre of London's East End it provided an expanse of open country and a marvellous breath of fresh air. There were wide lawns where families picnicked and little wooded areas to make a person feel they were nowhere near a busy city with its ever-present pall of smoke. There was a huge lake and neat paths that led strollers past clumps of daffodils, reminding them of little yellow carpets, and everywhere were small park trees just coming into pink and white blossom. Behind a wire fence deer browsed and, hidden at the very far end, an unusual edifice called the Stone Alcoves, once part of old London Bridge, which sat silent, mysterious, almost creepy, like a small part of some faraway Greek ruin.

More jolly were the bathing lakes and the Memorial Fountain, a favourite with children, today as always laughing and squealing as they banged the zinc cups on their chains against the stone trough surrounding the monument, the metal misshapen from years of children's not-so-tender handling. It had been presented to the park in 1862, the plaque said, by a Baroness Burdett-Coutts, and had since become a well-known meeting place. 'Meet you by the fountain,' was the usual comment.

Wearied by so much walking, Ellie and Dora had gone to a little café to have tea and cake on the pennies they'd been saving for weeks. Later they had fish and chips, a ha'penny bit of cod and a ha'p'orth of chips each, with plenty of salt and vinegar. The fish had been sweet and white and covered in crispy, oily batter, the chips so hot they burned the tongue, crispy on the outside, lovely and floury on the inside.

They'd taken their meal back to sit on a bench by the Regent's Canal and eat straight from the newspaper it had been wrapped in, washed down with a ha'penny bottle of sherbet fizz. Food fit for a king or for two young girls who usually had to eat in silence and with some haste at the kitchen table under Mrs Jenkins's watchful eye for any lapse of table etiquette, even below stairs.

Here, free of any restrictions, they had giggled, flicked bits of left-over batter at one another, bundled up the soiled, oily newspaper into balls to bat back and forth to each other, put their thumbs over the opening of the bottles to shake up the contents so that a minor release of the thumb would send the fine gassy liquid shooting in all directions. They finally settled down to enjoy a small cornet, licking with absolute relish the tiny ball of ice cream it held, by now keeping an eye on the time.

With the sun beginning to dip towards the west, they quickly tidied themselves, Ellie pinning up her hair again, which had come loose during their frolicking. In two weeks' time, she'd be sixteen, but already she was required to wear her hair up, not only denoting her as being considered adult now but also as being neater for her work. Dora's long tresses were still tied back with a plain brown bow, she being only twelve.

Tidied up, they made their way back to the narrow, three-storeyed house in Roman Road where Doctor Lowe lived and practised. Running down the steps to the basement area, they arrived breathless to find Mrs Jenkins waiting for them in the kitchen, hands on hips.

'So you've decided to come back home at last. It's four o'clock.'

'We ain't late, are we?' asked Ellie, seeing no need to apologize.

'Well, you're not early, that's for certain! You just about made it.'

'It *was* our day off.' This time Ellie did not sound so polite.

By the look on Mrs Jenkins's face she was in danger of overstepping the mark. But she felt confident. Yesterday Doctor Lowe had paused in the front hall as she was about to take a pail of dirty suds back to the kitchen to empty.

'How are you coming along?' he had asked.

She'd given a little bob. 'Very well, sir, I think.'

'Good,' he had said and continued on his way upstairs to find his wife. He hadn't spoken to Ellie since, but it was a start, she thought. And her wages had risen to five shillings a week – better than some in her position, she had found out, *and* without her asking, proving he must be thinking about her. Dora had been given a sixpence rise, bringing her wages to three shillings. It left both feeling almost wealthy. Ellie was making her sister put a bit away each week, while she was putting nearly every penny she earned into a little money box to start her on her way, one day, to seeking her father.

'Now, don't be cheeky!' came Mrs Jenkins's sharp retort. 'There's an ocean of difference between being back early and being back at a respectable time. Your supper's waiting, then off up to bed. You've had a full day. It's up bright and early in the morning, as usual. No lingering, saying you're tired. Now, get on with supper. I need to clear the kitchen ready for the morning.'

Supper was leftovers from their employer's dinner: a slice of cold lamb and bubble'n'squeak – potatoes and cabbage mashed together and fried – a slice of bread and a mug of cocoa. Food in this house was good and plentiful, far better than some Ellie had heard about. She wondered if she might not end up as plump as the rest of them here. But her thinness came from her mother. She'd never be fat.

'Who, may I ask, gave those two girls permission to take their day off both at the same time yesterday?'

Mary Lowe's small round face was contorted with fury as Mrs Jenkins stood before her in her sitting room.

Facing the smaller woman's wrath, Nora Jenkins's reply was respectful but dignified. 'I thought you were aware of it, madam.'

'I was *not* aware of it! I was not told. As cook/housekeeper you have full charge over the staff here. We do not have enough staff as it is without allowing two of them to have time off together.'

'Well, it wasn't me, madam!' Mrs Jenkins began to feel piqued. She wasn't accustomed to being spoken to as if she was a servant of the lowest order. She was housekeeper as well as cook. She ran this place. Each week she came to Mrs Lowe and went over the accounts with her. She was entirely honest in her management of the house, not like some, who craftily fiddled a bit of cash here, a few provisions there, and did nicely out of it. She was not prepared to have her honesty questioned.

'I wasn't told neither, madam,' she said huffily. 'I'd no idea – not until they both paraded past me all dressed up to go out. When I confronted them they said they'd been given the day off together. I assumed it was you who give them permission, being that the younger girl is mostly in your charge, so to speak, or I would've come and told you. But I can assure you, madam, it weren't me!'

'Then who?'

'All I can think of would be Doctor Lowe himself.'

'He said nothing to me. Are you sure he mentioned nothing to you?'

'Quite sure. They was off out before I could find him to ask. Anyway, he was in surgery and couldn't be disturbed – not by me any rate.'

Nora Jenkins's reply was terse. Being asked if she was sure indeed! She wasn't pleased and she made certain Mrs Lowe knew it.

She obviously did. 'Very well, Mrs Jenkins,' she sighed. 'I'll have a word with my husband. If it was he who sanctioned the two girls' day out, I will make very sure it will not happen again. We cannot have two absent at the same time with such a small staff. But thank you, Mrs Jenkins; I am sorry to have troubled you.'

Nora did not acknowledge the polite observance of her position in this house. Turning on her heel as abruptly as her bulk allowed, the cluster of keys, that housekeeper's badge of office, at her waist rattling sharply as if to emphasize her indignation, she left the room, closing the door firmly.

Mrs Lowe's annoyance was justified. She, too, was annoyed. Her authority had been undermined and she intended to have a strong word with those two young people.

'Mrs Lowe is very upset by the both of you taking your day off together,' she said after summoning the two girls to the little parlour off the kitchen reserved for her. The room was quite small, with hardly space enough in it to swing a cat, but she adored it. It was her home, her retreat after a long day. No one else came in here unless in need of a dressing-down, like today.

Hidden from view by a folding screen were a single bed, a wardrobe and a washstand with an oval mirror above. Her living area was cosy, with a rug in front of the little fireplace, a small table for meals, two chairs, one upright, one reclining, with arms and cushions for comfort – all of it given by Mrs Lowe – and a single wall cupboard for a few personal things.

'I've been put to great embarrassment,' she went on before they could open their mouths, glaring at Ellie.

'It was understood yesterday was your day off and I naturally took it Mrs Lowe gave your sister permission too, but that don't seem to have been the case. Who did? Speak up!'

The sharp command made Dora flinch, but Ellie stood her ground.

'It was Doctor Lowe. I asked if he minded us having our day off together and he didn't make no objection.'

'You asked the master . . .' Words almost failed Mrs Jenkins, but not for long. 'You went to him personally? How dare you, girl! You go through me in these matters. And if I'd known it was the two of you I would've said no – definitely no!'

'I didn't go to him,' Ellie protested. 'He spoke to me as he came out of his doctor's surgery. He said it was time I 'ad me day off, so I asked if my sister could 'ave her day off as well and he said he saw no harm in it. So—'

The rest was cut short by Mrs Jenkins shaking a fist at her. 'That's enough! Your sister answers to Mrs Lowe and should have gone to her for permission.'

'It all 'appened sudden, Cook,' Ellie said, leaning back from the angry gesture. 'I was off to bed. When Dora said the mistress would be out visiting the next day and wouldn't be back till six o'clock and wouldn't need her, I thought that was why the master said we could.'

It was no lie. It was how it had come about: a misunderstanding. But Ellie was already seeing her and Dora's employment here being terminated, her hopes of a good future dwindling. She needed desperately to put things right.

Next morning, despite Mrs Jenkins's warning that all requests must go through her, Ellie took her time cleaning out the grate and laying and lighting the fire in Doctor Lowe's study. There were questions she needed to ask the man; the business of her and Dora's day out together was now the least of her concerns.

His coming into his study, something he always did prior to his having breakfast, finally rewarded her slowness. Seeing her still there, he hesitated at the door, but to her relief came on into the room.

She stood up and bobbed. 'Good morning, sir.'

He was smiling. 'Good morning, my dear.'

The 'my dear' took her completely by surprise. Yesterday, around mid-morning, his wife had spoken to Mrs Jenkins to say that from now on Ellie and Florrie would be addressed only by surname. Florrie would be addressed as Chambers and Ellie as Jay. So his calling her 'my dear' so soon after his wife's request took Ellie aback a bit.

In larger houses with an army of servants everyone would answer to their surname, even among the servants themselves. The upper orders would address the lower ones this way, while they would require to have Mr or Miss attached to theirs, and cooks and housekeepers were Mrs, whether married or single.

In this house, with only four staff, this had never been the case, apart from with Mrs Jenkins herself. Now, suddenly, Doctor Lowe's wife had issued an edict that Ellie was to be referred to as Jay, and Florrie as Chambers.

But to Ellie's astonishment and anger her own sister would now be addressed as Miss Jay, since Mrs Lowe had also given out yesterday that Dora was now officially her personal maid – a kid of thirteen!

Ellie had been incensed. 'I'm not calling my own sister "Miss Jay"!' she raged when Cook relayed the mistress's orders. 'My own sister? It's daft!'

'Maybe,' Mrs Jenkins said sternly. 'But the mistress is the mistress and what she says goes.'

'Well, I ain't doing it.'

'You can call her Dora when you two are alone. Just not in public, that's all.'

Then last night had come a second shock as she and Dora lay side by side in their narrow bed. When they would normally have gossiped together in whispers about their day, Dora had been silent. Asked what was wrong, she had given several damp sniffs accompanied by little catches in her throat.

'I won't be sleeping here any more,' she'd managed between snivels. 'Mrs Lowe wants me to use the little room next to hers where I can be on hand. She says that a personal maid is elev— elevated, I think the word was – above ordinary servants. She said my wages will go up, but that I'm not to con— er . . . consort socially with you any more, because you're under-housemaid and ladies' maids don't associate with under-housemaids.'

As the gabbled whispers died away, Ellie had said, stunned, 'You're not having that, are you?'

Dora had given an enormous damp sniff. 'If I don't, she says she'll be ever so sad to have to let me go. Ellie, where would I go? I'd be all on my own.'

'You won't be on your own. I'll hand in my notice and leave with you.'

Dora had shot up in the bed, making the flimsy thing creak and sway. 'But we'd be out on the street, back where we was. That'll be just as bad. Ellie, I couldn't face that. We're comfy here. We've got a roof over our heads and plenty to eat and it's warm and we get a wage.'

Ellie hadn't felt sympathetic. 'So you're going to accept.'

'I've got to. Mrs Lowe says she wants to show me how to be a lady and speak nice . . . nicely.' Indeed her diction had improved since being with Mrs Lowe, but at this moment was letting her down.

'And I want to do that,' she'd gone on, gazing down at her sister still lying on her back. 'But I don't want to be parted from you. I'll be on my own. I won't have no friends, not even Florrie.'

Florrie, deaf to their hissed discussion, was snoring contentedly.

'Because someone in my position,' Dora had gone on, 'won't be allowed to mix with servants that are below my position.'

'Then that's your choice,' Ellie had said sharply. Already Dora sounded as if she thought she knew her place and Ellie's. It stung. She wanted to tell Dora to come down from this height on which she was suddenly finding herself. Instead she'd said huffily, 'Not much I can do about it, is there?'

She'd turned over, her back to her sister, simmering with anger against her. She had felt Dora slip quietly back down beside her, heard her plaintive whisper, 'I'm sorry, Ellie, there's not much *I* can do about it,' but made no reply.

As the hours passed she'd lain awake, knowing by little movements that Dora too was awake, and she felt resentment, fear, despair in turn creeping through her, and wondered if Dora felt the same.

It wasn't Dora's fault. What girl wouldn't be flattered by

a promotion like that? No, she blamed Mrs Lowe. She knew the woman disliked her. She had done it out of spite, perhaps thinking Dora's sister, who so reminded her of her dead daughter, might take offence and leave. Whatever it was, it was cruel to separate sisters in this way. Dismissing them both would have been kinder, but Doctor Lowe would have had something to say about that.

There was nothing she could do about Dora, though, and it would be miserable sleeping alone from now on. On the other hand, she didn't relish sharing with their new kitchen maid. She didn't much care for the girl, who never seemed to have a clean face and tended to sniff a lot, to Cook's annoyance.

'If I'd have known she sniffed that much I wouldn't of taken her on,' Mrs Jenkins had said. 'I thought it was just a cold she had at the time. But if she wants to remain here, she's going to have to curb the habit.'

Until now the girl had been sleeping in the kitchen – not unusual in quite a few households, her bed little more than a bench, situated at the far end of the kitchen where the staff ate or sometimes sat on their moments off between duties. Rose seemed happy enough with the arrangement, a girl who, prior to coming here, had slept in the damp cellar of another household, so she said. Even so, Ellie was prepared to refuse any suggestion that Rose Holt share her bed.

This morning she and Dora arose at six as always, dressing hurriedly against the chill. Neither spoke.

Florrie, too, dressed quickly. 'I think we're a bit late,' she said as she sluiced her face in the basin of cold water all three shared. Ellie didn't reply. Nor did Dora.

Dora was the first to leave, no doubt glad to escape the strained silence and get on with whatever new tasks Mrs Lowe was ready to face her with in order to prime her as a lady's maid.

Ellie's unenviable first task of the morning was always the clearing-out of ashes and laying and lighting fires in all the grates, her fingers then needing to be washed again to free them of ash and coal dust before she tackled anything else, while Florrie these days took the nicer jobs: dusting and tidying, laying the breakfast table ready for the master and mistress – all this before the girls had their own breakfast.

It was left to Ellie to wash floors, brush and beat carpets and rugs, lately polish brass and do all the dirtier jobs as under-housemaid, while Florrie waited on Sir and Madam at lunch and dinner.

One thing about Florrie: she could have started putting on airs and graces, but she hadn't. She was still the chubby, friendly, easy-going girl Ellie had first met. As they left their attic room together, Florrie said, 'Dora told me her good news last night as we met on the back stairs going up to bed. She said Mrs Lowe wants to train her to be a lady's maid. Lovely.'

'I suppose so,' was as much as Ellie could muster before hurrying off to gather up dustpans and brushes.

She needed to be in the doctor's study in case he popped in on his way down to breakfast. She liked to think that he might often need a bit of solitude to gather himself together in the quietness of this room on the second floor at the back of the house, away from everyone, before going downstairs to face his wife. Talk was that, after the loss of their daughter, Mrs Lowe had removed herself from his bedroom to sleep in another room. That, of course, had been before she and Dora had come to work here; but it suited her cause.

To her delight, he'd thought fit to seek his quiet study this morning. And now he had called her 'my dear'. She couldn't help wondering what his wife would have said about that if she'd heard him. But now she needed to take full advantage of his greeting.

She fought to find her voice – not to let it tremble.

Seven

Ellie swallowed hard. 'Begging your pardon, sir,' she began politely. 'It's good news about my sister.'

'Your sister?' he echoed. 'Ah yes, young Miss Jay.'

'I call her Dora,' Ellie interrupted before she could stop. She felt angry with herself. The thoughtless remark had probably spoiled what she was trying for. But Doctor Lowe was smiling.

'Yes, of course. And I shall call her Dora too, to you, my dear, but not outside this room. My wife has seen fit to lay down a few rules.' Ellie thought she saw a shadow pass briefly across his face, but he brightened instantly.

'And rightly so, and we should abide by them. You do understand?'

Ellie nodded. The voice had grown abrupt and, standing here with brush and pan in her grubby hands, she felt what she was: the under-housemaid, just once removed from the kitchen maid and not worth a candle.

She took a deep breath and forced herself to embark on her original quest. 'Beg your pardon, Doctor Lowe, but I wanted to ask, now that my sister – I mean Miss Jay, has been promoted to personal maid to Mrs Lowe, I wondered if there was any chance for me – in this house I mean.'

'In this house?' he cut in.

His expression had grown oddly alarmed and she realized that what she'd unwittingly said must have sounded as if she was prepared to leave if there were no prospects for her here. Sixth sense told her to play on it.

'I know I've not been here all that long,' she hurried on, 'but I've learned a lot and I hope I'm a good worker.'

'You are, my dear. I am most pleased with you.'

'But I don't want to stay an under-housemaid all my life.'

She gave him what she hoped was a pretty smile, despite a small streak of coal dust across her lips and cheek.

He did not return the smile. 'I would not like to lose you, my dear,' he said slowly.

It sounded like a threat and took her by surprise. She was about to protest that she didn't want to leave. Heavens, where would she go? And without Dora – Dora, who was now comfortably planted here? But his face had taken on a strange expression.

'I have become very fond of you, Ellie. I watch you from afar whenever possible, hoping you haven't noticed. If you were to leave, I would be lost.'

There was a wheedling note in his tone and she suddenly thought of her father, the way he'd look and speak before taking advantage of her.

She shrank back. 'No, please Doctor Lowe, I'm not that sort of . . .' She broke off, seeing him frown.

He looked shocked. 'My dear child, what are you saying? Oh, my dear child, is that what you think of me? Oh, my dear . . .'

His voice died away and for a moment a tense silence hung between them. Then he spoke again.

'I confess to watching you, but only because you remind me so of my daughter, my darling Millicent. Let me explain. I gain comfort from your close resemblance to her where my dear wife finds only grief from it. I think this is why she has laid down her rules and even taken your sister on as personal maid, looking to get back at you and make you so jealous that you will leave. I cannot allow that to happen. With you here I feel I have not lost my child, though you are more forthright than she ever was.'

He took a deep breath and drew his rotund figure up to its full, small height. 'I hope you haven't taken offence at what I've said. Please forgive me if there was any misunderstanding. And please, do not feel threatened by me.'

The moment of fear had turned to elation that she tried hard not to show. 'Of course not,' she said as evenly as she could.

'I am so glad.' He was still looking at her and she felt this might be the one and only time she would get to press home her request.

'And about my job?' she reminded him as gently as she could.

'Ah, yes. I have no intention of letting you go, if that is what you thought. On the other hand, we cannot allow you to continue looking like a little chimney sweep, can we?'

He smiled at his small joke, his moustache and short beard twitching. It was a nice smile, not at all lecherous, as she had first mistaken it to be.

'Leave it with me for a few days,' he was saying. 'I will talk to Mrs Lowe. I must, I'm afraid. She is in charge of the staff, not I. But I will deal with her.' The smile broadened to a roguish grin, one she'd not seen before. He seemed a different man.

'We might find you a pleasant position – parlourmaid, for instance?'

'That's waiting at table, isn't it? That might upset Florrie, being that's what she's doing. '

'Then she'll have to perk up a little. She tends to be rather sluggish, to my way of thinking. We need someone a little more sprightly. I think that would be you, my dear.'

Ellie was feeling flabbergasted but managed to give him a respectful bob of her head in acknowledgement. At the same time she wondered how she was going to face Florrie. 'Perhaps we could both take turns,' she suggested helpfully. 'I'm sure she wouldn't mind that.'

'For the time being say nothing to Chambers about our conversation,' he advised forcefully. 'Nor to Mrs Jenkins or your sister.'

Her sister? She was missing her already. From today she would probably hardly set eyes on her to talk about anything, much less about the conversation here in this room.

'Now I had better go down to breakfast,' he said, but at the door he paused and turned to frown at her, his mood seeming to darken. 'One more thing, my dear: I couldn't avoid seeing alarm in your eyes when I mentioned my feelings towards you? Why did you suddenly look so afraid?'

'It's nothing,' she said a little too quickly, betraying that it had indeed to be something.

He pounced on it immediately. 'Has someone in the past taken an unsavoury advantage of you?'

'Honestly, it's nothing,' she protested.

'I'm not sure I believe that, but I'll leave it at that for your own peace of mind. But should you ever need to confide in someone, I'm here. Whatever it is, it would go no further and I would support you in every way. I hope you feel you can trust me, child.'

She gave the suggestion of a nod. 'You'll be late to your breakfast, sir,' she reminded him.

'Yes, of course. And I have also delayed you, child. We will consider finding a replacement for you to relieve you of this sort of menial work.'

'That'll mean more outlay on wages.' She realized she was forgetting her manners. She hurriedly amended it. 'I mean I'd feel ever so guilty if you let Florrie – I mean Chambers – if you was to let her go. You won't, will you?'

'We shall see how it goes,' he said, and gave a little chuckle, his mood becoming visibly brighter as he left her to finish her work.

'I'm thinking, Bertram, of training Dora to dress hair,' said Mary at dinner one evening. 'She has made great strides as my personal maid. I am very pleased with her.'

He glanced up at a somewhat inattentive Chambers unhurriedly ladling consommé into his soup plate. The girl was no doubt tired, having been on her feet since five thirty this morning, but servants should be used to that. He found himself irked by her slowness – more reason for Ellie to stand in for her sometimes.

'Maybe we should discuss it later,' he warned Mary. He also needed to voice his idea regarding Dora's older sister, but not in front of Chambers.

'I think, my dear,' he went on cautiously as the girl moved back to take up a position by the sideboard until required to clear away the first course and serve the main one, 'what you are deciding to do could cause a little unrest among the staff. Jay is still under-housemaid. For her younger sister to be given such high status could cause jealousy and ill feeling.'

He cast a guarded glance towards the plump, apathetic Chambers. She seemed far from alert, but her ears could still hear.

It was expected of staff never to repeat anything they overheard of an employer's private conversation during meals or anywhere else. In fact it was assumed in larger houses that servants, footmen, butlers and the like grew suddenly deaf at such times. But the staff here were not highly paid or highly trained and he couldn't be certain that Chambers would not carry tales that might concern her. The subject of Ellie Jay must wait a while longer.

'It would save money,' Mary was saying, ignoring his warning of ill will and jealousy. 'You know my hairdresser comes to me two or three times a week.' She patted her newly done coiffure. 'But it does so eat into my personal allowance.'

Bertram gave a sigh. 'Then I had best increase your allowance, my dear, though I suggest you keep a stricter watch on what you spend.'

'I'm quite satisfied with what you give me, dear,' she said, huffed at being rebuked, even mildly. 'But it seems a waste of money paying to have someone come to do my hair when I've a capable young girl who is dainty and quite nimble and very quick to learn and one whom I could train.'

Having finished his soup, Bertram laid down his spoon. 'I suppose it would do no harm.' After all, he didn't believe in wasting money. 'Speaking of promotion, there is a matter I'd like to discuss with you, my dear.'

He paused as Chambers came to clear the first course. He waited as the main course was served before glancing up at the girl. 'Thank you, Chambers, you may go now. When we're finished, we'll ring for you to come and clear away.'

Was there disappointment in the girl's eye? But she gave a small bob and took herself off.

'It's about Ellie Jay,' he went on after the door had closed. 'I've had my eye on her. She works very hard.'

'Does she?' his wife cut in offhandedly. 'To change the subject—'

'Mary, hear me out, please! I was about to say that I think her hard work should be recognized. In the short while she's been here she has risen from scullery maid to assistant housemaid. I am thinking of her sharing the job of parlourmaid with—'

In sudden fury, Mary slammed her knife and fork down on to the tablecloth. 'No, definitely not! I won't have that girl anywhere near me. The less I see of her the better. And what about Chambers? She has been with us for over a year. What is she going to say?'

'I've no idea!' Bertram said lightly. 'But you must own she

is slow and inefficient. I've had tea slopped into my saucer before now, to mention just one mishap.'

'I find her efficient enough for the needs of this house,' Mary shot back at him, her voice beginning to rise.

'For a housemaid, yes,' Bertram returned. 'I admit she is efficient enough as a housemaid, but since Jay became under-housemaid she has begun to sit back and let that girl do most of the dirtier jobs. In my opinion she is not, and never will be, a pleasing parlourmaid and I consider it about time we found someone to take over that role.'

'Then by all means do let us advertise for one – if you think you can afford it!' Mary pushed her plate with its hardly touched contents away from her.

Her husband was fighting a losing battle to remain cool. 'Not when we already have someone here to fill that position. Jay is nimble and quick. She works hard and doesn't complain and has a pleasing attitude.'

'No!' Mary cried again, glaring at him through tears that trembled on her lower eyelids. 'I know why you want this, Bertram. You're besotted with the idea of the girl happening to remind you so of our dear Millicent.'

The very mention of their daughter's name had made her voice quiver. 'But for me, Bertram, it's the very reason I cannot stand the sight of her. She makes my very flesh creep.'

'That's a complete exaggeration, my dear,' Bertram said sharply.

'And my most ardent wish is for you to get rid of her as soon as possible,' she raged on.

'That's enough, Mary,' Bertram burst out, anger finally breaking its bounds. 'I will not get rid of her because you can't bring yourself to be charitable towards her. I'm sorry you feel about her as you do, but you will have to get used to her. I provide for this household, not you, and I will engage or dismiss whomsoever I think fit; and that is my last word on the subject, Mary.'

In a fit of rage, Mary let out a shriek and leaped up from the table. Drawing together the ample skirts of her grey-blue silk evening dress, she fled from the room, past Chambers, blinded by tears seeing neither her nor anything else as she hurried upstairs to her room.

* * *

Chambers had closed the door behind her and was about to make her way back to the kitchen area when she became aware of raised voices. Curious, she cautiously retraced her steps. The words were plainly audible through the door.

So intrigued was she that she was taken completely off guard by the door being thrown open, giving her no chance to excuse her being found hovering there. But instead of her finding herself challenged, Mrs Lowe passed right by her in full flight, weeping and stumbling in her haste to leave the dining room.

By the time Doctor Lowe followed, Chambers was back in the kitchen, having sprinted along the passage and down the short flight of stairs with amazing agility for one so fleshy.

Mrs Jenkins was asking Florrie why she was so out of breath as Ellie came into the kitchen with brush and pan to wash her hands and face clean of ash and coal dust before tackling cleaner jobs. Glancing across at Florrie, she saw she was indeed out of breath, chubby cheeks flushed.

'You orright?' she enquired, concerned. Florrie ignored her. Thinking she hadn't heard, Ellie repeated the question.

She was taken by surprise as Florrie turned on her. 'I've got nothing to say to you!' she flared. 'I know what you're up to. No wonder you don't mind doing grates, especially the one in the master's study. Hoping to catch him so you can wheedle round him to take my job away from me.'

'What all this?' cried Mrs Jenkins, but she was ignored.

'I'm not trying to take your job away from you,' Ellie hissed.

'You are. I just heard him telling Mrs Lowe he plans to give you my job. He wouldn't say it unless you put ideas into his head. It's really unfair. It's rotten of you trying to put me out of a job so you can have it for yourself.'

'I've done no such thing!' Ellie told her. 'It's as much a surprise to me as it is to you.'

'It's not fair! I've been parlourmaid for months and no one's ever complained. Then you come along and in a few weeks you're being offered my job.'

'No one's offered me anything,' Ellie said. 'And I don't suppose they will. You got the wrong end of the stick.'

'I know what I heard!' Florrie continued to rail. 'There's only one person could have put the idea into the master's head. I think it's sneaky and underhanded.'

'Surely this wasn't said in front of you, girl?' cried Mrs Jenkins.

'It was after Doctor Lowe told me I could go. I heard them arguing and the master saying he was thinking of *her* taking over from me. Her!'

Florrie's angry eyes flashed towards Ellie. 'Then Mrs Lowe came flying out of the dining room crying her eyes out.'

All Ellie could do was stare at her, trying not to show the elation she felt. Something had come of her chat with Doctor Lowe after all, though she'd not expected such quick results, nor that he'd propose her taking over from Florrie and that it would set her employers against each other.

But she felt sorry for Florrie. The girl must feel awful hearing it like that, but it was out of their hands now. Florrie might air her feelings down here, but she knew she couldn't complain or question her employer's decision lest he let her go altogether. This was an easy-going household. She might not get another as good.

Ellie's concern at this moment was hearing that Doctor Lowe's wife had burst into tears over what he'd put to her. It was obvious Mrs Lowe did not like her and might even guess what she was about. But if the woman did manage to influence her husband against her, it would put paid to hope of taking advantage of his obsession with her likeness to his beloved daughter.

From the moment she had realized the effect she had on him, her dream had been of taking that one's place in his heart, eventually becoming part of this family, learning to behave and speak nicely, with money enough to become a force to be reckoned with.

She'd woven dreams of being rich, confronting her father and bringing him down with her haughty condemnation of him, him grovelling before her proud bearing, begging her forgiveness. But was it just a childish dream?

Eight

It was no surprise to Ellie to be called into her employer's study two days later. During this time she'd not seen hair or hide of his wife. She only ever had glimpses now and again anyway, the woman purposely avoiding her.

She could only guess what she must be feeling after what Florrie had reported hearing, but she curbed any sympathy she might have had. Her own life was more important.

Not that life had been sweet these two days. Florrie wasn't speaking to her, Mrs Jenkins kept giving her looks and her own sister had long since been forbidden to associate with her. As to the kitchen maid, Rose, a timid little thing who couldn't say boo to a goose, the only words she ever seemed to utter were yes and no in a squeaky little voice; there was no alliance there.

She missed Dora dreadfully. Virtually ostracized, Dora would have been a life-saver, and Ellie found her dislike of Mrs Lowe for keeping the girl from her growing by the minute.

'Well blow the lot of them,' she told herself. But not Dora, she added hastily in her mind. Once she was established in this household, so long as she could develop the tenuous hold she appeared to have over Doctor Bertram Lowe, she and Dora would leave to a bright and certain future.

Now she entered his study to his summons. He was standing by the small window, gazing out over the open land around St John's Church. As she entered, he turned to her. She'd never seen him beam so widely; in fact it was the first smile she'd been given since Florrie's spot of eavesdropping.

'Ah,' he began. Coming forward he stopped three feet from her. 'I'll come straight to the point. I'll be brief, as I have my surgery to go to.'

The smile had vanished, leaving in its place an expression so severe that for a second Ellie felt her heart stop. She wasn't to receive promotion but to be told her services were no longer needed, that she must leave this house. His wife had got to him, twisting him around her little finger. Now she was to be dismissed. And what about Dora? How could she leave without her? What if Dora, now comfortable here, didn't want to leave? She'd be on her own with no money, nowhere to go. Having been here so short a while, she'd get no reference. Who would employ her? The future looked more bleak than she could ever remember – even worse than the time of the death of her mother.

All this went through her mind in a split second, her world collapsing about her. Only dimly did she hear Doctor Lowe's voice.

'I'm sorry that it has taken me longer to speak to you than I intended. Things have been quite hectic.'

For hectic he meant impossible, his wife eager to see the back of her, nagging him into dismissing her. He might proclaim himself master of his own home, but in truth he was as much under her thumb as any man who needed to see himself as the master. Women – even women downtrodden and knocked about by their husbands – were stronger than men would care to believe. She was strong. And now she prepared herself to meet the world completely on her own. But her heart shrank at the thought.

'You must have thought I'd forgotten you,' he was saying. 'I have discussed the situation with Mrs Lowe and have finally persuaded her that my decision remains unchanged, even though she is not happy with it. I have told her that in time she will become used to having you around.'

Ellie's mind snapped back into focus. What was he saying to her? 'You mean . . .' It was difficult to go on.

Perhaps she hadn't heard correctly, interpreting it only as what she would have liked to hear.

'I mean that there is too much work in this house for Chambers and yourself to cope with. I feel that our young kitchen maid – what is her name?'

'Rose?' Ellie supplied automatically.

'Yes. I feel she could take on extra work: laundry, simple housework. Chambers and yourself will share the duties of parlourmaid, neither one of you above the other. I'll speak to my wife and to Cook.'

Ellie was speechless. One minute she'd been devastated; now this.

'There is one stipulation,' he continued. 'Chambers will take on the sole duty of taking food trays up to Mrs Lowe, tidying, cleaning and dusting, making up the fire in her room, delivering bedlinen and making the bed. There'll be no need for you to set foot there.'

She knew exactly what he meant. 'I do understand, sir,' she said, finding her voice, and was aware of a look passing between them before either could help themselves. She hastily lowered her head.

'Well, that's settled,' he said briskly. 'However, I'm afraid I cannot raise your wages. Only my—'

'That's orright, sir,' she cut in quickly. Seeing him frown, she wondered what she'd said wrong. She raised her eyebrows enquiringly and the frown faded, to be replaced by an amused smile.

'There is one thing that concerns me, my dear.' He was still calling her 'my dear', which was also encouraging. 'I would like you to concentrate on your speech. I think it would be appropriate for you to try to learn the Queen's English and I shall endeavour to correct you as and when I can.'

'Thank you, sir,' she said meekly now, not quite sure why he should need to bother. Most working girls – even maids in big houses – had no need to talk proper.

'Well then,' he went on, 'as soon as Cook explains what duties are required of . . . er . . .'

'Rose,' Ellie reminded him.

'You will commence your new duties. Cook will draw up a roster, allowing for Chambers to wait at table for one day, you for the next, and so on. Now I must get on.'

Ellie quickly dropped a curtsey as he left the room.

Florrie was happy enough with the news, especially that no extra wage would be awarded to Ellie, so not promoting this virtual newcomer over her.

But if Ellie thought waiting at table was a picnic she'd got another think coming. It was, in fact, one of the duties Florrie disliked. While the master and mistress were eating, a maid had to stand perfectly still so as not to distract them. Sometimes in the evening Doctor Lowe would entertain guests, one or two medical colleagues and their wives, or maybe friends or family. Dinner could linger for ages, often going on till eight and there she'd stand, tired on her feet after a long day. Then it all had to be cleared away.

She was glad for someone to take over every other day and give her a rest. Ellie would soon learn it wasn't so easy. And with such a short time to learn the order cutlery must go in, where water and wine glasses should be placed, how to fold a napkin, how to properly serve food and to avoid drips when serving liquids such as soup, the port decanter always to be passed clockwise, and so on, she was bound to make a slip-up. Yet she had this sneaky feeling Ellie would shine at it. Ellie had that way with her.

As she and young Dora got into the hansom cab, its driver holding the door open for them, Mary Lowe felt sick.

She intended to visit her favourite West End department store, Lewis & Allenby, which specialized in silk, to choose a silk evening dress. On her way downstairs ready to leave she had seen Dora's sister Jay crossing the hall. For a split second it had been like looking at her darling Millicent and her heart almost stopped.

She'd let out an audible gasp and Jay had paused to look up at her. The shock of that moment had wrenched a cry of anger from her.

'What are you staring at, girl?'

When Jay didn't move, her voice rose even more. 'Stop idling and get on with your work!'

'Sorry, madam.' The apology caught her as sounding totally insolent and Mary heard her own voice rise to a screech.

'Do as I say, girl! Go!'

Jay had galvanized into action and hurried away, disappearing down to the kitchen. But Mary could not get the sight of her out of her head or the sound of her own shriek, making her feel like some fishwife.

Now, seated in the cab, the vehicle moving off, Mary turned suddenly to the girl beside her, who at this moment was very quiet – too quiet.

'Dora, if it can possibly be avoided, I would prefer you not to be found associating with Jay.'

Dora's voice was small. 'I don't, madam, just as you've told me.'

'Then I am reminding you again, Dora.'

'Yes, madam. But she *is* my sister,' she added timidly.

Even so, the remark sounded too bold to her – far too much like Jay.

'She is not a good influence on you,' Mary shot at her. 'You are a nice girl, Dora. I like you very much and if you remain a nice girl I shall see that you are educated and have a good future. She will only pull you down. And I warn you, child, that if you allow her to I will have no option but to let you go, and that will make me very, very sad.'

She was pleased by a compliant nod, but her day had been spoiled. That brief flash of likeness had upset her terribly, the insolent look on Jay's face even more. It stayed with her all morning, ruining the pleasure of her expedition.

Even the silk gown in a gentle shade of buttermilk that she ordered gave her no joy, seeming tainted by her harrowing experience. And to think that today, with an April sun shining in all its glory, she had actually begun to think herself on the verge of recovering from her grief.

After the bitter and devastating loss of Millicent she had been totally unable to leave the house – not even with Bertram. It was probably irrational and she could understand his impatience with her phobia.

It had taken a long time and only gradually had she improved. But she was still reluctant to venture out on her own. Not being one for making close friends with whom she could go shopping or take tea, Dora had come as a godsend. Gentle-natured, meek and respectful, she was fast becoming an admirable paid companion as well as personal maid. She dared not admit even to herself that to some small degree Dora's presence was beginning to lessen if not fill the void that the loss of her daughter had left in her heart.

Jay, on the other hand, was another matter. That girl knew exactly what she was about and it made Mary's blood boil to think of her trying to use that similarity to blind Bertram – he, foolish man, seeming to fall for it.

Mary wasn't quite sure what the girl hoped to gain, but something told her it wasn't good. From the moment Bertram had established his authority over having two maids share the work of parlourmaid, she had established hers by laying down a rule that under no circumstances would she allow Jay ever to set so much as one foot in her room.

'I won't have her anywhere near me,' she told him flatly. 'If you insist on her serving at table there is little I can do to stop you but my mealtimes will be ruined.'

'That's pure foolishness, my dear,' was his immediate response.

'You know how I feel. I don't like her. And if you insist on keeping her I shall eat in my room if need be.'

'I can hardly dismiss her without cause,' came the sharp retort.

'She is rude and discourteous to me! That's cause enough.'

'I'm sad you feel that way. I find her courteous and obliging.'

'You would!' she had flared at him. 'To my mind, Bertram, you find unnatural comfort in keeping sad memories alive. But what of my feelings? Don't you care that I feel differently? The mere sight of her makes my heart race so much that I feel quite sick and weak. It is making me ill.'

All he'd done was click his tongue and turn away, having made up his mind that the girl would stay no matter what she said, unwilling to let go of the past. Very well, he had his way of combating their loss and she had hers. But if he were not careful it could very well drive a wedge between them, for she'd never feel any different.

It was late May and Ellie was beginning to worry. Something inside her felt wrong.

The eighteenth of April had seen her turn sixteen – not that it had been celebrated in any way, she working through her day as usual, the long day not even being brightened by any sign of her sister.

She had told Doctor Lowe that it was her birthday. He'd smiled and wished her many happy returns, which was more than many a master would have said, though possibly many another servant wouldn't have dreamed of overstepping her position by even mentioning it. But she'd been beginning to feel confident of her position.

Two days later there was a small embroidered handkerchief on his study desk, a note pinned to it bearing her name and the words, 'For your birthday'. A flutter of elation had thrilled through her stomach along with a tiny prick of satisfaction.

Instinct cautioned her to say nothing to anyone about it as she secreted it in between the flat springs of her bed and the thin, hard mattress. No one would find it there; the mattress was seldom turned.

Though she sought to thank her employer, she'd only set eyes on him while waiting at table and then he had not once looked in her direction. Her attention had been more taken up with his wife, who also hadn't looked her way – it might have been a phantom serving her, there being not the smallest response to the food laid before her.

Doctor Lowe would give an almost imperceptible nod of the head as she carefully ladled soup, held the meat or vegetable dishes for him to help himself or replenished his wine glass. He hardly took his eyes off his wife when not concentrating on his meals. She, on the other hand, did not once glance up from her plate to look his way. It was indeed an atmosphere one could have cut with a knife. For Ellie, meal times were proving to be far from the privilege she'd imagined.

It wasn't only this that dulled the elation she'd first felt; it was a dawning awareness of something about her body not being quite as right it should be. The next morning, as she rose at six – in daylight now, which would normally have been heartening – she threw herself out of bed to grab the chamber pot underneath, just in time before bringing up last night's supper.

Florrie, already out of her bed, was staring as Ellie looked up from the receptacle. 'You orright?'

'I'm orright now,' she answered. 'I think,' she added, as another convulsion threatened, one that she managed to contain as she pushed the pot out of Florrie's sight. 'Something I must've eaten.'

It could only be that. She could think of nothing else that would have made her so violently sick completely out of the blue. Usually, when one is going to be sick, it takes some while, the sufferer tossing and turning and heaving before the offending food finally decides to vacate the stomach.

'I 'ad the same as you,' Florrie said. 'I feel orright.'

'Well, I'm orright now,' Ellie said sharply. 'We'd best get downstairs. We can't be late.'

She'd hardly got to the kitchen when a second attack, though not so fierce, had her running outside to the yard. She returned to find Cook gazing at her.

'What's the matter with you, girl?'

'I think it might be something I might've eaten.'

There came a deep, accusing frown. 'Are you saying I've given you something that's gone off?'

'No, Cook, supper was lovely and no one else is ill. It's only me.'

'That's true.' She jerked her head. 'Come over here a minute.'

Ellie came and had Mrs Jenkins look into her eyes. She saw her frown as she straightened up. 'When did you see your last monthlies, girl?'

'It was . . . I'm . . . not sure.'

It was rather late in her fourteenth year when she'd first realized she'd become a woman. But it had never been much of an inconvenience, arriving only spasmodically, just four or five times over that year.

When she'd spoken to her mother about it, the awkward, off-handed reply was that it sometimes happened that way when young girls first started, but people didn't talk about such things. She had continued to be irregular and thought no more of it, supposing it would always be this way with her.

'I can't remember either,' Mrs Jenkins was saying. It was she who took charge of the pail of salt water in which the soiled towelling squares were left soaking in salt water to lift the dried-in bloodstains. They'd then be boiled with the rest of the laundry, the skivvy's job to stand over the boiling suds and push the linen with the copper stick.

'I ain't got time to count months and days, but you should know,' Mrs Jenkins said in a distracted sort of way as she continued to study Ellie's face. 'But surely you must know.'

Ellie shook her head, trying to think back. It had been some time – maybe three months – but she'd been too busy to bother counting when and how long she was last on and even then she hadn't thought much about it.

'And now you've been sick,' Mrs Jenkins said in a low voice. 'Is there anything else that seems queer about you? Not quite right, I mean. Not ill, but not quite right.'

Yes, there had been something – something strange she wasn't sure of. Like an odd tenderness lately when she brushed her breasts with a careless arm when working. Small though her breasts were, they seemed to her to have somehow got bigger in the last couple of weeks and that didn't feel right either. She was sure she must be sickening for something. But what? She felt well enough in herself.

'Do you think there's something wrong with me, Cook?' she asked after answering Mrs Jenkins's question.

The woman was still looking at her, even more keenly now. 'Have you been seeing someone?'

'Seeing someone?'

'On your last day off. Someone you met or've been meeting behind our backs. Servants your age aren't encouraged to entertain young men. Have you been playing around with someone or other?'

'No, I ain't!' Ellie had begun to feel annoyed. It was her business if she did have a young man, which she didn't. What chance on one day off every month? 'All I done on me last day off was go and see an old neighbour where I used to live.'

She'd gone there to see if they'd had any news of her father. They hadn't. Not a peep. But Mrs Sharp had been pleased to see her and had her stay for dinner and tea. The woman had talked almost non-stop about this and that: the state of the area, the lack of policemen to patrol it, the crime, her noisy new neighbours, their horde of boisterous and unruly kids (not that her own youngsters were any better), the woman scruffy and her old man with the look of someone up to no good. 'Different when your family was there,' she said. 'Now the place smells something awful. I'm sure 'er ole man can't be bothered to walk two yards to the lav outside. I've seen 'im piddling up against me fence. I'll 'ave 'im abart it one day, see if I don't!'

The woman nattered on and on. Ellie would have made an excuse to leave much sooner if it hadn't been for Mrs Sharp's eldest son. It being Sunday, he wasn't at work and Ellie's mind was more taken up by him.

She'd never taken much notice of Ronnie Sharp when living next door. They'd grown up together as kids, but having been away for nigh on three months, she saw him in a new light. In that time he seemed to have grown taller and very upright. Dark-haired, dark-eyed, he'd always had a nice face. Now it caught her as being even nicer.

She listened entranced as he talked of his work in 'the

Print', as he called it, the *News Chronicle*. He'd started there at fourteen as an office boy running errands and messages, picking up mailbags from the post office. She hadn't been that interested in him then. Now she found herself all ears.

'It's a whopping big place,' he said proudly. 'They must have more'n a couple of thousand working there. Me – I work in the wire room, an important part of the paper. I'm still learnin' of course – sort of apprentice. One of the blokes, Mr Middleton, says he sees I'm very interested. I'll be eighteen in a few weeks' time and he's takin' on teaching me. There's lots to learn an' it's long hours – lots of night shifts – but it pays good. I get good overtime.'

After a while he had turned to asking her what she was doing.

'I'm a parlourmaid,' she told him as they ate the cakes his mother had made that morning. He had wrinkled his nose – a nice straight nose.

'No money in that and I 'eard they make you work 'ard.'

'I don't mind,' she'd said, taking delight in his attention.

'Do you still draw them pictures you used to?'

'Too busy.' She'd forgotten how she'd once enjoyed drawing – things like horses and carts, people, buildings, sometimes trees – not many around here.

'You used ter be really good at it,' he muttered almost sorrowfully. 'I used to think you was proper talented.'

She had thought so too. It would be nice to take it up again, but what time did she have? None whatsoever.

She had said goodbye reluctantly to Ronnie, having it in mind that on her next day off she would come and visit again, though it wouldn't be for another month.

As for Cook accusing her of heaven knew what, she had never done them sort of things. At last she'd realized what the woman was getting at, and told her so in no uncertain terms, saying that whatever was wrong with her it wasn't *that*! Her indignation stilled Mrs Jenkins into silence.

Nine

Listening through the open kitchen door this warm May morning to the sounds of vomiting coming from the outside lavatory, Mrs Jenkins made up her mind that Jay had certainly not told her the truth yesterday. If that girl wasn't around three months gone, she'd eat her hat.

Her first thought was to go straight to the mistress and lay her suspicions at her feet, but kindness of heart stopped her. Mrs Lowe only needed one excuse to get rid of Jay. But she wouldn't want to part with the girl's younger sister, and Ellie would be all alone out there in that wide world.

She had no doubts that, after a while, the girl would learn to fend for herself; but what if she was wrong and Jay hadn't got herself pregnant? She might be the cause of her losing her position. No, it was best to tackle her before jumping the gun. Then it might be better to take the matter to the master himself. After all, he was a doctor and level-headed. His wife would probably take off in hysterics or something.

As Ellie came back into the kitchen, looking white and strained, to faintly mutter an apology for absenting herself from her work for a moment or two, she said sternly, 'Come with me.'

Without waiting for a reply she made for her little parlour with Jay close behind, now with a hang-dog expression, no one being ordered into that holy of holies except for a dressing-down. 'Close the door,' she said abruptly.

'Now, young lady,' she began, turning to face her as Ellie did as she was told. 'What lies have you been telling me?'

'I don't know what you mean, Cook; I ain't told you no lies.' The tone was insolent and resentful.

Nora Jenkins tightened her lips. 'Oh yes you have! Now I want the truth from you, girl. The truth! Have you been up to tricks with a bloke? And don't you dare to turn your back on me!'

Her rather strident voice rose in volume as Ellie turned away. 'Walk out of this kitchen, girl, and I'll see that you're out of this house – you hear me?' she blared.

'Now,' she went on in a more moderate tone as Ellie turned back to face her, chastened, though the green eyes still stared resentfully from under the brows. 'I don't want trouble in this house, but if you are pregnant I will have to tell the mistress . . .'

She broke off as Ellie gave an alarmed gasp.

'Or maybe the master,' she added quickly. 'This matter is really for a woman to hear, but I know how things stand between you and the mistress. I've not been cook/housekeeper here all these years without knowing the goings-on in my place of employment.'

Nora Jenkins gave a half-smile, which was not acknowledged. She let the smile vanish. 'Now, before I do anything more, I need you to tell me exactly what's been going on. Who is the lad?'

'There isn't a lad!' The girl's voice came plaintive and desperate. 'I didn't even know me condition until you put the thought in me 'ead, and now I don't know what to do. You've scared me and now I'm praying to meself that it can't be.'

'Well, it looks to me like it can be,' Nora said, more gently now. The girl did look scared and obviously had no idea what could come of what started out as an innocent kiss and cuddle. 'I'm not going to fly off the handle at you. But if you know who the father is, you must tell me.'

'Father?' She seemed to cringe, then wilt.

'Father!' she repeated as if with sudden revelation, her eyes widening with something like revelation and loathing. 'Me father. Oh, God! Oh dear God . . .'

Her voice seemed to float away. Her hand had gone to her mouth. Her eyes widened with horrified disbelief. Her lips twisted as she shook her head from side to side in negation of what had entered her mind.

'What're you saying, child?' Nora Jenkins's voice quivered as she too found herself unable to credit the thought that had crept into her own mind.

She steeled herself to speak, trying to keep her voice steady, hoping against hope that the thought in her head was wrong. 'You said your father?'

Ellie's breathing came quick and shallow, her face as pale

as paper. She let her head hang, but she seemed to be nodding confirmation; yet even now Nora dared not think of it as that. 'Child, surely not.'

'It 'appened only three times.'

The girl hesitated, then went on, in a firmer tone. 'Me brother, Charlie came in and caught him touching me like he did before making me go upstairs with 'im. Me mum was out. So was Dora. Charlie was out too and we was alone. He always waited till we was alone. But Charlie came in unexpected and he went for me dad and there was a terrible fight.'

She seemed to gain strength in keeping away from the more sordid part. 'The furniture all got knocked about – we didn't have much as it was – me brother giving 'im such a pasting; and then he left. Two days after that me mum went down with pneumonia.'

Ellie glanced up, now taken up by her tale. 'Me mum hadn't been well with a terrible cold and cough for days. After me brother bashed him up, me dad 'ad a go at Mum – I don't know why, but he said he'd had enough of her always being ill and complaining and that he'd met someone else. He liked his women. And his drink. He was a beast. Then he left and he never came back. He don't even know Mum's dead and I don't know where he is ter tell 'im. Or me brother either.'

Lowering her head again as the tale came to an end, she looked thoroughly subdued and Nora Jenkins felt her heart go out to her. The first thought was to take the girl to her bosom, but she resisted the impulse. Her first and most important task was to sort out this business. It certainly couldn't be left as it was.

'Go and wash your face,' she told her brusquely. 'Then go on about your work.' As there came a look of doubt she added hastily, 'Leave this with me, child. I'll think of the best way of tackling it without you having to be dismissed. Go on now, child.'

She would speak to the master rather than his wife – catch him as soon as his morning surgery finished. She'd make sure he was in sympathy with the girl's plight. This child was a victim. She deserved justice. The girl was telling the truth – she was sure of it. She could only pray that she was.

After Mrs Jenkins left his study, Bertram Lowe sat unmoving behind his desk, staring unfocused at the opposite wall. It was hung with yellowing diplomas and certificates in their dark frames. They belonged to his father, also a medical man – a surgeon.

Beside them hung those that were his, fresher, unstained by time. His father had automatically seen his son through university, happy for him to enter the medical profession. He could have equalled his father, with a place waiting for him at the King's College Hospital, but events had changed all that. His father had died suddenly of a massive heart attack just as his son was due to leave university. His mother, deep in shock and pining, had followed her husband ten months later. By then he'd met the girl he would marry.

A timid, quiet little thing, Mary had stolen his heart, her quiet ways making him feel protective of her. When they'd had to marry rather suddenly, he'd opted to become a general practitioner, so as to be on hand. But the baby had been still-born, as were the next two. Rather than join his father's hospital – which would have meant long hours away from Mary who, having lost her own parents, feared the prospect of loneliness and pleaded not to be left – he had gone into private practice. It was sad not to have fulfilled his father's hopes and become an important man in the field he'd enjoyed. He might have opted for a Harley Street practice but felt his skills were of more use in London's deprived East End, though he often wondered if he'd been right.

Too late by the time Millicent was born. A healthy, pretty child, Mary's life had become wrapped up in her and he'd found himself put aside, Mary wanting nothing to do with her marital obligations lest another baby suffer the same fate as her first three. But he suspected it was more because she did not wish to share her love for her daughter with any other child.

In his own loneliness he too had indulged in overprotecting Millicent, feeling he'd been right to set up in private medicine. Working in hospital he'd have seen far less of her. It had seemed like a judgement on that overindulgence when what had been a perfectly healthy child had succumbed to tuberculosis.

Tears stung his eyes, misting the wall and the dark-framed testimonials at which he had been staring.

Bertram came upright in his swivel chair, leaned his elbows on the desk and rubbed the moisture from his eyes with his fists. As he looked up, the room came back into focus when what Mrs Jenkins had told him leaped back into his mind. He needed to think.

What should be done with the girl? There was no question of turning her out. That would be cruel and would sit in his mind for the rest of his life. But how could she remain here, his wife seeing the girl growing bigger each day with the child she carried? He dared not think how Mary would react.

Yet it would tear him apart to have her go from here. It helped to see her about the house, a salve for the emptiness that still lay in his heart even after eighteen months. The sight of her helped assuage that grief, kept him going, though even he knew he couldn't go on for ever pretending to himself this was his daughter he saw each morning. Now he was reaping the consequences.

What a fool he'd been to take the girl into his home in the first place. And what if the baby should prove to be not properly formed, or imbecile? There was every chance of that. Incest – its father the father of the mother who bore it, the child carrying the sin of the father in every way. What would they do with such a creature? God, it was a vile dilemma!

There came only one solution. For the mother's own salvation the foetus must be aborted, and soon. Mrs Jenkins reckoned the mother was around three months pregnant. There was still time.

He got up from his chair and rang for Mrs Jenkins again. Ellie hadn't come to do the study this morning – Chambers had instead; now he knew why.

'First, would you have someone inform my wife that I will be late down for breakfast,' he told Mrs Jenkins the moment she appeared. 'Then tell Jay to come here. I wish to speak to her. I do apologize, Mrs Jenkins, for asking you to play messenger, but I assume you understand?'

'I do, sir,' came the sober reply.

Alone in his study Bertram Lowe waited. He did not have to wait long. It could not have been more than two or three minutes before Ellie was bustled into the study with Mrs Jenkins holding her firmly by the arm.

'There you go, child,' she said and withdrew immediately, the door closing softly behind her.

Ellie stood in the centre of the room. The face gazing at

him had a drawn look. It made her look years older than she was and his heart went out to her.

'Come, my dear, sit down.' He gave her a smile and added, 'I'm not going to eat you.' The trite remark made him cringe inwardly. Fool! But his face did not change from the smile he had put on it and he was grateful to have her do as he had asked.

As she sat, perching herself on the edge of the chair opposite his, he leaned towards her. This wasn't the way he wanted it. What he really wanted was to go and put an arm about her, draw her to him, cuddle away that haunted expression; but he continued to stay where he was. How would he have behaved if this had been his daughter? But such a situation would never have arisen.

He gathered himself together. What he was about to put to this girl would have to be in the utmost secrecy. He dreaded to think what would happen were his wife ever to find out. He was already being torn three ways – between thought for his own safety, perhaps even the safety of his marriage if she were to remain here; a natural instinct to help any child in distress; and this overriding need to have her stay here, balm for his empty soul in seeing her every day in his home.

He was beginning to realize that there was a growing genuine fondness for her – not of any sordid kind, as she had come to know, but a fatherly affection while he pretended to himself that it was his own daughter whom he saw.

He took a deep breath, leaning forward on the desk, fingers interlaced before him. Ellie had been watching him closely and, as their gaze met, he said as soothingly as he could, 'Do you know why I want to speak to you, Ellie?'

She didn't move, didn't even shake or nod her head, putting him at a slight disadvantage.

'It concerns something you told Cook this morning – in confidence,' he added, hoping to coax her into speaking.

The hazel eyes had become wary and accusing. She frowned, but that was the only movement she made. It was disconcerting, and Bertram tried not to nibble at his lips or allow his face to give away the indecisiveness that was gripping him.

'Cook felt you needed help and so she came to me, in confidence, and I assure you, my dear, that what she told me will not go outside the four walls of this study.'

'But you want to get rid of me,' she said suddenly.

'No!' The word shot from his lips before he could stop it. 'No, my dear; I want to help you – do all I can for you. But I need your co-operation. I *can* help you, but in turn you must put your trust in me.'

He paused, but she didn't respond – didn't ask why she was being asked to trust him or what he intended to do to help her. She just sat rigid as a wooden doll.

'First, would you like to tell me exactly what you told Mrs Jenkins? It will help me to help you.'

'I don't know now what I told her,' she returned in a flat tone, almost as if she didn't care.

'You do realize your condition, don't you?' he went on.

She nodded and shrugged offhandedly.

'You told Mrs Jenkins whom you suspected.' Again she nodded, this time without the shrug. 'And is that the truth?'

Her gaze fell away and she lowered her head, but there came a faint nod, so brief as to be hardly discernible. There seemed to be no lie in the movement. A liar would surely have stared him out, but this gave the appearance of genuine shame. It was cruel. This girl had no cause to feel shame – a child at the mercy of a brutish, selfish father: what could she have done to defend herself. She had been wronged.

He leaned back, the movement making her glance up. What he saw in her eyes took the breath out of him: an arid gleam of utter loathing. It lasted for only a second and he knew it wasn't there for him but for another.

His mind conjured up the face, pugnacious, flushed – with drink maybe – its owner heavily built. What hope had this girl before such a man? The impression might be wrong, but even if he were a mere weasel of a man, his power over a girl like this was just as vile. But, having seen her hulking brother, his first impression struck him as probably more correct.

On an impulse, he stood up and came round the desk towards her. Seeing her lean away ever so slightly from his approach, he stopped himself just in time from catching her up in his arms and holding her close. Instead, he moved past her to pace the room, the only thing he could think to do.

Feeling a little more composed, he turned back to her. 'Listen to me, my dear. I need to explain certain things to you.' He spoke as kindly as he could, but serious matters needed to be dealt with.

'You are aware now that you are carrying a child inside you?'
Ellie nodded.

'And that it is . . . I am sorry to be saying this . . . that it is
the child of your own father.'

This time she did not nod but, as before, stared at him with
that arid, almost blank gaze. Again it was unnerving, but he
forced himself to continue, clinically, with no trace of emotion –
a doctor advising a patient.

'I need to explain to you the possible implications attaching
to such a situation. Certain things could affect the child's
chance of a normal life. At the best it would abort . . . You
could lose it quite suddenly, early on in this pregnancy. On
the other hand, it could go to full term; but what its condition might be is the problem. Do you understand what I am
saying to you, Ellie?'

She was looking confused. A child of sixteen – what could
she know?

'There are certain unions between man and woman nature
abhors. Between brother and sister, between uncle and niece,
between mother and son and between father and daughter. It
is in the Bible. Any such union can cause irrevocable damage
to the issue that may come of it.'

Still she stared as if uncomprehending what he was saying.
He began again, in simpler terms for her. 'If the child ever
goes to full term, it is almost a certainty it will be either
stillborn or will come into the world an imbecile, or
deformed, or both. I dread to think to what degree. Do you
understand now?'

At last realization of what he'd been trying to say had stolen
over her. Her eyes had grown wide, filled with fear. He hurried
to assuage that fear.

'Listen to me, Ellie; I can help you there. I can stop it if
you wish.'

'Oh, yes please!'

'But you have to put yourself in my hands, and not a word
can be breathed to anyone. And I mean *anyone*! – not even
your sister. I will explain. And if you are in agreement at the
end of it, you will abide by your word.'

'I promise.'

'Now, why you must never breathe a word of this is because
what I shall do for you is illegal. If discovered, I'd be struck

off the medical register, banned from the medical profession, never allowed to practise medicine.'

He had tried to say it in the simplest terms for her benefit, but there was no response. She merely sat listening to him.

'I shall need to perform a small operation on you, child – very simple and quick – and will relieve you of that which you are carrying inside you.'

It had been the only way to explain without becoming technical; being used to dealing with dull, uneducated patients, he had thought her brighter and quicker to grasp what he had been saying. Then he realized that she had been in shock; she had understood what he had been saying but hadn't been able to respond. He felt almost relief. But he needed confirmation.

'You know what I'm saying, child?' he said slowly.

'You're going to do something inside me and that will make me all right again, won't it?'

Good God! She had known all along. In her world she would have heard of back-street abortions. But if she knew all that, with the dregs of society all about her, why hadn't she realized her own condition?

He knew the answer to that. Even in such a world as she came from, mothers were too embarrassed to explain to their daughters the facts of life, many of which they themselves didn't know. Though even they knew how to prevent pregnancy, breast feeding for as long as possible – things like that.

The facts of life were usually learned from friends and then mostly from conjecture – babies could come about from open-mouth kissing; they came out through the belly button; you only got babies when you married; even the lingering children's ideas a mother had fobbed them off with, that the stork brought them or they'd be found under a gooseberry bush.

Many a girl of thirteen or fourteen was told that and believed it until later she went with a boy probably as ignorant as her about such things except that the sexual urge was probably one of the strongest instincts of nature, to end up horribly surprised a few months later. But one thing girls were aware of was the one thing they ought not to know about: that unwanted pregnancies could be got rid of by going to some woman or other for a few shillings. It was rife, it was dangerous and many a woman and girl had died from infection and shock.

'You will be in safe hands,' he reassured her.

She'd begun to look doubtful, probably from fear of the unknown, maybe having heard dire stories about fatal results.

'What if it ain't done?' she queried in a small voice. He wondered whether she was asking whether, if left in her condition, there'd be no place for her here, or whether something could go drastically wrong, ending her life?

She had no need to fear the latter. What she had to fear was that, left to go to full term, the child might be born in a condition not to bear thinking about. He had no qualms about his own skills, but she must be told what could come about were she to refuse his aid.

'I will answer your question,' he said sternly, 'and give you the truth in plain terms, but it may upset you.'

She listened quietly to all he said on the possible results of forbidden union. She listened with eyes closed and lips tight together. Only when he had finished speaking did she open her eyes to look at him.

'I put all me trust in you, Doctor Lowe,' was all she said, very quietly.

It was only after she had left that he allowed his own emotions to rise to the surface. He'd always been impeccable in medical matters. He had never practised what he was now contemplating doing. Assisted abortion – if he was discovered, he'd be struck off the medical register, or, worse, would face imprisonment.

More than that, this wasn't just any patient. This was a young person whom he'd become fond of. He was not alarmed by the operation itself but that their relationship might never be the same again. Would she always look on him as another violator of her person?

'I put all me trust in you,' she had said in her poor English. With those words ringing in his head Doctor Lowe felt his muscles momentarily weaken, so that he almost decided he couldn't go through with it.

He pulled himself up sharply. She had put her trust in him and he must make himself worthy of that trust. Going slowly from his study, he closed and locked the door and made his way downstairs to the dining room where Mary would most likely be waiting to have breakfast with him.

Ten

Physically Ellie felt she'd got over it better than she'd feared. Mentally it was hard: the memory, the pain, the humiliation, the one who had performed it, medical man though he was, being someone she must face every day. To have had to go through all that because of her own father's incest made her even more determined to make him pay, grievously, when she did finally trace him.

She could hardly look at Doctor Lowe – more than between doctor and patient, theirs was a secret between master and servant – she felt only embarrassment. Yet his own attitude towards her seemed to have become almost paternal, that of a father trying to do all he could to comfort her; he couldn't have been more considerate.

He had told Mrs Jenkins to inform his wife that Ellie had been taken ill and must remain in bed until she was able to resume her duties.

'Chambers will get suspicious, them sharing,' Mrs Jenkins reminded him. She wasn't worried about Mrs Lowe. The master could deal with her

He frowned. 'Of course. She must sleep elsewhere temporarily. Tell her Jay has influenza and that we don't want the whole staff down with it.'

'Where should I put her?'

'We'll clear out the old box room.' The box room was in the attic along from the two maids' room. Six feet by seven, it was a graveyard of discarded bits and pieces as well as housing a noisy water tank.

'With all this stuff out of the way,' he said, looking about him, 'we'd easily get a single bed in here. I notice there is already a commode in here and an old chest of drawers and there are door hooks to hang her clothes on. Yes, this will do admirably,' he concluded, ignoring the gurgling and rattling from the tank. 'After all, it's only temporarily, isn't it?'

'Why couldn't Jay sleep there till she was better?' Florrie grumbled in Mrs Jenkins's hearing, while avoiding making it a direct complaint; otherwise she would have got her ear bitten off.

For all that, Mrs Jenkins's tone was sharp. 'I don't suppose it crossed the master's mind and who am I to put him right? Anyway, it's done. You'll have to put up with it.'

Just the same, to Nora's mind the master's behaviour towards young Jay was looking glaringly odd, and she was worried. The only other one aware of the deed he'd performed on the girl, she was glad it had been successful and Ellie had suffered no lasting ill effects, the thing having been quickly disposed of. But should this business ever come out, she might be implicated, and that didn't bear thinking about.

As to his attachment to the girl, Doctor Lowe should be treading very warily. Yet as the days went on it seemed more and more that he was casting caution to the winds, not about the illegal operation – that was over – but in other ways and not so subtle other ways either.

No sooner had the girl got up from her 'sickbed' than he spoke of her needing to take things easy for a while longer.

'It would help her recovery if she had some time off work on one or two evenings a week,' he said to Mrs Jenkins, threatening to implicate her even more into whatever he had in mind for Jay. As she saw it, he was behaving almost like a father to her, and that was dangerous.

Chambers still slept in the box room with the water tank and was becoming frustrated and morose in her work, with no foreseeable prospect of returning to the room she and Jay had shared. In fact, young Rose was now sharing with her, leaving Jay with a room all to herself.

'We can't have Rose continuing to sleep in the kitchen,' he said by way of excuse. 'I know the lowest order of servants are little considered in some households, but that is not my way. We can squeeze a truckle bed in there for her – which will be an improvement for her, don't you think, Mrs Jenkins?'

Young Rose had relieved Ellie in doing all the more menial jobs: laundry, ironing, beating carpets, sweeping the outside area, sluicing the drain, cleaning the servants' outside lavatory and the like.

'And she'll be out of your way, Mrs Jenkins,' he went on. 'It can't be easy entering your kitchen first thing in the morning to see her getting up.'

It might have seemed a more proper arrangement had she not known different. It was only a matter of time before the mistress got to know about these strange changes and fell to wondering what was behind them. Lately she had hardly left her room, except for dinner and when entertaining, keeping to herself, speaking only to her as 'Cook' when she came to her room to discuss meals and purchasing provisions. Poor young Dora, closeted with her, must have been miserable. Mrs Jenkins felt sorry for her sometimes.

Then, a few weeks later, there appeared a new face in the house. Nora Jenkins wondered if the mistress was as in the dark about that as about Chambers' altered sleeping arrangements. But the young man was as much a mystery to her, except that she was told his name. Around seven thirty each Tuesday evening he'd arrive – by the front door, if you please – to be shown straight up to the master's study, giving her no time to quiz him. She felt a little irked that Doctor Lowe hadn't confided in her what the young man was doing here. She suspected it had something to do with Ellie, but what she couldn't think, even though she racked her brains.

It was Chambers' task to answer the tug on the door bell and conduct him up to Doctor Lowe's study, her complaining over sleeping arrangements pacified a little by this apparently important role.

'It's all very mysterious though, ain't it?' she said on the occasion of his second visit. 'He don't look like a doctor or lawyer or any professional sort.'

'Whatever he is is nothing to do with you,' she was reminded by Mrs Jenkins, by the third visit having been taken into the master's confidence.

'I've discovered young Jay is quite a talented little artist and I feel it might benefit her to be encouraged,' he'd confided after she had voiced her disapproval of being kept in the dark about the visitor. The ordinary staff had no need to know, but she had been with this family long enough to feel part of it, and not to be confided in struck her as grossly underhanded.

'I have asked the young man, the son of a colleague of mine and quite a talented painter himself, to come and give her a few lessons. But – and this is between you and me, Mrs Jenkins – I would rather my wife didn't know for the time being, and I know you will not allow this to go any further.'

She would dearly have liked to ask how he expected to keep his wife from knowing and what would happen when she did find out, as she was bound to eventually. Nevertheless, she would keep her eyes open and an ear to the ground. But she could see trouble brewing, even so.

By indulging the girl he was treading on shaky ground. Long ago she too had noticed the resemblance to his deceased child. It took only half an eye to see that what he was doing – trying to recreate one to replace the child he had lost – was tantamount to disaster. It could only bring trouble. But if trouble did arise from it, she would make sure she was there to help.

'I'll leave you with Mr Deel then, my dear.'

As Doctor Lowe withdrew from his study, Ellie smiled at the young man. His name was Michael. His surname was spelled differently from the English way, his father being Dutch. His mother was English, he'd told her when she'd first been introduced to him some four weeks ago.

Doctor Lowe had kept going on about her diction and how it would be so nice if she could learn to speak correctly. She'd tried, but her heart hadn't been in it, still disturbed, as she was, by what she'd been through at his hands.

It had had to be done and she'd been in the most capable hands, he being solely concerned for her safety and well-being; but it hadn't made it any less traumatic. For several days she hadn't been able to look at him. He was being so kind, and came into her room when the house was quiet to sit by her bed and talk to her – of his work, his student days, his childhood; it was like a proper father speaking, but she couldn't feel easy with him.

He would go to the window to stand there silently, having exhausted all talk but reluctant to leave. He'd sometimes glance about the room at this and that, everything in here her own stuff, Chambers resigned to remaining in the other room with her belongings.

The day before she was to get up, he had idly glanced at some bits of paper she'd been drawing on to occupy herself while being confined to her bedroom under this pretext of having caught a bout of 'flu.

'What are these?' he'd enquired. She had already asked if she could have some paper to draw on. She watched him scan her simple sketches: the view from her window, her own face as seen in the bit of mirror over the washstand, some bits from memory – cats, dogs, horses, carts, people.

'They are quite good,' he'd said. 'You've quite a talent.'

She knew that. Ronnie Sharp had told her that time she'd gone to see his family. She was aching to see him again, but this awful business had intervened and she wondered if he had more or less put her aside.

'I think,' Doctor Lowe had said slowly, as he put the drawings back on the side of the washstand, 'it might be good if someone showed you how to draw even better – perhaps even learn to paint.'

'I ain't never painted,' she told him. 'Couldn't afford paints.'

'Then we shall provide you with a box of paints and you can use my study when I am not using it. I will give you a key so you'll not be disturbed. After you have completed your duties, of course,' he'd concluded in a more formal tone, remembering his position.

'What if the mistress finds me in there, wasting me time?' she asked, still slightly taken aback by his offer.

'She never goes into my study,' he told her. 'If she needs me, then she rings for Chambers to inform me.' He gave a wry smile. 'We seldom see each other except for meals. There was a time we'd relax together in the sitting room, but not since the loss of our daughter. These days my good wife prefers her own room.'

His chubby features had dropped a little. They now brightened again.

'To this business of painting: it so happens that I know of someone who might help you – the son of an acquaintance of mine. He is quite a good artist, though he studied to become a doctor like his father. I will ask him. He may also care to help with your English at the same time – teach you how to speak more nicely than you do at present.'

'Why do you want me to speak better?' she'd asked and

he had looked at her for a moment before speaking. When he did, very quietly, she had heard a catch in his throat, his voice wavering a little. 'You must try to understand. You know that we lost our only child.'

Yes, she knew, but she'd let him continue.

'Forgive me, my dear, but I fear that, despite my better judgement, perhaps, I find that having you here does ease the pain of my loss. I hesitate to admit that I have a foolish need to keep her memory alive. Your being here has helped. My dearest wish was to have given her all the things she would have wanted, but I feel in retrospect that I was too busy in my work to give her the attention she should have had. Now it's too late . . .'

He broke off then began again. 'With you, my dear, I feel that perhaps it is not too late. I have a wish to do for you what I neglected to do for her, but I can do so little, things being what they are. You see, my wife—'

He'd broken off sharply, as if knowing he had said too much. Turning away quickly he didn't see the brief excitement that crossed Ellie's expression. By the time he turned back to her, it had been replaced by a sudden feeling of sadness for him, which she knew was genuine, despite her elation.

'I do apologize,' he'd said hurriedly.

'No, please don't,' she'd answered.

'Will you promise not to repeat to anyone what I have just told you?' he had begged, so pathetically that she had reached out and touched his arm.

'Cross me heart,' she'd said simply, making a concentrated effort to put the aitch in the word 'heart'.

That had been four weeks ago. He'd not referred to it again, nor had she, realizing that sleeping dogs should be left to lie. She saw Michael Deel on Tuesday evenings for about an hour and a half. Tuesdays were easier, the heavier work of the weekend having subsided a little before the build-up to the next weekend began. Ellie, Florrie, Rose and Mrs Jenkins could relax in the evenings, sitting around the kitchen fire reading, chatting, knitting or sewing, using the area in place of the servants' hall most larger establishments provided.

At eight o'clock Chambers would get up to go and answer the front-door bell's jangle and show the visitor up to Doctor Lowe's study. She'd come back down to throw herself testily on to her chair to pick up whatever she'd been doing and almost always pass some testy remark that Mr Deel must have something very private to do with the master to come so regularly. Her surmise was inevitably cut short by Mrs Jenkins telling her sharply that, whatever it was, it was none of her business, and that tittle-tattle and idle conjecture didn't go down well in this house.

Shortly afterwards, Ellie would casually get up from the chair where she'd been reading, with all pretence of going off to her room. It was exciting in a way to skitter along to Doctor Lowe's study, eyes darting about in case she was seen.

Doctor Lowe and her tutor would be there and as she entered, so Doctor Lowe would leave. For perhaps half an hour Michael Deel would help to improve her diction accompanied by chuckles and giggles at her pathetic attempts to get it right. The rest of the time – perhaps an hour and a half, which seemed to simply fly by – she'd sketch and paint in watercolour under his expert tuition, he pointing out little faults, better ways of doing things.

She looked forward to Tuesday evenings. They helped to dim the unpleasant, lingering memory of what had happened to her recently, though it dimmed none of her bitterness towards her father.

Drawing always helped her to lose herself. Alone in her room she'd sketch endlessly, her pencil moving at ever faster speed, often until what she had drawn became overlaid with increasingly wild and heavy strokes, as her feelings of humiliation, hatred and revenge came creeping back.

When working about the house, her thoughts concentrating on jobs to be done, it wasn't so bad; but once she was alone, her mind began to seethe. Her only relief from it seemed to be to immerse herself in sketching, sometimes little landscapes she'd seen in books or rough portraits of those around her – that was, until things in her head made her practically obliterate them. These she never showed to Doctor Lowe. Naturally he wanted to know how she was progressing. After all, he was paying for her tuition, for which not only was she thankful but also aware of a feeling of satisfaction. But if he had seen these other sketches, he would have been shocked. She shocked herself sometimes.

This evening, having finished her half-hour elocution lesson with the painful effort to pronounce words correctly, as out came pencils and paper and the box of paints Doctor Lowe had provided for her, the interest of both pupil and tutor perked up considerably.

'You know,' he remarked as he helped her get the correct perspective of the country cottage she was sketching ready for painting, 'you could go a long way once you've mastered a few more techniques. You have exceptional talent, Miss Jay.'

She wished he wouldn't keep calling her Miss Jay. It sounded so formal. She pursed her lips and studied the drawing. 'I won't ever be that good.'

'I'm sure you will be,' he said absently, falling silent to study the picture as, having now finished the sketching, she began mixing colours, applying a blue wash for the sky, several greens for fields and a rough suggestion of trees and bushes, and greys for the lane that would be filled in later, before she began on the cottage itself. It wasn't a large scene. The background work had taken some five or ten minutes before he spoke again.

'You've a fantastic insight into how things feel. Good artists need that, and you have got it.'

'What do you mean – feel?' she asked, paintbrush poised over her work as she studied what she'd done so far. 'Cottages don't feel.'

'What I mean is . . .' For a moment he seemed lost. 'How can I put it? It's like . . .' Again he paused, then pointed to the several bricks on the cottage wall she was colouring in. 'Look, you see these? Anyone can paint a brick. It's oblong, it's brownish, it sits straight in a wall. But it's more than mere brick – it has life in it, and you see that life, Miss Jay . . . Ellie.'

Her eyes widened at this sudden use of her Christian name, but he had his eyes trained on the cottage she was painting. His voice rose in a burst of enthusiasm.

'Don't you realize what you're doing? You're not painting every brick brown; you're instinctively adding different tints, touches of blue and ochre and umber – as if you *feel* what they are like: the texture, the roughness, the imperfections of brick. It's the only way I can describe it. Often something like that has to be taught, shown. You're doing it instinctively.'

'All I'm doing is painting!' she said, a little irked by the observation interrupting the flow of her brush. All she wanted to do was paint, not to be told the blessed ins and outs of what it all meant.

'No, don't you see what I mean, Ellie? You *are* those bricks.' He looked at her and noticed the pursing of her lips in confusion. 'Let me explain if I can. When I am painting, say, a horse, you know this soft part of the head?' – he touched his temples. 'When I am painting the head and my brush begins to perfect that part of the animal, I actually sense the brush against my own temple. Do you see what I mean?'

'I think so,' she said hesitantly. In fact, she had grasped what he was getting at. Her own temples seemed to sense something as he spoke.

'And what you feel is sympathy for the thing you are painting. You are one with what you are making on plain paper with a bit of paint. It becomes real to you.'

'Yes I see it,' she cried, and he laughed.

'Everything you paint will feel like that to you, Ellie: an animal, a human being, whatever – a leg, an arm; you'll sense those brush strokes on the exact area on yourself, like this.'

To her surprise, he had reached out and put a hand lightly on her upper arm, letting it slip over the material of her sleeve. He stopped, realizing what he was doing. She in turn felt her breath go for an instant and the warmth of the touch reached her flesh. Instinctively she stepped back.

'Ellie . . . Miss Jay,' he gasped. 'I'm sorry, I didn't mean . . .'

Ellie lifted her head and shrugged. 'It's nothing.'

'I was carried away – trying to explain.'

'It doesn't matter,' she said sharply. 'Look, let's get on with this. The time's nearly up.'

He took out his fob watch, as if looking for something to distract him. 'So it is. We might as well leave this to dry and have a go at it next week.'

Ellie nodded, but something inside her had stirred. The pupil–tutor relationship might very well be in jeopardy, and did she want that just now?

Eleven

W ithout her sister to talk to, Dora was feeling utterly lost. As a personal maid to Mrs Lowe she saw little of the other servants, giving her a sense of somehow being a prisoner, despite Mrs Lowe's kindness towards her.

The mistress could be demanding, if in a gentle way, and although she was always giving her little things – embroidered handkerchiefs, a ribbon for her hair, a modest little brooch – Dora suspected it was more to keep her at her side than from natural generosity.

'You know your position is a privileged one, Dora – much envied,' she had reminded her when she'd once shown signs of discontent by saying how she missed Ellie's company. 'You have only to look in the "Wanted" column in the newspapers to see that. Only those with excellent qualifications are invited to interviews for such a position as yours.'

'It's just that I'm not even to talk to her,' Dora had insisted.

She saw the woman's chubby lips purse irritably. 'I've taken you on as my personal maid and, I hope, companion, Dora, despite your tender years, and have taken great pains to teach you, because I can see great potential in you. You could go far in a position such as you now have.'

'Yes, madam,' Dora had obligingly agreed, too timid to mention Ellie again. She didn't want to jeopardize her job. She had all a girl could want – more than most servants got: comfort, little treats, the regard of her mistress, and a wage that had recently been increased. It had come to her ears that Ellie hadn't received any increase in her wages, even though she had apparently wheedled her way into the master's good books so that he'd even provided a tutor once a week to help bring out her artistic talent.

'Your sister's made sure she's landed on her feet orright,' Florrie had whispered to her out of everyone's hearing when

they'd passed on the stairs just after Ellie had got up from
her bout of 'flu.

'She never did it deliberately,' Dora offered defensively, but
Florrie gave a derisory sniff.

'I reckon you both worked it well if you ask me, 'er with
the master and you with the mistress, and not been 'ere but
a couple of months.'

Dora had gone on her way without replying to that. She'd
felt hurt, but she supposed they had both, in fact, landed on
their feet. She ought to have been grateful after what had lain
in front of them after losing their mother. She was – if only
she could just have been with Ellie now and again.

'One in your position does not associate with the lower
servants,' Mrs Lowe had told her, leaving her to wonder if
this was such a good thing.

This Sunday was Ellie's first day off in four weeks. Dora had
had her day off a few days before. Ellie had seen her from
the landing window as she was dusting the ornaments on the
narrow sideboard.

The poor thing, dressed up in a sombre cream summer
blouse and beige skirt, short beige jacket, cream gloves and
a light-coloured straw boater, had looked quite the young lady
as she'd left the house – only just turned thirteen – but lonely.
Ellie hadn't even seen her on her birthday; nor had Dora seen
her on hers.

She'd looked up as Ellie tapped frantically on the pane.
There was a lost look on her face. Ellie threw up the lower
sash window and leaned out.

'You orright?' She automatically spoke nicely these days,
but at this moment it seemed more appropriate not to.

Dora's face lit up. 'I'm fine. How are you?' She spoke
correctly and Ellie suddenly felt a pang of longing for the old
days when such things hadn't mattered.

'I miss seeing you,' she called in a stage whisper.

'Me too.' That was more like it. But the light in her face
had faded.

'Where you going?'

'I don't know. Walk round the shops, I suppose; have a bit
of lunch somewhere, I suppose.'

It sounded such a lonely idea: a thirteen-year-old all on her own looking around the shops to while away the time that should have been a pleasure, until it was time to come back here.

'Tell you what,' she hissed down to her; 'go and see Mrs Sharp, our old neighbour. She'll make you welcome. She might even give you a bit of dinner and you'll have a nice time. If you can, take her in a bunch of flowers. She'd appreciate that. When I have my day off on Sunday, I'm going to pay her a visit too.'

She was looking forward to calling on them then. Hopefully Ronnie Sharp would be there. 'And see if you can find anything out about Dad,' she'd reminded her on an afterthought. 'Ask her—'

'What on earth do you think you are doing?'

Ellie had broken off and spun round to see Mrs Lowe standing behind her. 'What are you doing?' she'd repeated, her plump little figure almost trembling with fury.

'I was just passing the time of day with my sister, that's all,' Ellie had returned none too politely. If there was anyone she detested more than her own father, it was this woman.

'I have explained to Dora that a lady's maid never associates herself with the lower servants and I would beg you to remember this.'

'It *is* her day off, madam,' Ellie had reminded her coldly. 'She can choose who she wants to speak to on her day off.'

Mrs Lowe's lips had tightened. 'I do not like your attitude, young woman. Nor servants leaning out of windows in my house yelling into the street like fishwives. I shall see about this. Now close the window and get back to work!'

The plump little figure had turned on its heel and descended the rest of the stairs to breakfast while Ellie had pulled down the window, giving a farewell wave to her sister.

Later she'd heard raised voices wafting from the dining room as Florrie came out with a tray of empty dishes. Her face was flushed.

'What's going on?' Ellie had hissed as they passed.

Florrie had paused, eager to relay what she'd overheard and see the other girl's face when she told her. 'The mistress is upset. She caught you hanging out of the upstairs landing window talking – yelling, she said – to Miss Jay, and she wants you dismissed immediately for rudeness and talking back. I think she really means to see you gone this time.'

Her expression was smug, but Ellie had ignored it. 'I don't think she'll get her way on that one.'

She would have said more, but caution had stopped her. The less everyone knew about her and the master and her now having a tutor, the better. They could tittle-tattle for all they were worth, so long as that was all it was.

She'd lifted her head and gone on past, but Florrie couldn't know how rapidly her heart was beating despite telling herself she was being foolish. She was sure Doctor Lowe would support her against his wife with her petty, irrational dislikes. Surely, after all he'd been doing for her – taking such an interest in her, engaging someone to teach her to talk properly and improve her artistic talents – he wouldn't see her go now, not even for his wife.

For the rest of the week she watched for him, but he seemed to be evading her. Once she glimpsed him opening the door connecting his surgery to the house, but he hastily closed it behind him as if he had already caught sight of her and wished to escape an awkward situation, leaving her to come to the conclusion that he was indeed trying to avoid her.

At least he hadn't called her to his study to convey the dread words of needing to dispense with her services. It could still come. Perhaps he was trying to compose himself for the awful moment.

By Sunday she still hadn't been sent for, which was encouraging, and she perked up a little. There had been more high words issuing faintly through the heavy dining-room door. No one had conveyed to her what had been said. Florrie said she'd been made to leave the room before anything reached her ears.

Since the window episode Florrie had been the only one told to wait at table. That in itself seemed ominous, but as the argument appeared to be an ongoing one, she'd taken heart a little more and fought off the fear that Mrs Lowe might even now persuade her husband that she was a bad influence on the staff. The longer it went on, the more likely it was that she would be allowed to stay here.

Hurrying off to visit her old neighbour, half of her glad to be out of the house today, the other half wondering if she would indeed come back to find herself dismissed, she turned her thoughts to Ronnie Sharp instead, hoping to find him there. Seeing him would take her mind off other things.

She returned home elated. Ronnie Sharp had asked her to go with him up west on her next day off to see George Robey, billed at the Pavilion as the Prime Minister of Mirth. 'I'll buy tickets for both of us – I can afford it,' he'd said, showing off with his decent wages from working at the press.

She'd had to decline, explaining that the younger domestic staff had to be back at their place of work by nine, but his offer made her feel good and he'd suggested that next time she came, if it was a Sunday, they'd go to Hyde Park, perhaps have a rowing boat out on the Serpentine. That, too, was questionable – her next day off might not be Sunday, and he worked all week.

Little wonder housemaids seldom picked up with a steady boyfriend except for one working in the same establishment or the local delivery boy, neither ever much of a catch; and if the couple did finally decide to marry, there was never much prospect of money.

It wasn't fair, being unable to go out when she pleased, for all Doctor Lowe was regarding her as more than just an employee – which was a good thing, she supposed, but she no longer felt comfortable in his presence, knowing how he'd seen and touched parts of her no one else would be allowed to, even though he'd done it as a doctor. She still cringed from the memory.

But she intended to marry well one day. Her goal was to work towards becoming something in this world and one day stand over her father, a proud lady of substance, and see him grovel before her. That was still a long way off, and might not happen, but Doctor Lowe was at least a stepping stone.

Meanwhile she felt excited as she made her way home. Ronnie was nice, well mannered for the family he came from, and quite handsome. Yes, she could take to Ronnie. He had a good job and hopeful prospects. But that too was a long way off. Early days yet.

She let herself in by the back door, glanced at the clock on the kitchen wall to find she was a few minutes ahead of her time to be back. Ignoring Mrs Jenkins's quizzical expression at her glowing face, she hurried by her before she could ask what a time she'd had and went up to her room.

There, however, she came back down to earth. Ronnie would never countenance waiting for her once-a-month day off to coincide with his. He would get tired and find someone else. Perhaps even now he had someone else in tow, someone freer than her. It was no good dreaming. Nor would she ever rise to become wealthy. Who'd want her, a mere parlourmaid, except someone in the same circumstances as her?

She began to feel suddenly depressed. Automatically her mind went to her father and with that the last shred of euphoria faded. To rid herself of the dismal feeling she found a small sheet of clean drawing paper and began to sketch, sitting on her bed, the paper propped on a book on her lap.

Without really thinking, she began to draw her father, as near as she could remember: the heavily handsome face, the full moustache and slick brown hair that made him look rakish, the muscular frame that under her pencil became even more muscular, the face growing ugly and brutish. At his feet she drew the outline of a crouching woman. The pencil strokes became steadily fiercer, making marks like blood dripping from his fists, spreading about his feet and the female figure, until the drawing was almost obliterating the original picture.

Of course her father – selfish, belligerent, callous though he was – had never been guilty of the sort of mayhem her pencil described; but the way he'd walked out when Mum had been so ill – that, and having his unnatural way with herself, was enough. For both these things she'd never forgive him.

She'd spoiled such sketches this way before and it always felt as if someone else was making her, though why was incomprehensible, except that it helped get some of this pent-up anger and hatred out of herself and left her with an odd sense of fulfilment, even triumph.

Laying aside the obliterated sketch, she got ready for bed. Stripping off skirt, blouse, straight-fronted corset and the rest of her undergarments, she washed herself from head to toe in the cold water poured from the cracked ewer into the basin on the washstand, each application of the flannel taking her breath away despite the warmth of the summer evening.

She washed methodically, each separate part scrubbed remorselessly with a harsh, faded flannel to be savagely rubbed dry with a rough towel. In a way it seemed to help erase every vestige of the memory the sketch of her father had conjured up in her mind – how her very soul would cringe from his approach even as she kept her face expressionless in case he got angry; that awful clutching at her heart as he told her what a pretty girl she was before leading her by the hand up the stairs, and what she'd recently gone through to get rid of the horrible result of his use of her. God! One of these days she would find him. She would watch him beg for his life. If it came to it, she would have no complaint about swinging for him.

Having dried, cleaned her teeth and donned her nightgown, she unpinned and brushed out her long hair, counting fifty strokes that would help keep the dark auburn tresses shiny, finally creeping into bed to think of pleasanter things: Ronnie Sharp, her art sessions with Michael Deel, the fact that no more had been heard from her employers about being let go. She felt a lot better.

In his study Bertram Lowe frowned at the drawing he held up before him – hardly a drawing, more a mass of heavy pencil marks, so thick that the picture beneath was almost unidentifiable.

Having given Ellie permission to use his study for this purpose, she often left her work here. This one had been among several other delicate pencil sketches and watercolours she'd done, pretty country scenes copied from a book he'd lent her. It came as a shock to find something like this.

Looking at the others she had done, he had felt pleased, the cost of a tutor being, he felt, well spent. She was improving with each visit. Her speech, too, had improved but could still be better. Not easy to get someone out of the bad habits of a lifetime.

Then, almost at the bottom of the little stack, he'd come across this. He could hardly make it out for the vicious indentation of the pencil over every part of what she'd drawn. There was deliberation behind the marks, not just a crossing out of something not up to standard.

He felt a sense of bewilderment as he held it up for a better look. If it hadn't been to her satisfaction, why hadn't she merely torn it up and thrown it away? Why this? and why save it? Quite possibly it had been left in this pile by mistake?

Bertram's medical brain began to question: had she often done this sort of thing? Even this one seemed to indicate a troubled mind – a confused mind, perhaps. It was possible.

The traumatic experiences she'd suffered: the death of her mother, the sexual abuse of her father, and for his own part, the abortion – who could say what such things did to the brain?

She seemed settled here, well adjusted enough, but what really went on in her head? Were these the outward sign of a traumatized mind?

Leaning closer, he could just about make out, beneath the apparent vandalism of her own work, what appeared to be the shape of a man with another figure lying at his feet, but little more than that. What had prompted her to obliterate the sketch so viciously?

He should have shrugged off the matter as showing mere childish annoyance about a sketch that hadn't turned out right, but something was telling him it went deeper than that. Oddly, it worried him every inch as much as if this had been his dear Millicent, even though he kept telling himself that it was none of his business.

He wasn't happy at the way he was beginning to feel about her. Ellie was not his daughter. If he grew too fond of her, she would break his heart in the end. The life of a cherished offspring was, essentially, forever bound up with their family, no matter how far in the world they roamed. Ellie's life was her own. She was beholden to no one; one day she would leave to get on with her own life and he would never see her again. The emptiness left on losing his daughter would be brought upon him again.

On the strength of this he told himself he had no right to question her as to why she'd so obviously and intentionally ruined what appeared to have been such a good sketch originally.

Moments later he knew he had to find out why, if only for his own peace of mind.

Twelve

Ellie knocked on the study door. She'd been sent for in such a way that the first thought in her head was, again, dismissal. She couldn't get over this constant dread that one day it might happen – her life here felt that tenuous. This bad blood between her and Mrs Lowe had her in fear that one day the woman would persuade Doctor Lowe to dispense with her services. Yet she had no cause to imagine he would allow his wife to rule him. He'd once said as much to her.

Early this morning Ellie had been in his study making up the fire. He would have made a point of being there to tell her without the fuss of asking Mrs Jenkins to send her up. With no sign of him this morning, she'd lingered to do a little rough sketch of his desk, concentrating on perspective, as Michael Deel had taught her to do.

She often brought a few sheets of paper with old sketches on the other side, economizing. As she'd put the drawing on to a chair with the others, to finish her chores, she'd heard cautious footsteps on the bare linoleum of the long passage, not like Doctor Lowe's ponderous tread. She had waited, not daring to breathe, and forgotten the drawings when she'd left, after the footsteps had receded, sure that they'd belonged to his wife.

Although she had been in Doctor Lowe's study for the purpose of housework, she had a fear of being seen entering or leaving because of the secrecy around her using it for other purposes than household duties.

She'd been concerned when Doctor Lowe had offered his study not simply for her tutor to instruct her but for her to practise her drawing and painting at other times. She recalled saying, 'What if Mrs Lowe finds me here?' to which he had replied with a wry smile, 'No need to worry; she never comes in here. We seldom meet except at meal times or at functions

or when meeting friends. There were times we'd relax together
in the sitting room, but not since our daughter died. These
days my good wife prefers her room.'

When she had pointed out that she didn't have a lot of time
off work to spend drawing and stuff, not even if she came in
here, his reply had been that young Rose would be doing more
around the house.

'That will give you an hour or so to yourself now and again,'
he'd said. 'Leave me to deal with anyone querying your occasional absence. So long as you don't abuse my generosity,'
he had ended with an almost playful frown. But she hadn't
felt comfortable about it and, on asking why he was doing all
this for her, had seen his face become grave.

It was then that he'd admitted that despite his better judgement, she'd helped to fill the void left by the loss of his
daughter and that he was deeply grateful to her for that. 'I
would like to have given her so many things,' he'd said, 'but
I *can* give them to you . . .'

His words had faded on one last word – 'compensation' –
mumbled as he'd turned away momentarily and he hadn't seen
the look of pleasure she'd felt must have been there on her
face. By the time he'd turned back it had been replaced by a
tinge of contrition, sorrow for him, despite her elation.

Now, as she knocked on the study door, she was sure his
wife had been spying on her this morning and was compelling
him to let her go. At the request for her to enter, she did so
almost belligerently.

When Mrs Jenkins had relayed the message that she was
wanted upstairs, her expression had been doleful. When Ellie
had asked why she was being summoned, the reply had been,
'You'll find out for yourself when you get up there. But the
master didn't look happy when he asked for you.'

Indeed he didn't. Ellie lifted her head in defiance. If this was
what it seemed, she wasn't going to bow her head in meek
acceptance, nor beg for a reference. He had no right to make
her feel as if she was a treasure to him, only to issue her
marching orders because his wife had taken against her. She
would certainly tell him his fortune before sweeping out of the
study to collect what bits and pieces of possessions she had.

Her only thought now was how to get her sister to come
with her. It would be one in the eye for high-and-mighty Mary

Lowe. That'd show her! That was if she could convince Dora to leave.

She was composing her plan to get her to come when she saw the sheet of paper Doctor Lowe held in his right hand. With his left he indicated the chair to one side of his desk. 'Come and sit down, my dear.'

The tone was so kind and gentle, despite the straight face, that she found herself doing as he asked. The next thing she knew, he had drawn up another chair to sit close in front of her.

'My dear,' he began quietly. 'I've been glancing through some of the drawings you left in here. I'm glad you took up my invitation to use my study for them. It gives you privacy to concentrate. And you are showing great talent, I must say. I am very pleased – pleased to have engaged a tutor. And I am very proud of you, my dear.'

This wasn't what she'd expected, but she said nothing.

'There is just one small concern that I have,' he continued. 'Among your drawings I found this. It worried me a little. I thought it might help me to ask you why it should worry me.'

It was an odd question, one she didn't understand. Unable to find whatever appropriate reply she was meant to give, she took what he was holding out to her and saw it was the sketch she'd made the day before of what she'd meant to depict as her father or someone like him. The amount of scrubbing out surprised even her. Had she done all this to it?

'Why have you kept it?' Doctor Lowe's voice broke through her confusion. 'Why didn't you throw it away if it was no good?'

Why hadn't she thrown it away? Was it that she needed to remind herself over and over how much she loathed the man? Anyway, what did Doctor Lowe mean by his question? How could she say why it should worry him? Surely he knew his mind better than she would.

'I don't quite know what you mean,' she said finally.

He smiled for the first time. 'To tell the truth, I don't know what I mean either. Perhaps I'm being a little over-reactive, but . . .' He reached out and took the drawing paper from her to scrutinize it. 'All this. Why? What thoughts went through your mind as you effaced what you'd drawn? – and so efficiently drawn, by what I can see is left of it.'

She wished he wouldn't use words she couldn't understand, but she had already grasped his concern.

'I ain't gone daft!' she said, reverting to her old way of speaking. He didn't correct her.

'I did not say you had.'

'But that's what you're thinking.'

As he continued to regard her levelly, she felt herself breaking down. All her rebelliousness leaving her, she was left unguarded against what was beginning to surface.

She could feel it rising up inside her, being caught, trapped in her throat. In a strangled voice she blurted, 'I didn't intend it to be my father when I started. I just drew a figure, but that's how it turned out, and I hated it. I hated . . . hate him! What he did, and I couldn't stop meself. I just kept on tearing at it with me pencil. I don't know why I didn't tear it up. I just felt I wanted to hurt him.'

'Child!'

The word interrupted the flow. He was holding out his arms and, as she burst into tears at the gesture, she automatically threw herself into them, felt them enfold protectively about her, felt herself being gently rocked, hearing him croon, 'There now, it's all over now. All over . . .'

It was odd being held this way by the man who employed her; yet he felt suddenly more like a father than any she had known. In the midst of her weeping came the knowledge that from now on she could get him to do whatever she wanted. She had achieved what she'd first set out to do. She'd schemed, planned, never getting very far, yet by this simple gesture of his it had come about, and she hadn't even done it intentionally.

'What do you think you're doing, Bertram? Have you gone completely mad?'

Mary was glaring at her husband, her rounded face suffused with the anger she could hardly contain. Giving him no time to reply, she swept on, 'If you think I am going to stand for this nonsense with that girl, you are sadly mistaken.'

She could hardly stop shaking as she stood facing him in the lounge. Whether or not the whole house could hear her raving, she didn't care any more. He had gone too far this time. She was devastated and so deeply hurt that she could hardly contain her emotions.

It felt utterly inconceivable that a man like him, a medical man with a background of sober habits could let a slip of a girl twist him around her little finger. How could he have been so foolish, refusing to see the dangerous situation staring him in the face?

He'd ignored all her warnings of trouble if he didn't get rid of the girl and, as the months had passed, little things had arisen to alarm her: Jay doing less and less work about the house, seeming to have more days off than she was entitled to. When she warned Bertram about it, he maintained that she worked hard to warrant it, which wasn't true and had even raised discontent with the rest of the staff.

Servants talked – were bound to talk. In larger houses containing a multitude of servants, tittle-tattle was rife, passing from mouth to mouth, especially if it concerned one of themselves or was of the juicy kind, and before long would reach their employer's ears. In this house there was only Chambers and that little kitchen maid who these days seemed to be taking on duties Jay should be doing.

It was that which had first alerted her that something wasn't quite right. Mrs Jenkins was the one who knew everything that went on, but Mrs Jenkins hadn't breathed a word of anything out of the ordinary, so she had assumed her fears to be all in her imagination. Mrs Jenkins, who had the family at heart, was very loyal but apparently misguided. She should have confided in her all she had gleaned, since it directly concerned the doctor's wife. She felt very angry towards Mrs Jenkins for withholding any information, even if it would have been painful to hear, with probably little she could have done about it.

Chambers had been the one to let it all come out.

'I'm not sure I should say, madam,' she'd said when asked why she was looking so glum.

'Say what?' she'd demanded.

'Well . . .' Chambers had looked across the bedroom to young Dora, but noting she was busy putting away the gowns her mistress had rejected for an evening out with the master, she went on cautiously, 'Well, what's going on between the master and Jay.'

Mary's heart had missed a beat. Surely it couldn't be what the words had put into her head. She had quickly turned to

Dora, telling her to go down to the kitchen and order tea to be brought up. 'Small ears carry tales' was the saying, especially when those ears belonged to Jay's young sister and the matter concerned them both.

'Tell me what you mean!' she commanded sharply after Dora had left.

'It's just that – I mean, Jay don't do any work now in the house any more.'

She hadn't noticed until then. In her wish to avoid seeing the girl she really hadn't noticed whether she worked or not, but Chambers had warmed to the subject, gaining momentum. 'She spends all her time, I think, in her room or up in the master's study.'

'The master's study! What does she do there?'

'Painting, I think.'

'Painting?' She recalled thinking that the questioning was becoming almost childish but found a pressing need to know what was going on. She also recalled feeling relieved that perhaps it wasn't as unpleasant as she'd first imagined; but even if innocent, why was it going on behind her back?

'What do you mean – painting? What sort of painting?'

'Pictures, I think,' had come the reply. 'It's 'cos she's clever at it.'

'And how do you know this is going on in the doctor's study? Tell me!'

Chambers had hung her head. 'I saw her go in there,' she mumbled. 'She had a key. She looked all around, secretive like, as she unlocked the door, but she didn't see me, and then she went in. I didn't see her come out 'cos I had work to do. Just lately there seems to be just me and Rose, the kitchen maid, doing all the work around this house.'

'Does Jay tell you about this painting, or what she's been doing?'

'No, not a word, but there's something going on we don't know about. She gets more time off than we do and she wears dresses I ain't seen before when she do go out. I'm sure the master gives her an extra salary. Then there's that man what comes every Tuesday around seven thirty. I take him up to the master's study. He's there until about eight thirty and then he leaves. I asked Cook about it but she said to mind me own business. If you ask me, madam—'

'I am not asking you, girl,' Mary had cut in sharply. 'That is all. Go on about your work now.'

Chambers had curtseyed and gone off, a little sullenly, she'd thought.

Now Mary faced her husband in a fit of anger that had had time to work itself up into a fury but had suddenly exploded this morning when she hadn't intended it to. She had planned to tackle him with coldness and dignity. Instead she was screaming at him like a harridan.

'You've no answer to give me, have you?' she cried, virtually at the end of her tether after stewing for days over this. His attitude, the way he was regarding her, as though she were a babbling fool, was all that had been needed to send her that last few inches. And she didn't care who overheard.

'Lies!' she shrieked at him. 'Lies! Painting be damned!' She saw him recoil at her choice of words. 'This talk of you finding her so like our . . . our dearest Millicent . . .' She stumbled over the word, trying to keep back the tears the mere mention of that dear name brought. 'All lies! In truth you're besotted with the girl and she's leading you on and you're fool enough not to see it. You're a silly, middle-aged man, carrying on with—'

'I'm carrying on with no one!' he interrupted fiercely. 'I find her sweet and caring – all the things I miss since we lost our cherished daughter. She is an inspiration to me, a boon. She fills that emptiness in my heart. If that is a crime—'

'Don't be so melodramatic!' Mary winced with embarrassment but quickly recovered. 'And I don't believe you. The truth is that you've found in her your own lost youth. You've allowed yourself to be seduced by her wiles. Painting! You and she have been deceiving me.'

'Mary, you are being ridiculous.'

Mary's eyes opened wide until they almost resembled saucers of blue set in her full cheeks. 'It is you who are being ridiculous, you stupid, stupid man! You beast! And she's nothing more than a little whore . . .'

'That's a terrible thing to say, my dear.'

'But true. And I shall not remain in this house a minute longer than is necessary to collect a few belongings. I shall stay with my sister Edith and her husband in Kensington. If and when you finally come to your senses, that is where I may be contacted. Dora is coming with me.'

Bertram hadn't shifted from the hearth where he'd positioned himself throughout her tirade. The only visible sign of his emotion was the clenching and unclenching of his chubby hands.

His voice, when he spoke again, was steady, though obviously being held in check.

'If that's how you feel, my dear, then I think you should go to stay with Edith and Edward. I can see that there is no way to convince you of my innocence. My only fault is the desire to seek solace for the void the loss of our daughter has left in my heart. I can only ask you to accept my apologies for failing to confide in you that need. But if you cannot see fit to understand my feelings, then I think it best you stay with your sister for a while.'

His outward calm had transmitted itself to her a little. In a haughty but more controlled voice, though still trembling on the brink of tears, she sought to clarify.

'And I can take it that you have no intention of terminating this relationship, whatever it is, with this person who is even less than half your age – young enough to be your daughter?'

Too late she realized her error as he nodded in ironic confirmation. It was too much for her. Turning, she fled from the room, the lightweight beige fabric of her day dress puffing out around her ankles as she went.

Bertram stood quite still. He could hear her calling for Dora in a high, frantic voice and wondered absently what the staff must make of it. Fuel for wagging tongues, no doubt.

His heart felt as though it had been drained of blood; yet now all he could think of, as his wife's door slammed to, was that Ellie – Elizabeth as he was wont to call her these days – would be near destroyed by the loss of her younger sister, whom she had brought here under her own far-too-young protection, seeking his protection for them both.

Thirteen

September: Dora had been away nearly three months. It felt more like three years, more like a lifetime. Bad enough when the mistress had forbidden Dora to associate with her. At least she had caught a glimpse of her now and again and they'd exchanged hurried smiles. Now there wasn't even that to console her. For the first time ever she felt ... well, orphaned.

She wondered if Dora was pining as much as she was. There'd been no word from her at all since she and Mrs Lowe had left. She had found where Dora was living from an address book in one of the drawers in Doctor Lowe's desk and written to her several times, no longer labouring over her spelling or her English since Michael Deel had spent time with her over it.

She was a quick learner, he told her. She hadn't realized it herself. Never going to school as often as she should have, with Mum always needing her help, she had thought herself a bit of a dunce. It had taken Michael Deel to bring out talents she'd thought she never had and, in fact, she had come to enjoy writing letters.

Writing got all the tension out of her and she had written pages and pages to Dora, full of hopes and fears – what she had been up to and how she was looking forward to hearing all Dora had been up to. Though her sister was really bad at writing, her spelling pitiful, written exactly as she spoke, she expected some sort of reply.

At first she wondered if Dora was too ashamed of her efforts to write, but soon came a feeling that her own letters were perhaps being intercepted and not passed on. Likewise she suspected Dora's letters were also being interfered with. She wouldn't put it past Mrs Lowe.

Poor Dora. All on her own, with only her mistress for company, at her beck and call and probably hardly let out of her sight. She must be feeling totally isolated, trapped. She could walk out, but Ellie knew she would never have the gumption: she was still only thirteen. But even at thirteen she could have found her way back here. If ever she did turn up, Ellie was prepared to give up all her plans to better herself here and go off with her to do the best she could in the wide world. Dora was worth that sacrifice.

Oddly enough, having got much of what she'd been aiming for, Ellie also felt isolated. Nothing was as she'd imagined it would be. She now ate her meals in Doctor Lowe's study, Florrie bringing her food there. Ellie could see she was far from being pleased about that, tossing her head when Ellie tried to make conversation or even smile at her; if Ellie addressed her, she was now calling her Miss Jay, as if they'd never ever been friends.

'You'll no longer be expected to work around the house,' Doctor Lowe had told her, which was exactly when Florrie had started showing off. And it was then that she had known things would never be the same again. Though she was on her way to becoming all that she'd planned to be, she didn't feel at all happy. She wanted Florrie to be her friend again, to have Mrs Jenkins scold her for small errors instead of behaving stiffly and correctly in her presence. But most of all she wanted Dora back here beside her, to confide in, protect, giggle and share thoughts with.

Then, last week, Doctor Lowe had said that he would be moving her out of the bedroom she'd used as a parlourmaid.

'Chambers and the girl Rose are to sleep there,' he told her with an almost fatherly smile. 'You will have my daughter Millicent's bedroom for your own.'

It was evening. His surgery had finished for the day and they were having a light supper together, seated opposite each other across the small round table in his study.

Ellie wasn't sure whether she enjoyed eating with him. Try as she might, she could never feel entirely at ease with him. Whether it was because at times he seemed just a little too fatherly, making it hard not to flinch away should he touch her arm, or whether it had something to do with the fact that she still cringed from the memory of the medical *help* he'd given her, a lingering sense of it being a little too personal, she couldn't say. But she always managed to disguise her feelings.

While he was working, she could enjoy her meals alone, even though it was becoming boring with little to do all day but draw and paint, read books or go out for a stroll. She could now come and go as she pleased, glad to be free of the place.

Sometimes she'd take an omnibus and wander around the big shops up west, sometimes go to visit Mrs Sharp, her only social contact with the outside world. With Ronnie Sharp at work it wasn't much of an outing, and she guessed Doctor Lowe wouldn't like her being out late, even though the early-September evenings were still light.

Mrs Sharp would always stop whatever she was doing to make her a cup of tea and to gossip, the gossip shallow and pretty uninteresting but a refreshing escape from the claustrophobic world her life had become. She'd hoped there'd be some word about her father, but though she questioned Mrs Sharp, the woman had heard nothing. It was as if he'd vanished off the face of the earth. Whether he'd ever learned about her mother was debatable. As to Charlie, no one knew where he was either. Probably it was just as well.

Mrs Sharp's most interesting topic was what her Ronnie was up to. Ellie had taken to writing to him, telling him about herself, and he'd write telling her about himself. That was as far as it had ever got.

She'd have liked to contact Dora, though it would only mean trouble for them both; but there were times when she thought she had never felt so lonely. Trying to become a lady wasn't as enjoyable as she had imagined.

At Doctor Lowe's revelation Ellie stopped eating and looked up at him in surprise. It was the first time he'd ever spoken his daughter's name without prefixing the word dearest or of having grief twist his podgy features. With his wife's departure he had begun to change.

'It's foolish to let the room lie empty,' he continued as Ellie went on staring. 'It should be brought to life again.'

'Didn't your wife want it to stay as it was?' she asked. 'After . . .' She let the words die away, fearing to upset him. Instead he gave a wry grin.

'Yes, and so did I. But time passes and the emptiness fills. I have you to thank for that. Yes, you, my dear,' he stressed as she tried to wave away his gratitude.

'It can in some ways be a comfort to keep alive a cherished memory, but there is a tendency to let oneself be dragged down by it with no wish or will to face the world again. I was in danger of that happening and until you came I was content to let it continue.'

He sighed and pushed his plate from him. 'I finally feel ready to come to terms with our loss and it is all due to you, my dear. I wish her mother could feel the same way, but there is little I can do about that.'

He seemed resigned to his wife having gone. It was almost as if a weight had been lifted from him. It struck Ellie that he was, in fact, glad of the freedom to spend more time with her without recrimination from his wife. Ellie had long guessed that they'd probably not enjoyed a close companionship for years.

She often wondered whether their marriage had been a love match or a contract between two families such as the better off were often said to indulge in. She imagined it to have been the latter, for she'd not seen the slightest glance of affection pass between them for as long as she had been here. It had seemed to her, as time went on, that his only show of such feelings had been towards herself, while his wife had bestowed hers on Dora. Almost like a contest between the pair.

She couldn't help feeling sorry for him. It couldn't have been much of a life, and to lose his only daughter too. Now, without his wife here, he was beginning to smother her a little too much, making her feel uncomfortable.

It was starting to feel wrong, playing on his good nature as a means to an end. She'd begun to hate herself, knowing she was treading on everyone for her own purposes. But what important purposes they were. It took all her efforts not to be reminded that he was a kind man, too kind to be taken advantage of like this. She didn't want to hurt him, but she couldn't abandon her scheme to find her father. This man was her only chance of attaining that goal; one day she would leave and it would break the man's heart.

His daughter's old room was lovely: spacious and bright – the bed covers, the matching drapes, the wallpaper apparently still as they'd been left. How doted on she must have been to have such a room. Ellie gazed about and thought of the tiny box she and Dora had shared in the two-up, two-down terraced dwelling in Gales Gardens. How lucky this girl had been. Ellie smiled. No, not lucky. She was dead. Ellie Jay was alive: she was the lucky one.

Yesterday, boxes of clothes and other things belonging to the girl had been put into storage in the attic room Chambers and Rose shared.

It all struck Ellie as something like sacrilege, as if Doctor Lowe was in a way trying to put away his daughter's memory. Of course he wasn't. It must have affected him, for he'd made himself scarce during the short procedure, down in his surgery, while two hired men shifted the lot in accordance with a list he'd previously written up.

Nor did he appear that evening, informing Mrs Jenkins that he'd be at his club and wouldn't be eating at home. Ellie felt disappointed as she ate alone in his study, but she understood. Of course it would have touched him very much. It must have felt to him as if he were sweeping away the past. Ellie found herself feeling quite emotional on his behalf.

But her transfer into Doctor Lowe's own household, as it were, had its price. Chambers had shown no gratitude in having her old room back, and now, coming into the study with Ellie's dinner on a tray – Ellie had yet to use the dining room downstairs – she didn't even glance at her as Ellie opened the door for her to come in. Stomping past her, she plonked the tray down on the small round table and busied herself setting out cutlery, condiments, napkin, water jug and glass, all without a word.

'That tray looked heavy, Florrie,' Ellie offered sociably, trying to break the ice; but an offended sniff for a reply conveyed exactly where Ellie stood with her as Florrie swept past her and out of the room.

'Done orright for herself,' Chambers complained to Mrs Jenkins downstairs. 'You should see her up there, standing there as if she owns the place while I set everything out for her. No offer of 'elp. Too much of a lady now to offer!'

'She's not exactly a servant any more,' was the reply, Mrs Jenkins being very busy making preparations for mutton stew for the next day, at the same time giving young Rose a sharp look to get on with her business as the girl paused in washing up to listen in.

Of course there was nothing to stop the pair of them swapping tittle-tattle tonight in their room, but not down here, in her presence.

'Who'd of thought she'd be such a scheming little so-and-so when she first came here?' Chambers went on, going back to cleaning the silver she had left in order to take supper up to the study for *her ladyship*. 'If the poor mistress was here now, she'd have a fit.'

'But she's not here,' said Mrs Jenkins with sudden venom. 'And there's nothing any of us can do about it, so don't go airing your views too loudly.'

'Well, I think it's a crying shame how she's using the master and he can't even see it.'

'What the master does is his business,' came the abrupt reminder. 'And you'd be well advised to mind yours.'

But Florrie wasn't finished. 'I'd say he's got ideas on her other than fatherly ones. Ideas that, if you ask me—'

'I am *not* asking you!' Nora Jenkins cut in almost savagely. 'So just you keep your mind on your work, girl!'

'All I'm saying is, she's got him round her little finger and I wouldn't bet he fancies her a bit more than making up for him losing his daughter.'

'Florrie!' The way Cook rounded on her made her start. 'That's quite enough out of you! Mind yourself. Get on with what you're doing and keep your thoughts to yourself or you might find yourself without employment.'

Florrie chose to show defiance – not too much, being tinged with alarm. 'Who's going to sack me? Her?'

'He will. And don't put it past him,' came the rebuke. 'Parlourmaids are two a penny these days and don't you forget it.' Modifying her tone, she went on, 'You've a good place here, and you're a nice girl – a good worker, after a style – and I wouldn't want to lose you.'

She grew busy again, turning away though still addressing the girl. 'The last thing I want in this messed-up household is to have to train someone else. Don't worry, that one will blot her copybook sooner or later and she'll be gone. Now finish what you're doing and off up to bed with you – you too, Rose. Be good now and mind what you say in this madhouse.'

Heeding the veiled warning, Florrie said no more, but it didn't stop her watching avidly for events to unfold as Cook was predicting. They all guessed what Ellie Jay was up to, wheedling her way into poor Doctor Lowe's heart and his purse. Day by day, no longer endeared to her one-time friend and workmate, she kept watch on every move Ellie was making, willing it to turn against the scheming little cat.

Ellie was coming to be aware of it. Things were not turning out the way she'd expected. Isolated from the rest of the staff, she found herself ostracized. Florrie, with whom there had been a time when the two of them had hardly stopped chatting together, would now drop what looked like a scornful curtsey without returning Ellie's efforts at a friendly smile but merely following her with her eyes as she passed.

Mrs Jenkins too seemed exceptionally haughty and correct in her presence, leaving her longing for the days when she would scold her for some little mistake.

Rose she hardly knew, so she didn't matter; but she missed the old warmth of below stairs. Nor did she feel at ease with Doctor Lowe. Instead of dulling the memory of his exploration in terminating her pregnancy, time seemed to be sharpening it.

It wasn't only being aware that he knew parts of her more than she herself did; since his wife had left he was beginning to see her as the centre of his world. It was in little things he said, the way he'd take her hand – she'd shrink inwardly from the soft, podgy feel, even though it was always offered in a fatherly way – the little things he'd buy for her – the small box of chocolates, the pretty little trinket, the somewhat expensive lace handkerchief and even a pair of lightweight summer gloves. He'd also arranged a small allowance.

'For you to buy yourself more personal items,' he'd said, telling her it was her right, that she was practically becoming his adopted daughter. 'At least in my eyes,' he'd said fondly.

It was so ironic. She had worked hard towards exactly this goal, but in fact she had never felt so lonely. Not even Dora to unload her doubts on, talk to about things. Not a soul in the whole world she could count on, except perhaps her tutor.

Maybe it was that Michael Deel was impartial, an outsider. They'd sit in Doctor Lowe's study, just the two of them, while he taught her how to speak well, doing his best to get her to lose those flat Cockney vowels of hers. He'd see the funny side of it when she put an aitch in the wrong place when she began to talk fast, as Cockneys do: 'It hain't 'alf good.'

They'd dissolve into peals of laughter, something that never happened with Doctor Lowe, his regard for her being far too intense. And when Michael put a hand on her arm to recover his composure, it felt so different from when Doctor Lowe did it. His touch was far too emotional and disturbing. Michael's was light and friendly and made her feel good.

She looked forward to Tuesdays with the eagerness of a child going on a jaunt. As summer waned they were spending less and less time on her elocution lessons and more on her painting. They talked a lot together. He was exciting to talk with and at those times never corrected her when she got the odd word wrong. She queried it once.

He laughed. 'You're quick to learn. You speak well when called on to do so, such as when the doctor's about. So long as he sees you coming along and pays me, I'm content.'

That had them both laughing. But a few minutes later, he sobered. 'It's your art that troubles me,' he said slowly.

She was still giggling. 'Why should it trouble you? You said I do well and you like what I paint or draw for you.'

'It's what you draw and paint for yourself that bothers me. It's weird.'

'Oh, that.' She made light of the words. 'Every exceptional artist has whims and fantasies – a dark side,' she offered in a lighter vein as he continued to look at her. She made another, feebler attempt at jocularity. 'I'm not an exceptional artist, of course.'

'I'm beginning to think you are,' Michael said, '– or have the makings of one.'

'Well, that's good,' she said, still trying to be merry; but she knew that Michael was not happy to leave it there.

'I've seen some of the drawings you've done lately.'

'You couldn't have. I never show them to anyone.' She pulled herself up too late, but he didn't seem to notice the error.

'The doctor showed me a couple of them. He said they bothered him and he asked for my opinion.'

'He's got no right!' she exploded angrily. 'That was private.'

'I agree, Ellie. But now I've seen some, it bothers me too.'

'I don't see why it should. It's what I fancied doing at the time and what I do in private is my business, no one else's.'

'But every drawing's the same: a male figure and a recumbent female figure. There are lots of them – and proper drawings: not sketches but meticulous drawings, done with care and full of detail. At least from what one can see for the black mess overlaying them.'

'It's just a bit of silliness.'

'But always the same picture?'

'What did Doctor Lowe say about them?' she challenged, alarmed.

Michael shrugged. 'He merely asked what I thought they represented. I said I had no idea and he put them away. But it has me stumped now. So why always the same drawing?'

It was Ellie's turn to shrug. 'Nothing. Just what I fancy doing.'

He lightened a little. 'Well, one thing. You draw the human form with great skill and accuracy, Ellie. You could become a portrait painter.'

Ellie too brightened. 'I wouldn't mind that,' she said. 'But different.'

'How do you mean – different?'

'The way I'd see faces.' She couldn't explain what she meant, but she knew there'd be dark, dark thoughts hidden, only hinted at with a brush, every twist of the features cruelly and starkly revealed. The idea brought a small thrill, but she couldn't tell that to Michael. It would have worried him.

Fourteen

E llie was having breakfast with Doctor Lowe when Mrs Jenkins brought the post. Nearly a month had gone by since he had told Ellie that eating in his study was rather silly.

'The staff are quite aware of the situation, my dear,' he'd said. 'I say that whether they accept it or not is up to them. I intend us to have our meals in the dining room together in future.'

Until now, other than breakfast in his study, he'd snatch a quick lunch in the dining room between surgery hours. In the evening he would eat there alone as he'd always done, though he seldom entertained since his wife had left. For Ellie those two meals had been taken up to her in the study.

Now it was being openly recognized that he'd practically adopted her, unofficially of course. He'd even started taking her on little outings now and again, maybe on a Saturday or Sunday afternoon.

So far he'd taken her to Hyde Park, where ladies and gentlemen on horseback would parade up and down the soft, well-trodden bridleway called Rotten Row, ladies riding side saddle, sedate and elegant, as they socialized with friends and acquaintances, a great attraction to others. In the still-light evenings of late summer, similar people would drive back and forth between Marble Arch and Hyde Park Corner while the crowds strolled by. Seeing it all, Ellie decided that she would one day have a carriage worthy of the upper crust.

Once, he'd taken her to visit a museum, which intrigued her; another time the National Art Gallery, which had her eyes boggling at all the wonderful paintings that put her own petty efforts to shame.

He had also taken her up west for a lunch at the Ritz. She'd felt out of her depth and, though vowing that one day coming here would be second nature to her, on that day with elegant waiters seeming to be looking down on her despite her nice dress and hat, and with all that tinkling of fine china and the hushed conversation, she was glad when it was time to leave.

They'd gone once by Underground, she having told him that up to the time of her mother's death she'd never been out of her own neighbourhood. She savoured the novelty of it with every inch of her being.

On a couple of occasions he'd taken a cab; other than that, they'd be in the small doctor's carriage used for making his rounds. Until then she'd never been in a carriage, private or otherwise, and felt quite the lady. But more than once, stuck in a seething jam of cabs and carts, carriages and horse buses, it seemed the Underground was probably quicker and safer.

On Sunday mornings he had begun taking her to church. In the old days it had been the practice of all the staff to attend at least once a month in an organized group while he and his wife and daughter, when she was alive, would attend separately. After his loss it had fallen away, so Ellie was told.

She knew their outings were the subject of much tittle-tattle from the staff, but she didn't care. She was making the most of it. The better she got on with him the more he indulged her. She was saving quite a tidy sum from the allowance he was giving her. She'd told him she wanted to open a post-office account, which pleased him, seeing her as an astute young person.

'But not a post-office account, a bank account,' he'd suggested. 'Far more interest to be gained.'

She'd never been inside a bank, much less opened an account with one. It had made her feel very important, but slowly she became quite familiar with the interior of the little branch that she now entered boldly to add her small but regular contribution to the amount already building in her impressive-looking savings-account book.

'But you mustn't let saving become your sole interest,' he'd advised. 'The allowance I give you, my dear, is so that you may dress nicely and make me proud to show you off to others.'

That made her smile, as if she were his little indulgence. Openly she obliged, but in secret hoarded as much as she could to further her plan when the time came. To this end she'd often tell him, while feigning a shamefaced expression, that she had overspent. She happily suffered his mild rebuke that she must learn to handle money better, knowing that he'd give her a little top-up with a warning to be more careful. This also went towards that day when she would track down the man who never left her mind.

This morning she sat over a simple breakfast, watching Doctor Lowe open his mail, each envelope slit with a silver letter opener, each carefully read before the next envelope was opened, each piece of mail methodically put on to its separate pile.

She never spoke while he was doing this; nor did he. But today he suddenly sat forward, his brows coming together in a frown.

'Oh, dear!' he finally exclaimed.

Ellie continued to sit quietly, though she itched to know what had so startled him. As he glanced up at her, she couldn't help a quizzical glance. It was apparently all he needed.

'Mrs Lowe requests to return home. It seems she has had a falling-out with her sister.' He shook his head in a sad gesture. 'It does not do to rely on the continuing hospitality of a relative. Sooner or later something comes to a head. It's bound to. Most married couples have differences of opinion. It is quite another matter when someone who is no doubt outstaying their welcome disrupts a marital relationship. I rather think her presence has most likely come between husband and wife.'

'Will Mrs Lowe come back then?' Ellie asked cautiously. She didn't want to be the one seen to be interfering in this marital relationship.

He returned his gaze to the letter. 'It seems she will have to. Little else one can do.'

Ellie felt her heart beginning to sink. Gone those little trips with him. Not that she enjoyed being in his company, but it gave him time to think of her as close to him; hence his joy in having her tutored, seeing her well clothed and, more than that, his generosity to her with money.

Placing the letter on its own on his desk, he looked up at Ellie again.

'It is only Christian to accept her back. This is her home. Though there is one thing that she will have to understand: no more complaints at my interest in you, my dear. I'll not have her say anything against you, nor snub you, nor expect you to resume your previous role in this house.'

'What about my sister?' Ellie ventured. 'She and me . . . I mean she and I weren't allowed to associate with each other, and I missed Dora awfully – even more when she went away with Mrs Lowe.'

Doctor Lowe smiled. 'Don't worry yourself, my dear; I will make sure that is rectified.' He got up and came round the desk towards her. 'It must have been such a very sad time for you to be parted from your sister.'

Ellie tried not to shrink from his embrace, fatherly though it was, his arm about her shoulders drawing her close as she sat. Releasing her, he patted her hand. 'I would never see you unhappy, my dear child. Never.'

Christmas at the Lowes' family home was like nothing Ellie had ever experienced and she revelled in every moment of it. She'd never seen so much food as was on that table and continued to be served during the entire evening until by bedtime she felt utterly bloated.

Mrs Jenkins and Rose were both included in the evening. Florrie had gone home to her own family in North London, but Rose, having no family, remained here. In larger establishments the staff probably would have had their own party below stairs, but since there were only two of them here Doctor Lowe had them to join in, Mrs Jenkins getting very happy on port wine.

Ellie did feel a little awkward before them, being addressed as 'miss', no longer one of them – awkward, too, having Mrs Lowe nearby while utterly ignoring her. But she was no longer bothered: she had Dora here now, and neither Mrs Jenkins's exaggerated deference nor Mrs Lowe's silent pique could get under her skin any more.

Only one other person she would have liked to be there: that was Michael Deel. He was, of course, with his own family. On any other Tuesday he'd have been here tutoring her and, despite the jollifications going on this evening, she found herself missing him. But at least she'd see him on the Thursday.

Since October he had come on Monday and Thursday as well as Tuesday, Doctor Lowe being eager to see her expand her talent as an artist. She hadn't seen him yesterday either, it being Christmas Eve, when his family had expected him to be with them. They did not consider what he did here as work and therefore an obligation.

'I come as a favour to my father's old friend,' he'd once told her. 'I studied medicine at university and am now with my father's practice.'

His father practised in Harley Street. Why Doctor Lowe himself didn't Ellie was left wondering but of course never asked, though his work here in the East End seemed to pay well enough.

'It was my father's wish that I study medicine,' Michael had once told her. 'I had an interest in art and found I had a talent for it. I would love to have been an artist, but it wasn't to be. I was never that good. So now I am teaching you.'

He had smiled wryly at that, a smile she had from the first found very attractive. The smile fading, he added, 'I really haven't the talent you have.' He'd waved away her protest. 'I know enough, technically, to teach a little, but one day you'll have to find a tutor who can give you more than I ever can. Eventually you're going to have to move on, Miss Jay.'

He no longer called her Miss Jay, but Ellie, and had asked that she call him Michael rather than Mr Deel. 'It's silly to be so formal,' he'd said.

She missed him today – could hardly wait for Thursday to come – and was sure he must be feeling the same about her. No word had ever passed between them of such feelings, but it was the way he looked at her, the way he guided her hand, would stand close to her as they surveyed the results of her evening's efforts.

It was nice to have him call her Ellie, since everyone else called her Miss Jay, apart from Doctor Lowe,` who mostly used the term 'my dear'. He had once asked what the name Ellie stood for, and when she had told him it was her mother's derivative from Elizabeth, he'd said he preferred that; but he seldom, if ever, spoke it. It was usually, 'my dear'.

He had no idea that she and Michael seemed to be growing slowly closer to each other, merely being glad that tutor and pupil were getting on so well. Today she caught herself time after time thinking of Michael Deel and how he was enjoying himself, wondering whether he was thinking of her in the same way. She would never have dreamed of asking him, but with her thoughts came recollection of his words: 'Eventually you're going to have to move on.'

Suddenly she didn't want to move on; but common sense told her that it was inevitable, some time or another. She had no fancy to stay with Doctor Lowe all her life and she had to find her father. That meant she'd need to be independent, which would mean earning her living. The only thing she knew was being in service and that she refused to contemplate.

One way was to develop her talent as an artist, enough to earn some sort of living, necessitating her moving on and losing touch with Michael. That thought made her sad – sad enough to almost ruin her evening. But then, who was she? No one. If their interest in each other did develop, his well-to-do family would never countenance a union with someone of no account. They probably already had in mind the right sort of wife for him, when he was ready.

Shutting her mind, Ellie took a quick sip of the drop of port Doctor Lowe had given her despite his wife's frown, and turned her thoughts to the party – Mrs Jenkins chatting with Dora and Rose, Mrs Lowe with her sister and brother-in-law. They seemed amicable enough, despite having had that falling-out, perhaps because now she wasn't in their household any longer. Next to Ellie, Doctor Lowe was talking of famous paintings and old masters – quite boring, but it would soon be bedtime and then she could dream of Michael.

As she had hoped, he arrived on the Thursday, though little work was done, with the time mostly spent talking of their separate Christmas experiences. She hardly stopped talking of the wonders of such a full table, the mounds of food there had been.

'When I was at home,' she said, as she attempted to make something of the picture she'd been required to paint, 'we weren't all that well off, so we just had what we could afford.'

She'd never told him of her real upbringing. It would have shocked him. But he knew her family hadn't been well off. After all, anyone who had been employed as a housemaid wouldn't have well-off parents. But, refusing to be ashamed of her roots, she had always been open with him, at least up to a point.

He in turn surprised her by saying how boring his Christmas had been. 'Just me and my parents and my sister and her husband. We all went to bed quite early, actually.' He made it seem such an ordinary day that she felt privileged to have enjoyed such a hearty time at the Lowes'.

'But I'm glad you had such a nice time,' he went on. 'I thought of you and hoped you'd be enjoying yourself.'

Suddenly he rounded on her. 'Ellie, would it be possible for me to ask Doctor Lowe if I could take you out one evening?'

'Take me out?' she echoed, a brush full of yellow paint in her hand in the act of adding tints to a sunset she'd been attempting under his guidance.

He had in fact taken her out before, with Doctor Lowe's permission. It had been a Monday, the twenty-ninth of October. With the Boer War having come to an end on the thirtieth of September, the soldiers had returned home one month later to a heroes' welcome.

Crowds had swamped the City of London. Ellie had begged Doctor Lowe to take her to see them returning, but he'd had his surgery to run. Nor would he let her go among the crowds unchaperoned, even with Dora as company. Unable to bear her disappointment, he'd suggested to Michael Deel that he might care to take charge of the two girls. But, with Dora there as well, she hadn't had the joy of having him all to herself. Now he was actually asking her if he could take her out – just her.

Although excitement gripped her, she had begun lately to feel more and more tied down. As Doctor Lowe grew closer to her, so he had begun to guard her as if she were his property. It seemed she could hardly go out unless it was with him, and if she did venture out alone, there were always questions as to where she had been and what she had done.

'What can you be doing all on your own?' he'd queried before now. 'I can take you to so many marvellous places.'

Sometime she felt almost a prisoner. It was true that, no longer employed by him, she was in theory a free agent, but there was this sense that if she were to try and kick over the traces, her future might become somewhat shaky, especially with his wife living back here and at his elbow, starting to nag about her all over again. If the woman did manage to get rid of her, it would be the end of it just when what she had so far saved was beginning to mount quite substantially. Another year over and she could sling her hook with a tidy sum to see her on her way. Until then she must be patient and not rock the boat.

It hadn't surprised her that he'd let Michael take her to watch the Boer War heroes return, a demonstration of an Empire's pride in its fighting men. But would he frown on Michael taking her out merely for pleasure?

'Where would we go?' she asked lamely.

Michael gave her a wily grin. 'Have you ever seen moving pictures?'

'Moving pictures?' she repeated – the second time she had echoed his words; she was in danger of looking like an idiot. She quickly gathered herself together. 'No, never,' she said as unhurriedly as she could.

'There's a little place that's been set up in Oxford Street where they are showing moving pictures, though they're put on at the end of music-hall performances. You've never seen one?'

'I don't go to music halls,' she admitted. 'I asked Doctor Lowe to take me but he considers them common. He'd prefer to take me to see plays.'

'What about before you worked for him. You must have gone then?'

'We didn't have money enough for music halls.' She felt instantly angry at herself for bursting out with that, but he didn't blink an eye.

'Then let's go to see the moving-picture show on Saturday. I hear it doesn't take long to show it. But it'll be an experience. Then we can have dinner somewhere afterwards. I'll bring you back here in good time.'

'You'll have to ask Doctor Lowe. I only usually go out with him. He might not like me being out with you.'

'I don't see why,' he said, puzzled. 'He did ask me to accompany you in watching the soldiers' homecoming parade, so why should he object?'

'That was Dora and me. This time it would be just you and me.'

Michael was frowning. 'He's not your father, Ellie.'

Nothing like my father, came the malevolent thought. Bertram Lowe was a good man, gentle and kind, if a little possessive of late.

'But he tends to see himself as my unofficial guardian,' she said. 'He's been good to me. He took us in – me and my sister – when we had nowhere else to go, and gave us work without any references.' Oddly, she no longer minded him knowing of her impoverished home life, so long as she didn't let it sound too squalid, which it had come near to being in spite of her mother's hard efforts to keep her family as respectable as possible.

'The doctor's protected my sister and me ever since,' she went on. 'And I think he's become very fond of me, so he's bound to be worried about me.'

She guessed he knew of the death of the daughter, Doctor Lowe being an acquaintance of Michael's father; but he could have no idea she'd become something of a substitute for the dead girl. Doctor Lowe would obviously want that part to remain secret. Poor man, she felt pity for him in a way.

Whatever Michael said to him, to her amazement he gave him his permission for her to be taken to the moving-picture exhibition. The only thing she could think of that might have persuaded him was Michael's intimating the benefit she might derive from it as part of her artistic tutorage.

Sitting in the dark of what was hardly more than a large room while others queued outside to fill up the chairs of those who left, it was a novel experience to see actual objects and people moving across a white screen as they were projected on to it.

Almost like magic – and indeed it was magic: a train that came at speed towards the audience, making everyone start back with a cry of fear, only to disappear before it came right out at them; a haystack that suddenly turned into a horse and cart, making people laugh but leaving them wondering how such magic could have been done. And when it suddenly became a troupe of female dancers kicking up their legs, everyone clapped appreciatively. And so it went on.

It was over all too soon, though the constant, jerky move-ments of the various images made her feel a little dizzy, and although it was something of a wonderful novelty, she was relieved to emerge into the daylight, where the stiff breeze that had seen them go in was now developing into a high wind, so that she needed to hang on to her hat despite the pins holding it to her nicely piled up hair.

'It was certainly very different,' she said, aware that during several alarming scenes such as the train one, she had clutched his arm. She tried to feign nonchalance. 'But I don't think it'll ever properly catch on. It's too harsh on the eyes and it could give people headaches watching it too long. But I'm glad I've seen it before it outwears its fascination.'

He laughed. 'The new century seems to be full of new ideas at the moment, even machines that can fly.'

Ellie looked scornful. 'People can already fly: balloons take them high up in the air and they go for miles looking down on all of us.' Looking down on people like her. One day she would be able to afford to go up in a balloon and look down on others.

'But these will be powered by machines.' Michael interrupted her thoughts. Then he laughed again. 'Whether it works or not, remains to be seen, I suppose.'

Dinner brought them back to normality, a nice ordinary little meal of lamb cutlets with fruit pudding and custard to follow, in a small restaurant, one in which she felt comfortable, a far cry from her grand ordeal at the Ritz.

Michael got her home by nine thirty. These days she entered by the front door, opened this evening by Rose. Obliged to stay up to let her in, she was blinking wearily after a long day and looking to her bed.

'Thank you,' Ellie said graciously, but received no reply except a brief and, it seemed to her, rather reluctant bob. No doubt Florrie was still intent on keeping the old grudge alive, probably with Cook's blessing.

Bidding goodnight to her, Michael startled her by dropping a tiny kiss on her cheek, turning immediately and skipping down the front steps and into the waiting cab before the eyes of an open-mouthed Rose. More fuel to fire staff gossip, came the thought, as she made her way up to her room; but on her cheek she could still feel the touch of Michael's lips. It felt so nice.

Outside her window the wind had whipped itself up, blowing almost a full gale. As she lay awake she thought about him, hoping he'd arrived home safely as she heard a chimney pot dislodged by the wind crash down into the street below. It was enough to have blown his cab over.

She didn't know until Monday that more than fifty people

had been killed in the floods and gales that had lashed the whole country. But with Michael calling on Monday evening as right as rain to resume her lessons, she gave no more thought to it. Her main interest was that he might ask if he could take her out again.

Fifteen

It was Thursday. Ellie had gone off to bed after her hour-and-a-half lesson, but before he left, Michael needed to speak to Doctor Lowe. Told he was on his own in the sitting room, his wife already having retired, Michael made his way there and tapped politely on the door.

Entering to the man's invitation, he found the doctor taking his ease on the sofa, enjoying a final nightcap. The man beamed up at him and motioned to the armchair opposite him.

'Ah, Michael. Take a seat.'

As Michael sat, he went on, 'My dear chap, what brings you here? Whisky?' He indicated a decanter on the small table beside him.

Michael gave him a smile. 'Thank you, but I'll be off home shortly. I need to have a brief word with you about Miss Jay, that's all.'

'Yes, she seems to be blossoming very well under your guidance. I am most pleased with the way things are coming along. Tell me how you yourself feel she is progressing. When I ask her how she is doing, she shrugs, says "all right, not bad", and appears disinterested. So how is she coming along?'

Michael gazed into the fire burning in the grate, its brightness boosted by a frosty January evening. This wasn't what he had come to talk about. He had to get down to the real subject. He had his excuse all ready, preliminary to a request he wished to make.

'She's proving to be a talented artist. I think she could go far.'

Doctor Lowe frowned suddenly. 'What do you mean – she could go far?'

'I mean she could become a great artist if she puts her mind to it – that is, if a lady artist can go all that far. But she would need a tutor who can teach her far more than I ever can. To tell the truth, sir, my own effort as an artist is very mediocre. I am nowhere near as gifted as she is.'

Bertram Lowe seemed not to be listening. He was studying his whisky glass. His voice had grown cool. 'I doubt she will be pursuing her talents to such lengths as could take her away from this house, where she has a comfortable home,' he said slowly. 'I don't think she would want that.'

'Whether that's true or not, she might one day marry and have a home of her own.' They were getting further and further from the real subject of his visit. He saw the man frown and purse his chubby lips, still regarding his whisky glass.

'Marriage. That will not be for a long time yet.'

'The truth is,' Michael interrupted with the matter he wanted to speak about, 'I don't know if you've noticed, but she seems to harbour some rather dark thoughts inside her. These pictures she draws—'

'Yes, I know of them,' interrupted Bertram. 'I've known of them for quite some time. She is probably frustrated with what she has drawn, no doubt disappointed and annoyed with herself.'

'But it's always the same drawing, over and over, and always heavily scored out, almost obliterated. If she isn't happy with the attempt, why does she not tear up the drawing? But she keeps it all, piles of it.'

The doctor took another sip of his whisky. 'I suspect all artistic minds have their odd ways and I expect this is her way of reminding herself to do better.'

'But always the same drawing?' Michael queried. The question was met with silence. The silence spinning itself out, he leapt on the opportunity to turn to what he'd originally come to ask.

'I've noticed she spends much of her time cooped up in this house. I do think she needs to be lifted out of herself.'

Doctor Lowe looked up sharply at him, his full lips growing tight. 'If she wants to go out more often, Mr Deel, she has only to tell me and I will take her anywhere she wishes to go.'

This was Michael's cue. 'Sir, I was very happy to oblige when you suggested I take her to watch the Boer War heroes' victory parade. I'd very much like to ask your permission to take her out again at some time, to a theatre perhaps, or to an art gallery, or wherever she wished to go. I know you're a very busy man and can't always find the time—'

He found his outpouring halted abruptly by the doctor suddenly leaning forward to put his whisky glass down with a loud thump on the side table and getting to his feet.

Politely Michael stood up too. 'I merely suggested, if I could be of help . . .'

'If I need anyone to take my dau—' There was a sharp hesitation; then he went on. 'If I need anyone to take Miss Jay out, I will ask. Enthusiastic as you are about her artistic talent, your task here, my dear chap, is to help her with her diction and give her tuition in drawing and painting, since that is what she enjoys doing. It is a pastime, a pleasant diversion for her – no more than that. So no more about her progressing to higher levels than she is capable of; and I would ask you as politely as possible, your father and I being close acquaintances, to leave Miss Jay's well-being and happiness to me, and your good intentions outside. It's often said the road to hell is paved with good intentions – a road to unhappiness; and my sole concern is to see her not made unhappy. Now, I thank you for your concern, my dear Michael, and though I am happy for you to continue to tutor her, Miss Jay's private life is better left to me. Now it is getting late. I bid you goodnight.'

With no other option, Michael gave the man a formal nod of the head and left, wondering why the man should feel so touchy about his asking to take Ellie out for a brief evening of freedom. Freedom – that was how it struck him. Something about her intimated that this house constituted a prison to her from which she seemed forever struggling to escape.

What mystified him more was the sudden and abrupt hesitation mid-sentence when he'd refused his help. He'd been about to call her something. 'My . . .' My what? Surely he hadn't been about to say 'daughter', though it had sounded as if that was exactly what he'd been going to say. Did he honestly see in Ellie a replacement for the loss of his daughter and, having lost her, was he terrified of losing the replacement? Was that why he was so reluctant to let her out of his sight?

Michael shrugged. He was probably being fanciful. But he liked Ellie a great deal. He wanted so to get to know her better. She'd told him she'd be seventeen in less than three months. He was twenty-two, a difference of five years: perfect, as far as he could see, for two people to get together.

Of course there were two obstacles: one, his parents, who had higher hopes for a future wife for him than a girl originating from the slums of the East End, though he didn't see her as such; the other, Doctor Lowe, who seemed to him to be quite obsessed with her.

Give it time, came the thought, as he hailed a cab to take him home. Be patient. Who knows what time can do?

The country was mourning the death of its long-reigning Queen – in deep mourning. With all entertainments closed, people were dressing in deepest black, as when a close relative has passed away.

Having ascended the throne at the age of eighteen, Victoria had reigned for sixty-four years – long enough for many to have known no other monarch but her. Though it was expected of one of her age, her death was still a shock. She'd become an institution.

With her many children having married into other noble families, she was known as the Mother of Europe as well as the Mother of Empire, her empire being so extensive that half the world on every globe in every school was coloured pink. Now, on the twenty-second of January 1901, she had died. Now they would have a king again. It felt very odd. A new king for a new century! Things would never be the same again.

Her funeral took place on the second of February. Ellie did not go to watch it, Doctor Lowe considering it more suitable not to go gawping at the solemn procession of one so dearly loved. To her surprise, however, on the fourteenth Michael said that instead of teaching her that day, they'd be going to see the procession of King Edward and Queen Alexandra on the opening of their first Parliament.

'Doctor Lowe thinks you're being stifled by not going out as often as you should. He would take you himself but will be with his wife. Apparently she wishes them both to go there on their own.'

In the midst of her delight at Michael taking her, Ellie mentally shook her head at the woman. In obedience to her husband's dictates, Mrs Lowe no longer treated her to the open loathing and disdain she had once shown, but still refused to give any sign of friendliness. Anyway, the feeling was mutual.

It was a sunny morning, but cold. Well wrapped up, Ellie stood beside Michael in the crowd. He'd given her his arm and she clung to it for warmth but derived a good deal more from their closeness than protection from the cold.

Even though she was of average height, it was almost impossible to see anything for the mass of heads in front of her as she heard the cheering coming towards her in waves when the new King and Queen in their state coach approached.

'I won't be able to see a thing from here!' she pleaded.

At her words, Michael chuckled and, easing his arm from her hold, crouched down. 'Here, climb on my back if you can.'

'I can't do that!'

'Of course you can,' he answered urgently. 'Hurry up now. There's not much more time and I can manage you. You weigh next to nothing, you're so slight.'

'What about you?'

'I can see well enough.' At five foot ten he would. 'Now come on, or you'll miss it all.'

It was quite a feat trying to clamber on his back, her skirt impeding her, her best hat in danger of tilting itself at an alarming angle.

'Here, love, up yer go!' She heard a man's voice behind her as a pair of hands clutching at her slim waist helped to hoist her feet off the ground. 'Yer young man's right, yer know: yer as light as a bloomin' fevver!'

She thought only momentarily of the imposition of a strange man's hands on her waist before she was hoisted up to a good vantage point. She couldn't even turn round to see the man's face, but his voice heartened her – a real, full-blown Cockney voice. The next moment a surging shock went right through her like a stab from a blade of hot iron. It was her dad's voice –she was sure of it.

She could only half-turn, getting merely a side view of a sea of globe-shaped faces, unrecognizably contorted with excitement as the magnificent gilded state coach came into view drawn by a team of plumed horses.

'Stop wriggling!' Michael scolded, laughing. 'Can you see?'

She turned back, her heart still thumping. 'Yes I can see!'

she said automatically. She had probably been wrong – it couldn't have been her dad, the man always on her mind; but it had been a strange feeling. Firmly she concentrated her attention on the spectacle passing before her.

Despite the splash of colour provided by the royal coach, the soldiers' uniforms and the silver and gold trappings of the household cavalry, black remained the prevailing colour in mourning for the late Queen, a solemn reminder of the country's recent loss. If anything, the gesture endeared the onlookers all the more to its new sovereign, the air being rent with cheering.

'That was really wonderful,' Ellie sighed as, with the departure of the glorious royal procession, the crowd began to thin and disperse.

She had slid down from Michael's back, with no one now to assist her, being careful not to have her skirt ride up and show the calves of her legs. The moment her feet felt firm pavement she looked around for the owner of the Cockney voice, but he was probably long gone. She'd never know now if it had been her father or just a figment of an oversensitive imagination. But if it had been him, what would she have done?

Better was the memory of her arm in Michael's, his laughter at her trying to scramble on to his back to see better, the way he now threaded her arm through his again and suggested they have a cup of tea and a bite to eat before returning her home.

'That's if we can find anywhere at all to eat,' he chuckled, patting her gloved hand. 'I expect everyone has the same idea.'

At that, she laughed lightly, forcing thoughts of her father from her mind for the moment.

That night she lay awake, thinking about the episode. What *would* she have done had it been her father? She could still feel those hands on her waist and in retrospect they felt horrible, as if pawing at her. Ellie felt herself shudder with loathing and the memory of that old clawing feeling she would get in her stomach as he leered at her. She had it now.

Angrily she turned over, trying to think of nicer things. Finally she fell asleep, but her dreams were of his weight on her, his grunting and sweating, the vile feel of him, while she was rigid, her mind numb, in fear that she might suddenly be sick over him and bring his anger down on her. It was a recurring dream, often waking her in the small hours. Next morning she'd remember and feel that shame, as she always did after such a nightmare, and make a renewed vow to find him, to make him pay as painfully and humiliatingly as possible.

She longed to see Michael, but it was Friday and she wouldn't see him again until Monday. Her weekend would consist of being nice to Doctor Lowe, whose obsession with her was becoming more irritating than alarming, of feeling the loneliness that weekends often brought, with the staff long ago having stopped speaking to her, and of trying to avoid his wife.

Her only escape was painting – that and hoping she and Dora could steal an hour together to enjoy a bit of a gossip.

It was so much easier these days. Mrs Lowe no longer held sway over Dora, though the girl was still her personal maid and companion. Since she had returned home, Mrs Lowe was less in her room and more with her husband, eating with him again, entertaining and accompanying him when out to dinner with friends and acquaintances. Ellie guessed it was a new ploy to let her see that she hadn't beaten her.

But it didn't matter. For her it was something of a relief, having his attention drawn away from her a little. He still made much of her, asking to see her work, hovering over her, enquiring whether she was happy and content, still calling her 'my dear' and, more importantly, making sure she was well dressed and had money enough to buy nice things with.

That was what she most wanted from him; the rest could go hang and perhaps, when she decided to leave here, it might not be so hard as it had once looked. He wasn't taking her out on so many of those uncomfortable and boring little visits to places of culture. Nor did she eat with him at table now his wife was sharing his company once more. That had been short-lived anyway and she ate in his study again. In a way she was glad not to have Florrie serving her in the dining room, her nose up in the air, being deliberately slapdash when serving her.

So the days went by. Spring came in fine and warm. Her seventeenth birthday had come and gone. A birthday cake had been made for her at Doctor Lowe's request, she and Dora quietly sharing it in his study. If his wife knew about it, perhaps from Mrs Jenkins, she made no sign.

The trouble was, being left more and more to her own devices was getting tedious, leaving her feeling lonely and isolated, her mind turning more and more to the day when she could get right away from this house.

She looked forward to seeing Michael three days a week. She wished it was even more and was beginning to feel a fear that Doctor Lowe might decide to terminate it, thinking she had learned enough. It was a dilemma. If she let him see her greatly improved work she might risk his saying that she needed no more tutoring; but to display her worst attempts might make him decide Michael was a waste of money. Either way she'd not see him again.

They no longer used the doctor's study. Now that she had progressed to painting in oil, the odour of oil, varnish and turpentine pervaded the room. A few weeks ago he had suggested they avail themselves of the little attic room where Florrie had once been obliged to sleep. From there would waft no smell of her work.

The place was small but bright. Light came in from a small dormer window in the roof during the day – perhaps not as bright as an artist's studio would have called for, but adequate enough for her. She spent most of her time here with all her materials to hand, as bought by Doctor Lowe. She and Michael were completely isolated from the rest of the house. They could talk and laugh without being overheard.

Better still, there was no Doctor Lowe to come barging in to interrupt them as he might have done had it been his study. Not that Michael ever behaved in any way improperly. He'd never even attempted to kiss her cheek again, but if he came close, she'd feel a thrill pass through her, wondering if his reaction was the same as hers. One thing did change – one secret thing.

One Thursday evening in May, with the twilight still lingering over the roofs of the houses opposite, it was almost time for him to leave when he gently took the paintbrush from her hand. 'You're so cooped up here,' he said softly. 'Don't you feel the need for a breath of fresh air?'

The words took her by surprise. The way he'd taken her hand had put her suddenly on her guard, even though his touch had for a second excited her.

She turned and gave him an enquiring look. 'A breath of fresh air?'

Why did she always echo what he said?

'We could creep out,' he whispered. 'It's a lovely evening. We could take a walk, find a coffee stall; then I can bring you back. What do you say?'

What could she say? The idea tempted her. 'How do we creep out?'

'Wait until the staff retire – which will not be long now, as it's getting late – and Mrs Jenkins is closeted in her room with a book and cup of cocoa. Florrie can let me out the front door as she usually does before going to bed. If Mrs Jenkins isn't still in the kitchen, you can creep out the back door. I'll wait for you there. When we return, I can leave you at the back door. No one will see you enter and no one will ever need know.'

He was like a small boy arranging to bunk off out of a school dormitory. But the idea was tantalizing – the exhilaration of risk, the prospect of being completely alone with him for the first time ever. She found herself nodding eagerly. Why not? She was her own mistress, virtually.

In the dwindling twilight, in an ordinary day skirt and jacket, not even a hat – but who would see her or care? – she walked with her arm through his, thinking that surely this must be the beginning of something between them.

From Roman Road they turned left into Cambridge Road, crossing over towards Bethnal Green Road, her old haunt immediately bringing back a host of memories that she hastily cast aside. Just as he'd said, there *was* a coffee stall on the corner outside the Salmon & Ball, busy serving a few customers. Many a time she and Dora, as children, had sat on the pavement outside that pub, nibbling a hard arrowroot biscuit and sipping a glass of lemonade while Mum and Dad had been inside enjoying a few glasses of beer. She'd been quite small then, Dora a mere toddler, her brother Charlie out with his mates.

That was when Mum had still had her looks and Dad had still been interested in her. It was only later that hard work, caring for her family, and poverty because of a man seldom in work preferring to gamble, drink and womanize away the money she earned, had aged her and brought her to ill health.

Memories she preferred to forget. But that was then and Michael was with her now. Slowly they sipped the dark, steaming Camp coffee from thick mugs, Michael talking quietly to her about his life.

'Even if my father had allowed me to study, I'd never have found the talent you have.'

'You could do, if you study hard enough,' she told him, jokingly taking a leaf out of his book when telling her always to study hard and dedicate her mind to her work.

He didn't laugh but looked at her in the fitful light of the coffee stall's kerosene lamp swinging in a light breeze. 'One day you'll be a good artist. You are now, but you need to think of spreading your wings, taking a chance and leaving the place where you are now living. You have all the talent. What you don't have, Ellie, is the courage and the hard shell required to face the difficult world that's out there. It's a difficult world for a woman where artists who earn their living are men.'

'Women paint,' she said, a little put out by what he'd said.

'Yes,' he agreed, '– ladies of leisure, I imagine. But it's as a recreation, much as they would embroider a pretty picture. They'd never dream of trying to sell the pictures. It's fine for a man but apparently frowned upon, as unsuitable to say the least, for a young lady to lower herself by selling her paintings.'

A sardonic note had crept into his voice and Ellie's brief moment of offended pride dissipated instantly. He was with her, not against her, had only been trying to point out the pitfalls to her.

'I can face anything,' she said defiantly. 'I wasn't brought up a lady and I know all about hard times, so I won't be upset by what others think. In fact, I mean to be the first woman artist to be famous!'

It sounded such a ridiculous statement that she expected him to laugh, but he didn't. He frowned. 'Then your work would have to be unique, different from anything else that's ever been. I often think that to get on in the world a woman has to be twice as clever, twice as talented and twice as astute as a man, who I guess can get away with anything. That takes hard work and courage and, as I say, a strong carapace.'

'Carapace?'

'A protective shell,' he enlightened her, laughing now. He put his empty mug back on the coffee-stall counter and, taking hers from her, put that beside it. He nodded his thanks to the heavily built, bewhiskered man who had served them, and guided her away.

'Time I was taking you back,' he said. 'Mustn't abuse my position.'

It was lovely walking through the darkened streets, again with her arm through his. It all seemed so natural. 'Can we do this again?' she asked, and he smiled.

'I don't see why not.' To her they were the most wonderful words she thought she'd ever heard.

Sixteen

Turmoil raged within Bertram Lowe's breast as he glared down from his study window. A small path led past the back gate. Beyond were the garden and churchyard of St John's, dim in the last light of this July evening.

For weeks Ellie and her tutor had been creeping out behind his back for evening strolls. Mrs Jenkins had reported it to him, saying that as head of the household he should be acquainted with the goings-on here. Yet what could he say? Michael Deel and Ellie were free agents. He could hardly forbid it without looking a fool.

Now this latest, innocent enough request from Michael Deel for permission to take her to view an exhibition of paintings by new artists.

'It will help her in her own work to know what is currently being shown.' A crafty ploy to be together. 'I'm sure she'll benefit from it, sir. You said you can't always have time from your busy surgery to take her to as many places of interest as you would like.'

There had been three similar requests these last two months, but how could he say no and not look as though he were jealous? For he was being eaten up by jealousy as he turned back to the young man standing there, awaiting his reply.

'As you say, I do find it rather difficult these days,' he'd said with an effort. 'It seems I will again have to leave her in your hands, as her tutor.'

'I promise to take good care of her,' were always the parting words.

Yes, he would! The young man could hardly keep the excitement out of his voice, blast him! Bertram found himself toying with the idea of announcing on the next occasion that Michael had nothing more to teach her and that a more skilled tutor needed to be found. But, rather than separate them, it might very well bring them closer. Absence, it was said, makes the heart grow fonder, and they would only start meeting in secret – he was sure of that.

Here he had some control over them, growing less and less he knew; but while this young man was teaching her under his own roof, he could keep an eye on them.

But now that this sneaking out of an evening had come to his ears, he was sick with anger and at the moment fighting to hide it. If he'd only made time to take her out himself, this situation would not have arisen. But he was no longer as free as he had been when his wife was away.

It wasn't so easy now she was back, ever watching him, just as he watched them. With Mary's eyes always on him he felt restricted, and there were times when he wished she had stayed where she was, with her sister. Nor had her carping ceased with her return.

'I have tried my best, Bertram, to tolerate the girl, but the sight of her makes my flesh creep. How can you even look on her as you do?'

'In the same way as you look on her sister, young Dora,' he'd retorted angrily.

'She is different.'

'How different?' he'd challenged her. 'They are sisters!'

She had turned away in a huff and said no more, leaving things as unsolved as ever. So when it came to this young man requesting to take Ellie to art galleries and museums as he himself had once done, he knew he had to reluctantly agree or heighten his wife's suspicions that there must be even more to his association with Ellie Jay than he admitted.

This evening Bertram remained glowering at the closed door after Michael Deel had left to tell Ellie that he had permission to take her to the latest visit on his menu.

A myriad of thoughts ran through his head. How far had this relationship gone? These secretive walks bothered him. Did they exchange furtive kisses, passionate kisses? Had it gone further than that?

He was sure Michael wasn't a man to take advantage of Ellie. Nor, he trusted, would she have allowed it if he had tried. She was a strong-minded young woman and the terrifying memory of her father would prevent her from allowing any man to touch her. But what about love? Were they in love?

The thought seemed to clamp his brain with an iron grip. It had to stop before it went any further. He might lose Ellie. Michael Deel had said previously that one day she would want to marry and leave this house – leave him. Nor would she ever come to visit him – he knew that instinctively.

Again came the thought that tormented him. She wasn't his loving daughter, no matter how he tried to pretend she was. He meant nothing to her. She could go off with anyone she fell in love with and he would never see her again. The notion petrified him. He had to put a stop to it before it was too late.

Making up his mind as the little dinner bell in the hall below buzzed softly, he made his way downstairs and, instead of proceeding to the dining room, slipped quickly into his surgery, just in time to avoid his wife on her way downstairs to dinner. What he was about to do would not take long.

Bertram sat in one of the many comfortable, leather, button-back armchairs in the gentlemen's club, his rotund figure dwarfed by the well-built, broad-shouldered man with the strong jaw, typical of the Dutch, sitting beside him.

Both lounged comfortably, both enjoying a cigar and sipping brandy brought to them by a silent, deferential waiter. The room was hushed, the low murmur of men's voices hardly breaking the silence. In this atmosphere Bertram fingered his glass and stole a glance at his companion.

'I can't apologize enough for putting this matter at your door,' he began.

'I'm very glad you did, Doctor Lowe. I do have my son's future welfare constantly at heart. I would have been happy rather that he did not have this idiotic notion that he is some sort of an artist and concentrated all his energies on his career as a medical man.'

Doctor Henk Deel spoke impeccable English, had come to England forty years ago to study medicine, had married an English girl of a good family and settled here after graduating. At sixty he was heartened to have his younger son Michael set to follow him into medicine.

His older son, Willem – known as Willy – was senior to Michael by eight years. Their sister Julia, born in between, was married and nicely settled. But Willy took after his mother – quite an accomplished artist in her way – and, having no intention of following his father into the medical profession, had taken himself off to roam the world, painting and falling into debt, forever sending distress calls home for help out of some financial crisis or other. Henk Deel had despaired of him years ago.

Fortunately, although Michael had also inherited his mother's artistic bent, he was far more malleable than his older brother. He'd studied hard at university and was his father's pride. However, not wanting to stunt the young man in his need to express himself artistically, he'd allowed him to study art. When Doctor Lowe, a friend of many years standing, had asked if the boy could help this odd child he'd befriended recently to speak better English and develop her own artistic skills, he'd seen it as an outlet for his son's hobby and perhaps a way of getting it out of his system. He'd tried to stop Willy, and look where that had landed the boy!

Thus he sat back to hear what was bothering his old friend. Lowe had revealed little over the telephone he had recently had installed on the wall of his surgery, leaving Henk to chuckle as the man rang off having uttered just a few words, no doubt unnerved still by the newness of the instrument.

'So tell me: what is on your mind?' he asked, laying his cigar in the ashtray to make it seem that he was ready to concentrate on what his friend had to say.

Bertram gnawed at his thick lips. 'First, I must thank you for allowing your son to tutor Miss Jay. As far as I can see, he has done a decent job.'

'Decent?' echoed Deel.

'I mean, an excellent job, obviously. But I think he has gone as far as he can with the girl.'

Deel leaned forward. 'Why are you taking such pains over this girl? After all, she is not connected with you or your family.'

Bertram hastily shook his head. 'It's merely that . . .'

He paused. Henk Deel had no inkling of his feelings for the girl. All that the man knew was that he'd taken in and employed her and her sister out of the kindness of his heart when they had been in dire straits. If anyone had asked Doctor Deel, he would have told them that Bertram Lowe was that sort of man: kind-hearted almost to a fault, a man with an easy-going nature and a querulous wife, who could have gone so much further in his profession had he been a different person.

Bertram's lips curled contemptuously at himself. '. . . merely that I feel such talent as she has should be nurtured,' he concluded. 'It seems an utter waste that a gifted person should be frustrated purely because she does not have the advantages others enjoy. Nothing more than that.'

That last was a mistake, as he saw a knowing smile appear beneath his colleague's moustache. There came an instant need to rectify the remark, but he realized any such effort would certainly add to whatever suspicion Deel might already have begun to form.

'But that isn't what I wanted to speak to you about,' he said hastily. 'It's not something that can be discussed on the telephone. As you know, young Michael has been tutoring Miss Jay for some time now. The thing is, I'm afraid it has prompted some feeling between them.'

He became aware of the blue eyes regarding him now with a certain amount of growing interest. He hurried on, but found it difficult to put into words that would not offend.

'I would say that it's beginning to develop into something more,' he said with care. 'A fondness towards each other? I would venture to say more than mere fondness, and I felt you should be acquainted with the fact.'

For a moment Henk Deel regarded him, then burst into a deep-toned chuckle, curbing it as those in the normally hushed room glanced up from their newspapers in startled irritation. He nodded a silent apology to those nearest to him and, retrieving his cigar from the cut-glass ashtray, leaned towards Bertram.

'My dear chap, I know my son. I very much doubt he would find a girl from some East End slum of interest to him in the way you describe. Michael is a well-brought-up young man and eventually will find himself someone of a good family to be his wife.'

He broke off and grew thoughtful. Willy had also been well brought up, had enjoyed the very best of education, a comfortable home, an affluent parent, a brilliant career awaiting him; and what had he done? Gone off into the blue to become what people liked to call a bohemian, wearing strange clothes, consorting with even stranger companions and no doubt partaking of substances that helped heighten his empty dream of becoming a great painter, always broke and even perhaps cohabiting with a woman or two of doubtful health – God knows what diseases he could have picked up from them. Henk fought off a shudder.

'Michael is very conscious that it would be folly to allow a fine future in medicine to be marred by such a girl,' he said slowly. 'Think no more of it, old chap. It is quite possible that you are growing a mountain from a molehill. They are possibly becoming good friends, nothing more.'

Even so, he would question his son when he returned home. Michael would not dream of covering it up if anything seedy was going on. And his features were as crystal: were he to tell a lie, it would show through on his face as clearly as if through glass.

'Now, another brandy?' he suggested confidently. 'Where is our fine waiter . . . Aah!'

In the cab taking him home Bertram Lowe felt thwarted. He gazed morosely from the cab window at the passing shops and occasional kerbside stalls, all lit up and still trading, with late-evening shoppers taking advantage of the dwindling twilight.

The man was a fool!

Listening to the regular clip-clop of the horse's hooves on the cobbles, the traffic congestion of a few hours earlier having eased, he mused. If Deel was too gullible to foresee the pitfall his son was heading for, then he was a blind fool and it was up to himself to do something about the two young people. He couldn't sit back and watch Ellie being led astray.

True, Michael Deel might have no intention of leading her astray. No doubt his feelings for her were honourable – that was until his father got wind of where it was leading and called his son to heel. If the boy was in love with Ellie, it might be hard to make him see his father's viewpoint, but in the end a dutiful son should take his father's advice and follow the career his father has preferred for him.

In the swaying cab Bertram suddenly felt a tinge of doubt. Had he done the right thing by going to Henk Deel? Lifting a hand, he plucked slowly at his top lip. What if things had already gone too far? If Ellie were to fall in love with him – if she wasn't already in love – and he was persuaded that it would be wiser to end the affair for the sake of his own future, her heart would be broken. He had to protect her from heartbreak just as if she were his very own daughter. He suddenly realized that he wasn't merely fond of her: he actually loved her like his own child.

It was a frightening dilemma. His first plan of dispensing with Michael Deel's services had held the danger of their meeting behind his back and it had seemed a better solution to speak to his father, who would wield greater power over his son. All the man had done was shrug off his suspicions. Fool! The utter fool! It seemed to him that, whatever he did, those two would find a way to continue their more secret meetings. But if he could persuade her that Michael wasn't all he seemed . . .

Bertram Lowe stopped plucking at his lip as a plan began to form in his head. He would make it his business to take up as many of her evenings as possible, taking her out and about, watching her face light up at the money he would spend on her. He would look good in her eyes by doubling her allowance. Meanwhile he would quietly let her see that Michael was from a totally different background from her – one upon which she would never be allowed to encroach He'd let her see that this young man was only dallying with her until the day when he would marry someone of his own sort.

She would be furious, feel used. Arguments would ensue, accusations fly, recriminations be batted back and forth; love's bliss would disintegrate, and who knows? – it might take just a single stern word from his father to make a disgruntled Michael Deel return to the bosom of his family. No need to dismiss him and no cause for ill feeling between himself and the boy's father. It was a good plan.

Ellie had never felt so cosseted. She'd never had so many clothes bought for her or been taken to so many places – even to the music hall, which she liked the most. Even her allowance had been substantially increased.

'I'm saving most of it,' she told Dora in secret. 'It'll be a tidy sum by the time I'm ready to leave here.' The only fly in the ointment was Doctor Lowe taking so much more interest in her than before. But so long as he gave her money she had to go along with it. After all, this was what she had planned for. More and more, however, these little outings were falling on the evenings Michael should have been coming.

She knew he was getting irritated as the weeks went by, asking what was going on. All she could say was that in time Doctor Lowe would tire of these needless outings. 'It won't be for much longer,' she coaxed. 'Then we'll be together again.'

But now he was openly impatient. '*How* much longer?' he had asked the previous week in a tone that rather took her aback. 'You could try to get out of it sometimes.'

'We still see each other on odd occasions, don't we?' she reminded him. 'I can't very well upset him. He's been kind to me and he means well.'

But Michael had become quite annoyed, refusing to see her point. It was a side of him she'd never seen before and she in turn had been huffy with him. They'd parted company that evening without him suggesting they sneak out together, and on Monday he hadn't appeared, a note arriving to say he was feeling a little under the weather, though she knew he was still angry.

She could see his side of it. She too missed their times together, but nothing could be done about it if she wanted to avoid suspicion of something going on between her and Michael.

She felt sure no one knew of their secret meetings and it did add a delicious touch of intrigue, her stomach churning with excitement every time she crept out of the back door into Michael's arms. Twice this month she'd made an excuse to Doctor Lowe that she had a terrible headache.

Doctor Lowe, now seeing himself as her guardian and asking that she call him by his given name in private, couldn't have been more concerned. On both occasions he had given her aspirin powder, told her to rest and had cancelled the evening's arrangement. But she couldn't play on that one too often. He had been so trusting and sympathetic that, in a strange way, it hurt to deceive him. She was aware that his fondness was becoming obsessive. If he found out about her and Michael, he might become bitter. If he sent her packing, her plans would fall apart. She couldn't expect Michael to keep her. She needed to stay here until she chose to leave.

To tell Michael her plans would involve explaining about

her father. Nor could she explain why she needed to remain in the Lowe household. What if he realized that she was using the man, and turned against her? If she lost him, her world would fall apart.

Dora's voice interrupted her thoughts. 'I don't know why you want to leave. I like it here. Mrs Lowe's awfully kind. She gives me nearly anything I want. And you don't do so bad out of the master,' she added slyly.

Dora, coming up to fifteen, was growing up quickly. Soon she would be having her hair up; the hemline of her skirts would be allowed to flare and sweep the floor. Whether she could constrict her waist to the extent some women were doing to achieve the new hour-glass figure would be up to Mrs Lowe.

'I know I'm still considered employed,' Dora pouted, 'but I get almost as many privileges as you do.'

Ellie, though, knew Dora would never be as spoiled as she herself was. She knew she should be grateful – now with a tidy bank balance and anything she asked for within reason instantly given to her. She wasn't, of course, able to come to the dining room with the master and mistress – Mrs Lowe saw to that; but she ate what they ate, meals brought by Florrie, who seemed to have forgotten that the girl she attended had once worked below stairs. They even talked together these days, Florrie sitting on the bed chatting while she ate, even helping herself to titbits off Ellie's plate, making them both giggle.

It was good to have her as a friend again. She was almost tempted to tell her about Michael but thought better of it. Florrie had a wagging tongue, and if Mrs Jenkins got wind of it, she'd be straight up to tell Doctor Lowe.

It was as if Florrie had read her mind this evening, as they sat side by side on Ellie's comfortable bed in the elegant room that had once belonged to the Lowes' daughter. They had been laughing about how lumpy Florrie's bed was becoming, and Ellie had promised to see if the master could find his way clear to getting his wife to see about a better mattress for her.

Suddenly Florrie's laughter faded. She grew serious. 'If the mistress was to find out what you've been up to, she'd send you away like a shot, much less get me a decent mattress.'

Ellie too stopped laughing to frown. 'What do you mean – what I've been up to?'

'You and that tutor.'

As Ellie stared, completely taken aback, she went on, 'Mrs Jenkins knows about it. It was one evening when she couldn't sleep, she thought she 'eard a noise in the kitchen. She said she went to investigate and saw you and him outside the back door, him with his arms around you, and you was both kissing. She said she felt she had to tell the master.'

'What she needs to do is mind her own business!' Ellie blustered, '– prying into my affairs. I'm nothing to do with her any more.' But her heart was racing.

He knew. He must have known for ages then, and had said nothing. It brought sudden goose pimples to her flesh. Surely, if he had been at ease with it he would have mentioned to her what he'd been told, but his having kept it to himself gave a feeling of menace, showing a side to him she had never suspected.

Had he spoken of misgivings about her and Michael's developing relationship, it would at least have been honest; but concealing what he'd been told . . . All the attention he had been showering on her, all this kindness, and all the time he'd probably been watching her like a hawk.

She hadn't truly realized how far he was eaten up with this obsession he had for her. Now she had no idea where she stood and her plans to leave, which had once seemed so simple and easy, suddenly made her wonder.

Seventeen

'I am thinking, my dear, it may be time to find you another tutor – one who can teach you so much more than you are learning at present.'

His tone was kind, his smile gentle, but Ellie was ready for him. 'Mr Deel is a very good teacher,' she said, trying not to sound too anxious.

'Maybe,' came the mild reply, 'as far as his abilities go. What you really need now is professional tutoring. There is many a fine art academy here in London, in Paris, Milan. With your exceptional talent any one of them will accept you. You could be a great artist at the end of it.'

He was warming to his subject. 'Think of it, my dear: to be considered among today's great painters. And I shall be there for you, to fund you, so you'll have no worry on that score. All you have to do is dedicate yourself to art. No, I fear Michael Deel cannot do that for you.'

'He still has a lot to teach me before then.' She had to be careful how she chose her words. 'And he charges you no fees, and he likes coming.'

She stopped. It was the wrong thing to have said. Of course he didn't charge fees and of course he liked coming here. And why? The answer stood out like a beacon.

'Any other tutor would be ever so expensive,' she said hurriedly. 'And I don't really warrant all that outlay. If I was really gifted then—'

'I consider you are.' His easy smile had vanished. 'Exceedingly so.'

'No, I'm not!' For all her efforts she couldn't help the sharp outburst. His false concern for her made her angry. 'I'm just a bit better than some, that's all. It's only you who think I'm some sort of genius with a paintbrush. Well I'm not! There's 'undreds and 'undreds of people can paint like me.'

In fear and anger she forgot for a moment what she'd been taught. She saw him frown and realized that this wasn't the way to go. 'I'm just an ordinary person, that's all I am,' she ended on a note of entreaty.

Was this his plan – to send her to some college of art, miles away, far enough away to make it impossible for her to see Michael – somewhere like Milan, in Italy? Beneath this mild mien of his there beat a devious heart. He wanted to keep her all for himself, even sacrificing her to a year or two away from him – anything to stop her and Michael seeing each other. But he didn't realize he was heading the right way to losing her.

It came to her suddenly. This *was* the time. It had finally arrived. She had enough money saved. She'd have liked more. For all his cunning, he had no idea how independent of him she was becoming. Yet . . .

In her breast conflict was beginning to rage. What if she did comply, manipulated him just a little longer? Michael would stand by her when he learned what really lay deep in this man's heart. He would wait for her. And if she did become a great artist – it might open all sorts of doors. She might even become wealthy in her own right. And she would stand over her father, see him a little man before her vast wealth.

Her father – he was never far from her thoughts. After all these months since the episode at King Edward's opening of Parliament back in February, it still played on her mind.

She'd chided herself so many times for having too vivid an imagination, telling herself that it couldn't have been her father who had clutched her around the waist from behind, unaware it was his own daughter; that it had to be too much of a co-incidence; that it couldn't have been his voice she'd heard. If he'd been in London, surely he'd have found out by then about her mother's death? Perhaps he had. Perhaps he didn't care. Perhaps he was only too glad to be free.

The thought brought a wave of hatred. And determination. She must work towards having more money, even if that meant being sent somewhere a long way off, or all her plans would fall apart.

Money had a habit of melting away before it could be put to proper use. Even with what she already had she might be broke in no time, trying to look after herself. If she wanted wealth and prestige, she would have to do Bertram's bidding.

But what if she lost Michael? Could she expect him to wait a year, maybe two years for her? Quickly she pushed away all her previous airy-fairy notions. She did have enough money to escape this man's cloying possession of her – now, the sooner the better. Anyway, she'd be out of her depth in some academy, here or abroad, and the thought of being alone in some foreign country was frightening. She would never be happy.

It was time she was gone, she and Michael together. His family was quite well off. He worked in his father's practice, in Harley Street, and one day he'd be well regarded in his field. With Michael behind her there was no need to worry about money. He loved her and she loved him and in time they would be married.

She looked at Bertram Lowe, his blue eyes alight with plans for her, unaware that she had her own plans, and smiled. There was a need to keep him in the dark just a little longer, to let him think she was content.

'Perhaps you ought not to dismiss Mr Deel too soon,' she said sweetly. 'It would look a bit rude and inconsiderate after his father has let him teach me how to talk nicely, and paint, and for no fees as well.'

A sigh of relief filled Ellie's lungs as this advice was met with a thoughtful nod. Reprieved. Time earned for her and Michael, so long as they could keep Bertram Lowe at bay.

She and Michael stood by the coffee stall in Cambridge Road. These days it seemed to be their only haunt, and the November chill crept into their bones; but they were together.

It was two months since Bertram Lowe had frightened her with sending her to another tutor or some distant school of art. No doubt he'd thought better of it, perhaps fearing Michael might defy his family's plans for his future and go after her.

He'd no doubt reasoned that those in love would follow each other to the ends of the earth and he'd lose her anyway. Here he could keep an eye on them and, Ellie guessed, be on hand to stir up feelings of doubt in each of them.

He no longer took her places. Maybe the effort had caused his practice to suffer, or maybe he no longer saw any point to it. But he was now refusing to sanction Michael accompanying her anywhere on his behalf as on those few occasions before he had become alert to the direction their relationship had begun to take.

He was now aware, of course, that they were continuing to meet, if not in secrecy any more, then discreetly; but there was little he could do about it. He could hardly lock her up or, she now realized, send her packing. It was probably tearing him apart, but she didn't care, deaf to his warnings that, though they might continue to meet, Michael's upbringing would never allow them to wed if that's what she hoped for.

Ellie didn't quite know what she hoped for. She knew she was in love with Michael. At the same time her need to find her father still occupied her mind, like a cancer lurking there in her brain, tormenting and ravaging her and spoiling any hope of happiness. She hated it and the one who caused it to be there. She wanted Michael so much – a smooth, contented life; but how could it be so when this blight was consuming her? Would it ever shrivel and die? Probably not – or not until this stubborn need for revenge was satisfied.

She huddled against Michael, more for reassurance and comfort than from the cold, and sipped the steaming beverage the coffee stall grandly liked to call coffee, trying not to think of her father. But now Bertram Lowe's words milled in her brain:

'You will never be his wife, you know, if that's what you are hoping. His family would never agree to a marriage between their son and someone of the poorest of poor upbringing. When he marries they will see he marries well. You will see.'

He had never used to refer to her background. It struck her as churlish and cruel, unlike him, and if he hoped in this way to earn her affection, he was going entirely the wrong way about it, driving her further from him, if he did but know it. That was bad enough. Worse were moments when he would express his fondness, say how sweet she was, how he wanted to shield her from harm and remind her just how much she owed him for taking her in and saving her from poverty. Such a kind man; but his kindness was cloying.

She shivered and felt Michael's arm come about her shoulders.

He glanced down at her. 'Cold?'

'It is cold,' she admitted, allowing an even bigger shudder.

'We'd best be getting back. Don't want you to catch a chill. I'd hate to be the cause of you going down with a cold,' he added with a light chuckle.

'You'll never cause me any harm,' she said earnestly, and felt his arm tighten about her.

'Come on then,' he said briskly. Releasing her, he took her empty mug and placed it with his own on the off-white, stained counter.

They walked slowly despite the cold, with its first thin curling of mist promising to develop into yellow fog by midnight. Her thick-gloved hand was through the crook of his arm, she not wanting to be seen in public with his arm around her; but she clung as close as possible, wanting so much to express how much she loved him.

He must have gleaned her thoughts, for he slowed to a stop where it was darkest between two of the sparsely spaced street gas lamps. There he took her by the shoulders and turned her gently towards him.

'I do love you very much, Ellie. I've not been able to say this before, not as I'd have liked. I've always felt it was a bit too soon, or too dramatic, or I'd take you by surprise and turn you away. But I really, really love you.'

It had taken her by surprise, but pleasurable surprise. 'I love you too,' was all she could find to say. It was hardly enough, but she looked up into his grey eyes and read the adoring glow in them.

'I was never sure if you loved me enough,' he whispered. 'You always seem so far away in your thoughts. I would wonder what you were thinking. And you were always so wrapped up in your painting. You seemed excited when you said Doctor Lowe was talking of sending you to some art school or other. You mentioned Milan at one time and my heart nearly stopped. I don't ever want to lose you, Ellie. Don't ever go away.'

He sounded so desolate at that moment that Ellie caught his face between her gloved hands and brought his head towards her. Kissing him on the lips and hanging on to the kiss, she felt him pull her to him.

'Oh, my sweetest!' she sighed as the kiss finally broke off.

'I'm so very happy and I'll never go away. No one can ever make me. I don't belong to him. I'm not his daughter. He can't force me to do anything I don't want to. I've always known that, but I've stayed with him because—'

She stopped abruptly, not daring to explain. 'I don't know why,' she lied, hating it. But to voice her motives could easily be the death of their love. He might even think that she was using him. Once again she shuddered.

'You're cold!' he said again. 'Let's get you home as quick as possible.'

Together they began to hurry. 'I'll leave you at the gate to the yard,' he said, as if their meeting were still in the utmost secrecy. 'And I shall see you again on Wednesday. Are you all right?'

'I'm fine,' she gasped.

It was a quick goodnight kiss, considering the passion of the last one, but somehow it seemed that any longer embrace would spoil that earlier one.

As she entered by the back door there came a scurry. She was being watched for. What would they, whoever it was, report to Bertram Lowe? she wondered idly as, with no one about, she quietly mounted the silent stairs to her room on the second floor, the room his daughter had once occupied, the room in which she'd taken that girl's place. The thought made her feel a little like a usurper, oddly and suddenly sickened by it. Quietly she closed the door on the silent hall, but the impression of listening ears remained.

Her mind changed: the quicker she got away from here the better.

Bertram held his breath the more clearly to hear the footsteps on the stairs, cautious though they were. He had been standing at his study window for around half an hour, waiting for the two young people to appear. When finally they did, the girl was holding the young man's arm, leaning close to him, as lovers do. They wandered slowly, reluctant, so it seemed, to reach that moment when they must say goodnight.

He watched as they stopped by the wrought-iron back gate. She still crept into the house by the back entrance, even though their secret meetings were secret no longer. Hastily he stepped back from the window as he saw her glance up at it; then, as her gaze returned to the young man, resumed his earlier position in time to see the man enfold the girl in his arms for a lingering kiss, the sight bringing a tight and distressing feeling of suffocation to his breast.

He'd stood here many times since told of these clandestine meetings, knowing that he was causing himself suffering yet unable not to wait and watch. He had tried to do all he could to part these two without being too obvious, but what they felt for each other was stronger than his will.

The girl was opening the gate, the young man walking away, turning to give her a final wave. Hastily Bertram left his study, hurrying along the long passage to his bedroom, hoping Mary wouldn't hear him from her room.

Carefully he closed his door and, with his flabby cheek to the wood, listened for the light step on the stair, the click of the bedroom door closing. As all fell silent, he slowly prepared for bed, knowing she would be doing the same. And all the time he was aware of the heavy beating of his heart, heavy with the weight of jealousy that lay there.

There had been another listener. Mary Lowe had heard the ungainly tread of her husband, out of breath with the effort. When they had first been married, he had been trim – not slim, but trim. She hadn't then noticed the promise of fleshiness to come. But then she herself had been slim and shapely.

Mary Lowe smiled mockingly at herself and went back to concentrating on listening. There came the quiet click of his bedroom door closing, then moments later the faint creak of a stair as the girl crept up to the room where she slept, the bedroom she now violated with her presence, occupying the very bed where once had lain her own sweet Millicent.

The girl had no scruples. She'd wormed her way into this house and into her husband's foolish, vulnerable heart, making full use of his grief to secure a comfortable little niche for herself. Wriggling her way into his affections, she was worse than a thief. But Mary wasn't prepared to let it go at that. She could never forgive Bertram for the way he had behaved – thinking to replace his own dearest daughter with an urchin from some poverty-stricken back street, indulging in her to ease his loss.

With no care how *she* felt about it, he'd set about selfishly filling his own emptiness by giving the girl whatever she asked for, completely blind to the fact that she was winding him round her little finger. Now he was letting himself be eaten up with jealousy because she had done what most young girls did – fallen in love.

He was in terror of losing her. That was how stupid he'd become, and he was doing all he could to break up the two young people. But she would make sure he'd fail. If he did but know, he had played into her hands with this obsessive jealousy of his. She had tried for so long to be rid of the girl and now this young man offered a way out that all her complaining, her nagging, even her temporarily leaving her own husband had failed to achieve. And now she had him. It was time to act. As the house fell silent, Mary crept back into her bed to think it out properly. It was so simple: make sure those two remained together – that was all she needed to do. She could hardly wait.

It had all come to her ears through Dora. Though Ellie had confided in her sister, she had sworn her to secrecy. Mrs Jenkins, however, being no fool, had discovered what had been going on and out of a strong sense of duty had reported it to her employers. The woman could usually be relied on to keep things to herself, but one chance word carelessly dropped had had that Chambers girl enlarging on it to the kitchen maid. Though everyone was aware of it, only she, his wife, knew of Bertram's fear that he was about to lose the girl to Michael Deel and intended to break up the young lovers with whatever means came to hand, no doubt even going to the boy's father.

What angered her was that he'd not spoken one word about it to her, still believing she was in the dark, for she'd been careful to keep what she knew to herself. Having him know what she'd found out would do her no good: he'd thwart her the moment she showed her hand. What a shock he was in for.

How she had managed to keep silent when he'd given Jay their own daughter's old bedroom had been beyond her, but her silence alone had spoken volumes and since that time they had hardly exchanged words unless there was need to. He didn't seem much put out by these long silences. He might, she felt, even be glad of them, as helping him to avoid occasional lies.

Since the death of their daughter they had more or less led separate lives anyway, meeting only occasionally at meal times, or when entertaining guests called for it. They went out together only when absolutely necessary – to a function or to dinner with a friend, maybe one of his medical colleagues. She had no real friends, had never been good at mixing. He'd thought otherwise when he had asked her to marry him but soon realized how wrong he'd been. Millicent had brought them closer, but now she was gone there seemed little point in it. Her only contact was her sister, but since having gone to live with her, if only for that short time, relations had grown strained. She blamed Bertram utterly for having driven her to leave home – he and his weird obsession for a child in whom he professed loudly to see such a striking likeness to his own dead child. Yes, loudly.

Mary couldn't help smirking as she lay on her side in bed with the covers drawn up over her ears. There were times when she wondered if this obsession with the girl was quite as fatherly as he made out. It didn't matter, for she was going to put an end to it. On this thought Mary Lowe drifted off to asleep.

She knew where her husband was this evening: in his club with Michael Deel's father. She had learned to be devious and earlier on had asked him innocently where he was off to.

'I've hardly set eyes on you all day, dear,' she pouted, having made sure to come down to dinner.

He looked up from his first course of salmon mousse. 'I can't exactly say that is my fault, my dear. My surgery is full to overflowing this time of year with autumn coughs and colds, lumbago and rheumatism, not to mention visiting time. This is the time of year when so many begin to take to their beds with pneumonia and pleurisy or are seen off with heart failure. My time is well taken up, leaving little time to myself.'

'Or for me, dear,' she cut through the rambling.

He regarded her with a puzzled frown. 'I thought you cared little for my company, my dear.'

'Because you are always so busy. I am loath to intervene.'

'You have Dora.' His tone had grown sharp. 'You seem quite content with her.'

'I would not be if I had more of your time. And where are you off to tonight, dear?' She hoped she was leading their conversation round expertly to its destination as he shrugged lightly.

'My club,' he said, resuming eating.

Her own food remained untouched. 'I do sometimes wish there were clubs for ladies. I might make friends there.'

'There are such places,' he answered, delicately cutting into the last few pieces of his salmon mousse. 'If you did but put yourself out a little more, Mary, my dear, you could find plenty of diversion rather than spending your time in your room with a paid companion.'

'We go out occasionally, shopping.'

She heard his brief, derisive laugh and his mumbled, 'Most exciting,' and felt she was losing track of her objective.

'I shouldn't think any clubs for women in this area would be to my taste,' she went on. 'Of course, yours being in the better part of London, those you meet are of your class – medical men, I suppose. Do I know some of them, their wives, whom we may have invited here for dinner at one time or another?'

'I expect so, my dear.' He leaned back while Chambers removed his empty plate ready for the next course.

She waved her uneaten mousse away as Chambers hesitated before swiftly removing it. 'And would I have met the wives of any of those you'll be seeing this evening at your club?' she asked innocently.

Again he shrugged, his gaze idly following the grilled lamb cutlets and assorted vegetables that Chambers was carefully transferring from a silver platter to the warm, gleaming plate she had put before him.

'Would I?' Mary prompted cautiously. 'If you named any you might be meeting there this evening to remind me?'

Unsuspecting, he formed his lips into a meditative puff as he sliced into his cutlet. 'Let's see. Wagstaff – you know his wife, I think: Harriet. He's always there, part of the fittings. The Pulmingtons, George – you know them. Henry Chauncey – I invited them to dinner last summer. Doctor Henk . . .'

She saw his eyes flicker towards her as he broke off, but she was pretending to help herself to vegetables and cutlets as if not really taking his words in. 'I really must make myself go out more,' she said easily. 'Wrapped up warm, Dora and I could pay a visit to Dickins & Jones, perhaps have tea at a

Lyons tea shop. Or, better still, a Fullers tea shop – a far daintier service and beautiful cakes.'

He'd played completely into her hands. Even the way he had cut the name short had betrayed him. She was satisfied. She knew what was in his mind. He would tackle Doctor Henk Deel about his son and this extremely unpalatable young person. The father would bring the boy to heel, put a stop to the relationship, remove his son from here, never to return, maybe even send him abroad out of harm's way. Would she be in time? Michael would be here tomorrow evening but, having been alerted, would his father prevent him from coming? She would have to act quickly.

Mary got up from the table, her second course untouched. 'Oh,' she groaned, holding her napkin to her lips. 'Oh, dear . . .'

Bertram looked up sharply. 'What is it, my dear?'

'I feel . . . so strange . . .' She let her voice die away, closing her eyes and swaying a little. To aid her collapse she let out her breath until there was nothing left in her lungs. Her husband was a doctor; he would see by the very colour of her cheeks if she were feigning illness. The loss of air to her lungs helped her legs to collapse easily under her, her cheeks turning pale, her face adopting a strained look, mouth open, eyes closing.

He was up from the table in a second, amazingly fast for a portly man, bending over her, loosening the buttons of the tight collar of the black gown she wore.

She felt her hand taken, her pulse being felt for. He'd know instantly that there was nothing wrong with her. She must not overdo it. She gave a little twitching movement, pulling her hand from his and opening her eyes.

'I feel so sick,' she stammered as if surprised by it. Seeming to come round, she made an effort to sit up. Now he was merely the concerned husband, kneeling beside her and helping her to sit, supporting her back. 'I've been off my food all day,' she sighed. 'I'm not sure I shall be sick,' she went on weakly, 'but I just feel . . . not well.'

'We must get you to bed,' he said firmly and signalled to Chambers, who had been hovering helplessly by. 'Help me get your mistress to her feet. Can you stand, my dear?'

As Mary gave an uncertain nod, a feeble, trembling hand going to her forehead, she felt herself gently helped to her feet by the two people.

'Can you walk, my dear?'

Again she nodded. 'I think so,' she sighed. Forcing all breath from her lungs had indeed made her feel giddy. 'I think I need to lie down.'

Allowing herself to be helped up the stairs to her room and laid gently on her bed, she lifted her head to Bertram. 'You won't go out tonight, will you?' she implored faintly. 'I don't want to be on my own.'

'Dora is here.'

At the commotion the girl had hurried from the little ante-room attached to her mistress's room, where she had been having her supper.

'What can I do?' asked the girl in partial panic.

Mary ignored her and held out a beseeching hand to her husband. 'Don't leave me, dear. I'm frightened.' This was true and rang in her voice.

'There's nothing to frighten you. You swooned, that's all. Perhaps you are catching a chill.' He nodded to Chambers. 'You can go now. Thank you for your help.'

Turning back, he said, 'Young Dora can use the telephone in my surgery to contact my club if there is an emergency, which I don't think there will be.' She having seemed to recover, he'd become brusque and impatient.

'She is terrified of that machine,' Mary gasped.

'She can tell Mrs Jenkins . . .'

'No . . .' Mary closed her eyes. 'I feel so odd. Please, my dear, stay here with me. You can – go to your club – any time.' She let her breath fail her again and saw him nod.

'Very well,' he conceded, and turned to the concerned Dora. 'You may go to bed, child. I shall stay here with your mistress.'

It was hard not to smile. She'd won. By the time Michael Deel's father spoke to his son she would already have got to the young lovers.

Eighteen

The moment Michael entered the little attic room where she practised her painting skills, Ellie flew into his arms in the joy of seeing him.

'Where is he?' Michael asked as they parted from a lingering kiss.

'He left to go to his club, just a little while ago. His wife wasn't well yesterday, so he had to stay with her. He's gone this evening instead. I think he wanted to meet someone, because as I passed his surgery door earlier, I heard him say he needed to meet whoever it was urgently this evening at his club. So that's where he's gone. We have the whole evening to ourselves. We don't even have to go out.'

She felt a certain excitement creep over her as she spoke. Usually they would have had to creep out of the house so as to be alone together. This time there was little to prevent a kiss from going further.

After for so long having had to embrace in darkened places there was no fear of anyone coming upon them. By the time Doctor Lowe came home Michael would have gone. Mrs Lowe was at home but wouldn't dream of coming near this room. They were safe here.

For a time they sat quietly together on the two stools the room held. There were long, awkward silences; what small exchange of conversation there was was stilted and Ellie knew instinctively what was going through his mind, as it was going through hers.

It had been wonderful. No words had been spoken, but she needed none. He had been awkward at first, this obviously being his very first time; but instinct had taken over and on the cold, bare floor, with nowhere else to go, they'd become one in love to finally lie silently in each other's arms before returning to the world and its mundane practicalities.

They dressed awkwardly, not looking at each other, neither sure what to say. Maybe there was no need. After a while, able at last to turn back to each other, Michael moved closer and took her in his arms, his words low and hesitant. 'Was it all right? I mean was I . . . I mean . . .'

'Of course,' she floundered, then grew slightly annoyed. 'Of course it was all right. We love each other, don't we?'

'I mean, it's the first time, and I didn't want you to think I was taking advantage of you, that I only wanted to be with you for – for that.'

'Of course I don't!' Catching the sharpness of her words, she repeated them more gently, 'Of course I don't. We're in love with each other.'

'It's just that I don't know where we go from here. I want to marry you, but I shall have to tell my father . . .' He hesitated. 'Ellie, I'm scared to tell him about us. I don't know how to put this, but my parents . . .'

He fell quiet, leaving her to wonder what he was trying to say. Before she could ask, he took a deep breath, ran his hand over her hair as if to steel himself for something he was finding difficulty in saying.

'I hope you don't find what I'm trying to say offensive, my sweet, and I don't mean it to be – not for the world. I love you so much, my heart breaks to pieces every time I think of you or say your name or imagine myself with you for ever. But it's . . .' He paused. 'I don't know how to say this.'

'And I don't know what you're trying to say,' she said. A chill began to creep over her. Had he indeed, having at last got what he wanted, felt the need to end it, perhaps even wishing that he hadn't been so carried away?

'What I'm trying to say,' he went on nervously, 'is that my parents have always planned out my life for me – what public school I should go to, what university, and that I would go into my father's practice. And they continue to plan for me to the extent that they hope that one day I'll meet someone whom they consider suitable to be a wife to me. That's how it's done, you see. I am introduced in certain social circles – weekend parties, society balls usually with debutantes from

nice families, suitable young ladies primed for good marriages.
Do you understand what I mean?'

She didn't reply, beginning to stand back from him as disil-
lusion set in. Her mind was in turmoil. She loved him so very
dearly, yet a sense of soured joy had begun to invade her
heart. She thought suddenly of her father. This was her father all
over again: soft words, cajoling her, in an effort to get her to
comply meekly.

Yet this was far more insidious; she had believed she was
being loved, truly, for herself, not used. But she had been
used, every bit as much as her father had used her – to satisfy
his own craving. Suddenly she felt defiled. But she loved him
so, and that was the worst part, her whole being torn to pieces
between an agonizing pull of love and that of disillusionment.
With an effort she held herself together.

'Then you can go, can't you?' she said coldly, moving away
from him. 'Go and obey your darling parents and find someone
– *suitable*, as you call it – to your taste and to theirs. I'm sure
I don't want to stand in your way.'

Her voice was beginning to tremble. 'But thank you for
your kind friendship. I hope I've been of service . . .'

'What the hell are you saying!' he cut in. Before she could
escape he had her in his arms, crushing her to him.

'For God's sake! I love you! I'm not going to lose you, not
for anyone. Ellie, you do love me? You do!'

She could hardly breathe. 'I do, oh, I really do.'

'And I shall tell my parents that I love you and that no one
will ever part us. I don't care what they say.'

He was covering her face with kisses, talking fast between
each kiss. 'We must go away together, darling. I want to marry
you.'

Delight had returned, yet behind it lay horrible practicalities. 'Where would we go?' she asked.

'Far away where no one will find us.'

'What about money? We'll need to live.'

For a moment he said nothing, as if this had never occurred
to him.

'Do you have any money?' she prompted quickly, hating the
subject, but it had to be raised. There was also her long-planned
promise to herself – what of that? He would have no wish to
follow her on that quest with its subsequent conclusion. It had

nothing to do with him. And after this long while she couldn't let it all slip away from her. She wanted revenge. Revenge was all she had ever cared about.

Michael was shaking his head. 'I've hardly any of my own. I've never felt the need to save money. I have only to ask and it's provided.'

Love him though she did, Ellie was not about to tell him that she had saved, and for an entirely different purpose. How could she use the money to keep both her and him after all she'd gone through? What she had wouldn't last them all that long, and having flouted his father's wishes, would he ever find work in his field enough to keep them both? He might regret it and so might she.

'Then what can we do?' she asked lamely.

Discovery of whether he had an answer or not was prevented by a quiet tap on the door. As they exchanged alarmed glances, Michael's lips silently formed the words 'Doctor Lowe'.

In a flurry they sat themselves back on the stools, now well apart, Ellie reaching for a small, half-finished canvas with the pretence of being absorbed in working on it.

'Yes?' she queried loudly and watched mesmerized as the door slowly opened. It wasn't Bertram Lowe's portly figure framed in the doorway but that of his wife.

'May I come in?' she asked.

Before Ellie could reply, Michael spoke for her. 'Of course, Mrs Lowe, do come in.'

'I've never been up here before,' she began. 'This is where you study.'

She was being far too polite, far too nice. Already on her guard, Ellie felt the rancour rise within her. She opened her mouth for a retort but felt Michael's touch on her arm, cautioning her to silence; but Mrs Lowe had seen the gesture and Ellie caught the brief smile on her face, a strange smile.

'What can we do for you, Mrs Lowe?' she asked stiffly, trying to make the woman feel like an intruder; but Mary Lowe's expression didn't alter.

She began to move around the tiny room, looking at this, glancing at that, fingering a piece of canvas, a brush, the palette – untouched, a drying skin of paint on each tiny pile of colour bearing witness to that fact.

'It appears very cosy up here. Even cosier, I dare say, my

husband being out tonight. At his club.' She turned her head towards the pair still sitting where they had been when she'd entered. 'I take it you are aware that your attachment to each other is common knowledge in this house.'

Ellie shrugged.

Michael's eyes hadn't left the woman's face. They now held a challenge.

'I imagine it is,' he said slowly. 'Is this why you've chosen to come up here to see us, Mrs Lowe, now, while Doctor Lowe isn't here? Do you intend doing something about it in his absence?'

Mary Lowe gave a tinkling, almost girlish laugh, at odds with her ample figure. 'It isn't up to me, Mr Deel. I rather think that must be left to my husband. But I feel for you both.'

She glanced at Ellie. 'That may come as a surprise to you, Miss Jay. I am aware of the dissension that exists between us. Nevertheless, I am not a hard person. I have some sympathy for young lovers and the problems they face and I think the problems in your case are particularly difficult.' She began to study her hands. 'And who am I to interfere in what Doctor Lowe thinks? He, on the other hand, does not see the matter in the same light as I.'

Ellie could have told her that, but the woman hadn't finished. 'I'm not sure if you know, Mr Deel, but my husband has, in his mind, adopted Miss Jay. He sees her as a substitute for the daughter we lost and has become very much attached to her – against my wishes, as you can imagine – and he fears losing her to anyone. I say *anyone*, Mr Deel,' she repeated firmly, looking straight at him. 'He does not look kindly on what is going on and is seeking to break it up.'

Giving them no chance to ask how, she hurried on. 'You see, at this very moment he is at his club talking to your father, acquainting him with what has been going on, and I imagine that once your father is made aware, he will put a stop to it.'

'Why are you telling us all this?' Ellie cut in at last.

'I felt it charitable to warn you both. I've no wish to see young people torn apart and made unhappy.'

'I'd have thought you'd be delighted to see me made miserable,' Ellie flashed at her. 'You've always wanted to get rid of me.'

'That is true. I've never liked you.'

'Then why are you helping us now?' asked Michael.

Mary Lowe regarded him directly. 'If you must know, I find no joy in this girl as the apple of my husband's eye. She is the bane of mine, and the sooner she goes, the better. You, young man, struck me as the solution, but now I see only that you will be banished and she will continue living here in my home to my continuing resentment, for I cannot see my husband letting her out of his sight ever again.'

The prospect of being a virtual prisoner in this house could have been terrifying if Ellie had still had it in mind to go her own way before long, with or without Michael. But it was the possibility of losing him that terrified her.

She turned to him in that terror. 'What are we to do then?'

Mary Lowe spoke for him. 'I will help you. I think the two of you should pack your bags immediately and go now, as far away from this place as you possibly can, before my husband returns.'

Michael's eyes lit up at the idea, but though the woman looked to be putting herself out to help the two young people, Ellie saw no point in gushing thanks, for she knew Mary Lowe was doing this for her own ends, nothing more. Still, it was the only course now, and by the start of next year she'd planned to go anyhow. This way she'd have Michael with her to look after her. Once away from this place they'd take up their lives together. Yes.

The moment of excitement faded as she realized what a foolhardy idea it was. Michael had no belongings with him and not all that much money about him. It was all too sudden, neither of them being prepared. She could only stare as Mary Lowe went on with a note of triumph in her tone.

'You must begin packing a few things immediately. Don't delay.' Never had Ellie seen her in such a hurry to get anything done. 'I shall leave you now to make your arrangements,' she continued, 'but do be quick.'

Throwing the two of them a bright smile of encouragement, she swept from the room, no doubt to a pleasant life, with no Ellie Jay to disrupt it.

Ellie gazed at the now closed door. 'Where do we go?' she asked.

When Michael didn't respond, seemingly stunned by the

swiftness of events, she gave an impatient little click of her tongue and moved past him, following in Mrs Lowe's tracks, but to her own room.

Michael had trailed silently after her and now stood watching her gather up a few clothes, together with her bank account book. But she felt she could detect a change in his attitude. She turned to him.

'Is something wrong, darling?'

'I've nothing with me but what I'm wearing,' he said. 'I've hardly any money on me and we don't even know where we're going.'

'I've some,' she said cautiously, '– in my bank book. I've saved up quite a decent bit and we can use some of it to find a place for tonight. Tomorrow we can take our time deciding what to do and where to go.'

'We'll have to pay for lodgings,' he reminded her absently as if still in some sort of daze. 'No banks will be open this time of the evening and a lodging house will want down payment before we are allowed in. And we can't sleep rough, even for one night. I wouldn't let you do that.'

'Well, we can't stay here,' she said sharply, pausing in gathering her clothes together. They lay in a heap over her bed. He was gazing at them.

'What are you going to put all this in?' he queried. 'You've no bag or case of any sort.'

Fraught with sudden mistrust, she turned on him. 'Why are you putting obstacles in the way, Michael? What is it? Have you changed your mind? Isn't it such a good idea now you've had time between that woman leaving us and you thinking about it?'

'No, I haven't changed my mind!' he shot back at her in a way she had never heard him speak before. 'I'm thinking about it – the logic. I think we should stop to consider what we're doing before rushing off willy-nilly.'

'But if Doctor Lowe gets back before we're gone, we're lost!'

For a moment she stared at him, trying to delve into his mind. What she thought she saw there sent a stab of panic through her veins.

'You don't want to do this!' she burst out. In a sudden fit of temper she grabbed up an armful of clothing and threw it to the floor. 'Oh, I know what's the matter orright. You've 'ad your bit of fun at my expense and now you don't 'ave the courage to take things any further.'

She saw him wince. Whether it was what she had said or the way she had pronounced the words, falling back on old verbal habits, she didn't care. She could clearly see the doubt in his eyes. What she'd said was true: he was backing out. It was too much for him, the product of a comfortable, wealthy existence, now asked to rough it on the street, for that's what he probably guessed it amounted to. Men were all the same. Fine when they had it their way – Michael, Doctor Lowe, her brother Charlie, her father – but as soon as it came to the crunch, it was back out quick!

'Then bugger off!' she said crudely without waiting for him to reply. 'I don't want you. Never mind, I was going to leave sooner or later and so it's turned out sooner. And anyway I'll be better on my own.'

'Ellie—'

'No, I don't need someone dragging after me, complaining about how they're missing their comfortable life. Where I'm off to it ain't going to be a bed of roses – not for a long while. But I've got plans that don't include you.'

Beside herself with anger she hardly knew what she was saying. She only knew that she was deeply, bitterly disappointed, as disillusioned as she had always been in her sort of life.

Seconds later she found herself pulled into his arms. 'Darling, please calm down! You must. You don't know what you're saying.'

Out of breath from her outburst, she stood in his arms, silent now, but his assurances didn't soothe her. She merely stood limp and sullen as his voice murmured against her ear.

'We have to be sensible about this. I've got only a few pounds in my wallet. That will take us nowhere. I don't intend you to use your savings for us. I'll get money somehow, but I have to go home if only to face my father. I can't walk away from my family without so much as a goodbye. We're a close, loving family.'

'Close, loving,' she mumbled. 'That's because you've never ever done anything to upset them.'

'I will do all I can to make them understand. My father has

always had my happiness at heart. He wouldn't wish to see me unhappy.'

'When you tell them about us, you'll see how just close and loving they are,' she said with bitter sarcasm.

'I'll make them see how much I love you. I'll make them realize that I could never live without you,' he returned, none of his enthusiasm dimmed by her words. 'When they come round to my way of thinking, we might not need to run away from anything.'

And I'll be rich beyond my wildest dreams, came the thought, but it was an empty one. His father, shocked at his son consorting with a girl from her sort of background, would talk him round to the wisdom of continuing the life he'd always been used to, perhaps even resorting to all sorts of emotional blackmail that would make Michael look about him and think twice about leaving it all behind.

'I shall be back before you know it,' she heard him say. She said nothing and, after a moment's faintly puzzled hesitation, he continued, 'I'll be back here tomorrow evening without fail after I've had a chance to talk to my parents. Doctor Lowe never need know about this evening, and of course Mrs Lowe will say nothing. I'll make sure we have enough money. I wouldn't dream of you financing us. And there'll be no need for you to pack everything – just a few items, as I can buy whatever you need. If you come as you are, no one will suspect anything out of the ordinary. I will be waiting for you at the end of the road, nine o'clock tomorrow evening.'

'What if you're not there?' she couldn't resist asking.

He seemed a little taken aback. 'Of course I will be there. Everything is going to be all right. I love you, Ellie. We'll go far away from here, and we'll be married and be together for the rest of our lives. Nine o'clock, darling, I shall be there, don't worry.'

But she was worried – by an insidious thought that wouldn't go away. He'd be reminded of his folly, persuaded to come to his senses. She'd be left standing at the end of the road for someone who would never come. And would he come here next Monday as usual, apologize for not having turned up, make excuses, new promises; would he say he needed just a little more time to persuade his parents? She didn't think so. His father would never allow him to enter this house again.

Bertram Lowe would say nothing. If she asked, he would tell her that circumstances had changed and he had decided she needed a better tutor. She would be expected to continue her life here as if nothing had happened, he no doubt assuming she had no knowledge of his meeting with Michael's father. Mrs Lowe's plan to be rid of her once and for all hadn't worked. She could very well be in danger of continuing to be saddled with her enemy's presence in the house. That, if anything, was the only consolation Ellie felt, though it was hardly one to make her smile.

No, she would not go and stand at the end of the road tomorrow evening to wait in vain as the hours ticked on. But she would leave. She would pack all she could carry into two large canvas bags she'd seen lying in the corner of the kitchen downstairs. She would wait until nine before creeping out of the house. She might hover for a short while at the appointed place. If no one came, she would walk off, find somewhere to sleep for the night, even if only some dark niche. Life had taught her that the body could accommodate itself to any situation if required to. At this moment it seemed that sleeping away a few hours on a darkened street held no terror for her.

Or perhaps she could go to her old neighbour, Mrs Sharp. She would not see her left out on the street and there'd be a warm place to sleep if only on an old mattress on the floor. Maybe Ronnie Sharp would be there. It had been a long time since she'd seen him or even thought about him.

Ellie chased him firmly from her mind, needing to think clearly. As soon as it was daylight she'd say her farewells and be off – go first to the bank and draw out all her savings: Bertram Lowe mustn't be able to trace her through her drawing it out little by little; then find a room somewhere.

After that the future was hazy, but one thing was certain: she'd have to make her own way in the world, buy a few painting materials. Her room would be her studio; what she painted she would sell to keep herself going. Meanwhile she would search for her father. He still had to be somewhere in London. She couldn't imagine him ever wanting to go elsewhere. London was his home. His haunts had always been here, his women local; who else would have him? There still lingered that moment when she had been sure he was there right behind her at the opening-of-Parliament procession.

It might take years – her whole life even – to trace him, but she would eventually. That she promised herself.

As Michael took her in his arms to enforce his promises, she realized that all these thoughts had taken only seconds. Swept back into the present she found herself wanting with all her heart to have him waiting there for her tomorrow evening, that single thought brushing away all others.

'Don't worry, my sweet,' he was saying. 'Everything will be all right.'

He said it with such conviction that she believed him implicitly as he kissed her with such passion that it made her head spin.

It was only in bed that night that darker visions came to plague her, playing tug-of-war with the fervent wish to see him waiting there tomorrow evening, ready to whisk her away to a new life.

Nineteen

This morning Bertram was being exceptionally nice to her, even more doting than usual. Ellie wasn't fooled. The pricking of bad conscience – that's what it was. His chat to Michael's father as to what was going on having apparently ruined their chances of finding love, maybe he now felt sorry for her.

Ellie smiled grimly. He didn't know that he'd be the one destroyed when he found her gone a few hours from now. She just prayed it would be with Michael. But her harder self knew it was wishful thinking, and it took all her reserves to hide the deep ache in her heart and pretend to be beguiled by Bertram's fatherly tones as she prayed Michael would be waiting for her.

He thought he was fooling her, but it was he who was being led on as she let him put an affectionate arm about her shoulders, his words probing. 'You are comfortable here with us, aren't you, my dear?'

Such a question! Ellie gave him a beaming smile. 'Of course.'

'I have done everything in my power to make you happy. If you are not, you would tell me, wouldn't you?'

'Of course,' she repeated. Fat fool, came an inner voice. Doting idiot, thinking he could replace his lost daughter with her. She felt no sorrow or regret for the further loss he would very soon suffer.

'Having a tutor as well,' she pandered. 'I really do enjoy those three days each week.' She couldn't resist dropping that in, but he evaded that.

'My wife and I will be entertaining this evening,' he said, gazing about her little studio, as he liked to call it, taking in the several finished studies. 'Saturday, you'll be alone, I'm afraid.' He breathed in the smell of linseed oil and varnish. 'But you are at home up here with your paints, aren't you?'

'Yes, of course,' she obliged yet again, eager to be rid of him now.

'Maybe a little lonely for you, but we'll see if we can remedy that. Well, perhaps tomorrow, if the weather proves clement enough, you and I can take a little jaunt somewhere interesting, perhaps after church?'

Was this supposed to be a consolation? And where would they go on a Sunday with most places of interest closed? Surely not a country trip in the chill of November! But she obliged him with a nod, only too glad to see the back of him, and in return received a tender, fatherly kiss on her brow.

After his morning surgery he would return, play the kind guardian again, call her 'my dear', praise her for her artistic talent, put an arm about her shoulder. Would he then carefully work around to how much more she could learn with a better tutor than Michael Deel? He'd no doubt enlarge on it, explain that Mr Deel's circumstances at home were beginning to make it awkward for him to come again but that it wouldn't take long to find another teacher, a far better one. She would be expected to smile and agree with him. She wasn't looking forward to the pretence at all.

The day spun itself out in a prolonged procession of endless hours. As she'd anticipated, Bertram came later on in the afternoon to act out his lies, she in turn lying, first with a show of surprise, then with questions to which his replies were no doubt well rehearsed, finally accepted by her with feigned resignation. It went just as she'd anticipated and he left reasonably comforted to prepare for his dinner guests.

About six, while Mrs Lowe was downstairs talking to Cook concerning the dinner arrangements, Ellie went to find Dora.

'I mustn't be long,' she said urgently. 'I've something to tell you.'

Standing in the little ante-room where Dora slept, she hurriedly told her what she was about to do. 'Whether Michael is there waiting for me or not, I'm off. I want to know: will you come with me?'

There was an astonished look on Dora's young face. The girl was now thirteen and a half – old enough to know her own mind; but that mind could be seen in her expression as she shook her head. She was scared.

'I don't know, Ellie. I've come to like it here. It's nice and comfortable and I don't have to worry about where I'll be tomorrow. I've learned how to speak nicely and be a lady. Mrs Lowe is kind to me. We're friends. I mean it, Ellie: we *are* friends. She looks on me as a friend.'

'Companion,' Ellie corrected her sharply, irked by her sister's stupidity. Any moment Mrs Lowe might come back before she could persuade her sister to run off with her.

'You're a paid companion. You can't call that being friends. And with a woman nearly three times older than you? You should have friends your own age. And there's me, saddled with a fat old man who wants to look on me as his child. Come with me. We'll go together, get out of this unnatural relationship that's going on here and find plenty of friends our own age.'

Still Dora shook her head. The delay was mounting. 'I can't just go without you, Dora. And I can't leave you here.'

She knew that this was just an excuse, hiding a sudden fear of the unknown that was assailing her. She needed company. Without it she'd be cast adrift on a sea she had become unused to by soft living.

Suddenly she was frightened. Could she really walk off alone into the wide world? With Michael, it would be no obstacle. Without him . . .

'Dora! You have to come with me! We've never been parted.'

There was a stubborn look on the girl's face. 'I want to stay here.'

'We might never see each other again.'

'You're not running away from prison. You can still come back and visit.'

'Once I'm gone, I'll never come back.'

'Not even to see me?' Moisture began to glisten in her young sister's eyes. The sight made her feel close to tears. Angrily she sniffed them back.

'Then stay here!' she shot at her, the words catching in her throat. 'See if I care!'

Mrs Lowe was coming – the tell-tale quick tread of short footsteps beneath a fleshy body, not plodding, like Bertram Lowe, for despite her weight Mary Lowe was light on her feet, as many chubby people are.

'Dora, I'm asking you one last time,' Ellie pleaded. 'Let's leave here now, together, you and me?'

Still Dora shook her head, her face creasing, tears now slipping down her cheeks. 'Stay here, Ellie,' she begged. 'With me. Please?'

'No, I can't!'

'I won't know what to do without you. I shall miss you so.'

'I can't help that.'

The door to the room opened. 'What do you think you are doing here?' came the high-voiced demand. Ellie spun round on the woman.

'Do you mind? I came to talk to my sister!'

The woman gasped, looking lost for words, as Ellie swept past her, only just managing to stop herself from saying, 'Goodbye, Dora,' over her shoulder and giving her intentions away.

It was dark as she let herself out through the kitchen and through the back gate to the alley, in a warm coat and with a veil keeping her straw boater in place.

Florrie was upstairs attending to her employers and their dinner guests. Mrs Jenkins was in the little cellar no doubt seeking out some special cheeses to go with the wines chosen for later. Only Rose had been there in the kitchen, bent over the sink washing up the used pots and pans.

The girl had looked up as Ellie passed. 'What's all that?' she'd queried, seeing the two big bags Ellie carried.

'Old clothes,' Ellie had told her. 'Doctor Lowe wants me to give them to someone who needs them. Be back in about half an hour, so no need to tell Cook. She'll be too busy seeing to them upstairs to listen to you going on.'

Now she struggled along the road, the bags swinging against her skirt. At the corner of Cambridge Road she put them down and waited. There was no clock nearby to show her the passing of time. If Michael had suggested she wait by the pub on the corner of Bethnal Green Road, there'd have been a clock there. But perhaps he thought walking that far on a dark November night might be a little risky for an unaccompanied female.

The cold began to creep through her coat as she waited. Leaving her belongings on the pavement, she started pacing to keep warm, up and down, a few yards this way, a few yards that, counting each turn. After forty turns her heart had really begun to sink. He wasn't coming.

Finally she stopped counting. What was the point? She should have known from the moment she arrived that he wouldn't be coming. Well, if the truth were told, she had known deep down inside her. Stupid fool to imagine he would. His creature comforts mattered more. Like all men: spineless!

Racked between anger and despair she continued pacing. Give it a little while longer, then she would go. But she didn't want to go. What if she missed him by a few minutes? She'd never forgive herself. Her mind's eye saw him now, waiting, disappointed; what would he do? Go to where she lived, or had lived, to see if she was there. No one had seen her go except Rose. What would she say? Where would he know to look? And she could hardly go looking for him. But if he'd wanted to be, he would have been here by now – would probably have already been here waiting for her, if he'd loved her strongly enough.

Saturday evening, Cambridge Road busy with traffic, the whole world looking for a pleasurable night out. Couples dressed to go somewhere threw glances at her as they passed. She felt conspicuous. Making up her mind, Ellie stooped and grabbed up her bags. But where to go? Her old neighbour, Mrs Sharp, came to mind again. She would go there – see what happened. Yes, that would be her best bet. Her heart like a sodden lump of clay, she turned her face in the direction of Bethnal Green Road, the place she had once known so well.

She was moving off when a cab rumbled to a stop by the kerb with the driver pulling energetically on the reins. A man leaped out and came towards her. ''Scuse me, your name Miss Jay?'

'Yes.'

'I've a note for you from Mr Michael Deel. He asked me to give it you.'

Dropping her bags she took the note from him, but before she could say anything he was back in the cab without asking if there was any reply, the vehicle moving out into the mêlée of other cabs and carriages.

Tears had already begun to well over. There was little need to read. She knew already what it contained; yet she had to open it, just in case.

> Darling, I'm so sorry I can't be there. Hope you haven't
> been waiting too long. There's been trouble at home. I

don't know how I managed to get this note to you, my
father is so beside himself. I don't care, I want to be with
you, but I can't, not tonight. He says I need not tutor you
any more, Doctor Lowe will be making arrangements for
another tutor to come. I want so much to be with you
but hopefully you understand how things are at the
moment . . .

Understand? Oh, yes, she understood, only too well.
Screwing the note into a ball she tossed it away from her,
seeing it land, a pale thing in the gutter. The last words he'd
written were: 'I love you, my darling, above all else. I'll sort
things out and come to you as soon as I can. Until then, I
love you, love you, love you, my own darling.'

Resolutely Ellie turned her back on the note slowly unfurling
among the other rubbish that lay there, and, picking up her
bags, she walked away.

'Ellie! Where'd you spring from?'

Mrs Sharp stood in the doorway, her gaunt figure in its
grubby apron faintly silhouetted by the feeble kitchen gaslight
that just about penetrated to the door. 'What you doing 'ere
this time of night?'

Ellie's tears had dried as she struggled the distance to
Bethnal Green Road and Gales Gardens. Now they threatened
to overwhelm her again. She bit them back hastily. There
would be a lot of explaining to do.

'Whatever you got there?' Mrs Sharp burst out, seeing the
two heavy bags she had with her. 'What's 'appened? You
orright, love?'

'No I'm not.' It was all she could say without bursting into
tears.

Seeing her distress, Mrs Sharp was all concern. 'You'd best
come inside, luv, tell us what's up.'

Sitting on a stool, a steaming mug of tea between the palms
of her hands, Ellie felt she could hardly tell her that she had
been left standing in the cold by the very man who had sworn
love for her and to take her away with him.

Instead she hastily prevaricated. 'I had to leave the place
where I've been working. I couldn't stand it any more.'

'Were they cruel to yer then?'

'No. It was just that I felt trapped. I left on a whim and now I can't go back. I don't really know where to go.'

'At this time of night, I should think so. Whatever possessed yer ter go walkin' out this time of night? And a Saturday too, wiv drunks an' all sort of odd people about.'

'Just things happening,' Ellie said evasively. 'I don't want to go into it more than that.'

'Oh, luv!' sighed Mrs Sharp. Her refusal to go into more detail had obviously got the woman thinking all sorts of things, but Ellie couldn't be bothered to set her mind at rest about what she was apparently imagining.

'If that's the case, love, you'd best stay 'ere tonight. Don't 'ave any bed ter put yer in, though.'

'Anywhere will do.' Ellie sipped her tea. It was strong enough to take the skin off her palate and not all that sweet, with only a small spoonful of condensed milk mixed into it, but it helped warm her. 'I don't mind even sleeping on the floor.'

'Good Lawd, no! There's the couch, such as it is. It's soft anyway.'

Fortunately the Sharp family went to bed early, Mr Sharp, if he was home, not having been bothered to get out of his when she'd called.

With the house fallen quiet by ten o'clock, Ellie lay awake on the sagging couch that her host had termed soft but was actually lumpy, with springs breaking through the stuffing.

The house had a peculiar smell to it, one she had almost forgotten – of stale cooking and clothes in need of washing. She thought of the clean smells of the Lowes' house, of furniture and floor polish and good fresh air.

Ellie wriggled to find a more comfortable place on the couch and thought of the soft bed in that lovely quiet room Bertram had given her – his own daughter's room. Part of her yearned to be back there, until she thought of her father, the old hatred rising up afresh in her. She knew she'd sacrifice it all just to find him. If only Michael were with her.

There was no sleep in her. Not only was her mind filled with the way Michael had let her down; her hope of seeing Ronnie Sharp, of pouring out her heart to him, had also been thwarted.

'Is Ronnie about?' she had asked as she ate the cheese sand-wich Mrs Sharp had offered her, the slices like doorsteps, the cheese – just parings – helped for taste by a generous dollop of yellow pickle.

'Ronnie?' had come the response. 'Oh, he's out, as usual. He won't disturb yer coming 'ome. He'll come through the back door into the kitchen when he does come. Yer know what it's like when people are courtin'.'

'Courting?'

'Didn't yer know? Been engaged since July. Nice gel she is. I expect they'll get married about eighteen months' time, soon as they've saved up enough for a place ter live. Probably round 'ere, I expect.'

Engaged! At the back of her mind, despite this terrible sense of despair over Michael, there'd been the faint hope that Ronnie Sharp might be there to show a little sympathy, even understanding, when told of what she'd been through. Not that she expected to fall into his open arms. After all, they'd never been remotely serious. Now, of course, his mind would be otherwise occupied, with no cause to concern himself with her. Anyway, if he'd been free, he'd never have taken the place of Michael . . .

Quickly she turned from that thought before it began to dominate her mind and prevent her sleeping. Burying her face in the cushion that served for a pillow, she closed her eyes tightly in an effort to think of something else, trying to conjure up some neutral vision of blue sky and green grass and trees – anything so as not to think of him, of how she'd been let down so abruptly without any heartfelt regret, it seemed, despite the words of love he'd written for someone else to deliver.

The scenes she tried to envisage behind her tightly closed eyelids were not working. Instead her brain began to play on how Bertram Lowe would react when he found her gone. That at least helped push away the thoughts that threatened to break her heart each time Michael's name stole into her head.

Twenty

B ertram closed the door on his guests, having seen them safely into their coach. Doctor and Mrs Sedley were old friends. He and Howard Sedley had been at medical college together and had something else in common. Both had married into moderately good families. Both looked with envy upon others whom they felt had done even better than they. Both had wives who tended to feel awkward in other people's company, and thus got on well together.

It had been a good evening, as always with the Sedleys, and for a while had swept away his present worries. Young Chambers had conducted herself admirably, waiting at table, and he intended to tell her so. It would make the girl feel well pleased with herself.

He slowly mounted the stairs to his room. Mary had gone up before him. In the hall, the long-case clock sombrely struck ten thirty. Mrs Jenkins was still bustling about down there. Once the house settled down she would turn down all the gaslights and retire to her own bed.

Reaching Ellie's door, he paused, then tapped on it with the knuckle of his forefinger – very lightly so as not to alert Mary. It occurred to him that Ellie might be in need of company for just a short while before settling down to sleep, having been on her own the whole evening. Very often they enjoyed a little chat during the evening, usually earlier than this, except of course when he and Mary were entertaining friends or out being entertained by them. Then, as tonight, he would tap on her door and enquire how she was. She would come to the door and allow him in. He would recline for a while in her little silk armchair while she sat on her bed. They'd talk until she yawned, he taking the hint that it was time to leave.

This time there was no answer to his knock. Softly he called her name. Maybe she was already asleep. It was rather late. The last thing he would have dreamed of doing would be to walk in unbidden. Would she still be in her studio at this time of night? Mounting the stairs to the attic, he stole past the maids' room to tap on the studio door. Getting no reply, he opened it and peeped in, feeling at liberty to do so, it not being a place where she slept.

Finding the room dark and vacant, he retraced his steps to her room. There was still no response to a fractionally firmer rap. Standing undecided, he gathered she must be asleep. Yet something didn't feel right – maybe it was the quality of the silence from the room, maybe just a feeling, a premonition; he wasn't certain, but there came an urge to speak to her.

'Ellie, my dear, are you asleep?'

A foolish question: if she were asleep, would he expect an answer? But if she were asleep, she wouldn't be aware of him if he crept into the room just to make sure. Biting his lips, he did just that, opening the door cautiously to peep round it. The curtains were drawn but the gas jet on the wall had been turned down to a spluttering glimmer behind its glass shade, just enough to see by. Ellie liked to sleep with some light in the room.

Bertram peered towards the bed. Suddenly he knew why he'd had that strange feeling about there being no answer to his knock: the bed was empty. For a second, alarm spread through him. Had Michael Deel come to the house and she'd stolen out to meet him? It was the only possible answer. But it was late. Surely they wouldn't still be out.

With a sense of panic Bertram hurried to the landing window. If they were outside, he'd see them. When she came in he'd demand to know what she thought she was up to. But there was no one there. It was nearly eleven.

Panic began to grow. They had got wind of his meeting with Michael's father and run away together. But who would have told them? Who could? A name hit him: Mary! But of course! She had always wanted to see the back of young Ellie. How could she have done this to him, knowing how he felt about the child?

Fury consumed him. This was absolutely the last straw with his wife. But before he tackled her, he would telephone Doctor Deel, though what he was going to say at this time of night he had no real idea.

The clipped tone of Henk Deel had no sleepiness in it. Bertram felt almost a childish relief. 'Bertram Lowe here,' he began tentatively. 'So sorry to trouble you this time of night, but would your son Michael be at home?'

There was a short silence on the other end of the wire, then the man's voice, a little surprised: 'Yes, he is; do you wish to speak with him?'

'No, not really.' Flustered, Bertram forced his brain to work fast. 'I merely wanted to confirm that he will not be tutoring Miss Jay from now on.'

'That is correct. But we spoke of this when we met.'

'Yes, we did. Of course we did. I forgot. But has your son posed any objections?'

Another small silence, then: 'I have spoken to him at length. I have explained the situation to him as it stands and he under-stands – that, and also where his duties lie. And now I think that is all we need to say on the matter, Doctor Lowe. It is closed.'

This last was said unusually tersely, a sharp reminder of the awkward meeting that had taken place.

'I'm – I'm sorry to have bothered you at so late an hour,' Bertram stammered. Muttering, 'Thank you,' he replaced the earpiece on its hook.

Glad to have done with the telephone call, his relief at having found Michael Deel at home was immediately clouded by anxiety. If not with Michael Deel, then where was Ellie?

With all sorts of awful thoughts going through his head, he puffed his way upstairs to Mary's bedroom and thumped on her door. He saw that she was still in her wrap, her hair loose where young Dora had been combing it for her, no doubt the one hundred strokes that took up a good deal of time – the poor child must be weary. But this wasn't the time to think of that.

'Ellie has gone!' he burst out. 'What have you said to her?'

Mary's expression was one of surprise but also a picture of innocence. 'Why should I have said anything to her? I have nothing to say to her, nor, if God is willing, ever will.'

He ignored that. 'Has Dora seen her?'

'When?'

'While we were at dinner. Has she seen her sister this evening?'

From the room Dora shook her head. 'No. I spent most of the evening chatting to Rose.'

Mary swung round on her. 'You know you are not supposed to chat to the lower—'

'It doesn't matter about that!' Bertram cut in. 'Ellie is not in her room or in her studio. I shall need to speak to the staff. Now.'

'It's late; everyone has gone to bed.'

'Even so . . .'

He turned abruptly and, going upstairs, thumped on the girls' door. As Rose came to it, sleepy-eyed, he leapt in: 'Have you spoken to Ellie Jay this evening?'

The girl shook her head; a sleepy voice called, 'What is it?' and Chambers came to peer over Rose's shoulder.

'Have you spoken with young Ellie Jay this evening?' he demanded, paying no more interest in the kitchen maid. Although most of Chambers' time had been taken up serving at table, after dinner had been cleared away she would have gone down into the kitchen while he and his guests had relaxed for the remainder of the evening.

'No, Doctor Lowe,' came the reply. 'I've not seen her at all.'

'Then Mrs Jenkins?' But before he could turn away, Rose spoke up in her slow voice.

'Sir, I did see Miss Jay, only for a moment. Cook had gone off to her parlour, leaving me to wash up the last of the pots and pans. Nine o'clock I think it was, or maybe half past nine – I'm not sure. She went out the back carrying two bags full of stuff. Heavy, they looked. She said they was old clothes what you said to give to the poor. I didn't take much notice of it, sir. I didn't see her come back. I was only too glad to go on up to me own bed. I said goodnight to Cook and I asked if there was anything else to do before I went up, and she said no, so I went. I didn't think to tell her about seeing Miss Jay.'

His mind now in complete confusion as he listened, one thought was that she had gone outside quite innocently and been seized by someone – a slip of a girl, gullible, pretty, alluring enough to give thoughts to a passing rogue. Minutes later that fear had been swept away: she'd been carrying two heavy bags, had told Rose a lie. Why would she run off, unless it was to meet Michael Deel? But he hadn't turned up. Why then had she not sneaked back here? Where else on earth could she go?

There was one place. 'Very well,' he said brusquely, trying not to look too eager. 'You can go back to bed.'

He didn't think it likely she would have gone to Michael Deel's home. She wouldn't have belittled herself; she was made of sterner stuff than that. But she might have gone back to her old haunt. That neighbour of hers – he couldn't recall the name, but if the family still lived there, would she not have gone to seek shelter? All the while his mind kept asking the same question: why had she not come back here if she had been let down by the man she had hoped to elope with, and if she hadn't, what had possessed her to leave? She'd been happy here. He'd done everything in his power to make her so. He loved her like a daughter, had given her everything – all she wanted: comfort, good food, people to care for her. Why then had she left?

All this filled his thoughts as he made his way towards where Ellie had once lived. He walked briskly, seeing not one unoccupied cab, and it wasn't so far to Bethnal Green Road; he was soon turning into the alley-like place grandly named Gales Gardens, with its soot-begrimed house walls and shabby doors that opened directly from living rooms on to the narrow, uneven pavement.

The number of the house he wanted eluded him for a moment, but the recollection of his visit to the house where she'd once lived brought him to a stop at the correct one. But on which side of it did the family reside? Gone eleven o'clock, none of this unbroken row of houses had lights showing in the windows. But he had to find out if Ellie had come here.

Choosing the street door, he rapped with his knuckles, there being no knocker. He waited as the minutes ticked by, growing sure that this must be the wrong house. What a fool he was. Then suddenly he recalled the name: Sharp – that was it.

Ellie was still lying awake when the knock came. She started up.

Mrs Sharp had said Ronnie would come in the back way, and anyway, he'd have a key. But someone knocking so late: she instinctively guessed the person.

A second rap on the door had her up from the couch and

tiptoeing through to the back room where the stairs led up to the two bedrooms.

'Mrs Sharp! Someone's at the front door,' she called up in a hoarse whisper. 'Mrs Sharp!'

'Who is it?' came the stupid, sleepy question.

'I can't answer it. It's not my house. You'll have to come down.' As the woman, sighing and grumbling at the hour, came down clad in a well-creased, off-white, flannelette night-gown, her greying hair hanging loose, Ellie caught her arm. 'If it's someone asking after me, please don't tell them I'm here.'

'Who'd be asking after you?' came the retort. 'I'll kill 'em, whoever they are, knocking at this blooming hour.'

'Then don't anwer it. It could be anybody.'

'I can't 'ave people banging on me door this time of night, waking all me neighbours up.'

'Then ask who it is first.'

Mrs Sharp went to stand behind the door. 'What d'yer want?' she queried, short of temper at the intrusion on her sleep.

'Are you Mrs Sharp?' came the reply.

'It's Ronnie!' Her eyes turned in panic towards Ellie. 'Somethink's 'appened to him. It's the police come ter tell me!'

But Ellie had recognized Doctor Lowe's high tone. 'It's my employer,' she hissed.

Mrs Sharp glanced at her. Ellie was shaking her head, one hand motioning negatively. To her relief, Mrs Sharp nodded reassurance and turned back to the door. 'What d'yer want?'

'I want to know if Miss Jay is there with you.'

'You mean the girl what used ter live next door? No, she ain't 'ere. Sorry. Ain't seen nothink of 'er. Who are yer?'

'It doesn't matter,' came the lowered reply. 'I apologize for having bothered you.'

'I should think so – strangers waking us up this time of night!'

'I do beg your pardon.'

'What's yer name anyway?'

Ellie's hand was waving frantically: no, please let him go.

'It's of no consequence,' came the voice, followed by silence as the owner walked away.

'He's gorn,' Mrs Sharp said unnecessarily.

Ellie looked at her as she moved past to go back to bed. 'Thank you for not betraying me. I feel so guilty coming here disturbing everyone. I shall be gone as soon as it's daylight.'

'You'll 'ave a bit of breakfast with us 'fore yer go.' The woman eyed her. 'One thing yer got from that employer of yours: nice, polite manners; and yer've learnt ter speak nice too. Beats me why yer want ter leave there. Unless yer've got somewhere much nicer to go.'

'I have,' Ellie lied. There was no point telling her that she had no idea where to go. She would find somewhere. She'd have enough money come Monday and in her bags were some small paintings. She already knew what she'd do: sell them if she could and, on the strength of that, plan her life.

She didn't hear Ronnie come in. She only awoke as someone came down the stairs, the battered little clock on the mantelshelf showing it to be nine fifteen. She had never slept so long, not even on a Sunday morning.

Leaping off the couch, embarrassed to be seen still lying there, though she had slept more or less fully dressed, Ellie pushed stockinged feet into her boots, frantically trying to do up the buttons along the outside of them.

She was sitting on the edge of the couch, the cover neatly folded and the cushion in an upright position, when Ronnie strode into the room one hand holding a steaming mug of tea from which he was sipping, the other hand holding out a similar mug to her.

'Mum told me you was 'ere,' he said as she gratefully took the tea, the brew as strong as ever. His voice, when it had broken, had been a deep one. Now it sounded deeper than ever, sending a little thrill through her. But it was all too late, Ronnie now courting and Michael still sitting painfully in her heart.

She'd tried not to think about what she and Michael had done. Why had she let it happen? But she'd been so sure of him – that they would run off together, be married; that their unforeseen moment of passion would be one of many moments. Hours later he had let her down.

She would never forgive him for that. She had even had a premonition after what they had done, but had brushed it away, foolishly believing every word he'd said.

'I never knew you was 'ere till this morning,' Ronnie went

on, his broad smile coming sudden and charming. 'Good job I didn't walk in on you in the middle of the night. We'd of both got a shock.'

Ellie didn't make such a good job of her answering smile, was even relieved to have Mrs Sharp come into the room.

'I've made you a bit of breakfast,' she said. 'No one else is up yet. Ronnie's sister's only too glad to get a lie-in, going ter work so early the rest of the week, and the other two kids just 'ate school, so they make the most of Sundays too. The ol' man, of course, don't hardly ever get up most days of the week. It's only Ronnie what's always up with the lark. Anyway, you said you wanted ter be off early so I made yer some breakfast – a bit of bacon and toast, orright?'

'I don't want to take your food, Mrs Sharp,' Ellie burst out, following her out to the kitchen, where the appetizing smell of bacon met her.

'Oh, we don't do so bad,' laughed Mrs Sharp. She nodded towards Ronnie following behind. 'That one brings in a nice little wage these days, a training reporter now. And my gel don't do so bad in factory work. They make up for what the old man don't bring in, lazy old bugger! No, we can afford a bit of bacon for a guest.'

She bustled about while the two young people sat at the cloth-covered kitchen table. 'Though when Ronnie gets married, I shall miss his money; but then I don't 'ave ter feed him or wash 'is stuff, do I?'

Teapot in hand she paused to look at Ellie. 'So where're yer going to stay on a Sunday? Friends, is it? Got a young man, have yer?'

As Ellie looked blankly at her, she seemed to deduce that her reply to all of it would be negative. She gave a sigh and, concentrating on topping up her son's half-drunk mug of tea, said, 'Then 'ave yer got any money?'

This time Ellie could answer. 'Not today I haven't. It's all in my bank account. I'll have to wait until they open tomorrow morning.'

Mrs Sharp gazed at her. 'Bank account, eh? Huh! But yer ain't got 'ardly a penny in ready cash ter bless yer name with now, 'ave yer?'

Ellie shrugged. 'So what yer goin' ter do till Monday?' she was asked.

'I don't know.' She had picked up a few pence she had about her when she'd left the Lowes', but that wouldn't go far. She hadn't really thought, had she?

'Then yer best stay 'ere another night till this bank of yours opens. 'Ope yer don't mind the couch again.'

'I don't want to be any trouble.'

'No trouble.' Mrs Sharp plonked another slice of fried bacon on Ellie's plate and turned to her son with a piece hanging off the fork she held. 'D'you want a bit more?'

'No, I'm full.' He grinned at Ellie. 'I don't eat a terrible lot. In my job, all the racing about I do, sometimes I don't get time to eat at all.'

Ellie smiled briefly back at him and turned her eyes to his mother. 'I will pay you back for the food.'

'Blimey! Don't come over all high'n'mighty, love. It's Sunday. We've got a shoulder of lamb. Surely one more mouth ain't goin' ter make a dent in that. And there's shrimps and winkles fer tea and a cake I made yesterday. I don't suppose what you eat would fill a fly, there's 'ardly any flesh on you at all. Like yer mother you are – thin an' wiry she was, bless 'er soul.'

That reminded Ellie. 'Have you heard anything of my father? Do you happen to know where he might be?'

Mrs Sharp pursed her lips and shook her head. 'Not seen 'air nor 'ide of him since yer mother went. I see Charlie about sometimes. He's living in Corfield Street, I think. Seems to 'ave got himself a proper gel. I often see 'em up the Bethnal Green Road of an evening when I'm there buying a few bits and pieces orf the stalls. Have you seen 'im lately then?'

Ellie shook her head. 'About my father: I do need to get in touch with him, but I don't know where he is.'

'Perhaps I can 'elp there,' Ronnie put in. 'You know, connected with the press an' all that, I might be able to pull a few strings, see 'ow we go.'

'Would you?' Ellie felt a rush of gratitude.

'Of course, I can't promise nothing. But I'll 'ave a try.'

She watched him get up from the table, downing the rest of the strong tea. 'Me an' Alice is off ter see one of 'er friends this morning. We'll be back fer dinner, then we're out again, so we won't be 'aving tea. See yer later then,' he said with a broad smile at Ellie.

It was a long morning. Ellie helped Mrs Sharp wash up the breakfast things, her husband coming down to his breakfast requiring more bacon to be fried, and then wandering off to wherever he was bent on a Sunday morning. A little later Ronnie's fifteen-year-old sister appeared, requiring more bacon and toast to be got. Once a friend to Ellie, she now seemed awkward, her smile shy, as if not knowing how to treat her, and she was soon off out. Last to come down were the two youngest, required to make do before disappearing out to play in the street.

Mrs Sharp went up to make the beds, leaving Ellie to amuse herself reading some of the several-days-old newspapers lying around. The place was a mess, but she could hardly start tidying up in case her host thought she was hinting.

Dinner found the family squashed around the big table with a need to make a place for her and Ronnie's fiancée. The afternoon was spent listening to Mrs Sharp's account of her life since Ellie had left. Tea was a little less crowded with Ronnie and his girl not there – though Ellie was put on her guard as Mr Sharp came sufficiently to life to ask what she saw as awkward questions about what she'd been up to since leaving Gales Gardens.

The evening dragged, Mr Sharp having run out of steam by then. Mrs Sharp, too, seemed to have run out of words, engrossed in darning socks or stitching away at seams that had come apart on anything from shirts and nightgowns to skirts and underclothing, all by the light of a large, ornate oil lamp she'd said earlier had been her mother's.

The two youngest children went off to bed at seven, protesting until their father gave an angry shout, making Ellie jump and them scurry upstairs. It was the only time he'd opened his mouth; otherwise his head was buried in a newspaper as he puffed away at a foul-smelling pipe. Finally he put the paper over his face and dozed off, filling the room with stentorian snores.

Ronnie's sister hardly looked up from reading her penny dreadful, and didn't speak at all. Knowing how they'd been only a year ago, Ellie was made ill at ease, the girl wary and distant. Perhaps it was the way she now spoke. She knew she had changed. Her life had moved on. It didn't seem possible that they had once all played together in the street.

She was glad when it was time for bed, delayed by having to wait until everyone retired before she could. As before, she slept with her clothes on, unable to wait for morning, when she could be off. She felt in need of a good wash. Her only wash the whole time she'd been here was to sluice her face at the scullery sink where everyone's ablutions were carried out. No bath, of course; the outside WC in the yard was a cobwebby place with a stained toilet from which she'd had to hurriedly avert her eyes the first time of using it, not caring to see the permanent stains of nature. Mum had been so clean.

Lying on the couch trying to sleep, Ellie listened to the sounds outside and inside the house: Mr Sharp's snores, seeming to shake the place; from the scullery the drip of a water tap into the battered, galvanized basin in the sink; the wavering yowl of cats, then a muffled shout; somewhere a dog barking.

Ellie turned her mind inwards, trying to seek sleep.

One thing she'd need to do would be to keep in touch with Ronnie's mother, for who knew? – he might come up with the whereabouts of her father and her quest would be over. But again came the question: when she was able to trace him, what precisely was she going to do?

One thing was certain: she had no intention of seeing him get away lightly with what he'd done to her and Mum.

Twenty-One

It seemed to Ellie that she'd been living on her own for ever. So far it had not yet been a week. It felt so much longer. She had never truly known loneliness before, not real loneliness. When Mum had died she'd felt alone, cast adrift, but Dora had been there, and her neighbours, and there had been the hope of Charlie coming back, perhaps even her father, and two days later she had been taken in by Doctor Lowe. But this – this was isolation completely and utterly.

She sat on the hard, broken-backed chair in this attic room in a back street not far from Euston Station. It had come to her that she should be where other artists were and she had been told it was mostly around Camden Town these days. But she knew no one. Sitting here gazing at paint dabs on the walls and floor, she'd been told by the landlord that the room had previously been rented to an artist; but, unable to pay his rent, he'd been required to leave.

'I hope *you* can pay,' came the low warning when she'd handed over a week's advance payment. 'I like my rent regular, in advance and on time.'

Ellie had nodded with a show of confidence and prayed, knowing she hardly had money left from what Ronnie had given her even to buy food for the next few days or coal for warmth, let alone pay a regular rent.

With the few sticks of smouldering firewood in the tiny grate scarcely sending out enough heat to combat the November cold creeping in through the ill-fitting window and skylight, Ellie shivered under the blanket draped around her shoulders. They let in plenty of daylight, which had probably suited the previous tenant, but plenty of draughts too. December a few days off, she couldn't remember ever feeling so cold. Still, with no means of paying the following week's rent she might be out of the place hardly having settled in.

Something she hadn't anticipated: having gone to the bank on the Monday morning after saying goodbye to Mrs Sharp, she had found that she would have to have Doctor Lowe's permission before she could draw out a single penny.

Alone in the room, Ellie offered up silent thanks to Ronnie for the half-crown he'd stealthily slipped into her hand as she'd left that Monday morning. Two shillings and sixpence was a lot of money. As soon as she'd felt the coin, she'd protested that soon she would have plenty of money; but he'd held her hand closed – how warm his had felt – and refused to let her open it until finally her protests had died away.

'You might have a bit of trouble getting your savings out,' he'd said.

When she had asked what kind of trouble, he'd said, 'I don't know, a bit of a delay maybe, or something of that sort.'

How right he'd been. But she wished that if he'd known what she was facing, he might have told her outright, rather than making a mystery of it. Maybe he'd felt he might be wrong and hadn't wanted to alarm her unnecessarily.

She'd been conscious of herself, a seventeen-year-old, standing in front of the bank manager's desk in his carpeted office, with him looking at her from behind steel-rimmed spectacles, his mouth firm beneath his neat moustache. He had made her feel as if she were a recalcitrant young pupil and he the headmaster, as he'd told her that, although the savings were in her name, as a young person, under age and a female to boot, she must seek the permission of whoever had charge of her. Without a traceable father, this was Doctor Bertram Lowe, in whose care she had placed herself.

'But it's my money!' Her protest had been cut short.

She'd been overthrown by his words. 'An allowance by whoever has been watching over your welfare is of concern to him as to how it is used.'

'But I was the one who saved it. I could have spent it all, but I didn't.'

'Nevertheless, without his obvious generosity to you, you would have nothing, and that is the way it must be seen.'

'But that's not fair! He gave it to me, so it's mine!'

'I'm afraid not, young woman. Until you reach the age of twenty-one you are beholden to your benefactor, who generously took responsibilities for guardianship, be they official or otherwise, of a young, under-age person, who enjoyed every privilege given whilst under his roof.'

'But I'm not under his roof any more. I've left.'

The man had fiddled with the pencil he held. 'Even so, young lady, he has responsibility for guarding your savings, for which I commend your astuteness for one so young; others of your age might have been tempted to spend instead.'

Seeing her set expression, ready to argue, he'd leaned forward to put his point across to her. 'I will explain. As a married woman is accountable to her husband in all things, he being considered responsible for her conduct and her welfare, so you are accountable to your – let us say, to the man who kindly took you into his home, provided you with shelter and food, clothed you and gave you money from his own pocket, not as wages but as an allowance. It was he who opened a bank account for you and it cannot be touched by you without his consent.'

'I'd have been better off spending it!' she'd retorted and had seen the hint of an almost understanding smile twitch the fair moustache.

'I suggest, young woman, that you speak with Doctor Lowe. He may see your point of view and be swayed by your argument. But until that time I am afraid I can do nothing.'

It had all left her feeling bitter, knowing how hard she'd saved.

It did occur to her in a moment of anger that her so-called guardian might even use her hard-earned savings for himself. But common sense asked why he should need to: he had plenty of money; he didn't need her paltry sum. And if she couldn't touch the money without his consent, most likely he couldn't lay his hands on it without her presence. She was ignorant on points of law, but it seemed logical. While it just sat there in the bank, however, she sat here with hardly a penny to her name and this Monday coming would be asked for rent for next week.

As they had done for the last three days these same thoughts left her with no incentive to shift herself, no ability to think things out. Gazing at the paint-splashed walls and the old table in the centre of the room, that too paint-splashed, she wondered if the previous occupier had had any luck in selling what he painted. It looked more as if he must have failed miserably, or he wouldn't have had to vacate the place. The thought opened up a moment of speculation. If she could sell just one of her own paintings, there might be enough for rent and a bit left over for fuel and food.

Coming suddenly to life, Ellie leaped up from the broken chair. Going to one corner where she had stacked the five small paintings she'd brought with her, she lifted them up and looked at them. None was framed, but she'd seen artists' work hung on the railings of Hyde Park in the Bayswater Road, some framed, some not. People hovered to gaze at them while a hopeful painter looked on. There were all sorts – some just splashes of colour and shapes, others beautiful landscapes she could never hope to emulate, some copied from old masters. Why couldn't she hang her small offerings on those railings? It was a bit of a walk to Bayswater Road certainly, but she had been brought up to walk. And at least her paintings were different.

Certainly they were a little out of the ordinary. Michael had told her they were brilliant, that she was tremendously gifted, but had queried why she chose such subjects. But he didn't understand and she had never been able to bring herself to enlighten him on why she painted what she did. She wasn't sure herself except that the finished work would leave a sense of fulfilment and relief.

Thinking of Michael brought on a heavy sense of aching regret and absolute emptiness deep inside, one that persisted in recurring but one she determinedly thrust aside. She thrust it aside now. Pining wouldn't help. Instead she concentrated on what she had painted in happier times, not all that long ago.

One of her most graphic works was of the man whose muscles bulged under his loose shirt, whose thighs showed strong beneath ragged trousers as he stood over the huddled figure that could be vaguely interpreted as that of a woman. It would have been a very striking painting had it not been for a hand in one lower corner tensely gripping a pencil, the scene seeming to have been almost obliterated by the thick black marks that pencil had made. Small though the hand was, it dominated the picture and, as if having come from nowhere, unattached to a limb, it seemed to hover, the fingers tight with prominent veins and sinews, portraying the hatred they contained.

Two others were portraits – one of Doctor Lowe's wife, the other of herself. The likenesses were recognizable enough, but while the lips on both faces bore a charming smile, the eyes, far from reflecting the smile, held malice in the one of Mary Lowe and contempt in that of herself. But the eyes themselves were so offset from the face as almost to have no connection with it, seeming to be floating. There was a disconcerting feel to them, as if the artist's hand had been jogged while painting in the eyes. The faces had a naivety about them, as if done by a child, but would hopefully leave a viewer wondering how deliberate was the expression in the eyes that didn't match the exquisite smile. Ellie had known just what she was about when she'd painted them. Whether anyone else liked them had been immaterial at the time.

Dressing warmly, she tucked the three paintings under her arm and let herself out of her room.

Despite her warm clothes she felt chilled right through, standing in one spot eyeing every person that chanced to glance at her work. As the overcast sky began to fade to evening and her fellow exhibitors were gathering up their work and moving off, she too prepared to leave. She'd sold nothing. Silly to think she would, with so much competition; and hers would be of interest to only a certain type of person. Another day gone and her funds were dwindling fast.

Perhaps she should have gone in for a few of a gentler sort of paintings, that didn't bite back when people stopped to look at them and have them gnawing at their lips as they struggled to make sense of what they saw. But she had perked up when a particular couple had pointed to them, approached with quick, embarrassed smiles in her direction, then resumed their study. They had glanced at each other with troubled expressions.

'What are they trying to say?' queried the young woman of the man beside her. She had sounded knowledgeable

The way she was dressed indicated an arty sort – floppy, fur-trimmed hat, extremely loose coat that concealed every trace of figure, a long, thin, squirrel-fur boa wrapped several times around the neck, the hands hidden in an old-fashioned but expensive fox-fur muff.

'I don't quite know,' the man answered. 'But it makes me feel a little uncomfortable.'

'I suppose that's what it's meant to do.'

'Well, I think it's very clever, but I wouldn't want it hanging in my hall,' came the reply as they moved off with another brief smile, almost like an apology for having dismissed her work after taking up her time.

The scenes might not have been to their liking, but at least they were proving food for discussion.

She went home as darkness fell, cold, with no money, her paintings under her arm, but with a determination to try again tomorrow, fighting off the disgruntled sensation in her breast.

One thing at least had come about. The young man next to whose exhibits she had placed hers, and who for most of the day had ignored her, had towards the end of the day moved closer to take a look at them.

'I like that,' he'd said, pointing to the so-called portrait of Bertram Lowe's wife. 'It's a real person, isn't it?'

'Yes,' she'd said a little guardedly, but heartened. He had recognized her interpretation of the inner person using characterization in a rather more vicious way, perhaps. But he'd said he liked it.

He'd said his name was Felix and she'd given him her name. Talk had fizzled out, a passer-by having stopped to question him about one of his pictures – one of a small brook trickling over stones through a leafy woodland glade – and had actually bought the thing. For most of the day, several passers-by had kept his attention diverted from her as he'd sat on the pavement, smoking the occasional rolled cigarette, at midday falling to eating bread and cheese and drinking from a bottle, though he'd been sipping from it for most of the day.

Ellie had had only water and some bread spread with a scrape of jam – jam that she trusted would last her a few more days yet. She had never been a big eater, even when with Bertram Lowe and there'd been the chance to be. Even so, the man's cheese sandwich had looked delicious from where she sat on a little folding stool from the room she rented.

In her room she returned the paintings to the corner where sat just two more, painted under Michael's tuition from earlier days and of a more acceptable type – pretty little country scenes. With no money in her pocket she brewed herself some tea and toasted another piece of bread, spreading it with another scrape of jam. At this rate she would end up starving.

Her only other source of income now looked like being a few bits of clothing. Bertram had insisted she clothe herself as ladies did, entailing at least three changes each day – morning, afternoon and for her, if called for, a nice dress for evening.

The clothes she'd brought with her hadn't included those for evenings; they were not needed and took up room. Instead she had stuffed the two bags with a couple of morning and afternoon dresses and a warm jacket, a second pair of button-up boots, necessary underclothing and toiletries, as well as the paintings she'd selected, plus what artists' requirements she could fit in. It was about all she'd been able to carry. The rest of her clothing she'd worn: warm coat, straw boater, gloves, shawl – the sort of things needed for winter wear. If she now sold two of her dresses, she would at least eat. She felt degraded – having expected her paintings to be snapped up, she was now reduced to selling the clothes off her back. It was depressing.

The next day, one of those early-December days that suddenly seem to recapture summer, she stood in her spot, the sun bringing her new hope. The weather seemed to have brought out plenty of Friday shoppers, no doubt beginning to browse in preparation for Christmas, and by lunch time the area had workers taking advantage of the unseasonably warm weather to enjoy their lunch in the park.

Ellie's was again bread and jam washed down with frequent sips of water. The meagre meal made her think of the money she'd so carefully built up in her savings book and how Bertram Lowe, having once praised her for her sound sense, was now preventing her touching one penny of it. Maybe unjustly, but she blamed him, and it made her blood boil.

If it hadn't been for him, she and Michael might have been together still. His fault too that she had come down to this. But if he thought she was going to go running back, he was mistaken. Even though her money was being withheld from her, she intended to thrive – somehow.

To this end she'd desperately included the two pretty landscapes. She wasn't very hopeful. Poor examples of her earlier work and not very well painted, who'd buy them? Comparing them to some of the talented works of art hanging from the railings, she felt almost ready to pack up and run back to her lodgings, though what good that would have done?

She was about to yield to temptation when two women, mother and daughter by the look of them, paused in passing. Their gaze riveted on her two landscapes, totally ignoring her three stronger paintings, they came nearer for a better look. Ellie held her breath.

'Just perfect, pet, for your bedroom,' she heard the older woman say, to which the younger one simpered, 'Can we afford them?'

'It doesn't matter,' she was told. 'If you like them, they can be part of our wedding presents to you and Howard. They're so pretty.'

Before she knew it both pictures were sold, the older woman not even haggling over the seven shillings and sixpence that Ellie boldly quoted for each one. So this was what people wanted. She felt oddly disappointed but heartened. Fifteen shillings! Unbelievable. For those nondescript pieces of nothing! Not only was there enough to buy some decent food, there would be enough for more paint, canvas, linseed oil, a little more varnish – crucial if she must do more paintings to sell. And she would have to forget trying to be clever. If people wanted pretty pictures, then pretty pictures she must paint, if she wanted to live – not only live but accrue enough money to enable her to look for her father. This, after all, was her main quest, and if she wanted to continue that, she would have to get down to serious work.

The problem was where to go to buy the things she wanted. She had never bought artists' materials herself before. Michael had always provided them, to be reimbursed by Doctor Lowe, as was right and proper.

'Do you know where can I buy paints and canvas?' she asked Felix when he chanced to look her way.

He had smiled at her as the two women had hurried off with their purchases. She thought at first that he couldn't begin to know the utter relief of having money in her hand, but something in that smile told her he knew exactly how she felt, that he had felt the same, perhaps many times.

Now he smiled again. 'When we pack up for the night I'll be able to show you. It's not far. Do you mind my taking you?'

'No, not at all,' she returned.

Having him with her, she wouldn't feel so out of place

buying her own materials with no idea what she should be looking for. She would be glad of the company too.

Since having come to live in the area she had met no one, talked to no one, except for a few words yesterday with this young man Felix. Tomorrow she'd try her luck here, hopefully pass the time of day with Felix if he turned up; but Sunday would be spent alone. Monday she'd have the privilege of a word or two from the landlord, looking for his rent for the following week. That was a thought: she must keep back some of her money for the rent. In buying her artists' materials she must be sure to have enough left for that.

'I've no idea how much canvas and paints cost,' she began, but was interrupted by the sight of an elderly man approaching. Short, chubby, for one alarming second he reminded her of Bertram Lowe, but he had a much bushier beard.

She stood by as he peered at each of her three remaining paintings, the scrutiny seeming to take ages. Suddenly he pointed to the one of the menacing male figure and said in a sharp, abrupt voice, 'This one tells a story, does it not?'

'Yes,' she responded, oddly abashed.

'Hmm! A lot of them these days tell a story. I get sick of seeing them.'

It didn't strike her as a hopeful remark. Why did people make such comments if they weren't interested in buying anything?

'Far too melodramatic for my liking,' the man went on, his voice carrying. 'Some bloody voluptuous, diaphanously clad female chained to a rock, sea foaming around her waist, the same damned painting of the same female gazing heavenwards and the same damned sea receding – bloody rubbish! But this one I like. This one has some strength to it. I'd say almost vicious. You didn't do this, young lady. Who's the artist?'

'I am,' she said, rankled that he doubted her abilities.

She saw his eyes squint with incredulity as he regarded her. 'You?'

'Yes, me!'

He was studying her as if imagining her to be lying.

'Why not me?' she shot at him.

His expression didn't change. 'You surprise me. How would a delicate young lady concern herself to paint such – I'd go as far as to say, *malevolent* themes?'

Ellie burst into laughter despite her initial annoyance. 'Rather than sweet little watercolours, pretty little landscapes?'

He didn't laugh, and although there came a glint of amusement into his pale eyes, he remained serious. 'I wonder what has caused you to choose such – may I say, strange subjects? – all three of them.'

Ellie sobered. 'That's my business.'

'Hmm,' came the response. 'They intrigue me. But I would like to buy the self-portrait.'

She was astounded. 'How did you know it was of me?'

The man smiled at last. 'Odd as it may seem, there is no mistaking it for anyone other than yourself. Though why you see yourself in that light I can only guess. How much are you asking for it?'

Taken by surprise, with no idea what she should be asking, Ellie hesitated. She'd sold those two earlier paintings for what she'd thought was a fair price, astounded that the price asked had been accepted without question. She could have asked more and, pleased though she was at having sold something, she'd wanted to kick herself. Incredibly, she might be making yet another sale almost on top of selling the two landscapes; but what to ask? He seemed to see her hesitation as a preliminary to a spot of haggling. His voice grew sharp.

'I don't intend to go to more than four pound, young lady, if you were expecting more.' Ellie gaped. Four pound – it was a fortune!

'That or I walk away!' she heard him say through what sounded like a buzzing in her ears. She nodded and felt four gold sovereigns drop into her hand. Never had she held so much money at one time – never even possessed so much.

The man was taking down the portrait, now his property, from the railings and tucking it under his arm. Turning to leave, he paused.

'One more thing, young lady,' he said slowly. 'You've talent – your work, expressionism, like Munch, Rouault, Ensor.'

Ellie had never heard of them. Her gaze was blank as he went on, 'My name is Hunnard – Robert C. Hunnard. I own a gallery. If when I return I find you've done nothing more than those two remaining works you have left, I shall assume you to be one of these artists who are too indolent to recognize that success only comes with dedication and sacrifice.

This doesn't mean dashing off a few dozen paintings just to sell to the public; it means putting your soul into each brush stroke, even if it takes half a lifetime. If you are of that mind, you will go far. If not . . .' He shook his head then gave an exaggerated shrug and, walking off very swiftly and elegantly for one of his build, left her staring after him.

'God, I wish I had your luck!' came a voice beside her. She turned to see the scruffy young man, Felix, now gazing at her last two paintings as if totally absorbed by them. 'Do you know who that was?'

Ellie shook her head and Felix went on, 'He owns one of the finest private painting galleries in London. My God, girl, consider yourself made!'

Twenty-Two

New Year's Eve. Ellie was alone, just as she had been at Christmas. At that time she'd missed the good company, celebration, laughter, good food, and had felt sad and lonely. Now, she told herself, all that was out of her system.

She stood now gazing at the half-finished painting she'd been working on. Her back was aching. With her mind riveted on the canvas, she'd let the fire die, and although she wore the thin blanket from the bed around her shoulders, her fingers were stiff from the cold as well as from gripping her brushes.

Her feet were freezing and when they warmed again would itch with chilblains. She'd have to stop, relight the fire, brew some warming tea and find something to eat. She didn't feel hungry but knew she needed to eat.

She had gone over this painting so many times, but it refused to go the way she wanted. For days she'd stood staring at the blank canvas, with nothing in mind but the words of that Robert C. Hunnard: 'Paint from the soul!'

She supposed she had painted from the soul when she had worked on those three other paintings, a soul full of hatred interpreted on canvas – of Bertram Lowe's scheming wife, of her own loathsome father, of herself and the way she felt about her life.

Now that she was on her own, trying to recapture that feeling was proving virtually impossible. A need to make money from her work was not enough to instil into her that clawing anger she should be feeling. She had tried hard to recapture it, but it just wasn't there. Hunnard's fear was right: when it came to it she was, after all, just one of those people who were ready to sit back on their laurels after one brief bout of inspiration.

But she *was* working hard. Usually cold, tired, hungry, aching from standing in one position all the time but unable to tear herself away from this present painting, she was trying so hard to reflect a bit of her inner self.

Surely that was dedication – giving of herself, her soul, to her talent. Yet there was something missing. There was no longer the stimulation that had come from desperately wanting to escape, live her own life, follow her quest for her father, seek revenge.

She still had every intention of finding him and her need to make more money in order to do so was there, but it wasn't enough. Something had gone out of her and she wasn't sure what it was.

Ellie shivered, the cold eating into her young bones. Putting down her brush and palette, she went over to the fire. There was the briefest glow from one of the coals. Gathering up a piece of newspaper, she coaxed it under the live coal and blew gently on it. It began to flare. She added a couple of thin sticks of firewood, and as they caught, laid some of the still-warm coals on top. Before long there was a bright fire again.

Sufficiently warmed, she made some tea. She would make herself a fried egg on fried bread. There was enough money left from the sale of her paintings before Christmas for her to eat and be warm. But it wasn't going to last much longer.

Since selling her so-called self-portrait she had only gone to her pitch three times with a few rushed landscapes done in watercolours. Oils took a long time to dry and varnish and people seemed to like her little landscapes, which she sold cheaply to keep herself going. But although conscious of what sold well to the general public, it was sapping her will to do the one she was at present struggling with. She was slowly losing that inner self this Mr C. Hunnard had spoken of. She'd not seen him since that first day. Maybe he had come while she wasn't there and had given up on her, assuming that he had been proved right about her.

That evening she and Felix Reese had gone off to the art shop he knew of, her day's takings of four pounds fifteen shillings burning a hole in her pocket.

It had been nice having a young man walking with her through the dark streets, even though he was thin and scruffy, so different from the young man who had once walked beside her. Michael – immaculately dressed and well-spoken but under the thumb of wealthy parents, destined to follow his

father's illustrious footsteps into the medical profession –
knew which side his bread was buttered on. All the more
reason to let her down. Her heart still felt dreadfully empty
without him, but she had to put him behind her, telling herself
that that part of her life was over.

Felix, with a cheap room not far from where she was living,
had been so kind, walking her back to her own lodgings.
'Young women should not be alone walking these streets after
dark,' he'd warned. 'Perhaps I can continue walking you back.'

She had readily agreed, but bad weather, with Christmas
approaching, had turned people off pausing to gaze at the
displayed efforts of casual street artists and she had only seen
Felix once more. Nor had Mr 'Celebrated' Hunnard shown
up. No doubt such an eminent person wouldn't brave the cold
even in a coach and, as Christmas came and went, she
suspected she'd seen the last of him, that it had been just a
flash in the pan.

Even so, she had been encouraged to buy some decent materials and so far had spent her time keeping to her room,
rushing off easier landscapes at odd moments while trying to
transfer her 'inner self' to canvas. All she'd achieved was this
uncompleted effort, trying to capture the endless shapes and
colours that invaded her head.

The portrait would be of her mother, or her memory of her
– thin-faced with care-worn features, the eyes, oddly misplaced
as with those others of her portraits, sad and empty from loss
of hope for the future, the mouth, though smiling, as Ellie felt
the need to portray, that smile false and bitter.

She painted her as she always did when these dark moods
took her – using heavy applications of purples, browns, dark
shades of green, black, and here and there streaks of stark
yellow and white and touches of vermilion, the shadows
always a sombre Prussian blue. The colours and the unusual
shapes that took her thoughts expressed how she felt. She
supposed this was what Hunnard had meant by that word
he'd used – 'expressionism'. She couldn't recall Michael referring to it. He'd tried to get her to emulate the old landscape
masters, with no idea of the secret images that lurked in her
head.

They were still there but refused to be transferred on to the
canvas, even though, time after time, she'd overpainted the

work in an effort to get them out of herself. At one time she'd even picked up the canvas from the broken chair on which it was propped to fling it across the room, spoiling the still wet image she had so laboriously worked on, so that she had to start that part again. Maybe she would be better off painting pretty pictures to sell until she saved enough to support her former quest.

Ellie gazed around the room, a far more comfortable one than when she had first arrived. She had bought a second-hand armchair, a table and two upright chairs as well as a passable mattress, another pillow, a pair of twill sheets and two blankets, all second-hand but clean. But her money was beginning to dwindle and she was growing a little desperate. The way things were going she would never have enough to go in search of her father.

The thought depressed her even to the point of asking the question why was she bothering. But it only needed her once to cast her mind back to those days when she had been help-less before him, and that other awful time having Doctor Lowe look on her private parts in helping her rid herself of the vile results of her father's attentions.

Where was Charlie now? Would he have found out where their father was? If she went to see the Sharps, they might have had some news by now. There was also a chance of seeing Ronnie again, but she doubted it, him being taken up with that girl he intended to marry.

Washing up the supper plate, Ellie prepared for bed, taking a last look at the painting she'd been doing. Perhaps in the light of day it would look better. She was just wasting her time trying to apply colour by gaslight.

Lying in bed, her thoughts zipped from one memory to another: Mum, Charlie, Dora – she'd have to write to Dora soon – Bertram Lowe and his wife, her time with Michael. At that her heart slumped, making her thoughts turn quickly to Ronnie Sharp, then to Felix, whom she'd not seen since being walked home by him over a week ago.

Bells began to peal, waking her from a half-sleep. They were pealing in a new year – nineteen hundred and two. People in the street below had begun singing and laughing and calling out to each other, 'Happy New Year!' over and over. And she lay up here alone.

She heard her own voice explode in a single intake of self-pity. A tear trickled from the corner of her eye.

In a flash she was up, sweeping away the tear and in her rough twill nightgown she ran to the window and threw it open.

'Happy New Year down there!' she yelled.

A voice yelled back, slurred and jolly, 'An' 'Appy New Year t'you too!'

Ellie's laugh gulped in her throat. So this was her new year, alone up here. She knew no one except Felix and he hadn't shown any interest in her other than by walking her home – as a sort of gallant duty, perhaps. Of his life she knew nothing. By the time she took her paintings out to sell – who knew? – he might probably have moved on. Dejected again, that brief but hearty exchange of good wishes behind her, she made her way back to bed, trying not to listen to the still pealing bells, the noises of hilarity in the street below that had set dogs barking from every quarter.

A tap on her door stopped her. 'Who's there?' she called in alarm. A muffled voice answered her. 'It's me – Felix.'

'Felix?'

'Reese. Surely you haven't forgotten me.'

'What do you want?'

'Open the door.'

'I can't: I'm ready for bed.'

'Come on!' There came another bout of tapping. 'I don't care! Open the door.'

Ellie stood hesitating. She was in her nightgown. How could she open the door to a casual stranger? But she couldn't just let him stand there. He sounded urgent. Perhaps something was wrong. She had to open it. Taking a hold on herself, she did so, peeping around the crack, one hand clutching the nightgown to her throat. 'What's the matter?' she queried.

'The matter? The matter, dear girl, is that it's a new year and you're in bed!'

His narrow features were lively, flushed with drink, but happily so. 'I haven't set eyes on you for a week. I even wondered if you might be dead. Get dressed, girl! We're going to a party.'

'I can't.'

'You can! Do up your hair,' he said, seeing it hanging loose. His eyes roamed appreciatively over the glossy, dark auburn tresses, never having seen her hair loose before; but his gaze didn't linger long. 'Put on something halfway nice, suitable for a party. Hurry up now. I'll wait out here.'

Suddenly excited, all morbid thoughts gone, quickly she dressed, selecting one of the nicer of her hoarded gowns and hurriedly pinned her hair up into some semblance of order.

She had washed her face for bed so there was no need to wash again. The scent of soap was still on her skin – cheap Sunlight soap, but it smelled nice and fresh. One day, when she was rich, she would have beautiful soap and beautiful perfumes. Casting dreams aside she scrambled into her winter coat, scarf and her straw boater and made for the door.

Felix was still standing there, a long, skinny form in a brown smock-like coat over green plaid trousers, a gaudy neckerchief and some sort of floppy cap of brown velvet, every inch an artist.

'What party?' she queried. 'Where?'

'Not far away. Friends of mine. Just a step. We'll be there in no time at all. You'll enjoy it.' He sounded almost short of breath. 'Let's go!'

Taking her hand he gave her no time to question him further as he ran with her down the two flights of stairs and out into the still lively street.

She'd had a good time but a strange one, one that had taken some time to get used to – certainly it was a side of life she had never seen before and had certainly never known. Poor and rough her upbringing had been before Doctor Lowe had taken her in – quarrelling neighbours, street fights, any person straying into the area often being waylaid, coshed, stripped of their cash, and sometimes even their clothes; petty thieves, fornication and adultery in the dark alleys. But people dressed as decently as they could. Not *these* people.

Having already welcomed in the New Year before she and Alex had arrived, they were most of them highly charged and very drunk. The rather vast artist's studio was thick with tobacco smoke, heavy with alcohol fumes and packed with perspiring bodies kicking up their legs to the thump of piano and drums or else slumped around the perimeter. The air was cloyed with cheap scent and body sweat. No one had taken any notice of her as she and Felix had entered, leaving her to melt in with the general noisy mêlée.

As he walked her home, her arm through his, mostly to keep herself steady for she'd had a little more to drink than was good for her, she couldn't stop talking about it all, how strangely most of them had dressed and behaved.

It seemed to amuse him when she spoke of her horror at seeing women in a state of partial undress, showing no shame in exposing too much of their bosoms as they and their partners openly kissed and cuddled in such a liberated way – and not always their partners, even women with women, men with men, so that she had a job not to gape.

'No one seemed put out by it all,' she said, which made him burst out laughing.

'Why should they be? There's nothing wrong doing what's natural. Let's face it, everyone does it, though the so-called respectable majority do it in secret, thinking others don't know. They were having fun, a good time. So, what if one gets carried away? Nothing wrong in that.'

She hadn't referred to it again, thinking of her father. He'd enjoyed himself – at her expense. There was more wrong in that than she cared Felix to know about.

'You were glad you came?' Felix queried her silence.

Ellie perked up. 'Yes, of course I was.' She'd had a good time, her eyes opened to another world. 'Thanks for taking me.'

'That's all right,' he said perkily. 'There's always something going on somewhere. I'll take you whenever you like. We all need company; painting, sculpting, writing – it's a lonely business and most are only too glad of a little company at the first opportunity.'

She knew about loneliness and, despite her having been so taken aback by what she'd seen this evening, the idea of finding friends among these people was tempting. At least they were honest about what they were, every one of them steeped in their art and to hell with the world outside their sphere, spirits unto themselves.

But one thing Ellie still couldn't get over. There had been a corridor leading off the studio where now and again a couple would wander off, their intentions vividly obvious

At one time she had lost sight of Felix and felt herself

giving way to sudden panic. Then she saw him, his lips almost eating those of a shaggy-haired female with hair shaded an alarming red. Used to elegantly pinned coiffure, Ellie felt quite shaken by the sight as well as by seeing her apparently inoffensive escort practically sucking the girl to death. She'd gone over to them, by then the alcohol inside her creating courage and some annoyance.

At her approach he had let go of the strange female, who had commenced upon a sinuous, gyrating dance all on her own with slow head and body movements as if her mind was somewhere in the clouds. It was then Ellie realized that alcohol wasn't the only stimulant being consumed here.

As she went to turn away, she'd seen Felix give a sheepish grin.

'What's the matter?' he'd asked, but her annoyance had dissipated and she remembered turning back to him, thinking it suddenly very funny.

She dimly recalled wondering on the way home in the cold, fresh air of the small hours of nineteen hundred and two, whether she might allow him to take the advantage, if he so felt inclined. But she'd thought of Michael. She'd let her guard slip with him and been made a fool of. She still felt horribly abashed and humiliated by it.

Surprisingly, Felix had conducted himself well, even though there had been no apology for his behaviour with the red-haired girl. This morning Ellie was left wondering whether, if she hadn't been there, he and the strange red-haired girl would have stolen off along that dark passage together? As he'd said, it was perfectly natural to follow one's instincts in certain circumstances.

Like most she had met last night, he had no prim notions about life, had likely had his fill of women when the chance came, had no trouble drinking himself into a stupor; nor could she really see him drawing back from an occasional dip into drugs, hemp or a pipe of opium. Yet she did like him. After all, it was well known that in society circles many a lady kept a neat little small-bowled pipe on her person for a puff or two to steady her nerves, and laudanum wasn't always taken merely for medicinal purposes.

Ellie felt she must have derived something from that evening, for she had awoken this morning feeling unexpectedly lively, not even with a headache. Going over to the portrait of her mother, she knew she could finish it.

Better still, where the painting was concerned, surveying her mother's likeness rekindled the old pain and instinctively she knew that this portrait was going to be the best work she had ever done.

Twenty-Three

At the sound of Mrs Lowe's voice calling her Dora looked up sharply from the book she was reading in her little side room.

She wished she had a room like Ellie used to have. This one, coming directly off Mrs Lowe's room, gave her no privacy at all. She had made one or two tentative approaches, asking that she might use the now vacant room, but Doctor Lowe had refused on the grounds that it had been his daughter's room and was not to be disturbed, which made no sense. So it had been all right for Ellie to have it, but not her.

Mrs Lowe, too, had found obstacles to put in the way. 'I cannot go running to that room whenever I want you. Dora, I need you by my side.'

It seemed that she was constantly needed, that Mrs Lowe would have sewn her to her skirt if she could. Forever at her beck and call, she felt that the woman was using her to vent her self-inflicted loneliness upon. Dora's role, as a maid as well as a lady's companion, was one that never seemed to let up for a moment. She felt more a slave than a paid companion. Even slaves would probably have had some time to themselves, but she . . . she was expected to be on hand at any moment. She was meant to have days off, but Mrs Lowe seemed to view their days out together as being sufficient.

'I don't know why you wish to go off on your own,' she had said many times when the question arose. 'Don't you care for my company, Dora? I do my best to make you happy. I buy you nice things. I take you to select little restaurants for lunch. We go together to the most fashionable shopping streets and to the finest emporiums, such as you would never see if on your own. Isn't it enough? Is it so boring being with me?'

'No, of course not,' Dora would assure her.

'I have tried to be a good friend to you, Dora. Do I not do enough for you – is that the problem?'

'Yes, you do.' She felt that her reply had to be meek, grateful.

'And am I not kind to you?'

To this Dora would nod in an abashed sort of way. But Mrs Lowe was not all that kind. Dora had known that when she had first taken her on to train her to be a lady's maid; but when Ellie had apparently become the apple of Doctor Lowe's eye, so to speak, Mrs Lowe had become quite sweet towards her.

She guessed now that it had been only to make Ellie jealous because, since Ellie had left, Mrs Lowe had changed completely and for the worse. She'd quibble over the least thing and nothing seemed to please her, often being sharp with her – and nothing Dora did was right. Yet the woman clung to her as if she would be utterly lost without her, maybe because she was so ill at ease in social circles.

'I'm afraid it is inconvenient,' she'd snapped when this morning Dora had timidly asked yet again if she could have a day off.

It had led to yet another bewildered tirade. 'I don't know why you feel the need to go off on your own. Where can you go that I cannot take you? It's not as if you've a family you can visit.'

That last cut deep. 'On your own', Mrs Lowe had said. Lately she'd never felt so alone – Mum gone, never a word from Charlie. And Dad? God knew where he was and he seemed unlikely to ever show himself again. As for Ellie, she'd been gone nearly six weeks and hadn't come nigh or by to see how she was. It was like she didn't have a sister.

Ellie had sent her a Season's Greetings card at Christmas, saying she hoped she was coping all right at the Lowes' without her, but there had been no address to write back to.

The card had come with Doctor Lowe's post and been handed to her by Mrs Lowe, having been opened. To Dora it seemed she had no privacy at all, but complaining would have evoked a prolonged and hurt reproach so cleverly designed that she'd immediately feel ashamed at having complained, the reproach so subtly manipulative that it trapped her every time.

She sometimes wished she'd taken up Ellie's offer to go with her. If she'd known where her sister was, she'd have upped and left as Ellie had done. But she wasn't like Ellie. She couldn't have upped and gone off all alone out into the wide world like she had. She hadn't her courage and, with no idea where Ellie was, she was stuck here.

Dora put down her book and hurried to answer Mrs Lowe's call.

'Why did you take so long answering me, child?' The reprimand was aggrieved but had a sharp edge to it. 'What were you doing?'

'I was reading, madam.'

'Haven't you anything better to do, Dora? Doctor Lowe and I will be out this evening. Come and help me choose a gown. Something warm. It is such a chilly night and our host's home is always so cold. I do believe they are not so affluent as they like to pretend and I am sure that they must be trying to save on fuel. I am not at all looking forward to this evening.'

Going to the great satinwood wardrobe, she opened it to gaze at the row of gowns she possessed. There were dozens, all of them beautiful. They made Dora's mouth practically water to see them, but though Mary Lowe adored buying, she rarely wore what she bought.

'I wish Doctor Lowe would not accept these invitations,' she went on. 'But I suppose as it is in connection with his profession I must suffer to meet people in whom I myself find no interest.'

She sighed mightily, surveying the row of gowns. 'Now, which do you think would be suitable for this evening?'

Dora glanced along the row. What Mrs Lowe was already wearing looked to her to be as suitable as any, but it was a house gown. Of grey watered silk, the fashionably pouting bodice was all tucks and frilled lace, the lower part of the skirt ringed with a swirl of ribbon, the sweep of the hem trailing the carpet as she walked. The sleeves, following the mode, were puffed, narrowing down to the wrist – not a gown for an ample figure like hers but in Dora's estimation beautiful enough to indeed be worn for a social occasion rather than just around the house; but then what did she know about it?

Mrs Lowe was running her fingers along the row, making

each gown shimmer. Her fingers paused at one particular gown of pale-blue silk, its length striped with evenly spaced tucks, the skirt decorated with artificial flowers. The décolletée, not as low as some were, had a bertha, a small fichu and epaulettes of cream silk and deep-blue velvet with more artificial flowers. At the waist was a huge bow edged in deep-blue velvet, again not something that flattering to the shorter, plumper figure like Mrs Lowe's, but again a really lovely thing.

Dora took her cue from the pause. 'What about the blue silk one, madam?' she suggested cautiously.

She had learned always to suggest, never to inform. Mrs Lowe might be indecisive about what she should wear, but to be told would immediately put her back up, no doubt because she felt she could be easily belittled. The only times she became set in her views were when she felt put out, such as in her ongoing dislike of Ellie.

Dora thought again of her sister as she helped her mistress prepare for her apparently miserable evening with Doctor Lowe's colleagues, easing her into the gown, doing up the hooks at the back, making sure the slightly greying hair was dressed nicely, the way she had been taught.

Last week Ellie had written to her, this time with an address. It had been delivered by hand and passed to her by the new housemaid Sarah.

'The gel give me sixpence ter give it ter you only an' no one else,' she said, beaming, enjoying the conspiracy. 'Said she was yer sister.'

The new girl was nice but Mrs Lowe's diktat that a lady's maid didn't fraternize with the lower servants had made it doubly difficult to pass on the letter. But Sarah agreed to post an answer. Florrie might not have done. She no longer worked here, having left not long after Ellie to look after her mother, who had fallen sick following the death of her father. Dora was glad she had gone because after Ellie had left, Florrie had become very full of herself.

The next day Dora wrote Ellie a letter, handed it to Sarah and set herself to wait hopefully for her sister to reply.

Ellie stood back to survey her work. It was finished. It was everything she had envisaged, as if a ghostly hand, perhaps even her mother's, had guided her brush strokes – the hazel eyes staring out of the canvas straight at the viewer as if defying anyone to try to look down on her.

It had taken several weeks to finish. This one she would frame and take with the other silly little landscapes to display to the public. Would that man Hunnard come by? It was a slim hope. Yet if he did, would he turn up his nose and tell her it was a piece of rubbish? Oddly enough, it was him she had painted it for as much as for herself. The man haunted her just as her paintings did, refusing to be flushed out of her mind. Why did he find the painting he'd bought from her so interesting? She'd only put them out for the public because she had needed money and could only hope someone would buy, but she had never expected someone to practically drool over them.

This Monday morning she parcelled up a couple of water-colours of scenes she'd taken from a poster advertising trips into the country and two small oil paintings of street scenes, hopefully quite saleable. She also included her mother's portrait, which she knew would be given no more than a few odd glances from passers-by and would probably end up being brought back here the same way as she was taking it.

In the dingy hallway she handed over next week's rent to the scruffy-looking landlord.

'Letter for you,' he said shortly, handing her the envelope with the single blue stamp on it, and disappeared back into his room.

Recognizing her sister's hand, Ellie put down her parcel and ripped open the envelope. Her first thought was that Dora might be in need of her, but scanning it gave no indication of anything wrong – just an ordinary account of daily goings-on.

But something about the letter wasn't quite as it seemed. Ellie began to read it over again, more carefully. Dora had written that she missed her so and wished she had left at the same time as her. That was odd. She'd been so adamant about staying.

Slowly Ellie began to realize, reading between the lines, that though Dora seemed to be making light of all that went on, little things – the odd word dropped here and there – appeared to reveal that Dora was not at all happy.

Refolding the letter and putting it into her pocket, Ellie

hoisted the somewhat bulky tied-together canvases under her arm and turned towards Bayswater Road. But her mind kept going over all that Dora had written, bit by bit deciphering it until by the time she arrived there she was convinced something must be done about the girl. That evening she'd go and see her – not slink there as she'd done on delivering her letter, but arrive openly, and brave whatever unfriendly reception she would get from Dora's employers.

She was ready for Mrs Lowe, but how would Bertram Lowe deal with her sudden appearance? What would his reaction be? Hurt, bewildered, angry? Or would he keep well out of the way, unable to confront her? She would face that when she got there.

The next move would be to get Dora to come away with her. That was if she meant all she had put in her letter. It could have been a moment of upset when she'd written it. By the time she got there, Dora might have changed her mind, feeling better. It was an uncertainty that dogged her mind as she began to set out her few paintings against the park railings.

Felix was already there. She'd not seen him since the New Year party, being too engrossed in her work and he probably in his. Whether he'd been here she didn't know, not having come here herself. But she had thought about him a lot since the party. Despite his scruffy looks he was certainly handsome, his face smooth and gentle – she would have said 'sweet'.

She felt her heart race as he lifted a hand at seeing her. His light-voiced salutation – 'Hullo there, love! Are you all right?' – had her replying that she was fine and experiencing a little thrill of excitement as he came over.

The sensation surprised her. It seemed to her that it never took long for a man to be lured by her: Ronnie, Michael, now Felix. Had she in some way been instrumental in luring her own father to do what he did? As she smiled at Felix, her mind flew back to those days. Had it been her fault? Had she the right to look for revenge for what he'd done? Was she so pure that she could blame him entirely? She shuddered and pushed the thought away.

'It certainly is cold this morning,' Felix laughed, misinterpreting the shudder. His laugh was high, musical. 'All I hope is that this bit of sunshine, cold as it is, will bring out a few punters. Can't wait for spring.'

Pausing, he eyed her for a moment, seeming about to say something.

'Yes?' Ellie prompted.

He gave a small shrug. 'Oh . . . it's nothing really.'

'Tell me.'

What had he been about to say? Ask her to go out with him? Mention going to another party? She knew that artists frequently met together, maybe in a café, or someone's studio, being ever in need of company after working alone for hours on end. Some shared accommodation, and not only to eke out the rent. Most artists were hard up. Paints cost, and paintings were hard to sell. Normal working men, poorly paid as they were, could never know the sort of income some of these people often had to subsist on.

It was obsession for their art that drove them to live as they did – pure obsession, and the hope that one day a painting would make them suddenly rich. For her, all she'd wanted was enough to be able to stand over her father and humiliate him. Now she wasn't sure. She, too, wanted to be blessed by that one big success. But her sights had been set long ago: to find the man she loathed so much. She couldn't give up now.

'Tell me what you were going to say,' she said again.

Felix nibbled at his top lip. He had such lovely white teeth. 'It's just that . . .' He paused again, then went on with visible determination.

'Just that I went to Hunnard's galleries only to see if that self-portrait of yours was there. And it was.'

'Did you?' Ellie cried excitedly, unable to curb the thrill of knowing that something of hers was actually hanging in an important art gallery. 'Was it? What did it look like?'

He still seemed to be playing for time, again nibbling at his lower lip. When he spoke, his words were stilted. 'Well . . . it was small compared with some, but it looked very special. But what I'm trying to get at – and I think you ought to know it – was the price being asked.'

'Yes?' she prompted as he hesitated.

'Well, it was fifty guineas.'

This last was blurted out. Ellie stared at him, unsure what her mind was deriving from his news. Her picture hanging in an important West End gallery: for a second that sounded absolutely wonderful; then slowly it began to dawn. She'd been paid four pounds, thinking that a marvellous sum. Now it was being sold for fifty bloody guineas! A sense of having been robbed, of having been taken for a fool, sent her suddenly livid with indignation.

'He swindled me! How dare he!'

Felix's laugh was filled with relief at having rid himself of the news. 'That's how it goes, love,' he said lightly. 'We're only the bricklayers – no matter how much the finished building sells for.'

She didn't see the wit behind the wisdom. 'I've a mind to go there and tell him just what I think of him, the thieving old bugger!'

He smiled. 'It's not worth shedding blood over. Be glad that someone important took that sort of interest in it. Some would give their eye teeth for that.'

'I don't care how important he is. He cheated me and I'm going to give him a piece of my mind!'

'I'm afraid, love, you'll be better off just grinning and bearing it. You'll only show yourself up in front of everyone. The sort who visit those galleries are usually well off and they'll merely think you mad.'

'I don't care!' she said defiantly. But his advice brought her feet back on to the ground. She let her anger subside. She'd already been taken for a fool – no use adding to it.

'But he'd better not show his face here again,' she griped sullenly. 'Because if he does, I'll give him what for.'

'At least someone of importance taking notice of your work must count for something. Anyway, I don't suppose he'll be back.'

But Ellie wasn't so sure. If Mr blooming Hunnard thought he had got away with it, he could come back looking for more from her, seeing her as an easy touch. And she'd be ready for him.

She managed to sell just one painting during the afternoon, for only a few shillings, which was no more than she'd expected. She'd had little heart in painting it and it probably showed. Her mind at the time had been solely on the portrait she'd been working on.

The people who'd bought the watercolour had glanced at

the portrait and quickly looked away, their exchange of grimaces making it hard for her to hide her contempt for them as she took their money and handed over the poor piece of work.

'At least you've sold something today,' Felix put in. He seemed very sensitive to how she was feeling. 'I've not even had a nibble.' He glanced along the row of others trying to make a living from art. 'There's too much competition.'

'Not down on your uppers, are you?' she asked, suddenly concerned for him.

He gave a small shrug. 'We manage.'

'We?' She pounced on the word, her heart sinking. Someone with his looks had to be married or perhaps sharing his place with a girl.

'Didn't I tell you?' he said. 'I share a room. We share the rent and – well, everything else. He sculpts. He sold something recently, so we aren't too badly off. I'd just like to sell something so I can pull my weight. Though he's very good about it.'

He. Ellie couldn't help a sense of relief. At the same time she felt sorry for him having to put up with sharing, both no doubt getting under each other's feet. But then, it was probably better than going back to an empty room, with no one to talk to or go out with to meet others.

She'd made no friends apart from Felix. The way he'd smile at her, she still had hopes that he might ask her out at some time, maybe to meet his friends. That would be nice. And maybe there might come about a more lasting union, though she wouldn't make the same mistake as she'd made with Michael Deel. Or with her father.

She would need to keep him at arm's length where that was concerned, at least until she was very, very sure of him. Odd, though, that while he'd been very free with that red-headed female she'd seen him kissing with gusto on New Year's Eve, he hadn't made a single advance towards her so far.

Perhaps she wasn't his sort. But she was pretty and lively and if he looked deeper he'd find that she liked fun. Perhaps he preferred the more unconventional artistic type, the bohemian type of woman who dressed outrageously, dyed her hair and made free with men without a qualm. She, with her conventional dress, stuck out like a sore thumb amid such flamboyance. If she dressed like them, would he take more interest in her? Ellie vowed to try and make an effort so as to get closer to him. She needed companionship more than anything at this moment.

As Felix accompanied her home, he carrying her unsold paintings along with his own, showing more strength than his thin physique would have had people believe, Ellie took his arm. But when she made to snuggle against him, he pulled away.

'Whoops-a-daisy!' he laughed. 'You'll have me over, carrying this lot.'

She immediately let go his arm. 'It must be heavy. Let me carry mine. There'll be one less for me to carry now.'

'Doesn't matter; we're almost here,' he said, his old self again as they turned a corner into her street.

'Would you care to come up for a cup of tea?' she asked eagerly as she took her canvases from him.

He pursed his lips. 'Thank you, perhaps another time. Ginger, who I share with, will have got something in for us. I'll see you tomorrow though?'

'Yes.' She felt a little deflated. But now her mind turned to Dora. If she could get Dora to leave, then they could share this room and she'd have companionship, someone to talk to; and as Dora had no interest in art, she wouldn't get in the way.

One problem would be that if she and Felix did become closer, Dora might be a stumbling block. Even so, her sister needed to get away from the place where she was, being virtually trapped by that woman. Paid companion indeed! – a girl her age playing companion to someone of Mrs Lowe's years who should have had contemporaries as friends.

Tomorrow evening she would go and demand Dora's release from her job, and so long as Dora was still willing to come away with her, there wasn't much they could do about it.

Twenty-Four

What was it about best-laid plans? Whatever the saying was, Ellie realized that rushing off to visit Dora would do no good at all. To turn up out of the blue could cause all sorts of problems and her chances of enticing her sister away could go all wrong.

It wouldn't take five minutes for that woman, Mary Lowe, to talk Dora round with a bribe of, say, another nice dress or something like that. What had she to offer? An attic room, the constant smell of paint, the leak in the corner from a broken tile, a lavatory along the hall below whose flush was as if a battle had broken out and which, if used in the middle of the night, would wake up the whole building; tenants who kept themselves to themselves, whom she saw so little of that they might have been ghosts, who often, out of a misguided courtesy for others asleep in the house, avoided pulling the chain after bedtime, the morning revealing a pan full of all that had passed in the night.

This is what she had to offer her sister. On top of that, food would be plain and not plentiful. No more nice gowns. She'd be out all day trying to sell her work and what would Dora do with herself in the meantime? Not a very attractive offer. Ellie scratched miserably at her itching chilblains.

She still intended to visit Dora, but best to leave it for a while longer. Instead she used the evening to write to her, keeping it light-hearted so that should anyone else open it – and she wouldn't put it past Mrs Lowe to do just that – there'd be nothing significant to be gleaned from it.

Another reason for not going to see her was that this afternoon had been a little traumatic, and special, not to say surprising.

As usual, she had sat on her stool beside her small display of pictures propped against the park railings, eyeing the passing public despondently. Not much interest in works of art. The weather had been miserable, the end of January as cold as could be expected, heightened by a sharp wind bearing the odd flurry of light snow whenever it felt inclined. Who'd want to come out?

Huddled in the expensive but now gradually deteriorating winter coat she'd brought with her from Doctor Lowe's, Ellie got up off her stool as she recognized the man coming towards her. Her lips tightened.

'So you've shown yourself at last,' she began. 'What've you got to say for yourself, Mr C. Hunnard?'

She might have been talking to the wind. He utterly ignored her as he took in the two oil paintings she'd set up, the one of her mother, the other, still unsold, of Mary Lowe, the rest just a couple of watercolour scenes.

The painting that was supposed to represent her father she had left behind, no longer being able to look at it without experiencing a new feeling: that the figure at his feet wasn't her mother but herself. It made her feel strangely ashamed now to look, and it stood propped with its face to the wall. She wanted no one to see it now and many times had thought to paint over it, but was somehow unable to bring herself to. Though why she couldn't have said.

'This one,' Hunnard was saying, indicating the distorted likeness of her mother. 'This is new. It's very good.'

He looked from the painting to her. 'You must keep going with these, young woman. Get rid of this other rubbish.' He waved his silver-topped cane towards the landscapes, then swung it back to her mother's portrait. 'I should like to buy this one.'

Strangely she felt loath to sell it, though if she wished to settle the rent and buy fuel and food, she would have to. She was no nearer to having all that money she'd dreamed of, enough to further her plans to find and confront her father.

The man had moved even closer to the painting to peer at it. Ellie watched him with growing indignation. Who did he think he was, taking in her work as if he were some blooming judge or other at a competition?

'How much?' he asked suddenly, standing back.

Now Ellie flared. 'A bit more than the measly four quid you gave me for my last one! Someone saw it in your gallery, marked up at fifty guineas, and you gave me four pounds. Well, no, Mr Hunnard, this one's not for sale – not at what you're offering.'

He regarded her for a moment, then quietly said, 'What if I offered a sum you couldn't refuse?'

Ellie's anger died a little, but she still stood her ground. 'It depends on how much.'

Her heart was beating so fast it was making her feel a little sick. What if he named a price around the fifty guineas that the previous one had been marked up for? – should she stick out for more? After all, this portrait of her mother was special to her. She wasn't sure she even wanted to sell it.

She needed the money, desperately. All that she had made earlier was practically gone and next week's rent still to pay. But what if he laughed at her price and walked away? She'd be in the soup.

She took a deep breath. 'What about what you're selling my other picture for? This one's even better . . . I put my heart and soul into my work and you treat it as if it's just a business. You're the one with no soul.'

He interrupted her with a laugh. 'My dear child, I am appreciative of the work you people do, and art *is* in my soul. That is why I am proprietor of an art gallery. But business is business and my establishment does not run on hot air. It is costly, there are massive overheads and risks taken, and at the end of the day I am not a charity. I also need to make a profit from what I love selling. Is that enough for you, child?'

Ellie wasn't impressed. She was incensed. 'And what about my overheads, as you call it?' she demanded. 'I've got to find the money to buy paint and canvas and food, and pay for the room I have to live in and coal for a fire to keep warm with. At the end of the day what profit is there for me?'

'So what are you asking for this?' Completely unmoved, he looked back at the portrait. 'Who else is going to buy it other than myself? You have a client here who is interested in your strange interpretation of the human form and I happen to think it may have a market. But your price must be a viable one.'

She didn't know what viable was. All she wanted was her due. Ellie tightened her lips. 'I want half of what you sell it for.'

'That means I take it away and pay you nothing until it is sold. That could take months, or might not happen at all. Maybe people are not ready for work such as yours.'

'You sold my other one.'

'No-o-o.' The reply came slow and exacting, almost patronizing. 'That hangs in my gallery still, awaiting a buyer. That is the risk I take. Therefore I will not meet any exaggerated price, and your suggestion is not sensible, to my mind. I shall give you twenty pounds for it.'

Ellie stood dumbfounded in disbelief, but he continued to talk.

'Here is my proposition. I will give you twenty guineas, here and now, and take this away with me. I will give you my card. And if I find a buyer I'll give you ten per cent. That is a generous offer. Take it or leave it. Leave it and I will not buy your painting.'

Ellie thought quickly. Ten per cent of fifty guineas wasn't all that generous – a little over five pounds – but she'd have the twenty in hand. Dared she take up his offer? He seemed very keen to possess her painting. She might even up the price.

'Come on, young woman!' he prompted. 'Make up your mind. I'm paying a lad to keep an eye on my vehicle. He'll be wondering where I am.'

'Vehicle?'

Unable to help herself, she queried the word and saw him grin behind his beard. She was informed that he had one of these automobiles that were beginning to be seen on the roads, frightening the horses.

The revelation chased away what she'd had in mind to tell him and she found herself blurting out the words, 'All right, I agree. If you take me to see your showrooms.'

Instantly she realized how childish she must sound, proving her not to be as adult as she assumed she was. 'I'd just like to see the other one I did hanging there.'

To her surprise he nodded. 'Very well.'

'Twenty guineas,' she reminded him before he could move to take up the picture. His smile broadened as he reached into his heavy, dark-coloured, astrakhan-collared topcoat. Extracting a leather wallet, he took out several large, crisp, white banknotes and handed them over.

'Bring the painting,' he ordered and strode off rapidly, Ellie following.

She saw Felix with both his thumbs up and displaying a broad grin. In reply she indicated a plea for him to keep an eye on her other pictures, and he nodded, still grinning. She could trust him. He might even sell one. But with interest being sparse, she reckoned not. Anyway he had his own to sell.

This was the first motor vehicle she'd ever been near enough to touch, much less ride in. Slipping a sixpence to the young lad he'd enlisted to keep an eye on the vehicle, Hunnard took the painting from her to place behind the long, leather seat before taking her hand to assist her into the vehicle. She had to gather her skirts so as not to trip on them as she stepped tentatively up into the thing, bending her head low so that her straw boater did not collide with the hood that had been unfolded to shield the inside from the weather, very much like the hood on a baby's pram or on a bath chair.

'Are you comfortable enough?' he asked. Ellie smiled and nodded, feeling not at all comfortable but very much on edge in case she might topple out on to the ground the moment the contraption started up. Her heart was in her mouth, but she held her smile.

Closing the little door on her, Hunnard went round to climb in beside her, spreading a thick rug over her knees, making her feel strange sitting so near to a man she hardly knew; but he took little notice of her as he began adjusting things that probably worked the engine.

He seemed quite at ease with it all, but Ellie clung with clawed fingers to the edge of the seat, unsure what would happen as they moved off, sure she might be flung up into the air. At a signal from Hunnard, the young lad began to energetically crank the engine, part of the task he had been paid to do. His job done, he scurried off, a silver sixpence richer for his pains.

As the engine started up, Ellie gave a little squeak of terror. Hunnard gave a deep chuckle.

'It's quite safe. Safe as houses,' he remarked and she held her breath, so as not to show herself up any further. As they started away, she felt the breeze hit against her cheeks with the increase of speed, but the machine wasn't as noisy as she had imagined – none of that rumbling, clanking, banging of the very few she had so far seen frightening the horses as they rattled past far faster than a trot.

His galleries were situated near Brompton on the other side of Hyde Park. They didn't look nearly as big as she had expected but seemed to have quite a few people moving in and out of the main door. Leaving the vehicle in a side street, he conducted her through a side door, along a short corridor and into a long, brightly lit room where people were wandering with intent expressions as they gazed at what was being shown.

No one noticed them enter from the side door and Hunnard seemed to prefer it that way. Unobtrusively he guided her to one side.

'Your self-portrait,' he announced, quietly indicating it, now in a plain, light-coloured wood frame. A little removed from a collection of modern art, it looked isolated, as if it had no right to be there, making it look amateurish and stiff against the flowing lines of the others. It looked different and out of step with what he told her was the work of post-impressionists.

When she said nothing, Hunnard went on. 'There have been quite a few new schools of thinking springing up these last fifty years. Yours is just another way of looking at life and it takes time for the public to adjust to something new.' Gazing at her forlorn little painting, Ellie could see why.

It did look out of place. Perhaps it would never sell. Then why had he bought it and then even come back for more of her work?

Hunnard led her away from her forlorn little picture to move between the rows of hung paintings. What he was saying meant nothing to her – all about post-impressionism, primitivism, expressionism. As she gazed with feigned knowledge at what he was pointing out, it was going over her head. All she knew about painting was what Michael had told her, no connoisseur himself, and her natural talent and sensitivity for what she painted. All this grandiose allusion to all these different schools of painting was only making her feel inadequate and very naive.

'Your work is very different,' he was saying. 'It falls into the category of neither impressionism nor expressionism, though maybe leaning towards primitivism.'

Ellie had never heard of any of this before, having no idea what he was going on about. But she wasn't going to display her ignorance.

'However,' he continued, 'your work is new, refreshing, and for a young woman your brushwork is surprisingly strong, which adds to its charm. It presents a puzzle and the public may think that; but I firmly believe it will eventually be accepted.' If this was meant to be encouraging, she didn't feel it; but he continued with hardly a pause.

'It was the same with most of our impressionists in the beginning as well as with the expressionists and primitives. Consider Vogeler, Fritz Mackensen, Charles Maurin, Lovis Corinth, Paula Modersohn-Becker. She is a woman, by the way, like yourself, but is of course well established.'

She was glad to hear of at least one woman among all these male painters. She wasn't alone, then.

'What you lack, young lady, is experience, good grounding. You need to study under a good tutor, another painter of merit. I strongly advise you to consider it. But you are very young and have hardly begun to live.'

Ellie wanted suddenly to laugh but managed to curb it. If anyone had done enough living, as he called it, she had – enough for someone twice her age: living in fear of her own father, watching her mother working to keep her family together, watching her die, being thrown out of her home at the age of fifteen to fend for herself and a younger sister, and they could well have been sent off to an orphanage to work like little slaves for all the good her own brother had been . . . No, that was unfair. Charlie had given Dad a good bashing when he'd caught him abusing her. But then he had walked out. They'd both walked out, leaving her at fifteen to cope with a dying woman.

She became aware that while she'd been going over the past, the man standing beside her was still talking, unaware of her wandering thoughts.

'In time you could develop into as fine a painter as Modersohn-Becker, if you apply yourself. You have time on your side. Even Paul Gauguin did not begin to paint seriously until he was nearly forty.' He shook his head sadly. 'But now his health is failing him. His paintings no longer sell as once they did. Virtually penniless, yet he is producing some of his finest work. He now lives far away from France, you know, on one of the islands in the Marquesas. Such is the fickleness of public taste.'

He gave a deep, dramatic sigh before turning to regard her. 'But you have still to reach your peak, and this is why your single piece of work is here. It takes up room, but I pride myself on being far-sighted and have faith in it. And that is why I have bought your second painting.'

Ellie found herself being conducted back to where her picture was hanging. Someone was now gazing up at it, briefly consulting a catalogue he held, then looking back at the picture in deep study. Ellie dared hope that he would suddenly say to Hunnard that he wanted to buy it, but the man moved on and Ellie felt her heart sink a little.

'You see,' Hunnard began, 'I am interested in the subject.'

'You mean my mother?' Ellie queried. 'She was—'

'No, child, the subject matter, the technique – symbolic of your world as you see it, the way you approach your subject. It is filled with pain,' he added as she began to look confused. 'I cannot put it in any simpler terms.'

'No, of course not,' she had said stupidly, trying to look learned.

She had still been unsure of what he'd been talking about as she finally came away, left to find her own way back to where she had left her other pictures. Even so she had felt good about herself and, with money in her pocket, she actually took a cab, if only one of the cheaper ones, known as growlers because the driver was seldom polite, as if he begrudged his job, and might become quite surly if pressed to do anything out of the ordinary such as carry someone's parcels.

With her head full of all the nonsense Hunnard seemed to talk, Ellie had approached a grinning Felix. 'Well?' he'd asked.

'Well,' she had shrugged. 'He did talk a load of rubbish, but at least I gathered he thinks my paintings have promise.'

She hadn't told him of their deal. It might not come off and she might find herself landed with unsold pictures and nothing to show for it. But the man wasn't going to get his twenty quid back and that was certain.

After a moment's thought about the letter she was writing this evening, Ellie added a bit about this afternoon's event, unable to keep it to herself any longer. And it would look good to Dora, perhaps make her feel even more discontented with her lot and want to come and live with her instead. What fun they'd have if she did: no restrictions, doing what they liked without having to ask anyone, going out together when they felt like it. It would be just lovely. And she did miss Dora so.

Twenty-Five

'You've been among us for almost two months,' Felix was saying as he lifted her exhibits along with his own on to the old perambulator he used to get his work home after a day of trying to sell them. 'But you don't mix.'

That was true. Other than at the New Year party, he was the only one she really knew. Perhaps she could have pushed herself forward more, but she felt she was still an outsider.

She thought he might have given his support, introduced her to a few of his friends, at least the man he was living with, but he hadn't. Perhaps to him she did appear to prefer her own company, but it was only because she didn't quite know how she, a stranger, could break through what she saw as a barrier. By nature she *was* lively, but on strange ground, and she didn't want to show herself up in a community whose only conversation seemed to revolve forever around its work, the outside world being another sphere.

'Not much I can do about it,' she said huffily.

'Don't you want to?' he queried.

Yes, more than anything she wanted to. 'Well, I don't know anyone. And no one seems to want to know me, apart from you.'

'Well, with Robert C. Hunnard buying your paintings, they'll soon want to know you. We're all struggling. One or two make it, but not many.'

'I haven't made it,' she retorted. 'All I've done is sell a couple of paintings to him.'

'Which now hang in the Hunnard Gallery. He doesn't buy paintings that he doesn't think will bring him a good profit. You don't know, but he could make your name for you. Lucky girl!'

'Or perhaps he won't!' she snapped.

Felix gave a little chuckle. 'There's that to it, I suppose. Meantime you're stuck in that one little room of yours like some anchorite, seeing no one except when you're here hawking your work, and even then you don't talk to anyone but me.'

'I know you,' she explained. 'I don't know anyone else.'

He looked at her quizzically. 'Then do you want to meet some of us?'

'Of course I do, but I can't just push my way into other people's private conversation. Anyway, they're men artists and I'd feel out of place.'

Felix became serious. 'Is that what you're worried about? Well, my love, there are quite a few lady painters. This evening I'm off to meet a few friends. Come along with me. I don't guarantee another female painter will be there, but most of us do have female friends . . . They're nice,' he added hurriedly as Ellie grimaced. 'One or two even have wives. Will you come?'

Ellie lifted her head and nodded. Some had lady friends. Some were married. It made her feel better.

As Felix walked her home, she wondered about the person he shared his room with. Surely it was really a woman and not a he? Was she more to him than just a room mate? He hardly ever spoke of her. But Ellie knew these people by now – sleeping together didn't seem to worry them overmuch and it could be that Felix and this woman shared the same bed as well as the same room. Still, it could be only a casual relationship, a natural consequence of living there together, say until the woman moved on, found someone else. If it was only that, then perhaps she had a chance with him. He was likeable, considerate, not rough or brusque. Yes, she could be happy with someone like Felix.

As he helped her home with her paintings Ellie made up her mind to have him herself, and luckily, not having met his partner, she'd feel no guilt. It did occur to her that going with Felix could spoil her plans for tracing her father, but she couldn't go on turning down love and making her own life a misery. It would only be adding to the damage he'd already done to her and she didn't see why she couldn't enjoy life yet still keep to her plan. Only lack of money, not lack of someone to love, was stopping her. Why couldn't she have both?

As she and Felix reached her destination, she took her paintings from him, and looked up into his face. 'You really are kind to me,' she whispered, moving close to him. She saw him shrug.

'How else would one be to a friend?'

'Not more than just a friend?' she prompted coquettishly. She saw him smile, a sort of secretive smile she couldn't interpret.

'A good friend then, a very good friend,' he conceded; but as she lifted her face up to his, her lips ready to meet his, already guessing how soft and gentle they would be, he surprised her by moving back a little.

Ellie tried not to let her gaze harden as she too moved back from him. She'd made a mistake. He was being loyal to this partner of his. Moments later, determination to get him away from the girl took hold of Ellie even more. But she could bide her time. 'About you taking me to meet some other people this evening,' she reminded, '– is it still all right?'

'Of course.' He seemed a little embarrassed by the incident of a few moments ago. 'I'd be thrilled to have you come along. Shall I collect you around eight, if that's all right? Come just as you are. We're quite informal.'

'Will you be bringing your other friend?' Ellie couldn't resist asking.

'I expect so. See you later then.'

Ellie tried not to frown. His friend!

She had already promised herself that the girl wouldn't be his friend much longer, but what if she turned out to be sweet and unassuming? – could she still try stealing her man from her?

She almost wanted to call after Felix that she had changed her mind, didn't want to go, but he had already turned the corner out of sight.

To Ellie's relief, Felix was alone when he arrived. Ellie wondered as she looked beyond him if they might have had a row. Maybe he'd told his girl about her and she'd become jealous.

Yet he didn't seem disturbed when she enquired, 'Your friend not with you?' as they moved off together.

'No,' he said lightly. 'Other things to do, I'm afraid. He's in the middle of completing a piece of sculpture and has got very wrapped up in it. He's awfully good.'

He, Ellie almost echoed, but bit her tongue in time. Her heart soared suddenly as light as a feather. She had no reason to feel guilty at all. Why had she assumed his room mate to be a woman? She couldn't remember now what had happened to make her think that. She felt so happy that she linked her arm through his, and didn't notice the instant tension in the muscle.

It was a wonderful evening: a noisy little café, almost everyone having something to do with art of one sort or another, all talking shop, as it were.

Felix introduced her to his own circle of companions; and there were women there, mostly clad in colourful, flowing garments. Where conventional fashion was for the nipped-in waist, the puff-pigeon bosom and formal neckline, these gowns were loose, as tea gowns might be, but brilliant in colour, many with really low necklines and wide sleeves; and instead of wearing stiff hats, they were bareheaded or wore brightly patterned bandanas that bound the hair and forehead, some with a dyed feather or a cheap and gaudy brooch, while coloured beads festooned the neck, and earrings clanked. But they were all happy, noisy, talking non-stop. Ellie felt she'd never enjoyed an evening so much.

At first she was hesitant, but was so quickly welcomed that she soon relaxed – especially after Felix had brought her a small, milky-coloured drink he said was absinthe.

'It can be a little strong if you're not used to it,' he said as she took it from him. 'So I had some water added. Hope you like it.'

Water or no water, the first sip tasted so strongly of aniseed that it took her breath away, but by the time she'd sipped it for half the evening, she had unwound enough to join in with all the conversation, giggling at silly jokes, trying in fact to focus on the faces before her.

'So you've caught Robert Hunnard's evil eye, have you?' someone said to her, at which she proceeded to tell those around her about her experience; and, to her delight, everyone listened avidly, pitching in from time to time with enthusiasm and snippets of encouragement, genuinely delighted for her.

'You're made,' she was being told. 'God, I wish I had your blasted luck! You won't forget us when you're rich and famous, will you? – us poor, bloody, struggling, Godforsaken daubers!'

She promised them that she'd never forget any of them but protested her 'luck' might be just a flash in the pan and she'd never be rich. But she preened herself about the fact that it might happen. She told them all that, but for them, she wouldn't have been there today, thanking them profusely for all they'd done for her. Before she knew it, Felix was helping her to her feet, laughing.

On the way home in the small hours, he let her lean against him for support as the world moved around her in a giddy spin. He had his arm about her waist, and when she came to a sudden standstill, not quite sure which foot to put in front of the other, he held her close.

All she could think about was that the person who shared his room wasn't a woman. It was wonderful. She lifted her face to his, her arms about his neck as their lips met in a lingering kiss, so it seemed to her befuddled mind, until suddenly he pulled his face away from her.

'Don't, love!'

She felt suddenly angry. 'Don't? After that sort of kiss, what d'you mean – don't?'

'I mean don't, Ellie. What else can I say?'

She tried to turn from him in her anger and if he hadn't held on to her she'd have fallen.

'What's wrong with you?' she blared at him, trying to pull away from his grasp. 'Aren't I your sort? Well, I'm sorry I don't please you. I s'pose you prefer women what dress like them in the café, like that female you were slobbering over at that New Year party.'

'Woman?' he said stupidly. Of course he'd forgotten since then.

'The one with the red, dyed hair, showing half her bosom and plenty of her leg. The one you kissed in front of everyone. Not that they cared. They were all drunk. If I hadn't come up to you, you'd have been off with her to where all the other lovers were going for a good time.'

Felix was staring at her. 'Ah, the New Year party.'

'Yes, that. And I'm sorry I can't match the likes of her sort, nor do I think I want to.'

He was silent for a moment, then said slowly, 'Ellie, it wasn't a her.'

Ellie tried to focus her eyes on him. He was still holding on to her to prevent her from toppling sideways. Surely she wasn't so drunk that she had misheard him. She wanted to giggle at the ludicrous admission, yet her heart seemed to be falling down into her boots.

'What – what d'you mean?' she stammered.

'That one you saw me kissing. It wasn't a woman. I'm sorry, I thought you understood.'

He spoke so calmly, his voice so gentle, a naturally lovely, gentle person: now it all came together. She'd secretly fallen in love with him and now she must fall out of love. Her heart felt so heavy in a way that she'd never expected.

'Oh,' was all she could say.

'I'm sorry,' he said again. 'I thought you knew.'

'No, I didn't.'

'Does it matter to you?' What a stupid question to ask. Of course it mattered.

'No, it doesn't matter,' she said automatically. The street had begun to slow its whirling. 'It just took me by surprise, that's all.'

'We're still friends?'

'Yes, of course.' She wanted to get away, put the door between them, go upstairs to her little attic room and throw herself on the bed to burst into tears. But she wouldn't make it on her own. She had visions of losing her footing on the bare flight of stairs and rolling back down them. 'I need help getting upstairs,' she said weakly.

There was a need to sort her life out. It was like being forsaken, just as she'd felt when Michael Deel had let her down. Then she'd felt insulted, belittled, betrayed. This time it was no one's fault, no one was to blame, it was out of everyone's control – like a sort of an act of God that nothing could be done about.

After days of moping, when she couldn't even find heart to take her pictures to sell, Ellie pulled her thoughts together. She wasn't doing herself or anyone any good behaving like this. The worst thing was that she couldn't even bring herself to pick up a brush, her mind being utterly blank.

With fitful February sunlight picking its way through the grubby windowpanes, she set up the old easel she'd bought second hand and propped the partly begun canvas on it. Once a little more paint was applied she might find the impetus to continue.

Standing back from it, Ellie contemplated what was already there. It was going to be a portrait of Felix. She had begun it only a week ago with love in her heart – a beautiful, gentle face, this time not sharp and thorny and stark, with no harsh angles but gentle curves, the eyes, offset as was her trait, to be full of appeal. And now in the dark background a face, shrouded in shadow, like a spectre, looking on – the face of his lover as she saw him.

After staring at it for a few minutes she began to squeeze precious colours from half-empty tubes that would soon need replacing; money must be found for these at the expense of other essentials. But, of course, she had much of Hunnard's twenty guineas left.

The palette dotted with small circles of oil paint, Ellie began mixing a touch of white and blue together on her brush. Reaching out, she laid the contents thinly under what would be the shadow beneath the smooth chin. It went on far too thick.

Damning her folly, she angrily scraped off the offending effort. Forcing herself to calm, she slowly and painstakingly reapplied the paint.

It seemed to work this time, but after a couple more efforts she put her brush and palette down. Something was missing inside her; there was no feel for what she was doing, just sadness – against the tricks that life can play on people, a man that a girl could love was someone beyond her reach. The one he cared for – not the one he'd casually embraced in a miasma of opium and alcohol at the New Year party, but a loving and steady partner – had all the affections she wished *she* had.

She somehow felt that this portrait of Felix would never be completed, but there were no other ideas in her head at all and there was no point in forcing herself.

Ellie turned away from the unfinished work and instead proceeded to brew a pot of tea. She'd not eaten, but didn't feel hungry. Sipping the mug of tea, she went over to the picture that she now saw as that of her father, still with its face to the wall, and turned it round towards her.

The sight of it was as good a cure as anything for taking all else out of her mind. As she gazed at it there came the thought that she must go and see Dora. But first she would drop in to visit her old neighbours. They'd be surprised to see her. And

she did need something solid to hang on to – real people with
their minds on living as best they could. It was probably the
tonic she needed to get her feet back on the ground.

That Sunday morning Mrs Sharp opened the door to her knock,
her eyes opening wide with surprise and pleasure at seeing
her standing there.

'Gor bless me, it's you, young Ellie! We ain't seen you fer
ages. 'Ow are yer? All right?'

'I just thought I'd pop in to see how you all were,' Ellie
said, and seconds later was ushered into the back room, where
the entire family was gathered, the remains of Sunday breakfast still littering the table with its tea- and food-stained cloth.

To her delight, Ronnie was there, but without his fiancée.
He was lounging back on his chair when Ellie entered. Seeing
her, he got to his feet almost as if she were a lady and he a
menial. He looked so tall, so handsome that Ellie's heart did
a little flip despite herself; but it settled immediately, knowing
he had a steady girlfriend now. No doubt he'd shortly be
leaving to go and meet her.

It came to Ellie that if she had struck earlier instead of
being so set on finding her father, and had settled down to
normal life, she might now be his fiancée instead of this girl
he now had. But at the time she had not wanted anything to
get in the way of her search. It was ironic that at this moment
it no longer seemed that important. Just the same, she couldn't
help asking him if he had ever found out anything through
the *News Chronicle*, where he worked.

'No, not yet,' came the easy reply. 'But yer never know,
something could come up one day.'

As she had anticipated, it wasn't long before he was up,
taking his leave of her to get himself spruced up ready to
meet his fiancée.

After he had gone, it no longer seemed all that important
for her to stay. With a promise to pop in more often, she too
left, aware that she had missed her chances with him. At seventeen, she should have had a boyfriend, but she had no one.
All because of this stupid obsession of hers!

Twenty-Six

This was the right time to visit Dora – she was sure of it as she left Ronnie's house: Sunday, a day of rest for most people, mid-morning, Mrs Lowe either taking her ease or at church – so long as Dora hadn't been required to go with her, in which case she'd wait for them to return home.

An attack of the collywobbles began to start up in her tummy as she approached Old Ford Road. By the time she gained Doctor Lowe's house and surgery, they were really having a go. At the small flight of steps up to the front door Ellie hesitated. It would be better to go round the back, past the surgery entrance. She'd tap on the kitchen door. Mrs Jenkins would be there, preparing the Sunday lunch. No church for her.

Ellie's knock was tentative. Even so, she had hardly removed her knuckles from the figured-glass portion before the door burst open as if in a fit of anger to reveal Mrs Jenkins ready to give a piece of her mind to whichever unwelcome caller this was on a quiet February Sunday morning.

'What do you . . .' The harsh voice trailed off as the woman frowned down at her in surprise. 'You!' Another pause, then: 'What d'you want, coming here?'

Collywobbles gone, Ellie lifted her head in defiance. 'I've come to see Dora.'

'Oh, you 'ave, 'ave you. Then you can just go away again, miss. She don't need to see you.'

'I rather imagine that to be my business, Mrs Jenkins.' She spoke in the nicest accents, the way Michael had taught her. 'Is my sister at home?' She said it as if Dora was part of the family.

Mrs Jenkins blinked, but her round face remained hard. 'She usually goes to church with Mrs Lowe, but she's been a bit poorly.'

All pretence fell from Ellie with her alarm. 'Poorly?' All sorts of awful illnesses raced through her mind. She should have come here much sooner. 'How poorly?'

'She's had a bit of a cold all week. She's getting over it now but Mrs Lowe thought it was best she didn't go out this morning.'

That was a relief. Ellie regained her confidence if not her artificial airs. 'Then it's a good job I'm here. I'd like to come in to see her, Mrs Jenkins.'

There was a short hesitation as the woman glanced over towards the big, plain clock on the kitchen wall. 'Well, they won't be home for another half-hour so I suppose you can. She is your sister. But you've got to be gone before they get back.'

With this she moved aside, still not quite friendly, but resigned to letting the girl in. 'You stay here. I'll go and get her, then you can go into the parlour to talk. But not for long, mind.'

Dora looked washed-out when she came into the room. She hadn't done her hair and it hung loose almost down to her waist in a mass of gleaming auburn almost like a shawl about her shoulders.

Her nose still looked sore from constant blowing into a handkerchief and when she spoke, saying how good it was to see Ellie, her words were thick.

'You should have written to me that you had a bad cold,' Ellie scolded as they sat on the sofa in the parlour, careful not to disturb the cushions in case Dora's employers noticed and asked questions. 'I'd have been round here straight away if I'd known.'

'I didn't feel much like writing,' Dora said quietly, '– much like doing anything really.'

'You could have been at death's door and I wouldn't have known.'

'Nothing like that,' Dora said quickly. 'Mrs Lowe was very kind to me and Doctor Lowe was on hand to give me some medicine and keep an eye on me in case it got worse. I couldn't have been in better hands.'

'And I wasn't needed.'

'I didn't mean it like that, Ellie,' came the plea. 'I've wished so many times that you was here. I even wished we was all together back home, with Mum and Dad and Charlie, just a family.'

Dora's eyes began to swim in tears. 'I do miss everyone so much.'

'Then come and live with me. I've got a nice room. I use it as a studio to paint in, but there'd be room for the two of us. And I might soon be able to afford something bigger.'

Gabbling on, she told Dora about the gallery owner who had taken a liking to her paintings.

'So it looks like I might be well off before long,' she ended eagerly; but Dora was biting her lips.

'I can't leave here,' she said. 'Not really.'

'But you're not happy.'

Dora gave an indifferent shrug. 'I've got used to it here. I know Mrs Lowe can be a bit of a trial, but it is safe here. What would I have done last week if Doctor Lowe hadn't been here to look after me? I keep thinking of Mum and how she got worse and worse without anyone to get her better.'

Ellie felt her resentment begin to rise. 'If Doctor Lowe had found it in him to see her, Mum might be alive today,' she said sullenly. 'But no, we didn't have any money. We were just nobodies. Now, of course, you're in his care and his wife doesn't want to lose you. You're very convenient for her!'

'It's not like that!' Dora protested. 'What I mean is, I'm comfortable here and safe and I've more or less got most of what I want.'

'And if you come to live with me, you won't have them comforts.'

Dora was silent, her pretty young face turning sulky. Ellie got up sharply in a fit of annoyance. 'Very well then, you stay here. But one day it'll get stale and you'll find yourself not wanted. What then?'

Still no response. The girl's head was bowed. She had her hanky to her nose, the cold still bothering her; or was she crying silently? Ellie couldn't tell with the girl's hair fallen forward, hiding her face. But she was still angry.

'So that's it, is it? In that case, I don't know why I bothered to come.'

She walked to the door but, with some of her anger dissipating, turned back to her sister, still sitting silently on the sofa. 'At least you can write to me now and again, let me know how you are. And if you do change your mind, Dora, if anything goes wrong, I'll be here for you. All right?'

Dora managed a nod and sat up to look at her. Her eyes had become bloodshot and tears ran down her pale cheeks. 'I don't want to be a nuisance to anyone.'

Ellie felt all her anger sweep away. She ran back to her sister. Sitting down again beside her, she pulled her close, rocking her gently and making comforting sounds as the girl broke down. She found she too was crying.

'Look, I understand,' she crooned. 'I won't ask you to do anything you don't want to. But if you do want to, let me know straight away and I'll come and collect you. Any time.'

With a deep, fortifying intake of breath, Dora sat up and, giving an almighty sniff laden with mucus, lifted her head. 'I'm all right, Ellie. But it's all taken me a bit by surprise – you coming here out of the blue. I need to think about things. And I will let you know. I promise.'

Ellie looked at the little bowed clock on the cloth-covered mantelshelf over the low fire in the grate. 'I'll have to go now,' she said gently. 'They'll be back soon. I didn't know the time could go so fast.'

She gazed at Dora. 'Will you be all right?'

As Dora nodded, Ellie stood up, bending to kiss her sister's wet cheek. 'No more crying, or they'll see your eyes all red. I'll keep in touch with you. And you keep in touch with me, and—'

She was stopped by loud voices: Mrs Jenkins's harsh tones and Mrs Lowe's high, bleating ones. Before Ellie could take a breath the door flew open and three portly figures stood there: Doctor and Mrs Lowe, dressed in formal Sunday wear, as well as Mrs Jenkins. He was in his black frock coat, black striped trousers and stiff high collar, his high silk top hat no doubt left on the hall stand. Mrs Lowe's hat was huge and plumed. Her sombre grey day dress also had a high collar with a jet brooch at the neck and a festoon of jet beads falling to her full bosom. Like her husband's top hat, her warm wrap had most likely also been left with their maid. Mrs Jenkins stood behind them, her full face full of concern.

Mary Lowe's blue eyes were trained on Dora. 'What is the meaning of this?' she burst out. 'What do you think you are doing, girl?'

'It's my sister. She came to see me,' Dora said in a small voice as she rose from the sofa.

'I know who it is!' came the sharp reply. 'What is she doing here? Why are you entertaining her? You were apparently too under the weather to attend church; yet here you are, chatting away to your sister. Was this some sort of conspiracy – making excuses not to attend church and, as soon as I am out of the way, going behind my back? I request you go up to your room and wait for me . . .'

Ellie stepped forward, her face blazing. She knew she looked every inch a woman. Her wavy hair was piled up and carefully puffed out. The black toque she'd bought especially for today with some of the money Hunnard had given her for that last painting went with the dark winter coat she'd brought away with her from here. Black gloves and well-polished boots finished the ensemble.

'My sister's not your property, Mrs Lowe,' she began. 'If she wants to quit her job as lady's maid and so-called companion, you can't stop her.'

'Who do you think you are talking to?' squealed Mrs Lowe, coming to confront her like some aggressive, puffed-up pigeon. 'That girl is in my care until she reaches the age of independence. Then she can do what she likes.'

'You mean she can be thrown out when it suits you?' Ellie finished hotly. 'With no idea of the world after having been tied to your skirts for years? – told what to do and what not to do.'

Not knowing what to say, the woman hesitated, appealing to her husband to speak up for her.

He did. 'Dora, do as your mistress says and go on up to your room, like a good girl.'

Dora's eyes had dried. 'What?' she said indignantly.

'I said, like a good girl!' he repeated. 'Now do as you are told, Dora.' The tone of his voice, instead of startling her, made her eyes blaze.

Suddenly, it seemed, she made up her mind. She turned towards her sister, her lips thin and set.

'Right, Ellie, I'm coming with you,' she said and threw the others a truculent glance. 'I shall be staying with my sister for a few days.'

'Dora, did you hear what I said?' thundered Bertram Lowe, but she took no notice, as if he hadn't spoken at all.

'And if I decide to stay for good, I'll come back to collect the rest of my things.'

She sounded so grown-up for someone only fifteen years old that it took Ellie's breath away and she felt a great surge of pride go through her. But then, she'd been only fifteen, too, when she'd been forced to suddenly grow up.

Bertram Lowe was looking at her, his piggy eyes baleful. 'This is your doing,' he blared, his moustache waggling with indignation, his face suffused with a rush of rage.

'I've done all I could to make sure of your happiness and safety under my roof. I took you in when you had nowhere to go. I gave you a good home. I had you taught to behave like a lady. I paid out of my own pocket for your tutoring. And what did you do? – threw it all in my face, running off with your tutor, and thank heaven his father made him see sense. I gave you all my fond affection –' He pulled himself up sharply as his wife shot a startled glance at him. '– and this is how you reward us,' he went on quickly as if he hadn't noticed the confession he'd just made. 'By disrupting my home and enticing away a girl my wife has become equally fond of.'

He glanced again at his wife as if that last statement vindicated him.

Ellie stood her ground, even found herself enjoying the argument. 'I am grateful for all you did for me,' she said calmly. 'But you must have realized I wouldn't stay with you for ever – that one day I would leave to live my own life.'

She almost said that she wasn't his daughter, bound to his family, but thought better of it before any more damage was done. He was a good man. He didn't deserve to have his nose rubbed in it. She suddenly felt unkind to have been so pleased with herself.

'I am sorry, Doctor Lowe,' she said now. 'I am truly grateful for all you've done for me and Dora. But it did have to come to an end eventually. You can see that. I really don't want us to be enemies.'

'That is exactly what you are!' cried Mrs Lowe, but he put out a hand to quieten her.

'Nor do I, Ellie. And I understand your feelings. If I can be of any help to you in the future, please do let me know.'

There were tears in his pale eyes – tears she hoped his wife hadn't seen – and she felt her own tears start to spring. He had been kind to her. That he'd allowed it go so far as to see in her a replacement for his dead daughter was no one's fault.

But it had become too claustrophobic and she'd have had to escape at some time, even if Michael hadn't persuaded her away. Now she felt as if she was betraying him. She had used him. She had used everyone, it seemed, to further her plan to get even with her father. Had it all been worth it? She wasn't sure now.

'I'm so very sorry,' she managed to say.

'We don't want your sorries!' shouted Mrs Lowe vehemently. 'Just get out of my house! And take that ungrateful little brat with you!'

Mrs Lowe had no idea that she'd unwittingly broken the spell, in which Ellie had almost found herself ready to run into Bertram Lowe's arms to kiss his cheek and thank him for being such a good man to her. How would that have been received?

Instead, she nodded to him and gulped, feeling her heart about to break as he returned the nod, and saw him step back to let her and Dora pass.

Not so, Mrs Lowe. Ellie was half aware of a sudden sharp movement from her. Dora gave a little cry and ducked as Mrs Lowe's hand connected with the back of her head.

Ellie's first instinct was to swing round on her, to return the clout, knock her fine hat off her head. But she refrained out of what in that second felt like a surge of love for Bertram Lowe. Her hand fleetingly touched his, feeling it warm, the fingers momentarily curling about hers, and she was out into the hall, Mrs Jenkins already having the street door open for her.

So she and Dora emerged into the cold February air, which hit them like a fierce dash of cold water.

Dora was crying, not from the clout but from the upset of the whole affair. Ellie realized the girl had no coat, no hat or gloves, her hair hanging loose and uncombed, and that she only had a pair of indoor slippers on her feet and no stockings.

Letting go her hand, Ellie swung round and raced back up the three steps to the door just before Mrs Jenkins could close it.

'Dora's things!' she shot at her. 'Please get them for her!'

'I don't think—'

'Get them!' Ellie blazed, her tone bringing stares from two passers-by.

The door shut on her. She waited, Dora shivering with cold, sniffing with the remains of her own cold. Had Mrs Jenkins closed the door for good or just closed it to keep her out while she collected what was necessary?

Her ear close to the wood, she could hear Mrs Lowe's raised voice, Doctor Lowe trying to pacify her. How must he be feeling? Ellie put the thought from her. She couldn't concern herself about that just now.

There was one thought in her mind: if Dora's outdoor clothes weren't forthcoming soon, she might catch pneumonia, just as Mum had done.

What if Doctor Lowe wouldn't come out to her? But of course he would.

What had she done, going off half-cocked on the spur of the moment? Had she made things worse? But if this door didn't open soon she would kick at it with her foot, hammer on it, bellow for all the street to hear.

Then suddenly Mrs Jenkins was thrusting a shabby carpetbag into her hands. 'If she don't come back, you can come and collect her things for her. That's what I was told to say. Mrs Lowe don't want to see her any more. She says to say she's deverstated, she's really deverstated.'

The door closed abruptly. In the street, Ellie opened the carpetbag and pulled out coat, scarf, gloves, and quickly got Dora into them. She made her draw the stockings on only as far as her calves – no woman should be seen putting on stockings in the street – and eased her boots on over them.

With her arm about the girl, trying to get her warm, she walked her along Cambridge Heath Road, crossing the wide junction into Bethnal Green Road and continuing down along Gales Gardens.

'Good Lord, luv,' gasped Mrs Sharp as she saw the two standing on her doorstep. 'What in Gawd's name . . . Come in, yer both look perished.'

By the warmth of Mrs Sharp's back-room fire, and with hot mugs of cocoa clasped between their hands, the chill slowly oozed out of their bones. Ellie hadn't realized how cold she herself was, though it was more from the trauma of what had happened than from the cold February weather.

Quickly she told Mrs Sharp all that had happened. 'So you see, you were the only one I could think of coming to.'

'You two should stay 'ere tonight. It'll be dark soon and yer can't go all that way back to where you live on a day like this and in the dark. You'll 'ave no fire to heat up yer rooms and yer can't go ter be in the cold – not this kind of cold. Yer'll both catch yer death. I'll make up the couch and yer can sleep top ter toe, if that's all right. I'll keep the fire in all night. It's orright: I got money enough ter burn a bit of coal. Ronnie brings in good wages nowadays. The girls too. We don't live too bad these days. Not like when they was kids.'

She chatted on as she pottered about, cutting up the still-warm joint of lamb from their midday Sunday dinner to make sandwiches for the two girls. 'I've got some prunes and custard left over, so yer can 'ave them for yer afters. Sorry, there ain't no 'taters and greens left over from dinner, but my lot don't 'alf know 'ow to scoff.'

'Did Ronnie have dinner with his fiancée's people?' Ellie enquired while Dora was in the girl's bedroom putting her stockings on properly and doing her hair with brush, comb and hairpins that Mrs Jenkins, sensible woman, had thoughtfully put in with the clothes.

Mrs Sharp grimaced. 'Him? No, he 'ad it 'ere, what he et of it. Had a bust-up with his girl. I think it's orf fer good now.'

Ellie felt her insides give a leap. 'What happened?' she managed to ask calmly.

Again Mrs Sharp pulled a face. 'Oh, they was always arguing. It's bin on an' off fer months. Bit of a la-di-da, she is. Wants ter move to the country, wants 'im ter rent a blooming big 'ouse – more'n he can afford. Wants the bloody moon, I think. And 'im, silly sod, bin puttin' up with it for months. Too soft, that one. She wants everything 'er way. He don't 'ave no say in it. Well, I think it's finally come ter the crunch, and bloody good riddance I say. I didn't go much on 'er anyway.'

It was hard to speak without her voice trembling. 'Where is he now?'

'In the front room. Said he wants ter be left alone. So that's that for the while. You feeling warmer now, you two?'

'Yes thank you. And thank you for letting us stay the night,' Ellie said smoothly; but her heart was singing.

Twenty-Seven

It was marvellous having Dora with her. At last, someone to share her room, a room that had been so lonely. True, it was somewhat cramped, but so it had been when they had lived at home, the two of them having to share the one bed, as they now did. But as the weeks passed, Dora began showing signs of becoming bored.

At first she had been excited at not having Mrs Lowe to restrain her freedom and wanted to go out nearly every other day, Ellie finding herself having to leave her work to take her to see different places. It was almost as if the girl was up from the country and had never seen London before. No one would have taken her for a Londoner born and bred.

'When I was with Mrs Lowe,' she told Ellie, 'we'd always go out in a closed cab straight to one of the bigger department stores or to a small milliner's or a gown shop, and it would be in, out and straight home. I never saw anything of London, really.' And, of course, when they had been children they had been too poor to go roaming London and seeing places of interest.

But it couldn't go on for ever. Sooner or later she had to get down to some serious work. It was then she began to notice how bored Dora was becoming.

'We never go out anywhere,' she complained after only three weeks.

'We go out to sell my paintings.'

'What's the point of that? Not many people buy them.'

'Some do.' Hearing the sharpness in her tone, Ellie hated herself.

It was difficult to concentrate on painting, with Dora looking over her shoulder or walking aimlessly around the room, staring out of the window and sighing as she gazed down at the street below, blocking the light until Ellie had to tell her to move aside. She knew, too, that Dora felt in the way on the few occasions Felix called in, making her feel foolishly guilty.

He didn't call all that often, but when he did he was a welcome sight. He'd said he wanted them to remain friends and she went along with that, surprised how quickly her initial infatuation with him had faded. Now he was just a friend, but a very constant one.

He was even able to bring his partner with him now. A short, stocky ginger-haired young man named Jock – not the sort of person she'd have imagined Felix would have shared his life with: maybe someone slightly built and gentle-natured like himself; but she sometimes caught the looks that passed between them and saw what true love and affection lay in those glances.

Dora had no idea and Ellie didn't enlighten her. Her hard start in life hadn't included this side of it and she had been living a sheltered life with Doctor and Mrs Lowe. Ellie supposed her own had only opened up since she'd come to live here.

Sometimes she and Dora would go with Felix and Jock to the cafés or whatever small party was going on. One needed to escape the enclosure of four walls and let a little light into the mind.

She felt that, since having painted Felix's portrait, her zest for this sort of painting was waning, her ideas becoming arid.

With two months gone by she'd heard nothing more from Robert C. Hunnard either, and took it that he had not sold her paintings. Money was running low even though she knew how to be careful with it, and there was little coming in from any other pictures she sold, none of them being what she would have preferred to paint. She worked solely in oils now, good paper for watercolours being expensive. Her worst worry was how to support Dora if things began to get really bad. With that in mind she painted as if her life depended on it, but her soul seemed to have forsaken her. She needed a goal, a certain feeling of anger; but it wasn't there any more.

Oddly, her fierce resolve to find her father was fading. Funny how time mellowed things, shaved off the harsh corners. If it hadn't been for her quest to avenge what her father had done to her, she might never have become a painter, might have remained with Bertram Lowe for years – and what then? Even if she had stayed, Michael Deel's father would never have let them marry. What would have happened to her? Would she have become a painter, hanging out with the sort of people she'd come to know? It was odd how time mapped things out for a person.

Now, what her future was she had no idea except that every so often that old hatred would climb on to her shoulders and poke a hole in her skull to nibble at her mind. Then she would look for the sort of painting she needed to do to evict the ogre from her brain again.

One portrait she'd started working on, which was helping to sustain this odd sensation, was of Dora, showing her as a lost child, fear of the unknown emanating from the oddly positioned eyes, though the mouth – a thin line of a mouth – smiled tremulously but bravely at the world, while, in the dark background, misty faces looked out at her – faces with menace in their dimly distinguished expressions.

'It's absolutely horrible!' Dora burst out when at last she was allowed to see it. 'That's not me at all.'

'It depicts your inner self,' Ellie tried to explain, but Dora turned away in a huff.

'All that sitting like a blooming statue and that's the result. Is that how you see me? The way you've painted me makes me feel you don't even like me.'

'Of course I like you. I love you. You're my sister and I love you.'

'Then why make me look so ugly?'

'You're not ugly. You're pretty. It's how I see you deep inside: worried about being your own mistress after having been at your employer's beck and call.'

'Well, I think it's horrible. You make me feel that I'm just a blooming nuisance to you, that I'm only in the way.'

'You're not in the way, Dora. I enjoy you being here.'

'And those faces behind me – it's enough to give anyone nightmares. Who'd want to buy something like that? No wonder you don't sell much!'

It was hopeless trying to explain to her. She was her father's child, with no depth of imagination.

'If I *am* in the way here, perhaps I'd be better going back to work at Doctor Lowe's,' she pouted.

'You are not in the way,' Ellie told her, the words uttered slowly.

Dora shrugged and let it go at that while steadfastly refusing to even look at the painting, and not at all happy about Ellie taking it to display alongside her pleasanter ones. Ellie let it go at that. It was up to her what she did or did not display. And one day it might hang in Hunnard's galleries. But that was just a pipe dream. There'd been no sign of him for ages.

By May she was mildly surprised that Dora had stayed this long with her. She'd expected at any time to have her say she wanted to go back to the Lowes' whenever some small disagreement or other came up. But time had cut the girl off from them and there was little Dora could have done about it.

No longer was it hard trying to keep the girl's mind occupied. Finally having succeeded, Ellie couldn't believe how easily Dora had suddenly begun to mingle with those whom she herself mixed with, enjoying the witty talk and laughter, though any serious discussion went completely over her head.

Lately she had begun trying to copy the flamboyant dress of some of them, starting with haunting second-hand stalls for cheap bright clothes like they did, until Ellie had to stop her.

'You're not wearing that!' she exploded as Dora appeared in a well-worn, shapeless red-and-black skirt and bright, shabby blouse with a low, baggy neckline, '– wasting hard-earned money on that sort of rubbish.'

Dora pouted. 'A few bits and pieces – it hardly cost a fortune.'

'We have to eat, pay the rent, and what's left, if any, I need to save for a rainy day.'

'You don't do all that bad. Those nice paintings sell all right.'

Yes, they did sell – just enough to keep body and soul together. Where was the wealth she had dreamed of, the plan to revenge herself on her father? And where was Hunnard who'd promised to sell her other paintings? He had lost interest – that was the truth. She could forget him.

'And what's more,' she told her angrily, 'I won't have you showing yourself up dressed like that. You're showing *everything*!'

'Other women wear clothes like this. And I'm not showing *everything*.'

'Most of that type like to look eccentric. They're usually no better than hangers-on, not serious painters. Women artists have more interest in their art than in dressing up. And one day someone is going to take you for a prostitute.'

Dora looked shocked, her pout fading, and Ellie's anger diminished.

'You've not yet turned sixteen, Dora, and I feel responsible for you. No one will think wrong of you if you dress as you've always done.'

There seemed to be more women painters than she'd first noticed. It wasn't just them: women everywhere were looking towards recognition, freedom of expression – to be accepted as having brains. Like those whom the newspapers called suffragettes, shouting the odds from street corners and at protest gatherings; but none flaunted themselves in garish clothing.

They didn't interest her, but she was heartened to find women like herself taking their art out of the drawing room and into public view. Maybe they had always been there – she just hadn't noticed. Now, with Dora here for company, she felt more at ease and found it easier to fit in. But she did intend to put her foot down about Dora's choice of dress.

The girl was beginning to behave a little too grown-up. That was well apparent when she noticed her half-stupefied one evening. Dragging her from the café, she knew instantly what the girl had been imbibing: the man she'd been talking to had been pouring her another glass of green liquid that turned a milky colour as he added a little water to it.

'How dare you take advantage!' she shot at him, halting the babble of conversation around them for a moment. 'She's not even yet sixteen.'

The man had grinned up at her. 'Sixteen's old enough for more than a drop of absinthe. And I wouldn't mind if—'

What he wouldn't have minded was cut short by a loud slap around the face.

With a roar he was up, his fist drawn back ready to hit back, whether she was a woman or not. It was Felix who leapt between them and somehow, with a gentle word, brushed away the man's rage. How he did it Ellie didn't know, but she felt deeply indebted to him.

If only he'd been different from what he was, she thought as he and Jock elected to help her get a befuddled Dora back home.

'Don't you ever touch that stuff again!' she berated her after the two men had left, having seen them safe and settled. 'You'll end up in the gutter.'

'But everyone drinks it,' mumbled Dora. 'Felix does.'

'He knows what he's doing,' she argued. But that wasn't always true. She'd seen him slumped beside Jock, and not only from absinthe and other concoctions: from the opium that she'd come to realize he was addicted to.

He saw no wrong in it. 'It's relaxing,' he'd told her at one time. 'Takes away the cruelty of the world for a while, let's me weather its condemnation.'

She knew what he meant. She too had felt that, her portraits viewed with distaste by those who sought something less worrying.

Talented painter though Felix was, his days as an artist were most likely numbered. It was sad: good-hearted, young and handsome, but for an accident of birth he could have married, become a good father. Instead he was doomed to fade away unnoticed. Did he have a family somewhere? He never spoke about himself. She just hoped that Jock would stand by him through his life. If only . . .

Ellie sighed as she put Dora to bed to sleep off the absinthe. Why did she fall in love with the wrong people? – thinking she'd found love with the wealthy Michael Deel, weaving dreams of confronting her father as a wealthy woman; falling for Felix, who could never give her the love she'd hoped for.

Then there was Ronnie Sharp. She'd always had a soft spot for him. He'd have been her ideal, but he'd found someone else. When that had fallen apart she'd hoped he'd turn his attention to her, but he hadn't.

It hurt and it had made her think about him more and more. Some would have said out of sight out of mind, but for her the longer time went on, the more she thought about him. For the last few weeks she'd been popping in to see Mrs Sharp, on a Sunday when she knew he wouldn't be at work so that there was more chance of finding him there. So far she'd had no luck.

'Out wiv his mates,' was his mother's usual reply to the inevitable question.

'No, 'e ain't got a gel at the moment,' had been the heartening reply to her casual, apparently innocent enquiry a few weeks ago. 'But he's got plenty of mates.'

'So he's not pining about his engagement breaking up?'

'No,' had come the reply. 'Seems to 'ave got over it orright. I expect he'll find someone else, given time.'

If only that someone else could be her. She was working at it as hard as she could, but if he was never there, what could she do?

'Give him my love,' she told his mother on leaving. She needed to be bold. 'Tell him I think about him a lot.' Even that seemed too forward.

It was easy to say to his mother, would have been impossible to his face, but she could only hope he'd take the hint if Mrs Sharp thought to pass it on.

This Sunday she got dressed up as usual, taking Dora with her as usual, not expecting to see him, but living in hopes – though if he had any thought of her, surely he'd have sought her out after the message she had left with his mum. She'd even told her the address where she was staying, but he obviously hadn't picked up on it. Arriving at Mrs Sharp's door, her heart leapt to see his bike leaning against the house wall. In fact it was he who opened the door to her knock and, to her delight, he smiled down at her.

'Wotcher! I was just about ter go. Only 'ad ter put me coat on.'

'Oh,' she said weakly, her expectations flying off into the blue. 'Did your mother tell you that Dora and I often . . .'

He seemed to step back mentally from her and she realized that *Dora and I* must have sounded so stuck-up and affected. Perhaps he felt he wasn't good enough for her, or that *she* thought him not good enough for her.

Hurriedly she began again. 'Me and Dora often come round to see your mum. Old neighbours – that sort of thing.'

Was it her imagination that he suddenly seemed to relax? Now he gave an easy chuckle. 'She did mention it.'

The statement sounded tongue-in-cheek. Maybe his mother had said more than that, hinting that she was forever asking after him, with all its implications. She felt suddenly foolish. What must he think of her?

'So where you off to?' she asked firmly, reverting in part to her old way of speaking, hoping it might help.

'Meeting a couple of mates of mine in the local.'

Of course! No girlfriend now. 'Just hoped you might still be here, that's all,' she said lamely.

He stepped back from the doorway. 'Well, I'm still in. Might as well hang on a bit. There's no set time.'

He was being warm and friendly and now, thoroughly at ease with her, sitting down and telling her all about his work, asking what she was up to, listening intently as she talked about her life, her struggle for money.

'You're looking very nice,' he said appreciatively at one time, but went no further than that. Finally, after half an hour he said, rather reluctantly it seemed, that he had to go or his friends would be wondering where he was.

'But I might see you here next week,' he said as he put on his coat and his cap.

Ellie's heart felt light as a feather as they left. He'd not gone as far as saying he'd like to see her again, much less take her out. All he'd said was that he might see her here next week. Perhaps it was a start.

She wished she could help things along a little, but it wasn't proper for her to make the first move. Decent young ladies didn't. If only she could tell him her true feelings; but that would be too forward of her.

All week she was on tenterhooks for next Sunday to come. But when it did, she found him not there after all when she called.

'He said ter tell yer he's sorry,' his mother informed her. 'One of his mates 'ad an accident fallin' orf a roof what he was working on yesterday and he went with the other blokes ter see 'im in orspital this morning. But he said he'd be 'ere next week if you come.'

Despite her disappointment, it was like music in her ears; but the following Sunday, something totally unexpected occurred to stop her going – something very important, even though it left her wondering afterwards if he might have taken it to mean that she wasn't that interested in seeing him.

Twenty-Eight

Sundays would see hordes of strollers pausing to gaze at paintings hung on park railings by optimistic artists – rows and rows of them, large and small, some framed, some not, in a variety of subjects and styles. For some it was a Sunday-morning or afternoon diversion before another working week; for the artists there was the hope that at least one painting sold, meaning food for another week.

Lately it had been a day Ellie missed out on, taken up with hopes of seeing Ronnie Sharp. Going all the way to Bethnal Green to chat over a cup of tea, then journeying all the way back, gave no time to show her work, any money she might have made being lost. But seeing Ronnie made it worthwhile.

She'd been so excited about her date with him – if that was what it was – this Sunday. He'd said he'd wait in to see her and she'd been reading meanings into his words all week.

She was ready to go. She would be going alone. Thankfully Dora had decided to stay behind, since rain seemed not far off – heavy rain at that, the air already turning sultry, promising thunderstorms before long. But Ellie shrugged. Nothing was going to stop her.

'I'll see you later on then,' she said to Dora as she took the old, faded black umbrella off the chair where it lay. She frowned as a knock came on the door.

'If that's the landlord,' she snapped as she went to answer it, 'he can wait until Monday morning. He's been coming it lately – frightened we'd run off.'

Opening it, she was surprised to see Felix there, his face full of smiles. 'Someone to see you. He didn't know where you lived, so I brought him.'

Stepping to one side, he revealed the smartly dressed, bulky figure of Hunnard in a light-grey, single-breasted morning suit, the coat open to show a well-fitted waistcoat with a thick, gold fob chain. He wore a grey-silk top hat and beneath his trim beard a starched white collar seemed to be holding his neck in a vice. The cane he carried had what looked like a silver top.

He looked so immaculate that, for a second, Ellie stared at him with her mind racing idiotically to the shambles of her humble room and what he'd think, seeing where she lived. Even so, she couldn't keep him standing there. Without speaking, she stood aside for him to enter, which he did, deftly removing his hat. Felix followed him in, his face still wreathed in smiles.

Ellie's eyes were trained on her main visitor, but with nothing coming to mind to say to him, she just stood there, feeling like an idiot.

'I've not seen you lately,' he began. He was gazing directly at her, not around at her poor surroundings, thank God. 'I've looked for you on several Sundays, but you don't show up – a fine way to sell your work, eh? But this young man says you've completed another two paintings.'

His gaze began to roam the room. 'So I should be happy to see them, if I may, young lady?'

Ellie felt her scepticism start to mount. Obviously he had it in mind to buy them, not just to gaze at them. It would mean money wouldn't be quite so tight for a little while if she sold them to him. But if he thought he could fob her off with another few pounds, he had another think coming. And what about those he'd already had from her? Had he sold them and wasn't telling her? If he hadn't sold them, why was he after more of her work?

'What about those other paintings you bought from me?' She came out bluntly with it, almost rudely, seeing Felix's mouth drop open. 'Are they still hanging on that wall in your gallery?'

Hunnard smiled. 'As a matter of fact there has been a great deal of interest in them. If your two new paintings are of the same standard, I have in mind to include them in a small exhibition I'm planning. It should prove a success, as all my exhibitions are, though small.'

Ellie's eyes remained hard. 'And I suppose you want to buy my others from me for another few pounds, like you did before.'

From the corner of her eye she could see Dora, now up from the chair by the window where she'd been looking down into the street for something better to do as Hunnard entered, tensing with interest at the mention of money. Felix, too, was looking attentive, sensing the possibilities here; but she knew that his interest was centred unselfishly on her welfare.

'I take it you're after buying them?' Ellie went on. 'If you've plans for them, I think I should get a bit more for them than last time. I've seen nothing of that last proposition you spoke about.'

Maybe she was being rude, but she felt angry. Months of eking out the last few pounds he'd handed her to have him lord it in here, dressed like a millionaire, on paintings no doubt bought for a song from other struggling artists – she'd rather throw her own in the Thames than hold out a servile hand for his measly few quid!

'No, so far you haven't,' he answered, still smiling. 'But if your recent work comes up to the standard of the previous two, I may give you cause to take that frown off your face for a long time to come.'

Laying his cane and hat on a chair, he took hold of the one Dora had vacated and brought it to the table where she and Ellie would eat.

Indicating for her to sit on the one on the opposite side of the small table, he glanced up at Felix.

'I'm much obliged to you for guiding me here. I shall find my own way when I leave. Now perhaps you could take Miss Jay's young sister for a little stroll – say for half an hour or so while I speak to Miss Jay.'

'I want them to stay,' Ellie interrupted sharply. It sounded just a little too forceful and she glanced out through the window. 'It's started to rain and I think we're in for a storm.'

She'd hardly spoken when a low, prolonged growl of thunder rumbled in the distance. Hunnard regarded her for moment, then nodded and turned his back on the other two to rivet his attention on her.

Looking a little awkward, Dora went and sat on the bed in the far corner, Felix going to sit beside her.

'Now then,' Hunnard began, leaning towards her, his elbows on the table's scratched surface, 'if your recent work is of the same standard as your previous work, I have it in mind to put on an exhibition at my galleries. I am certain it would cause quite a stir. Your paintings are revolutionary to some extent and there are those with money looking for something different. We've had impressionism, expressionism, the violent colours of Fauvism.'

He spoke the word almost contemptuously. 'Your work, young lady, falls between all three. And now, getting down to business.'

He glanced over his shoulder at the other two and turned back to her, lowering his voice. 'Let me explain in simple terms you might understand. An exhibition will cost money, for which I foot the bill. Therefore I take all the risks. You don't. I therefore take a commission on every painting sold. So you see, I have to feel confident the paintings will sell well.'

'You think they will sell?' she asked, still not quite sure what he was talking about.

'For quite a lot, if I'm any judge of art. Young lady, you may be pleasantly surprised.'

Surprised! Did he mean rich? She dared not guess. But this talk of commission was worrying. Was she about to be diddled again? Before she could stop herself, she came out with it and saw him smile.

It was a strange smile. 'That's a rather odd remark, but I understand,' he said. 'You are very young, alone in a world about which you have very little conception. But I can offer you protection – be your patron, so to speak.'

'Patron?' she echoed. The smile hadn't diminished.

'I find your work interesting. I find you interesting, and exceedingly brave. You are destined to go far as an artist, but you need the right backing, the protection of an influential patron. I have influence and you'll not find me lacking in that if you allow me to take you under my wing.'

Ellie had her eyes fixed on him. What was he proposing? She'd seen that same smile on Bertram Lowe's face – one that could be taken as fatherly and protective, yet seemed to hint at something else not quite as it should be. It made her uncomfortable and she was glad Felix and Dora hadn't gone out for the stroll he'd suggested.

That oily smile – Ellie felt herself squirm. She'd seen it now on three older men: her father, Bertram Lowe and now

Hunnard. What was it about her that made them look at her
this way? Had she stayed with Bertram Lowe, would he have
shown his true feelings for her? Would that happen with
Hunnard? And her father – the same had been true of him,
but he'd made no pretence about his intentions, the father
gradually turning into the lecher.

But was it her fault? Did she unconsciously seek to attract
such men? Had it been her doing that her father had developed an unnatural attraction towards her?

She became aware that Hunnard was still speaking. 'You
show great promise,' he was saying. 'With the right teacher,
who knows how far you could go? As your patron, I would
finance your—'

'You said you charge commission on whatever you sell,'
she broke in harshly. 'What sort of commission are you
thinking of?'

She saw the smile vanish and he again became business-like.

'I suggest fifty per cent? Half of what each painting takes,'
he added when she looked confused.

Ellie's mind was working. If one of her special paintings,
as she liked to call them, made roughly thirty pounds and he
took half, she'd end up with fifteen. It sounded a lot. If they
all sold, it would be a lot more.

She had six such paintings. Six times fifteen? Multiplication
of that sort was beyond her, but it sounded as if it could be
a fortune. But what if they only sold for a couple of pounds
and he took half of that? She could sell her work on the street
for more.

Again his voice cut into her thoughts. 'Of course, I'll have
to see the others you've done,' he said briskly.

Ellie came to herself with a start, her suspicions immediately roused. He'd talked of selling her paintings even before
seeing them – a ruse to get her excited with talk of money,
then to say they weren't good enough and offer to buy them
for some paltry sum. Well, she hadn't come down with
yesterday's rain.

But she said nothing yet, as she went over to the corner
where the two portraits lay, propped face to the wall: the one
of Dora and the other of Felix.

'There!' she said tartly, propping them up before Hunnard's
eyes.

She saw those eyes widen as if with appreciation; then they narrowed as they turned towards her.

For a while he didn't speak. Then he said slowly, 'These are amazing. I really don't know how to express it. They are . . . brilliant, like the rest of your work: unusual. The depth of expression. With my backing these will sell. And I mean sell! They're virtual masterpieces.'

Ellie wanted to laugh out loud, but something in his face stopped her. Dora and Felix, caught by his exuberance, had come over to see what it was all about.

'If I am right,' Hunnard was saying, 'you've a fine future ahead of you. I'll take these away with me and begin organizing something at once. Leave everything to me. All you need to do is apply yourself to finishing as many of these as you can over the next month or so. Work day and night if you must. And keep away from those awful, slushy, sentimental pictures you've been hawking. Don't even think of going out to sell such mush! Concentrate on more of what you are doing. I wish to see enough to make an exhibition worth its while.'

'Paint costs money,' Ellie blurted out. 'I haven't got—'

'Don't let that deter you,' he snapped, and before she could say any more he fished into his breast pocket, drawing out a fine leather wallet, and extracted several white banknotes. 'Buy whatever you need.'

Thrusting them into her hand, he grabbed up his hat and cane and made for the door. 'I shall send someone tomorrow to collect these two. I shall see myself out,' he added, as if she was living in a mansion instead of some attic room.

When he'd gone, Felix looked at her with wonder on his thin face. 'God!' he breathed. 'I can hardly believe it.'

'Neither can I,' she replied. 'Do you think it's genuine?'

'Of course it's genuine. Look, I'll help you buy whatever is needed. Me and Jock will run whatever errands you want.'

'But I can't paint to order. I need a subject. I can't conjure up the feeling I get, not out of the blue. I need . . .' She paused. She couldn't say 'anger': he wouldn't understand. 'I need passion,' she said desperately, '– something in here.'

'You'll find it when you need to,' Felix said and, kissing her on the cheek with excitement, he grabbed one of the banknotes and sped from the room. 'I'll be back shortly with everything you need,' he called back.

She could hear his footsteps running lightly down the two flights of uncarpeted stairs, the door to the building slamming as he let himself out into a virtual cloudburst, a great boom of thunder rolling overhead as if to proclaim her future.

She hadn't seen Hunnard for nearly three weeks but letters arrived every so often telling her to keep working, that all was well, that he'd made some very interesting and opulent contacts.

Ellie had persuaded Felix's Jock to pose for her. What she saw in the young man's eyes that appealed to her senses was a sort of vacancy coupled with a soul that had been hurt in the past. What he was, the way he had behaved, had been condemned, maybe from childhood. It struck her that he must have had a miserable childhood and it made her feel for him – so much so that the finished work made her almost want to cry.

She dragged her second subject off the streets – a ragged individual she'd seen begging. In him she found pure, unadulterated despair and painted him, dirt and all, so that anyone viewing the subject would almost have felt they could smell the filth on him. He went away happy with the money she handed him, and she just hoped it would give him an incentive to wash.

She'd painted it far too quickly to feel happy with the results, but Felix enthused over it and Dora looked sufficiently sick to make it impressive.

There was also a little girl, not much more than seven or eight, apparently the sole provider for a mother left widowed and desolate and two younger siblings, one only a baby, the girl told her.

Ellie hadn't asked her name. Somehow that would have made her too real. She just sat the child down in her room and painted her, the wan little face with eyes so terribly empty for one so young, when they should have been bright with childish laughter. Ellie had found her trying to sell pitiful little bunches of flowers she'd gleaned from those dropped by more proficient flower sellers who sat around Piccadilly Circus with baskets of flowers got from the Covent Garden itself. The girl must have thought heaven had smiled on her as she finally left with an apron pocket heavy with the handful of silver coins Ellie gave her.

By the time Hunnard called with news of the approaching exhibition and the numbers of well-feathered clients eager to view his new protégée, all Ellie had to offer was these three paintings. Although, for her, all three had turned out to be immensely satisfying, she felt drained, as if the suffering of her subjects had seeped into her.

'It's not a lot,' she accepted.

'Enough to be going on with,' he said, not noticing how pale she was, her shoulders stooped from exhaustion, with sleepless nights, hours on her feet.

She was beginning to feel that if she continued working like this she'd end up going off her head. With Felix and Jock setting themselves the task of providing her with all the paint and canvas she needed, she hardly saw the outdoors, felt the hot summer sun beating on her face, heard the babble of people she'd have passed in the street.

'I've got to get out for a while,' she told Dora, who was going off on her own these days to enjoy the company of friends she'd made from those she now associated with.

Left to herself, Ellie began to feel trapped. She hadn't even been to see Mrs Sharp, hadn't set eyes on Ronnie, and guessed he'd given up on her, seeing her as too snooty for him. She wanted so much to get into contact again, but Hunnard was giving her no time to herself.

What was it all about, if she found herself deprived of a normal life, of happiness? Yet if she didn't make the money Hunnard kept referring to, how would she ever be able to search out and confront her father – if she ever did find him. And if she never found him, then what was the point of doing what she was doing?

Perhaps in time it would all come to an end, leaving her free to contact Ronnie again, explain the cause of her absence and hope to goodness that he might ask her to go out with him – that was, if he hadn't by that time found himself another suitable girl to propose to.

Twenty-Nine

'We need more,' Hunnard was saying. He'd been surveying the three further paintings she'd done and said they were exactly what he needed.

'These will have them begging to buy,' he had said; then, as bold as brass, had added his need for more.

'I can't do any more,' she told him wearily. 'I feel worn out.'

Hunnard turned on her almost savagely. 'That's not good enough. Your work is all-important.'

'I said I'm too tired,' she said. 'I've worked myself to a standstill.'

She received no sympathy. 'You've no time to feel tired when a golden future could be staring you in the face. Perhaps after the exhibition. Even then demand could grow, though I would recommend we keep them wanting by holding back a little. That way your work will become even more sought-after, with buyers ready to pay whatever we ask.'

He spoke as if he shared her talent. 'To make the exhibition work we must have more than these three.'

'That's all you're going to get!' Ellie flashed at him, exhausted to the point of showing her anger. 'I'm worn out.'

Hearing her raised, desperate cry, Dora came to put her arms around her and Ellie was glad to lean against her. 'I can't do any more,' she sighed.

For a moment, Hunnard regarded the two girls, perhaps noting for the first time how pale and washed-out Ellie was; then he quietly took hold of a chair and, with Dora helping, eased her down on to it.

'I do apologize,' he said, 'for my brusqueness. I, too, am weary from the work entailed by setting this exhibition up. I don't wish it to fail.'

Ellie looked up, alarmed. 'Do you think it could?' All her hard work!

'No.' He smiled, whispering the word with reassurance. His stern lips behind the trim beard could look quite pleasant when he smiled.

'This exhibition will be a roaring success,' he went on. 'Every one of my invitations has been eagerly accepted and all know they will be viewing an exceptional talent with an entirely new concept.'

Weariness fell from Ellie like a cloak. 'When will the exhibition be?' she asked, her gaze on the paintings he'd propped against the table. She asked with no sense of enthusiasm for the event, which mildly surprised her: all she wanted was for it to be over, leaving her at last free to visit the Sharps, hopefully finding Ronnie there.

She would say sorry to him for having let him down that Sunday and hope he would understand. Surely he would, after she'd explained the reason.

He was always on her mind lately. The more time painting had taken up, the more she thought of him, wanted to see him. It was almost like an obsession, the best of reasons for her to work even harder so as to be able to go and see him.

To her delight and relief came the words, 'A fortnight from now.' Hunnard was apparently taking her question as a sign of impatience. 'Then you may relax, Ellie, for a while at least.'

She couldn't ever remember him using her first name before and she looked sharply at him. He was smiling benignly – a smile she'd seen on his lips before, and she hastily looked away.

When she looked back, the smile had gone.

The exhibition was proving a huge success, the place full of people almost immediately the gallery opened. Hunnard had done a good job, seeming to have lots of contacts.

For Ellie, unused to such attention, it all had a dream-like quality, everything happening as if in a mist. She tried to keep out of the way, but Hunnard kept dragging her out from whatever corner she was hiding in to introduce her to this and that person – they with their educated manner of speech making her own, even though she'd learned to talk nicely, sound flat and uncouth.

All wore expensive clothes. At Hunnard's request she had bought herself a well-tailored dove-grey costume with a smoothly flowing skirt and double-breasted jacket, the high neck of her pin-tucked blouse being fastened with an art-nouveau brooch in silver with blue enamel that he had bought her to celebrate her coming-out, as it were. She had protested, secretly fearing he might be trying to buy her favours. But he waved away her protests and that oily smile was absent.

Nicely dressed as she was, she felt a fish out of water. These people weren't her kind. This wasn't her world. She loved painting, but having to do it to order wasn't what she'd looked for. She was grateful for Dora's support today and the company of Felix and Jock, though they seemed to prefer to keep to themselves, happier with each other's company.

Hunnard was dominating her and she began to acquire an awful premonition that from now on he would start to dominate her in all she did, a father figure, taking over almost as her guardian, as Bertram Lowe had done, and whatever else might ensue from that. He hardly left her side, guiding her about, his hand on her elbow, until she almost felt stifled.

It was an immense relief when the day was over. She hadn't enjoyed being dragged about the gallery, introduced to this one and that one as the newest discovery in the world of art.

The next few days saw her being wined and dined, paraded around by Hunnard, who indeed seemed to be taking over her life.

'Your fame will grow,' he'd said. 'I'll see to that. No more scrimping and scraping for Ellie Jay. *Elizabeth Jay* will be lauded among the famous of today's artists.'

Odd how those words suddenly terrified her. That she now had a rapidly growing bank balance of several hundred pounds in her name, able to be withdrawn as and when she fancied, with no guardian to take charge, was strangely no comfort. She still couldn't quite take in this change of fortune, didn't even know what she could do with that kind of money. There was still this quest to find her father, but strangely it seemed to be taking a back seat.

She stood at the window, alone for the moment, Dora sitting on the bed reading a penny dreadful, contented in knowing she too would benefit from her sister's good fortune. It was all too sudden. She felt unprepared.

'I shall procure a fine studio for you,' Hunnard had said

when the exhibition had finished and she realized she was a moderately wealthy woman, destined to become wealthier as he handled the work she produced. 'Separate living quarters, of course. I'll start looking for suitable accommodation within the next few days.'

She didn't want him arranging where she should live. She didn't even know herself what she wanted. She stared down at the street below. It was Sunday again, the street quiet. She thought of the times she had had to struggle off to Bayswater Road with her efforts. Felix still did so.

She determined that she would attempt to offer him and his Jock a little of her new-found wealth, if they weren't too proud to accept it. Felix had done so much for her – befriending her, helping her when she'd lost heart.

She'd be sad to move away from him – from here even. She'd become attached to this squalid room with its broken, second-hand furniture, the landlord with his skinny hand held out for his weekly rent. Could she ever keep in with the group she'd come to know and like, or would she drift away, expected to mix with people of standing, moneyed people, people she felt she could never become part of, would always feel awkward with? Or would she eventually rise to their heights, her nose turned up at the lowlier sort? Would she forget her humble beginnings?

That thought turned her mind to her father, to her original plan to take her revenge on him, to belittle him, to see him squirm before her. She could do that now. But did she still want to, wherever he was?

And there was Ronnie. Would he want to associate with her: the artist who had made good, the grand lady? As she would feel outclassed by those in society circles, so he would feel outclassed by her. She'd give him her new address when she moved; but would he feel too embarrassed to visit it?

Still gazing down at the quiet street below, beginning to feel quite desolate about this new future looming before her, she found the view swimming through sudden moisture collecting in her eyes.

A knock on the door interrupted her reverie, disconcerting her for a moment. But it might be Felix. Turning from the window, she went to answer the knock, hurriedly wiping the tears from her eyes as she went.

Opening the door, Ellie gasped. There stood the very man she'd been thinking about.

'Ellie! I think I've got some good news for you,' he burst out without even greeting her, '– about yer dad! Sorry it took so long ter find anything out. I even thought I'd come to a dead end, but . . . Look, can I come in?'

She felt no shame in him seeing the state of the place where she lived. His home wasn't much better. But that wasn't what occupied her thoughts at the moment. Her heart had begun beating rapidly with heavy, sickening thuds at mention of her dad.

Ronnie gave her no chance to speak. Without a glance around the room he carried straight on talking. 'After all this time I think I've traced yer dad's whereabouts. Got it through the newspaper I work for. What I did was ter put advertisements in from time to time. Then the other day someone answered – said they knew of 'im; so I thought I ought ter come and let you know.'

Ellie wanted to hug him, not because of his news – that held nothing to lighten her heart, but with the joy of seeing him. But to throw herself into his arms and probably alarm him wasn't proper, even though her heart was now racing with delight, pushing aside that first heavy beat at news of her dad.

She made herself calm a little and asked as evenly as she could, 'Did they give any address?' though what she would do when she saw him she had no idea. It had been such a shock, coming out of the blue like that.

Ronnie was frowning. He seemed reluctant to oblige.

'Is it a long way away?' she queried.

'No, not far,' came the reply: 'Whitechapel – but it might be better if I take you meself.'

It was all she wanted to hear: Ronnie going with her, walking beside her, perhaps letting her hold his arm.

'I wouldn't want you dashing off there on yer own,' he was saying. 'It's a bit squalid where he's living. I say squalid: it's a dump.'

Ellie bit her lip, grew serious. This wasn't what she'd expected. She didn't quite know what she'd expected – her father perhaps living it up with that woman he'd left her mother for, he dressed up to the nines, her with paint on her face and common as muck.

'When I say dump . . .' Ronnie paused to scratch the side of his head as if giving himself time to say what he had to. 'To be truthful, according ter what the person said who answered me ad, I think it might be a dosser – a doss house. Not a fit place for a young lady to wander into on 'er own. I'll 'ave ter come with you, Ellie. You don't mind, do yer?'

Did she mind? Not only did she want to have him with her, it seemed she *needed* to have him with her.

'Should we go now?' she asked.

'If yer want to.'

'I do.' Dora was standing by, looking anxious. Ellie turned to her. 'Stay here, Dora. I shan't be long. I just need to speak to him, then I'll be back. I don't think it wise for us all to go barging in wherever your dad is.'

Dora nodded dumbly. Ellie didn't think she, having heard the conversation, would have wanted to come along anyway. She herself was feeling a little sick, wondering what would confront her. Her father was obviously down on his luck for the moment – as he'd been many times before; but he had always bounced back. In a way, it did make it easier to say what she planned to say.

While Ronnie waited for her outside the door, she changed into the expensive dove-grey costume and fashionable matching hat she'd worn at the exhibition, bought with the money Hunnard had advanced her.

Ronnie looked at her with rapt amazement as she came out of her room, making her feel she'd dressed too smartly for him, especially when he took her by the hand to help her down the stairs as if she were a real lady, incapable of nego-tiating their steep descent without assistance. In the street he threaded her arm through his; and now he even seemed proud of being her escort.

'I'm afraid we'll 'ave ter catch a tram,' he said as if excusing himself.

'That's fine, I don't go any other way,' she told him, happy to lie.

It had been raining hard this morning and, though it had now stopped, the interior of the horse tram still smelled of damp clothing – wet umbrellas brushed against skirts and trousers and dripping forlornly on to the fluted boards.

Beside her, Ronnie was talking brightly about his recent

promotion and wages rise and how he intended to get on in the world. She said nothing about the money coming from the exhibition of her paintings. Best he didn't know just yet. It might turn him off and she dared to foster high hopes of resuming their friendship of so long ago, this time more seriously.

At the same time she couldn't stop thinking of where they were going. Her tummy kept going over as she thought about it. Now it came to it, what could she find to say to her father? It was making her feel sick.

The sun was peeping through the parting clouds as they got off the tram. They turned in the direction Ronnie indicated, he now holding tightly to her arm. It felt wonderful.

Whitechapel was much like the rest of East London, with cheap shops, busy main roads, poorly clad shoppers absorbed in finding the cheapest food for the table. Whitechapel had its alleys, too, and it was into one of these off a dreary, run-down side street that Ronnie led her.

It was narrower even than Gales Gardens; the pockmarked nameplate on one wall read 'Spectacle Alley'. Ronnie paused. He seemed embarrassed and anxious as if the state of the place was his fault.

'I'm sorry about this,' he said. 'I ought to have warned yer.'

'You did.'

'But I should 'ave made it more plain – I mean, where they said yer dad is supposed ter be staying.'

Even Ronnie, where he was living and where she'd once lived, found this place disgusting.

Rubbish of all sorts littered the broken pavement, the walls being blackened by years of soot. There were two or three tiny, dingy shop fronts, signs dangling over brown-stained doorways advertising wares such as cigarettes, beer, Colman's starch, matches, and above that windows set deep into the brickwork.

None seemed to be doing any trade and only two people passed them as she and Ronnie made their way down the alley, he consulting a piece of paper, the name on which he hadn't let her read.

As they reached a sign saying 'Good Beds – Single Men Only', hanging from an ornate bracket over a black-painted door and window sill, Ronnie stopped.

He looked at Ellie, nibbling his lower lip. 'This is the place. I'm sorry, I didn't know. All I was given was the number.'

'What is it?' she asked, bewildered.

'It's . . . Well, it's the place I told you about – a dosser.'

For a moment she was sure he'd got things wrong. She had been sure he'd been taking her to the wrong place ever since they'd got off the tram. In her mind she had seen her father living in moderate comfort at least.

He'd always been a gambler and, though not always lucky, he'd made money as well, a snappy dresser even though Mum had had to slave taking in work to try to make ends meet. True, he liked his drink: she and Mum had suffered the results of that, both of them in their separate ways; but the money he made gambling had adequately covered his spending on drink. Now Ronnie was saying he was living in a dosshouse, filthy and bug-ridden by the look of it, despite the sign grandly proclaiming 'Good Beds'!

'This can't be right,' she burst out. 'They must have got it wrong, the people who gave this address.'

Ronnie looked at the piece of paper again. He seemed as devastated as she felt. 'Perhaps we'd better go back home. Perhaps there is a mistake and this ain't the right address.'

As they stood looking at the door, a man lurched out. On an impulse Ellie called to him. 'Do you know of a Mr Albert Jay?'

The man paused, swaying a little, peered at her, then began pouring out a string of beery oaths, finally making some sense.

'Ol' Bert – 'im wot's ill? Poor ol' bugger ain't long fer this world if yer asks me. Bloke wot runs this place wants 'im art – says 'e don't keep no sick people wot ain't even on the charity, and 'e don't run 'is doss 'ouse on any charity neiver . . .'

His words faded away as he lurched off, while Ellie and Ronnie gazed after him, disappearing into the grog shop they'd just passed.

She looked at Ronnie, lifting her chin. 'I'm going in anyway.'

'You can't,' he cried. 'It might not be the right Albert. And I'm not letting yer go in there. You could catch something.'

Without answering, Ellie pulled free of his arm and ran in through the half-open door. The smell of urine that met her almost knocked her back as she covered her mouth and nose with a navy-gloved hand.

The place was dim, the dirty windows giving hardly any light, but a thin shaft of weak sunshine, washed-out after the rain, coming through the doorway gave enough to distinguish a flight of bare, rickety stairs, a piece of candle burning low in its holder at the top.

As Ronnie followed her in, a door along a dark passage opened. 'Yus, wha' yer want?' came a hoarse demand.

Ellie looked towards the voice, frightened by the sudden sound, but it was Ronnie who answered. 'You've got a Mr Albert Jay staying here. I've just been told he's ill. This is his daughter come to see him.'

From somewhere Ronnie suddenly became well spoken, perhaps to impress the owner of the uncouth voice or perhaps because he heard his own way of speaking being aped.

Maybe this was how he spoke at work, it being expected of him – only falling back into his slipshod ways when at home.

It sounded nice, hearing him speak like this, but the thought was swept away as the lodging-house owner emerged from his cubbyhole.

'Oh, she do, do she? Well, tell 'er that 'er ol' man owes me money fer the bed what 'e's occupying and is she gonna pay me?'

'If he's her father,' Ronnie replied, 'she'll pay you. If he ain't, then she won't. What room's he in?'

'Top o' the stairs, turn right, second door along!'

The man went back into his room and Ellie mounted the stairs that creaked and shook to each step, the banisters dangerously wobbly. She was glad to have Ronnie hold her arm, not only supporting her physically, his touch immediately boosting the courage that had threatened to fail.

She had known for years just what she would say to her father. It was why she had put on her best clothes, so he would see that she'd risen above his humiliation of her. She had rehearsed the words so many times: what she thought of him over what he'd done, and for walking out on a dying woman. She would take delight in watching him squirm under her haughty contempt. But she hadn't expected to find him in such a place as this, and apparently ill. Now her courage was failing her.

At the door, Ronnie's hold on her arm tightened. 'I'll come in with you, give you support.'

The words brought her mind back to her quest. She lifted her chin with recaptured resolve. 'No. I need to do this on my own.'

Ill or not, there would be a reckoning – she knew that now. All the scheming, planning, the hard work – it mustn't go to waste. She wanted to see his expression when he saw her, tall and elegant and self-assured.

She wanted to see his face blench, twist, his eyes unable to meet hers as she gazed steadily down at him with venom in that stare. She'd stay calm as she belittled him, condemned him to eternal remorse, finally to turn from him with dignity, knowing she had accomplished all she'd set out to do. She knew just how to go about it, and now she could hardly wait to carry it out.

'Stay here. I won't be long,' she said firmly, Ronnie stepping back.

Without knocking she turned the handle of the door. Her intention was to walk quietly up to where he sat, to look straight into his amazed face. She would not rant and rave. She would be calm and cold – ice-cold.

The state of the house should have forewarned her. As she opened the door to the room, the smell made her clap her hand to her mouth and nose yet again. She felt herself quail.

A man lay on a filthy bed. It wasn't her father, this emaciated wretch whose face she could see covered in sores. All this effort and she'd found the wrong man. She stood quaking, staring from the door at the apparition.

Her father could never have looked like this, even if he had been ill – the tall, burly, handsome man she remembered, with the handlebar moustache, the fair hair always slicked down, face ruddy with health, arms bulging with muscle, the whole belligerent attitude of him that would never have allowed him to be reduced to what this man was like.

'I'm sorry . . .' she began.

The body stirred, the head turned and the eyes opened to look towards the voice.

'I'm sorry,' she said again. 'I think I've made a mistake.'

Flustered, she could hardly wait to get out of the room, back into Ronnie's strong, comforting, healthy arms. He'd got the information wrong, but if nothing else it had brought him and her together.

Making towards the door, wanting only to escape this horrible place, she was stopped by the man's cracked voice. 'Ellie? Is that you?'

Ellie froze. It was a while before she could turn to face the stricken man as he said again, 'That you, Ellie?'

Thirty

As Ellie stood transfixed, he spoke her name again, the voice just a croak, hardly above a whisper. Then she heard him say, 'Come 'ere, so's I can see yer.'

She didn't want to go near him, wished she hadn't been so full of resolve in telling Ronnie to wait outside. Her determination had collapsed into crass fear, wanting only to have Ronnie hold her hand.

'I'm sorry,' she managed to say, 'I don't know who you are. I've made a mistake.'

A skinny hand and forearm rose from the bed. 'Come 'ere.' Though the voice croaked, little above a whisper, it bore a note of command, just like her father's requests had always done. *'Ellie, come 'ere, yer silly little fool. I ain't goin' to 'urt yer.'*

The voice came now, weak and croaking: 'Ellie, I'm ill . . .'

Yet as the words trailed off, an unexpected feeling of pity overwhelmed her, as it would have done at seeing any poor wretch in these conditions. Not knowing why she obeyed, Ellie moved towards the bed.

At close quarters the state of the sick man was even more alarming. The hair was thin and patchy, revealing the scalp beneath. There were ugly weeping ulcerations on the face and scrawny neck. The eyes looked red and sore. The arm and fingers that had been held out to her were partly covered in a strange rash, the rest of the skin showing brownish-red stains.

She almost felt relief that this was no one she knew. 'Who are you?' she asked, her voice sounding small. 'How do you know my name?'

His whisper came haltingly. 'Don't yer know me? I'm . . . yer dad.'

At the words, panic swept through her. 'You're not!' she burst out. 'You can't be!'

Her voice trembled then broke; fear and disbelief combined into denial that this apparition might once have been a strong man, her own father.

'I don't know you,' she whispered, trying to convince herself. But he'd spoken her name. Who else in this awful place would have known it?

He made no reply. A sigh issued from his blotched lips as if the whole of his breath had been pumped from his frame in a single, slow exhalation. It was like the sound her mother had made when she'd died, though hers had been a gentle, shallow breath, drawn in like all the others before it, then to be quietly exhaled into silence, no breath ever to be drawn in again.

It had been that strange silence that had made her collapse in grief over her mother's body until Dora, a mere child, had solemnly coaxed her away. There had been no more tears for a long time after that, as if they had all been expelled with that last breath flowing quietly away from her mother.

There was no grief here as she gazed down on the man who had said he was her father. If he was dead, then he was dead. She felt only a passing regret at having been robbed of her revenge. Yet revenge hadn't been on her mind as she'd stood beside the filthy bed, the thin body covered by a dirty and threadbare blanket, its head on a thin and stained pillow.

A second or two later a sudden great intake of breath startled her. She saw the eyes open and swivel in her direction.

'Please 'elp me . . .' he pleaded in a pitiful whisper. 'I think I'm done for.'

How she got through the weeks that followed Ellie was not sure, her time being divided between pity for him and a feeling that she should be gloating over his plight, telling herself he had only got what he deserved.

She wanted to remind him of his abuse of her, how she'd felt and how devastated she'd been when his perverted selfishness had made her pregnant, and how humiliated in having it got rid of. She wanted him to see, too, that despite what he'd done to her she had made a life for herself and had come up in the world, that she was only caring for him as any decent person would care for some poor wretch in his state. But she didn't. What he was suffering was revenge enough.

His illness sickened her, knowing that his debauched life since leaving his family had brought it about; and it served him right, as far as she was concerned. Yet she couldn't have brought herself to walk away and leave him in the state in which she had found him.

At her own expense she had him moved to a clinic. No one could have left such a sick man in that horror of a place, no matter what he'd done. At least she was able to let him see that she had money enough to pay for his care in a private hospital, despite his having left her destitute and her mother dying. This in itself gave her satisfaction.

Not that he was aware of it, his condition deteriorating so rapidly despite proper medical care and clean conditions.

'He cannot last but a few more weeks, you understand,' the doctor had informed her impassively, only his eyes betraying his feelings about a well-dressed young woman with a father in such an appalling condition.

She nodded without emotion, hiding a shrug. She felt neither hatred nor pity any more, and maybe that was the culmination of her revenge: that she felt nothing.

He'd no doubt picked up the disease not long after leaving home. The way he carried on with women, she wasn't surprised at what he'd contracted. Poetic justice, if you like – far more than she could ever have dreamt of doling out; yet she was increasingly and uncomfortably aware of indifference as she watched him fading, neither sad nor triumphant. Rather it was keeping it to herself that was telling on her. She had to confide in someone.

She told Ronnie as they came away from her father's bedside. Ronnie had been her constant companion and support these two weeks. She could not imagine how she could have coped without him and it was only fair to be honest with him, especially when he remarked this evening how stoical she was, having to stand by and watch her dad slowly dying before her eyes.

'I'm not being stoical,' she'd said tersely. 'There's just nothing there.'

The confession prompted her to go on. 'If you want to know, I've hated him for years. But now it's all over. He's dying and I'm glad he is!'

She wasn't prepared for the change in Ronnie's face,

fondness turning suddenly to shock. She'd said too much or hadn't properly thought out what she'd intended to say. She had been hoping that he would understand. That was going to mean explaining everything in detail, but she hadn't been prepared for this initial look of horror before she'd even started.

How could she tell him now? If she did, and he refused to understand, she'd have to walk away, never seeing him ever again. She would have to learn to get on with her life, maybe one day find someone else, though she couldn't imagine who.

Meanwhile she would learn to work hard, do all Robert C. Hunnard's bidding to become a great painter. The thought of losing Ronnie was tearing her to pieces. Yet she needed to explain.

'I'm sorry if you think that's an awful thing for me to say,' she began.

To her dismay, Ronnie made no reply. She was losing him, her life stretching out before her lonely, filled only with work, with looking after Dora, Dora perhaps finding a young man, eventually marrying – and being utterly alone.

She wanted to plead for him not to think too badly of her. Instead, she released her hold on his arm and moved away a little, seeking to find a little spark of dignity in her step as they walked; but inside she was crying.

'Perhaps I should explain,' she began coldly. Was she ready to bare her soul to someone who'd suddenly revealed what little faith he had in her?

Still he said nothing. The silence between them grew as they walked on through the twilight, she on the very verge of turning back and walking off. If she did that, she would never see him again; but do that she felt she had to.

'Explain what?' he said suddenly, bringing her back to herself.

'Nothing!' she replied, cold and distant.

'No, Ellie. Whatever it is you're bottling up, I'm here to 'elp. Yer know I am. I can't bear you looking so lost and upset over something I said.'

Something he'd said! He'd said nothing. But his tone was warm and comforting and he reached out and drew her to him. Suddenly she was leaning against him, her face buried in his shoulder as she sobbed fit to bursting. Through a welter of tears she let it all out: how her father had abused her; the indignity of having the doctor, who'd taken pity on her, seeing in her a likeness to his own daughter, help rid her of the thing her father had left her with; how she'd worked so hard yet always failed to save enough money to enable her to trace her father so as to take her revenge for everything he'd done to her. All the time she could feel Ronnie's arms growing tighter and tighter about her as he listened.

Slowly her weeping died away and he loosened his hold on her to thread her arm firmly through his again, a support for her. Like this they walked on in silence, not too fast, she dabbing with a small handkerchief at the tears that continued to threaten.

'Are yer going ter be orright?' he asked as they turned into her street. They were the first words he'd spoken since her outburst. It was as if he hadn't been able to cope. He hadn't kissed away her tears, had just held her to him, as anyone would a girl in distress.

Was he still alarmed by her attitude towards her father? Had he really understood? Was he trying not to show how he felt about her now he knew? She wasn't prepared to ask as she looked up at him.

'I do feel a lot better,' she said. How formal that sounded.

'Good,' he said. 'I could see you up to yer room and tell Dora you was feeling a bit upset over yer dad. Otherwise she might wonder why you've been crying.'

'No, I'm fine,' Ellie said, still formal.

'I'll leave yer then. I'll take yer tomorrow evening to see yer dad – if yer want to go, that is.'

'Yes, thank you.' She moved away but turned back, her smile now defiant. 'By the way, I'll be moving from here next week. Mr Hunnard is looking for a place for me with a decent studio where I can carry on with my painting. As you know, he says I have great talent and could become quite famous one day.'

Why had she said that? She saw his face drop, heard him say, 'Oh.'

'But I'll still see you?' she hurried on. 'I'll still be living in London.'

'Yeah, of course.'

It was all so stilted, like passing acquaintances unsure of each other. He had held her so firmly, so comfortingly as she'd wept, but he'd not kissed her or said he loved her. She'd been so sure he loved her even though he was shy of saying so. Now he'd seen another side to her and probably felt it best to back out of this awkward situation he found himself in.

'Well,' she said lamely, trying to smile. 'I'll see you tomorrow evening if that's all right?'

'Yeah, of course,' he said again. 'OK. 'Night then.'

She returned the parting words, saw him step back, step by step, still facing her as if unsure of going. Then, swinging round on his heel, he walked off. Ellie stood watching him until he turned the corner. He hadn't looked back. It reminded her of someone going out of her life for ever. But he'd said he would see her tomorrow. She had to be content with that. But what if he didn't turn up? She thought of Michael Deel. He'd said he would be there to meet her, to run away with her. But he hadn't come.

Slowly she went inside the building and closed the door.

A voice accosted her, making her jump. 'I take it you'll be paying me next week's rent before you leave.'

She turned abruptly. 'Obviously!' She hated the man for breaking into her unhappiness. 'I've always paid regularly.'

'Just want to make sure,' he went on, grinning at her, the slimy little beetle. 'Course, you're well off now, ain't you? and things like that can slip the minds of them with money.'

'I'll settle before I go,' she said curtly and hurried on up the stairs, her heart empty.

Her father was dead. All the things she had wanted to say to him, all those things she'd rehearsed for so long, had remained unsaid in the end.

She'd sat well away from the bed as he faded. When Mum had died she had held her hand until the last and remained holding it long after that cherished soul had passed away. But him – she couldn't bring herself to give him that comfort. Why then had she felt guilty at not doing so when she had carried this loathing of him for so long?

Watching him, hating the minutes ticking by as she waited, she'd just wanted to run from the room and leave him to it. And all the time Ronnie had stood behind her, a comforting hand on her shoulder. As if he knew.

Now her father was gone. Trying to smother this peculiar

guilt of hers, she'd forked out for an expensive funeral, an oak coffin lined with white silk (she hadn't gone to look on him as he lay there), a hearse with black-plumed horses. She and Dora, her brother Charlie, whom Ronnie had traced by an advert in his paper, and Ronnie rode in the chief mourners' carriage.

The following carriage had held her old neighbours, the Sharps, who'd been so good to her. In the last carriage, Felix, Jock and several of those she'd made friends with, friends she would soon be leaving behind as her wealth grew. That saddened her, but more than anything else she harboured the fear of losing Ronnie.

Hunnard had told her she was spending far too much on the funeral, funeral clothes, the new studio, furnishings, leisure. But suddenly money had no value. The thing she really wanted was swiftly becoming out of reach.

Ronnie had been a staunch friend when she most needed him, even taking time off work to be with her; but he was keeping his distance.

This Sunday morning in the chill of autumn he stood with her by her father's grave.

She'd had a huge headstone erected, a towering thing, of white marble embellished with frowning angels. To the stone-mason's raised eyebrows she had specifically ordered they should frown. There were also a marble plinth and base, cold and impenetrable, as if holding the soul down for ever.

On the base were engraved the words: '*Albert Charles Jay, born 1860, died 1902*' – nothing more. He deserved nothing more, no sentiments, not even the day and month of his birth or his death. She didn't want to know, cared even less.

Nearby was her mother's grave. With her money she'd had her mum's body exhumed from the poor little graveyard where it had lain all this time and reburied with great ceremony in this lovely cemetery, not beside him but further away.

She, too, had a headstone now, a far humbler one, but more important by its very simplicity, with all Ellie's love borne out by a kindly stone angel smiling down on the quiet resting place. At her mother's grave she had wept, letting her love fall with her tears on to the new, clean soil in which she had planted beautiful flowers and would continue to plant them until her own life left her. Her father's grave, despite the elaborate headstone, would always remain bare.

'I just want to look at my mum's grave before we leave,' she said to Ronnie as they stepped away from the cold headstone and bare, solid base where no flowers would ever grow, not even a blade of grass.

She felt Ronnie's arm come around her shoulders as they made their way towards the other grave. If only, she thought with a pang, that arm had been about her waist rather than her shoulder.

For a while they stood there in silence. Then she said quietly, 'You know, Ronnie, I'm alone now. Truly alone.'

'You've got Dora,' he said in a flat tone, dampening her spirits even more.

Silence fell on them again, and then he said quietly, 'And you've got me.'

Ellie looked up at him. 'Have I?' she queried, wanting to add, 'Yes, as a friend,' but she let only those two words fall.

He was gazing down at her. 'And I've got you – if you want me.'

As she looked at him enquiringly, he went on, 'I'm . . . not good at this sort of thing. I've been reluctant ter say anything, what with all your troubles and all that money yer'll be getting from your paintings from now on, and you moving in finer circles than what I'm used to, it didn't seem right to . . . well, to tell you . . .'

Again he hesitated and then too took a deep breath, the words halting and awkward. '. . . to tell you I love you. And to ask you if you would . . . well, if you'd consent to be my . . .'

He broke off yet again, swallowing hard. His broad, handsome face twisted with what seemed like fear of the words he wanted to say.

Suddenly they began to pour out in a torrent. 'Ellie, yer must never be alone. Yer won't be. What I want ter say is, you don't ever need to be alone. Ever! I'll be with you. Ellie, will yer marry me?'

Ellie wanted to laugh, wanted to cry too, wanted to say, 'Yes, oh yes, my darling, more than anything!'

Instead, she threw herself into his arms and now she was crying tears of happiness. The kisses they shared as they stood locked in each other's embrace, in the middle of the cemetery, needed no words.

*   *   *

Hunnard was beside himself. He had worked hard to make a killing from the marvellous, strange paintings by Elizabeth Jay.

They'd now all been sold and he needed her to paint more – not too many at a time, of course. 'Keep them wanting, so to speak,' he said, filled with confidence in her compliance. 'While the craze for your style lasts, we'll have people clamouring for them and we'll make a fortune between us.'

How wrong he was. 'I can't paint to order,' she told him heatedly after telling him of her engagement to Ronnie, which he conveniently ignored.

'It'll soon come back,' he said. 'It's been a rough time for you, nursing your father, but now you must get back to work. We need to make money.'

He meant *he* needed to make money.

She faced him defiantly. 'To do the sort of paintings I did I have to feel the pain inside me. I don't feel that way any more, so I can't do them. I'm sorry.'

He argued with her until he was blue in the face but she was adamant.

It wasn't long after that she removed herself from the art world. There had been a simple wedding, Elizabeth Jay becoming now Mrs Ronald Sharp.

Hunnard did not come to the wedding and she didn't care. That part of her life was behind her. She didn't even inform Doctor Lowe and his wife, though she often wondered about him, feeling a little sad for him.

Living on her husband's modest income, she had arranged for some of the proceeds from the sale of her works to be put in Dora's name – she having come to live with them – for when she eventually met a partner and married.

Some she let Charlie and his wife Carrie have in memory of Mum and to buy themselves a house, though she guessed he would help it on its way gambling. That was up to him, and up to Carrie to put a stop to it. What was left she made Ronnie take care of, knowing he'd manage it well.

'First thing we'll do,' he'd said, 'is find a nice little place somewhere out of London, with plenty of fresh air for the kids when they come.' He was also anticipating another promotion and rise and Ellie expecting their first baby.

It was as it should be. In time the money from her paintings would dwindle. With no more forthcoming, Elizabeth Jay's work would probably be forgotten, a flash in the pan, with new movements and interpretations, new artists pouring on to the scene all the time.

'I don't think I ever want to pick up another paintbrush,' Ellie told her husband. 'The need has gone right out of me,' she added as she patted her rapidly swelling stomach.

It was true. That strange need that had made her paint the way she had wasn't there any more, she told herself, and she laughed as she felt the baby kick.